SHOT IN THE DARK

NICOLE HELM

TEXAS BODYGUARD: BRAX

JANIE CROUCH

MILLS & BOON

First Published in Great Britain 2023
by Mills & Boon, an imprint of HarperCollins*Publishers* Ltd
1 London Bridge Street, London, SE1 9GF

www.harpercollins.co.uk

HarperCollins*Publishers*
Macken House, 39/40 Mayor Street Upper,
Dublin 1, D01 C9W8, Ireland

Shot in the Dark © 2023 Nicole Helm
Texas Bodyguard: Brax © 2023 Janie Crouch

ISBN: 978-0-263-30717-7

0323

This book is produced from independently certified FSC™ paper
to ensure responsible forest management.

For more information visit: www.harpercollins.co.uk/green

Printed and Bound in the UK using 100% Renewable Electricity
at CPI Group (UK) Ltd, Croydon, CR0 4YY

SHOT IN THE DARK

NICOLE HELM

To good moms and dads of all types.

Chapter One

Sarabeth Peterson was eleven years old. She had done a lot in her short life. Moved from Florida to Arizona and then to Wyoming. She'd helped protect her mother from all the varying family who wanted to hurt her.

And then, a month ago, she'd killed her father.

Self-defense, of course. And she hadn't really known him anyway. Mom had kept her as far away from Rob Currington as she could, but he'd found them last month. Hurt Mom. Used her.

And Sarabeth had shot him. Saved them.

But she knew they weren't safe yet. Mom thought the fact the old bank robbery gold had been found meant people would stop looking.

Sarabeth knew better. There was more—so much more—and someone was going to figure out she was the one who knew about it.

Luckily, there was someone who could help her.

The problem was finding a way to talk to Henry Thompson without her mother finding out. Mom would find a way to talk Henry out of helping them. Sarabeth had to keep it a secret. Usually not easy to do, but Mom had been busy the past month—talking to the police, and family services, and getting a job at a company that offered people stagecoach rides so they could pretend they were back in the old days or something.

Adults were weird.

But they were staying in Wilde, Wyoming. Sarabeth was happy about that. She liked it here. Better than Florida and Arizona. She liked the mountains and the ranches and all the *space*. It was like an adventure.

Adventures were fun, but they were also dangerous. They were going to need some help. They were going to need some protection.

A phone call wouldn't work—she wasn't sure anyone would listen to her over the phone. Mom didn't let her use the computer without supervision, so email wasn't on the table.

It had to be done face-to-face.

"Sarabeth."

She had to turn her attention away from her plans to the man she didn't trust sitting in front of her. She liked the lady from family services. Maybe she didn't always agree with Ms. Angie, but the social worker had a nice smile. And she didn't talk to Sarabeth like she was a dumb little kid.

The family counselor, Dr. Evan, was another story. And she didn't like his eyes. Flat and brown and too…something. She didn't like the way he looked at her. It made her angry.

Sarabeth was used to being angry, but she usually understood why. She didn't know why Dr. Evan made her angry, only that he did. And Mom had always said to listen to her gut feelings. When you didn't, you ended up tied up in a basement.

At least, that was what had happened to Mom. After ten years of keeping them away from Sarabeth's dad, Mom's luck ran out and Rob had showed up at exactly the wrong moment and brought them to Wyoming against Mom's will.

Sarabeth hadn't liked her father, but she *had* liked trying to find the gold. She'd hated that Rob had hit and hurt her mother, but Sarabeth had done something about it. Hadn't she?

"What are you thinking about?"

She fingered the piece of gold in her pocket. It had been her dad's. Well, technically, he had stolen it from a man who was maybe *his* dad, but dead now. Because of her father.

Who was dead now, because of her.

That was kind of weird, wasn't it? It was a thought she would have shared with Ms. Angie. She wasn't about to share it with Dr. Evan.

"I don't like it when my mom's not in here," Sarabeth said. She didn't scowl at Dr. Evan, even though she wanted to. Because sometimes you had to pretend to get what you wanted. And she wanted to not have to come to these dumb appointments anymore.

Dr. Evan's face changed. It got kind of pinched like he was irritated with her, but his smile stayed put and his words weren't mean.

"We thought maybe you'd feel more comfortable talking about your father without her in the room."

"I'm not," Sarabeth returned flatly. She didn't want to discuss anything with Dr. Evan, but especially her father.

"All right."

Sarabeth didn't believe his smile for a second, but he pushed a button on his phone and asked somebody to send Mom in.

"I think we've got about as far as we can today," Dr. Evan said to Mom. "We'll see you at your appointment next week, Sarabeth."

"Thank you, Dr. Young." Mom put her arm around Sarabeth and started leading her to the door.

Sarabeth knew she shouldn't. Mom told her to be nice and polite to people who wanted to help, but Sarabeth couldn't always resist poking at somebody. Especially a somebody she just didn't like.

"Bye, Mr. Evan." He *hated* when people called him Mr. instead of Dr. She'd found that in her first appointment with him.

She'd said it once every appointment since.

His nice smile fell and Sarabeth had to hide her grin behind her hands as Mom led her outside.

"That was wrong, Sarabeth," Mom muttered as they waved at the front desk lady and then left.

"I'm sorry, but I don't like him. You said I don't have to talk to people I don't like." Sarabeth squinted at the summer sun as she looked up and down the street.

Wilde was by far the smallest town they'd ever lived in. There wasn't even a grocery store here. It was a strange place, but that was what Sarabeth liked about it. It felt odd and out of place like she did.

Still, she preferred the ranches out past town. All that land. Horses. Big sky and space. Sarabeth felt alive and in control out there. But town was okay too.

One of the Bent County stagecoaches went by and Mom waved at the driver. They started walking down the road. They lived in an apartment above a hardware store just down the block. Mom had lived there when she was a little kid with her grandma.

Before they got very far, Sarabeth saw a familiar silver truck. She looked wildly around for any of the Thompson brothers, hoping for one in particular to materialize. But wherever they were, they weren't in or around their truck.

That truck would eventually go back to the Thompson

ranch, where Henry was—if he wasn't the one driving it. Sarabeth slowed her pace and pulled her hand out of Mom's grasp.

"Jessie!" someone called. Mom tensed, but she plastered on a smile. Sarabeth knew Mom couldn't stand nosy Mrs. Caruthers who ran the hardware store with her husband, but Mrs. Caruthers had not picked up on it.

"What have you two been up to?" Mrs. Caruthers asked, smiling her big, toothy smile. Her eyes were beady though. And always watching.

Sarabeth shifted to stand behind mom. "Hello, Mrs. Caruthers," Mom greeted. "How are you today?"

Mom was good at that. Not answering questions. They'd spent a lot of time hiding, lying, *not* answering questions that might make her father or Mom's family come after them.

Mrs. Caruthers was talking about some foot problem she had, but Sarabeth wasn't listening. She was looking at the silver truck. She knew it was one of the Thompson brothers'. *Knew* it.

Her lucky gold piece was giving her the chance. She let go of Mom's hand. "Mom, can I go buy a piece of candy?"

Mom looked down at her, eyebrows drawn together. She looked into the store window they were standing in front of, then sighed and gave a little nod.

But Sarabeth didn't go into the store. She backed slowly away, toward the truck, watching Mrs. Caruthers's mouth move and move and move.

Sarabeth scrambled up into the truck bed as quiet as a mouse. She curled herself into a little ball in the corner and waited, hoping against hope the Thompson brother would return soon and drive off. Before Mom realized she wasn't coming back.

She didn't think of how worried Mom would be or how much trouble she'd be in. She just thought about how she could finally get the help Mom needed.

HENRY ROYAL HAD been more than happy to leave his last name behind when his superior officer had informed him of the military leak that necessitated he and his team members be killed on paper, then sent to the middle of nowhere, Wyoming, to ranch with a new last name.

Royal held nothing but tragedy and bad memories attached. Thompson was like a new start.

He wished the new start included a little less cow waste, and really wished it included a lot less of his military brothers bringing *women* into their lives. Zara had been fine enough. A ranch woman, always ready and willing to go toe to toe with his bad temper and scathing sarcasm, and Jake was happy so that was that.

Kate, on the other hand, was a softer sort, and Henry didn't care for *soft* even if Brody did. And if Kate was soft, Hazeleigh was downright pillow fluff, the opposite of her sister Zara. But Landon was dedicated to the sweet woman.

All their love bull gave Henry an itch between his shoulder blades. Only bad things could come of *love* and committing your life to each other. He'd learned that lesson early and not a damn thing in his life had ever changed his mind.

Jake didn't agree as he and Zara were now engaged. No doubt Brody and Landon would fall into the same trap soon enough.

Luckily, his other two brothers were as likely to form romantic attachments as Henry was to sprout wings. Taciturn, injured Dunne. Stick-up-his-ass former commander Cal.

No, the three of them were safe. Thank God.

Henry parked the truck in front of the big house that now

felt too dang crowded. Though Landon and Hazeleigh had moved into the cabin across the yard, Henry had still been conned into the big house, agreeing to give Brody and Kate the little shack outbuilding he'd redone into a nice room.

Henry still complained bitterly about it, though Kate being an amazing cook made it worth the while. Zara took a turn washing dishes—which was one less turn he had to take. It wasn't all bad.

Not that he'd let anyone know that.

Henry preferred to focus on the bad. That way when it came and bit you on the ass, you were ready.

He slammed his truck door, headed for the house, but then he heard a strange…sound. He looked back at the truck, and there was a little girl.

The little girl they'd helped last month. "What are you doing here?" he demanded, taking in her windblown brown hair and red-cheeked face.

"I need your help," she said, hopping out of the truck with a child's ease.

He looked in the bed of the truck, trying to figure out where the hell she came from. "You didn't ride in there all the way from town, did you?"

"I absolutely did."

He was losing his touch. That was concerning. There'd been a day he wouldn't have driven an inch without knowing, instinctively, there was a stowaway in his truck.

Of course, he wasn't used to stowaways asking for help rather than wanting to kill him.

She fisted her hands on her hips and looked up at him. She was fierce, he'd give her that. But she was a tiny thing— far too skinny for her frame, all angles and vinegar.

He'd been impressed by her vinegar, in awe of the way

she'd calmly killed her father to save Landon's—and her mother's—life. She was *something*.

But she reminded him of too many things to name, and no matter what she'd done, she was still a little girl.

"Does your mom know you're here?"

She shook her head, casting a guilty glance at the ground. "But she doesn't understand. Mom thinks she's safe here, but she's wrong."

Henry's military training jumped to alert. *Danger*. He was good at stopping danger. But he also knew that poor woman who'd been tied up in a basement would be worried sick that her daughter was missing.

He pulled out his phone and texted Landon inside.

Call Sarabeth's mom. She stowed away in truck. Out here now.

"What are you doing?"

"Telling Landon to call your mom. He's got her number, doesn't he?" He hit Send on the text.

The little girl's face flickered for a moment. A wince, a moment of guilt, then sort of resetting herself. Focusing on him and this bizarre little stunt rather than all the trouble she'd no doubt be in.

"You have to protect my mom. She's in danger."

"How do you know that?"

She crossed her arms over her chest, a stubborn pout on her face. "I know."

He shook his head, trying to remind himself who he was, where he was and how little this was his problem. "Look, kid…"

"I may be young, but I killed my father. I don't feel much like a kid."

He understood where she was coming from. She didn't have a clue how much, but boy, was this little girl *not* his problem. "That doesn't make you Wonder Woman."

"See. This is why I need you."

"No, if you need anybody, and I'm not convinced you do, you want one of my brothers. Landon helped you before. He'll—"

"No, I need you."

"Kid—"

"You're mean."

Henry had his mouth open, but no words came out. Mean. He was indeed mean. Had been called it in a lot more colorful language than this little girl had employed.

"You're the mean one," she insisted. "Your brothers are nice, or at least nicer than you. Whoever wants to hurt my mom is mean. And real bad. She needs someone who can protect her from that. I'm mean, but I'm small. I need help."

Henry tried to harden his heart—after all, he wasn't sure he even had a heart anymore. Or if he'd ever had one to begin with.

But it hit close to a home he'd spent a lifetime running from. A failure he'd tried to make up for his entire military career.

And failed, more times than he liked to count. The failures always outweighing the successes, no matter how the scales tipped in his favor.

"Please," the little girl said, big eyes on him imploringly. "You're the only one who can help."

Chapter Two

Jessie Peterson knew she was driving too fast considering the last thing she wanted to do was get pulled over by the cops—God, she'd had enough cops this month to last a lifetime. But she had to see for herself Sarabeth was okay.

What had she been thinking, letting Sarabeth go into that store by herself? Never again. Never again.

You want her to have a normal childhood now, remember?

Well, that was stupid. Who got to have a normal childhood after they'd killed their father?

Guilt waved up and threatened to swallow her whole. She'd ruined Sarabeth's life. The past few months had been hell and she hadn't been able to save her only child. After ten years of keeping her safe—from Jessie's own father, from the man she'd thought would save her from all that who'd turned out to be just as big a monster—Jessie had failed.

Her breath was coming too quickly and she squeezed the steering wheel too tightly. She was letting guilt take over, and that was something she was working on in therapy.

But Jessie knew she'd failed her daughter. Because Sarabeth had run.

After some thought, it had all made sense. Sarabeth didn't like her therapist. Dr. Young had been the only choice for a child psychologist in the area, and Sarabeth had made it clear she didn't like him.

Jessie shouldn't have insisted. She should have worked with the social worker for another alternative. She should have done everything—

No, we're not going to spiral, Jessie. Because that doesn't help Sarabeth, does it? And your daughter needs help.

She would pick Sarabeth up from the Thompsons', thank them for watching after her and then she would have a long, calm talk with her daughter. Together, they would come to a conclusion that suited them both.

One that included keeping the Thompsons out of their lives.

Jessie knew she owed everyone at the Thompson Ranch. Landon Thompson and Hazeleigh Hart had both risked a lot to help Sarabeth. When they were under no obligation to do so. When they hadn't even known who she was. Sarabeth might have pulled the trigger that kept Rob from killing them all, but Jessie owed her life just as much to Landon and Hazeleigh as to her daughter.

It was Jessie's whole embarrassment at the situation that made her want to keep her distance. Her *and* Sarabeth's distance.

But Sarabeth was fascinated with the brothers, with the ranch and…

Well, if Jessie hadn't made her see Dr. Young today everything would be different. That was the problem, and that was a problem they could solve.

Jessie pulled to a stop next to a big silver truck in front of a beautiful old ranch house. The Thompsons' house— which had been the Harts' when she'd lived in Wilde—had been well tended, repaired and looked cozy and homey.

Or might have, if one of the imposing Thompson brothers wasn't standing on the porch like some kind of bad omen. Now she had to try to remember which one this was. Not Landon. Him she knew. The rest of them all kind of blended together.

More importantly, Sarabeth was nowhere to be seen.

Jessie got out of her car, trying to fix a smile on her face. "Hello, again."

He tipped his black cowboy hat. "She's in the stables with Landon."

Jessie let out a breath of relief. She didn't have to try to make small talk with the big, dangerous-looking cowboy. "I'll…go get her." But she might as well say the rest first while Sarabeth was out of earshot. She took a few unsure steps toward the brother on the porch stairs. "I am so sorry for her interrupting your day."

"No harm done." He flicked a gaze down at her. "Except maybe to you."

Jessie laughed, but it came out bitter. She didn't want to be bitter. She had to be a good mother, so Sarabeth could break this awful cycle Jessie had gotten herself sucked into.

"Yes, well… I was a little frantic. Landon's phone call was a relief. I'll just fetch her and leave you to it."

"You don't want to know why she was here?"

Jessie blinked. She looked at the man in the chest. He wore a black T-shirt that clung to, well, admittedly well-formed muscles.

She looked at the ground. She'd learned faking a kind of meekness kept anyone from looking too closely underneath. "I think I know, Mr. Thompson."

"Henry," he said. "Call me Henry."

She didn't plan on calling him anything. Because she was getting her daughter and leaving.

"You can look me in the eye," Henry said when she didn't say anything. When she kept staring at the ground.

Temper flared. It was a bad one, but she'd spent eleven years of motherhood learning how to deal with it. Hide it.

Funny how it seemed to show up inside her daughter anyway. And made Jessie proud, though it shouldn't. Still, Jessie wanted her daughter to be strong. To be a force of nature who'd always know how to stand on her own two feet.

But as for herself, she still had secrets to hide. She lifted her eyes to his, hoping none of the temper showed.

His gaze was a soft brown that seemed an odd contrast to the hardness around his mouth. The hardness of him.

"Sarabeth seems to think you're in danger. That you need help."

Jessie shook her head, panic darting through her, but she held a placid smile. Made it a little sad around the edges. "She's been through a lot."

"Yeah, that's what I figured." But he studied her face, and *that* was another reason she hadn't looked him in the eye. There was a watchfulness about the Thompson brothers she didn't like and didn't trust—no matter how they'd proven themselves.

"I'll go get her now." She started forward for the stables, just a few yards away. She could even see Sarabeth and Landon's forms next to a pretty black horse.

"If you need help, though…" He trailed off, but she kept walking. "Whole passel of us here have your back. And Sarabeth's."

Jessie stopped. They'd said that before. In the aftermath of Sarabeth's shooting Rob. The brothers, the nearly identical sisters, they'd offered help. But Jessie had thought they were just…being nice. Finding something to say in the middle of a bad moment.

But the bad moments were gone. She turned, too puzzled to pretend meekness and avoid his gaze. "Why on earth would you help us?"

He seemed to give it some thought, then shrugged. "Because help is what we do."

HENRY TRIED TO stop thinking about the Peterson women. The little girl meant nothing to him, her mother even less. Jessie had collected Sarabeth, and the girl had trudged guiltily to the car. She'd given Henry one last plaintive look as she'd crawled into the back seat of her mom's sedan.

He'd never answered Sarabeth's request. Landon had come out and Henry had let Landon handle it. Handle the girl.

Henry figured Sarabeth would get an earful from her mom on the ride home, and that would be that. Because clearly, Jessie didn't think she was in danger the way Sarabeth did.

Henry had to let it go.

But he couldn't get over the way Jessie had looked at the ground. Or the flare of temper in her eyes when she'd looked back up.

Not totally beaten down by life yet. Good for her. And God knew Sarabeth had enough life for twenty eleven-year-olds. They'd be fine.

No help needed.

When he walked into the kitchen the next morning, though, it was only Landon sitting at the table drinking his coffee in front of his computer. Henry figured he might as well mention it.

Maybe then he could stop thinking about Sarabeth's imploring expression and Jessie's spark of temper.

"Can we expect any visits from little girls today?" he

asked, crossing to the coffeepot. Not quite enough to fill his mug. He scowled. Too many damn people in this house.

"Didn't know you cared," Landon drawled in response.

Henry merely grunted and took a seat across from Landon. He wouldn't push, because this concerned him not at all.

"After what you said Sarabeth told you, I looked into Jessie a little last night. Just to make sure she wasn't in any major trouble," Landon said, without Henry having to push at all. "Just trying to get an idea of what kind of danger she might be in considering the evil husband is dead. And interestingly, Jessie Peterson never married Rob Currington—and there's no record of her anywhere after Sarabeth was born."

"Interesting or concerning?"

Landon shrugged. "Hard to say. Sarabeth didn't ask *me* for help, if you recall." Landon studied Henry with some suspicion. "Why *did* she ask *you*?"

Henry grinned the way that had people who didn't know him scurrying to do whatever he asked. "She said I was mean enough to handle it."

"Yeah, such a tough meanie, worrying about it the next day."

"Not worried."

"Sure." Landon grinned, and Henry knew better than to be riled up by that grin. It would just prove Landon's point, and Henry didn't plan on proving anyone's point.

"Don't you have your own house to steal all the coffee from?"

"Hazeleigh *does* make an excellent cup of coffee, among other things," Landon said with such self-satisfaction Henry couldn't hide his scowl.

Smug bastard.

"But I was turning it over with Hazeleigh last night, and she pointed out something. Hard to say if it's connected, if it means anything, but Rob Currington died thinking there was still some of this stupid bank robbery gold out there."

Before Rob Currington died. Before Sarabeth shot him.

"I can't help but think it's possible there's still someone out there after it," Landon continued. "You wouldn't think it'd be important, but Rob killed his own father over it. He might not be the only one."

"What does that have to do with Jessie and Sarabeth?"

Landon frowned. "I don't know, but anyone connected to it? I'd be careful if I were them. Maybe Sarabeth knows something about the gold, and that's why she thinks they're in danger. Hard to say. She didn't talk to *me*."

Henry scowled deeper. "I'm not getting involved."

Landon leaned back in his chair and studied Henry. "She asked for *your* help."

"You just said it's about mythical gold and old-ass bank robberies. Count me out. I'm interested in real problems."

"You have to go find out what Sarabeth might know, Henry. So we can all sleep at night."

"Got nothing to do with me," Henry insisted. "Some of us prefer to keep our nose clean out here hiding from the man. Besides, she saved *you*, Landon, not me."

Landon kept his gaze level, his expression bland. "If that's how you want to play it." He pushed away from the table and began to whistle as he washed out his mug and then sauntered out the door. "But I think we both know that's *not* how you want to play it," he called as he disappeared outside.

Henry scowled at the door, wishing he could prove Landon wrong.

Knowing he wouldn't.

SARABETH *HATED* BEING GROUNDED. She *hated* when Mom was mad at her. Most of all she hated when adults acted like they knew better when she was the only one talking any sense.

Sarabeth had been the one who'd been able to listen to her father's plans. Because he hadn't thought she was a threat. Mom had been hurt and tied up, but Sarabeth had been able to do whatever she wanted.

She knew things. But even she knew the things she'd overheard sounded, well, over-the-top. Adults would think she was exaggerating or making things up. Even Mom would be skeptical.

Sarabeth looked at the gold piece in her hand. She traced the rigid edges. It had been her good luck charm ever since she'd found it. Mom had survived. They were free of her father. What was better luck than that?

The problem was the rest of it Rob had been looking for. Sarabeth knew someone would come for it eventually, and likely her or Mom in the process.

The doorknob to her room turned and Sarabeth hurried to shove the coin under her pillow and sat up.

Mom stepped in. "I'm sorry," Sarabeth blurted. She wasn't really. Not about what she'd done, exactly. She was sorry about Mom being worried. Sarabeth figured it amounted to the same thing.

Mom came and sat next to her on the bed. She reached out and slid a hand over Sarabeth's hair. "I am too."

"You are?"

"I didn't listen when you said you didn't like Dr. Young because… Well, I don't really like talking to anyone about my problems. But it's supposed to be good for you."

Sarabeth didn't have a clue why they were talking about

Dr. Evan, but if it got her out of having to talk to him, she'd go with it.

"Still, you should have someone you can trust to talk to. I'm quite certain family services will require it."

"I only trust you."

Mom's eyes got watery and Sarabeth didn't know why that was the wrong thing to say, but clearly it was. "Okay, I kind of trust Ms. Angie." Sarabeth looked carefully at her mother. "And the Thompsons."

Mom's mouth got tight and she sighed. "The Thompsons are very nice, but—"

"They've got the most amazing horses. I like talking to horses. Horses listen and they don't say dumb stuff about girls needing to be nicer than boys."

Mom stiffened and she got that look in her eye—the one that usually turned into yelling. Sarabeth always kind of liked it when Mom yelled.

"Did Dr. Young say that to you?"

Sarabeth nodded. "Yes. Yesterday. He wanted to talk about Dad when you left, and I didn't want to. But he kept asking and asking and asking, and I finally just said he was mean. And I said you're not. And he said that's because women aren't supposed to be mean."

"Well." Mom huffed. "We definitely won't be going back to him, will we? We'll have to talk to Ms. Angie about alternatives. But he is out. I'll put my foot down if I have to."

Sarabeth snuggled into Mom. She liked it when Mom put her foot down about stuff. It started to feel like the old days, before her father had taken them. When their life had just been theirs.

But then things had gotten bad and now… Now things could be good again. As long as no one came after them. As long as they were protected.

Which meant she was going to have to try to find a way to talk to Henry Thompson again.

And beg him to help.

Chapter Three

Jessie had always loved horses, and she might have considered it luck, if she believed in such things, that she'd been able to secure a job that involved them. Driving the stagecoach around Bent County was like all her childhood dreams come true. Plus, she got to bring Sarabeth.

Who was currently pouting on her little perch on the roof of the coach because she hadn't been allowed to help hitch the team. Because she was still grounded.

Jessie climbed into the old-fashioned stagecoach and settled herself into the driver's seat, trying to ignore the wiggle of guilt. What Sarabeth had done was wrong, and she needed to learn that lesson.

Jessie clicked the horses into a slow walk. There were little stops around the route where she'd pick up people, but otherwise her job was to simply ride in and out of town. The advertisements on the stagecoach their own mobile billboard.

Wilde didn't look much different than it had when she'd been Sarabeth's age. This had always been the goal. Home—because Wilde had been stability. She'd lived with her grandmother for the first thirteen years of her life in the little apartment above the hardware store. When Grandma had died, there'd been nowhere to go. So her uncle had collected her and taken her to the Peterson compound in Idaho that had turned out to be hell on earth.

Such hell, she'd believed in Rob Currington's foolish promises and run off with him—thinking he'd save her. But he wanted the same thing her father did.

Gold.

It was still hard to believe the gold had been real, but she'd seen it herself. And now it was with the FBI or some museum and good riddance. The pursuit of it had turned all the men she came into contact with into maniacs.

She'd escaped that for almost eleven years. Running out on Rob in the middle of the night before she'd been stupid enough to say I do to him. But not before she'd gotten pregnant.

She sighed, sneaking a glance up at Sarabeth. She had Jessie's auburn hair and stubborn chin, but her father's hazel eyes and fair complexion. She had a sulky pout still on her face, but those eyes danced with anticipation. She loved her little seat on top of the coach, and she'd be grinning by the day's end.

Sarabeth was the single best thing that had ever happened to Jessie. Given her a strength and a purpose she didn't think she would have found without someone completely vulnerable who needed protection from the world.

But the girl was getting older, and less inclined to be protected *or* vulnerable. Jessie thought of Sarabeth's stunt and scowled at the horses in front of her.

Less inclined to be protected by her mother, but certainly happy to ask a perfect stranger for help.

Jessie scowled even deeper thinking about Henry Thompson, and the way he'd said she could look him in the eye like he understood *anything*. The way he didn't seem to believe the adult in the situation—*her*—could take care of herself.

She'd been doing nothing but taking care of herself. And now the gold was gone. There was no danger anymore. No one needed her for anything. She could just...live.

Without big males and their quiet, condescending studies. Without cowboy hats and soft eyes on a hard face. She did not need protecting—because she was safe. And if it turned out she wasn't, she'd handle it.

As if stewing about him conjured him, Henry Thompson was there. Right there. Waiting at the next stop. Big and broad. She had had her fill of dangerous men and he was clearly in that same camp.

But her body was not getting her brain's messages. Luckily, her brain was irritated enough not to listen. She pulled the stagecoach to a stop and glared at him. "You don't really want a ride."

"Sure I do." He flashed a smile—one that seemed utterly devoid of warmth or charm. It was all surface and made her a little too interested in what he might be hiding underneath.

She supposed that was why it was effective.

"Enjoying the ride, kid?" he asked, shading his eyes as he looked up at Sarabeth.

Sarabeth scowled at him. "I'm grounded."

"Probably should be," Henry replied with a shrug. Then he moved like he was going to climb onto the stagecoach.

Oh, *no*. "You can't get on. You need a—"

He pulled the bright green paper out of his pocket. "A ticket? Here you go." He plopped himself next to her.

"This is the driver's seat. You're supposed to sit in there." She pointed to the actual coach. She caught her daughter studying Henry a little too intently.

Ugh.

"This'll do," he replied.

She wanted to argue with him. She was half tempted

to push him out. But he seemed like the kind of man who lived to do the opposite of what he was told. So she'd have to swallow down the urge to bicker with him. She could play the boring, shy woman to be ignored when it suited.

She gave the reins a flick and pulled back into the street. Henry shifted, trying to spread out his long legs, but there just wasn't the space for his large frame.

Served him right.

"This is one weird town. You guys really make enough to cover the cost of the horses?"

"Yes, Bent County Stagecoach Company does just fine, thank you." She had no idea what the financials of the company were, but they'd hired her and paid her, so surely just fine. "What are you doing here?" she demanded, when he shifted again, taking up entirely too much of her space. And she didn't manage to keep the snap out of her tone.

His eyebrow winged up as if surprised by her temper. Oh, damn him anyway.

"Well, Sarabeth's little field trip yesterday got us a little curious."

"I told you, we're fine," Jessie managed between gritted teeth.

"Yeah, sure, and maybe you are. The thing is it's a little odd."

"What is?"

"You two don't seem to exist on paper."

HENRY WAS SOMEWHAT gratified to see Jessie's temper come up. Her eyes flashed. Her cheeks turned a pretty shade of pink. But it wasn't embarrassment. It was fury.

Good. Fury was good. She wasn't totally beaten down by life. He knew what that looked like.

"You looked into my *background*?" she asked on a hissed whisper.

"Technically, Landon did."

"None of you have any damn right."

Henry shrugged, unbothered. "Just making sure the kid was in an okay position."

"An okay position? An okay position?" He thought she was going to start yelling, but she disappointed him a bit. She sucked in a breath. Let it out. Her shoulders slumped and her eyes tipped down so he couldn't meet her gaze. She flicked the reins and expertly moved the horses along.

One more long breath and then she spoke. Calmly. Quietly, with just a hint of apology in her tone. "Sarabeth is just fine. If you have concerns, you only have to discuss them with our social worker."

"Social workers," he muttered with disgust. "What can they do?"

"Plenty, if you let them."

He supposed that was the difference. A mother who might want help. His never had.

This wasn't about his mother. He looked up at the girl sitting cross-legged on a little perch on the roof of the rickety old stagecoach. She was studying him closely, and he—a man who'd faced down men with guns, entire terrorist organizations—wanted to fidget.

Her frank, childish gaze seemed a little too insightful.

Ridiculous.

"Look, if you don't exist on paper, you're hiding from something. If you're hiding from something, it usually means you're in danger. Why not let us help?"

She didn't say anything to that for a very long time. Her chin came up a little, but she didn't look at him. Her grip on the reins was too tight, but she kept her movements re-laxed and easy.

She was a woman of strange dichotomies. Ones that didn't quite add up.

"The person we were hiding from is dead," she said after a few moments, in that same calm voice almost as if she was asking permission for it to be the truth.

He studied her profile, but she was careful of the angle, never giving him much of a view of her eyes. The color hadn't gone from her cheeks.

"But Mom…"

Henry looked up at the girl. She was chewing on her lip. Clearly torn between telling him whatever her mother was hiding and getting the help they obviously needed.

"There are no buts," Jessie said very calmly. "All this foolishness about this…old gold. I don't understand it. Even knowing it's real now, I still don't understand it. But the gold has been found. Rob is dead." She swallowed. "Sarabeth is dealing with the aftereffects of that." There was a hesita-tion, and then Jessie's voice lowered and she leaned close enough he could smell the flowery scent of her shampoo. "Her therapist says it's normal to still feel some danger, but I can assure you there is none."

Henry flicked another glance at Sarabeth. She was frown-ing, but he didn't think she'd heard what her mother had said or there'd be more outrage or hurt or arguments.

Jessie's shoulders were stiff, her eyes on the horses, and everything she said made sense. It seemed reasonable Sara-beth would have some paranoia. She had a social worker and a therapist on it, plus a mother who apparently cared.

He didn't need to stick his nose in their business.

But his instincts hummed that there was something miss-ing. He should let it go. Really let all those military instincts

go. He was a rancher now. Nothing more. Nothing else. Just
Henry Thompson, cowboy.

He kept trying to convince himself of that as the horses
clip-clopped along, the coach rattling behind them. It really was a bizarre town. Stagecoaches and old bank robbery
gold, and some murders when there were barely enough
people to murder and *be* murdered.

She pulled to a stop at the next little bench. She turned
and smiled at him, eyes not quite meeting his. "Here's your
stop."

He figured the ticket was probably for a round trip, but
he didn't mind walking back to his truck if she wanted to
get rid of him that badly.

He would be gotten rid of. He'd forget Sarabeth and her
mother and *gold*.

But he glanced up at Sarabeth as he climbed down from
the coach. She was frowning at him, and he remembered
the calm way she'd recounted killing her father to the cops
that night last month.

*He was going to kill us all, so I shot. I didn't mean to kill
him, but it's what had to happen.*

Henry had envied her. A strange, twisted kind of envy,
he knew. But it explained why he couldn't quite let this go,
no matter how he should.

She'd done what needed to be done. Eleven years old,
she'd ended the threat to her mother. And now she wanted
his help, as if she hadn't solved all her problems.

Jessie cleared her throat and Henry looked at her. She
nodded at where his hand was still clamped on the coach
even though his feet were on the ground. "I hope you enjoyed your ride."

He said nothing, and he didn't let go. He wasn't sure...
And that was the problem. This woman made him un-

sure when he'd never been unsure. She seemed to defy all his instincts.

"Sarabeth and I can handle ourselves, thank you." Her smile was that same placid, timid thing, but something about those dark eyes didn't match. Almost like it was all...an act.

She flicked the reins and the horses moved, and he finally let go of the coach. It rattled away, and Henry frowned after them.

He had the very uncomfortable realization he might have read her wrong. That all his well-honed skills at first impressions and making snap decisions might have been completely off when it came to Jessie Peterson.

Worse, he had to agree with her daughter. They were in some kind of trouble.

It wasn't his problem. It wasn't his *responsibility*.

But that didn't seem to matter.

Chapter Four

The plan was simple. It would get her in a lot of trouble, it would hurt Mom's feelings, but it was simple.

Sarabeth studied her packed bag. She had everything she'd need. It would be a long, hard hike. It might even take days. But Sarabeth knew how to keep going, and she knew how to protect herself.

She was going to find the rest of that gold, *and* force Henry to help her mother. Because if Sarabeth went missing, Mom would ask Henry to come looking for her. She'd think about going to the police, but Sarabeth was pretty sure Mom wouldn't trust them no matter what. She might not trust Henry, or even Landon, but she'd ask them for help.

That was what Mom needed. And Sarabeth needed to find the rest of that gold. Rob had told her enough. She was pretty sure she could do it.

As for the Thompson brothers… She knew they'd find her. She had no doubts about that. She didn't mind being caught—as long as she got done what needed to be done before she did.

The hard part was getting out of the apartment without Mom waking up. She was a light sleeper, but Sarabeth wasn't stupid. She'd planned and practiced.

The first step was the pillows. She threw them on the

floor, then eased off her bed and onto one. She pulled her backpack onto her shoulders, fastened the headlamp she'd gotten as part of a camping kit for Christmas last year around her head. She didn't click it on yet. She could get out of the apartment with her eyes closed—and might need to when it was all said and done.

She stepped to the next pillow, then crouched down and grabbed the first. She used the two pillows to soften her footfalls to her closet—which she'd purposefully left open. She pulled a sweatshirt off the pile, sat on the pillow and got her hiking boots on, then she was on her way.

She'd figured out the pillows softened the sound of her feet—and kept the floorboards from creaking if she stepped in the right place. Her biggest challenge was going to be the doors. She'd spent time testing and practicing how to hold and apply pressure at just the right way to keep the doors from squeaking, but it was still nerve-racking.

By the time she made it to the front door, sweat was sliding down her back. Her heart was beating so loudly in her ears she wouldn't have heard Mom behind her at all.

But she kept moving forward. She had a plan. The plan was going to help everyone.

She held her breath as she unlocked the front door and snapped the dead bolt. She squeezed her eyes shut when the click of the lock seemed to echo through the room and maybe the entire town.

But no lights flashed on. Her mother didn't appear. So she opened the door, and it didn't squeak. She was careful as she closed it, no matter how her hands shook.

She let out a long breath once it was shut. She wanted to run. To scream. But she knew she couldn't, and if she'd learned anything when her father had had her mother tied up, it was that she knew how to survive. How to handle scary things.

She had to be calm and careful. She couldn't rush and she couldn't panic. So she took each stair down with careful precision until she reached the door that would lead outside. She didn't have to worry so much about this one making noise since Mom was upstairs with a door closed, and the hardware store was empty for the night.

Still, she reminded herself to be careful. To be smart. And when she was finally outside, she allowed herself a moment to stand still. To settle herself.

She had a long way to go. This was only a first step, and there was no time to celebrate it. But she grinned to herself anyway.

Looking out at the town, all she saw was darkness, and though she could picture it in her mind's eye and knew where she needed to walk, things looked...weird in the dark. The shadows seemed to ripple with movement. They meshed together to form figures.

Sarabeth clenched her hands into fists. She bit her lip until it hurt so much her eyes stung. And then, she set off.

Sarabeth was brave. She was smart.

And she was going to make everything okay, once and for all.

HENRY WOKE UP to the odd sound of thudding. He rolled over in his bed, sure one of his brothers was doing something stupid. And hopefully not... He grimaced and sat up in bed.

The thumping kept going on, muffled enough it seemed to be coming from downstairs. Muttering to himself, he tossed the covers back and opened his door.

If anyone else sleeping upstairs heard it, they weren't interested in investigating. He thought of grabbing his gun, but if someone out to do harm was doing it this loudly, Henry doubted he'd need a weapon to take them down.

He walked down the stairs, wishing he'd grabbed a shirt. This drafty old house even made summer evenings cold.

It became clear as he got to the bottom of the stairs someone was knocking on the front door. He even heard the faint sounds of…shouting, maybe? A woman shouting?

At the same time he entered the living room, Dunne—whose bedroom was downstairs—was limping in. He was rumpled and looked as irritated as Henry felt.

"Who the hell is that?" he growled.

"Hell if I know."

Henry crossed to the door and opened it. Jessie Peterson stumbled inside as if she'd been leaning against it while pounding frantically. She righted herself and looked at Dunne, then at him. She seemed to decide he was her target.

"Where is she? Where *is* she?" She punctuated the demands by drilling a finger into his chest.

He grabbed her hand, because while her poke didn't hurt it didn't feel *great*, and he wanted to be annoyed and yell right back at her, but her hand was shaking. He kept it in his.

"Calm down, now. Where is who? Sarabeth?"

"Yes, of course, Sarabeth. She has to be here. She has to…"

Henry squeezed Jessie's hand hard enough to get her gaze to focus on him—no matter how angrily. "Take a breath," he instructed firmly, "and explain."

"She left. She ran away. She has to be here. She has to be…" She looked around wildly, her hand still caught in his.

"Dunne, why don't you go call the police and we'll—"

"No." She used her free hand to grab on to his hand holding hers. "No, you can't."

"Is your daughter missing?" he asked. Interrupted sleep

and her sad brown eyes irritating him enough to have far
too much snap in his tone.

She tried to pull her hand away, but he wouldn't let go.
"You don't understand."

"So help me out here."

She licked her lips and looked around. Everything about
her was panic and poor choices. They needed the police,
but…something about her panic kept him from signaling
to Dunne to do it anyway.

"I need you to find her, okay? Or Landon or whoever. No
one can know she's missing. You don't know what kind of
danger she'd be in. Who might find her."

"Who might find her, Jessie?"

She sucked in a shuddering breath. And ignored the question. "She'd come here, I think. Maybe? Oh, I don't know.
I don't know what she was thinking. She's never run away
before."

"Before the other day you mean?"

"Yes, and she ran to *you*."

It was an accusation he didn't care for, since he hadn't
done anything to encourage Sarabeth to come to *him* for
help. Except maybe the whole stagecoach stunt.

"The police have the resources to—"

"So do you," Jessie said, cutting Dunne's calm words
off. "I may have only been around town a short while, but
I've heard at least six people tell me about how Brody found
that little boy everyone thought was missing. And helped
someone with their missing father or something. You guys
find things, help people and have convinced my daughter
you'll help. She has to have tried to come here."

Henry agreed with her on Sarabeth's likely target being
the Thompson Ranch, and as much as he believed the correct course of action was to call the police, he was also fairly

convinced Jessie was hiding something—and *that* was why she didn't want to go to the police.

Figured. Not the protective mother she pretended. Just out to protect herself. He should have seen that coming.

Well, regardless, Sarabeth was likely in trouble. Trouble of the girl's own choosing, but that didn't mean he was about to leave an eleven-year-old to the wolves—metaphorical or literal. "Dunne, wake everyone up. Start a search from here. I'll take Jessie back to town and see if we can find a trail of some kind."

Dunne nodded, and Henry took Jessie's arm and led her outside. She went willingly, but of course not silently. "I don't know why we'd go all the way back to town. You and I both know she'd be coming here."

"Maybe," Henry agreed. "But what if she's not? We need the full story, and you were likely too panicked about whatever trouble you've gotten yourself into to worry about what Sarabeth was *actually* doing."

"Excuse me?"

He jerked his chin toward the truck. "Get in and wait. I'll only be a second." He hurried back into the house and up to his room where he grabbed a shirt, muttering under his breath the whole time. Jessie and her daughter were becoming trouble he didn't like.

When he returned to the truck, he was almost surprised to see her sitting patiently in it. He thought she might have bolted. Like her daughter.

She didn't argue with him when he got in, and she let him pull out onto the gravel road before she said anything.

"What do you think Sarabeth was actually doing?"

"Hard to say when you won't tell anyone the full truth."

She seemed to think that over. "There isn't much to the full truth. Some people who'd like to hurt me would hurt

Sarabeth in my stead. I mostly think we're safe here, as long as we don't make any waves. Cops are waves. Besides, if the cops get involved, so does the social worker, and I think we all know what happens then."

"Seems to me if she was happy with you she wouldn't keep running away."

"Why are you acting like I'm the bad guy here?" Jessie demanded, and when he flicked a glance at her he was just a little puzzled to see actual confusion in her expression. Not defensiveness or outrage.

"You can't even call the cops when your daughter runs off because of some trouble *you're* in?" He shrugged. "Seems to me you should be more concerned about her over yourself, so sorry if I don't crown you mother of the year."

SHE HEARD THE buzzing in her head, knew she should breathe with it. Look down, look away. It didn't matter what Henry Thompson thought of her mothering. Reacting wouldn't help Sarabeth any, and that was all that mattered.

Her little girl out there wandering around trying to get to the Thompsons for reasons Jessie still didn't understand. Not mother of the year? Oh, she knew exactly all the ways she'd failed as a mother. They looped through her mind every night when she went to bed.

But she also knew worse mothers. She knew abandonment and neglect, and she knew parental abuse at the hands of her father. So no, Henry didn't have any right to judge her on this.

She couldn't breathe, and she couldn't look away. She could only say all the things she shouldn't. "You have *no* idea what I've done to protect my daughter. You have *no* idea what kind of danger she would be in if the wrong people find her. You think I care about me?" She laughed so bitterly it seared her throat. "You don't know a damn thing."

He was very quiet for a very long time. So quiet the only sound in the truck was her own ragged breathing as she attempted to rein her temper back in.

"Not half the shrinking violet you like to pretend to be," Henry said after a while.

She looked away from him, stared out the window at the inky dark. Somewhere out there her daughter was walking around. Alone. Somewhere out there, her daughter had run away because…

Why? *Why?* Didn't Sarabeth know if the social worker found out about this that she could be taken away? Didn't Sarabeth know…?

Jessie closed her eyes. She couldn't go through all the what-ifs. She just needed to find Sarabeth—through whatever means necessary. And if that ended up meaning the cops, so be it.

But not yet.

"She's very worried *you're* in danger, you know."

Jessie whipped her head to look at him. He had a contemplative look on his face, and he drummed his fingers on the steering wheel as he drove. His eyes were sharp and focused on the road ahead, but she could tell he was thinking everything through. "That's why she came out to the ranch the first time. She thought *you* were in danger."

"I'm not."

He turned those eyes on her. Something skittered in her chest, like fear but not. "It sounds like you are."

"You don't understand."

"You keep saying that, with no effort to tell me what it is I don't understand."

"Because it's none of your business."

"And yet you woke me up in the middle of the night to look for your daughter."

"Because *she* is fixated on *you*. And let me remind you I didn't encourage you to come hijack my stagecoach, look into *my* background. If you would have butted out—"

"What? Sarabeth would have just accepted that? Because she strikes me as a stubborn little thing."

Jessie hated that he was right, and she could hardly argue with him. He wasn't stupid, and no matter how much she wanted to blame him, what was going on with Sarabeth had nothing to do with Henry Thompson.

"She ran away. Clearly. So as much as I can think of a hundred terrible things that might have happened to her in the middle of the night in *Wilde,* Wyoming, I also know she's a smart girl who knows how to take care of herself." Jessie sucked in a breath. "She had a plan. A very well-thought-out plan."

"Then let's see if we can't figure out what it is? Maybe there's a clue in her room. Meanwhile, my brothers will start looking for her from the ranch moving outward. What time do you think she ran?"

Jessie looked at the clock. Three. She went to bed at eleven, sure Sarabeth was sound asleep in her bed. "Three hours ago tops. She would have planned it, and I'm predictable enough. In bed at eleven, usually asleep by midnight."

"Not enough time to get to the ranch. Too much time to still be in town. She got a phone or anything like that?"

Jessie shook her head. "She doesn't have a phone, and I put all the electronics away at night. I checked to make sure she hadn't taken anything before I came out to find you."

Maybe he was right. Maybe it did make her a terrible mother for thinking it through enough to go to the Thompson brothers over going to the police. But all it took was a police report, an overheard radio message. Petersons after Sarabeth. Social workers taking her away.

Henry pulled up in front of the hardware store and Jessie immediately jumped out, her entire body buzzing with adrenaline and panic. "We live upstairs. She snuck out of her room, out of the apartment—my front door was unlocked—and then down the stairs and out this door. Which was also left unlocked."

"Show me."

So she did. She led Henry upstairs and tried not to get frustrated when he lingered or studied something as inconsequential as a smudge on the wall. Of course, the only reason she managed to hold her tongue was the fact he looked so...serious. Tense and ready to act.

It reminded her too much of those years in Idaho with her father.

She swallowed down that foolish skitter of fear and opened the door to her apartment. She let Henry inside. His large frame was so incongruous in the small, feminine space.

Jessie pointed to the pillows on the floor. "She used these pillows to muffle her steps, I think. She'd been messing around with the doors lately. I thought it was just a game. I should have realized she was testing how to open and close them without making a sound."

Henry surveyed the room. "She really put some thought into it."

"If you're going to use that as another reason to tell me how horrible I am—"

"Honestly? The opposite. This her room?" He started forward, but Jessie stopped him. "No, that's mine. Hers is down the hall."

Henry studied her for a second, and she didn't know what

Shot in the Dark

that was about, but he nodded, then went down the hall and into Sarabeth's room. He immediately began to look at things, and then through things. He pulled her pink-and-purple plaid comforter off the bed.

"What are you doing?"

"Seeing if I can find a clue. A diary. A map. A list of some kind. Something that might clarify her plan."

"But her plan is probably just to get to you."

"When we returned her to you last time?"

Jessie felt the blood drain from her head. She had to reach out and steady herself with the wall. "What?"

"I'm sorry. I know it's not what you want to hear, but there's more to this than her coming to us. I think that's *part* of her plan, but it's hardly all of it." He pulled the pillowcase off her pillow, scrunched up the pillow then placed it on the comforter. He matter-of-factly searched her bed.

When he pulled out a little purple notebook, Jessie leaped forward and took it out of his hand. "No. No, we can't read that."

"Why the hell not? It might be an answer."

"But it's her personal, private thoughts. That she hid to remain personal and private. I don't go through my daughter's things."

"I respect that. When said daughter isn't running away in the middle of the night and we need to find her."

Jessie knew Henry was right, but she held the notebook to her chest. Tried to hold in those old, ugly feelings, but... "I know what it's like not to have any privacy. To have nothing that's your own. To feel violated and..." She was giving far too much away—of her past, of herself. But the idea of going through Sarabeth's things the way her things had always been gone through—to possibly make her daughter feel the way she'd felt like a prisoner, like she couldn't make a wrong move or she'd risk her *life*—it made Jessie sick to her stomach.

"She ran away, Jessie. Either you want to find her, or you want to protect her privacy. It can't be both."

Chapter Five

Henry didn't understand this woman, and that would be fine in just about any other scenario, but not this one. Not where he didn't know whether to suspect her of something or not. Not when he couldn't tell if she was fierce, protective mother or uncertain victim or even cowardly criminal using her daughter as a shield.

Henry always knew what he felt about people right off. He trusted his gut. He believed in his observations and conclusions without fail—and without question.

Until Jessie Peterson had come into his life. Who *was* she?

He'd thought she was protecting herself over her kid, not going to the cops. But she'd picked the smaller bedroom closer to the front door—and maybe it was coincidence, but Henry had enough tactical training to know if you wanted someone safe, you'd choose their bedroom farther from the door.

He'd thought this privacy crap was about protecting herself, but then she'd gone on about feeling *violated*, and he realized she likely just had some childhood hang-ups.

Join the club.

Bottom line, Jessie Peterson didn't make sense, and he didn't like it.

Jessie swallowed. She still clutched the sparkly little notebook to her chest. But slowly—too slowly for the current situation—she loosened her grasp and then held it back out to him. "I can't do it. I can't. But you can."

Henry took it. He certainly had no qualms about an eleven-year-old runaway's privacy. He flipped the diary page open.

And then he couldn't help but laugh, when it wasn't a laughing matter at all. In different colors, in different fonts, on every *single* page she'd written:

Like I would ever write down my plan.

"Why are you laughing?" Jessie demanded.

Henry held up the book, pages out, and flipped through.

Jessie sighed. "God, she'll be the death of me." But the word *death* seemed to sober her and certainly did him.

"But we do know there's a plan. She spent some time making and hiding this. She's a smart, resourceful girl. So we start from here. I do believe her end goal is the Thompson Ranch, but there's something else. There's something more. Isn't there anywhere else she'd try to go? Something else she'd want to do?" He continued to look through her things—because while the diary may have been a fake, that didn't mean she hadn't left some clues. No matter how smart or resourceful, she was still eleven.

"No. We haven't been here very long, but she says she likes it. She still has this…need to protect me. There's no imminent threat, though, so I don't understand. I thought she knew I'd protect her no matter what."

"Maybe that's the point."

"What?"

Henry focused on rifling through her dresser rather than the growing feeling of…understanding or connection. The girl was nothing like him. She'd *killed* the man who'd threatened and hurt *her* mother. "She knows you'd protect her no matter the cause, so she's going to beat you to the punch."

"But there's no imminent threat," Jessie repeated.

Henry gazed up at her and gave her a pointed look. "You keep saying *imminent*, which means there *is* a threat. Or could be."

Jessie closed her eyes and blew out a breath. "I just want to find her," she said, and her voice wavered like she was *this* close to crying.

He really didn't want to deal with *that*. He wouldn't even have the first clue what to do. "We will," he said, with that old military certainty. Because he had no doubt he could find her, and he thought it unlikely she would have done something stupid enough to be irrevocable.

"She wouldn't have run away for the fun of it. Or to get away from me. I know that. I do." Jessie began to pace, and thank God kept those tears locked down. "There has to be a purpose. More than having you help me. Like you said, she'd have to know you'd just bring her back home."

There was nothing else in the room to give any clues. The girl was definitely too clever for her own good. "Unless she's stubborn enough to think enough tries could change my mind."

Jessie studied him, far more obviously than she'd done before. Again showing off that side of her that was far stronger and more in control than she wanted people to see.

"I guess." She scrubbed her hands over her face. "I guess you're right. In which case we should go back to the ranch. Or try to follow whatever route she would have taken? We have to find her." But she watched as he sifted through the stack of books on Sarabeth's little desk—choose-your-own-adventure types, mostly about pioneer girls in the Wild West.

Jessie inhaled sharply.

"What is it?" he demanded when she offered nothing.

"When…" Jessie cleared her throat. "When Rob had me tied up, he let Sarabeth roam around. Obviously, she was worried about me, trying to get me free, but I think… I got the impression she liked it. Being on her own out in the wild. Like a pioneer girl, she said. And she does love those types of books." She pointed at the book in his hand.

He looked at it. There was a young girl in pioneer garb, all windswept, hands fisted at her hips, looking determined. "What types of books?"

"Oh, the historical girl out in the middle of nowhere on her own, making her own way. It's a whole genre."

Henry grunted and set the book down. He didn't know much about little girls' reading genres, so he'd have to trust Jessie knew what she was talking about.

"But that's not the point. I think she got into the whole… gold thing. She wanted to find it too. I know she wanted to me save more, but she liked those gold stories, and I think she believed Rob when he said there was more." Jessie chewed on her bottom lip and Henry found himself having to look away.

"Where?" he asked gruffly.

"That was the problem. He didn't know. And I don't know how Sarabeth would know."

"She wouldn't have to *know*. She'd just have to think she could figure it out."

"The Peterson house is still out there. That's where Rob was set up. Where he held me. I suppose she could think… there's a clue there. But it's falling apart. Dangerous."

"Yes. Falling apart. *Abandoned*. Which means she likely wouldn't be found, if she didn't want to be. Not too terribly far from our place," Henry mused.

"Maybe it's genetic," Jessie muttered. "And skipped this generation," she added, pointing to herself. But she shook her head vigorously. "Surely she's not out there chasing fake gold stories."

"It connects though. Doesn't it?" Henry asked. "The gold story and this not-imminent threat to you?"

JESSIE KNEW SHE was going to have to explain herself. She just didn't know how to find the right combination of words that would keep Henry from telling his brothers, the right way of framing it that would make it sound…a little less insane.

She'd tried before. When she'd run away from Rob. When she'd been pregnant and scared, she'd tried to tell people what she'd escaped.

No one believed her. No one took her seriously. Because a bunch of men in Idaho dedicating their lives to searching for lost bank robbery gold from the 1800s in *Wyoming* and hurting anyone who might stand in their way *was* insane.

"Jessie."

"Yes, it connects. Sort of. But that isn't the important thing right now. The important thing is getting to Sarabeth before she hurts herself in that old place." She gestured to the door of the room.

She could see a slight hesitation and was worried she'd have to just leave him here, taking up too much space in her apartment, but he gave a firm nod and then strode out of the room.

She let out a long breath of relief and then followed him, out the front and down the stairs into the cool night. But he paused right in front of the building. He looked back up at it and then at her, the harsh angles of his face looking dangerous in the faint streetlight. "You should probably stay here. In case she comes back."

"No, absolutely not."

"Jessie, be reasonable."

He sounded so *aggrieved* her temper responded in kind. "Reasonable? My daughter is *missing.*"

"Yes, and the reasonable thing is that someone stay here in case she comes back. Like we've established, she's a smart kid. Maybe she'll come to her senses."

"And like we *also* established, she's stubborn. I know my daughter. She won't come back until she's done what she left to do."

"And what's that? Because it seems to me you don't exactly know what she's left to do, for someone who knows her so well."

"You keep throwing out accusations, but you don't know me. Why don't *you* stay here and wait for her to change her mind and come back? *I* will go find my daughter. It was a mistake to—"

The sound of a car door had them both looking over to the street. Hazeleigh Hart stood there, staring at them both. Jessie didn't know her well enough to interpret what that expression was, but Jessie didn't think she wanted to know.

"Hi," she offered, walking over to them.

Jessie tried to smile. Everyone involved had been nothing but kind to her, but old habits and mistrust died hard. It wasn't that she thought they would do anything to hurt her—on purpose—it was just that she couldn't let her guard down with anyone.

You already have with Henry.

Yes, because her temper had gotten the better of her. It had been a long time since someone had brought that out in her, and she didn't appreciate it. At all.

"Landon thought someone should wait here in case Sarabeth came back, but he figured Jessie wouldn't want to."

"Landon is right," Jessie said firmly.

"And he figured you wouldn't let Jessie go looking on her own," Hazeleigh continued, looking at Henry.

He nodded silently.

"So I'll stick around just in case. If that's all right with you, Jessie?"

All right was maybe a stretch, but it was better than no one. And while Jessie might not be able to trust anyone, she knew Sarabeth liked Hazeleigh. If she did come back—which Jessie estimated at a less than one percent chance—Sarabeth wouldn't run away from Hazeleigh. "Okay."

Hazeleigh smiled reassuringly and Jessie handed her the keys.

"Call Landon and tell him we think she might be headed for the Peterson place," Henry instructed Hazeleigh. "We don't want to miss her, so we want to fan out. Jessie and I will start here. A few start at the ranch, and a few go straight to the Peterson place."

"All right. I'll tell him. They've all got walkies, but you'll be too far out for that and for your phone for a while if you walk from here."

"We'll be all right."

"Good luck." She passed Jessie and gave her arm a reassuring pat. "She's a smart girl. Brave. She's going to be fine." Hazeleigh went past and into the building and Jessie felt like her heart was in a vise.

The more people assured her that Sarabeth was smart and brave, the more anxiety began to curl itself in her gut and solidify like a heavy weight.

She'd been smart and brave too. Careful and certain. And Rob had still found her, kidnapped her. Smart and brave was all good and well, but it didn't mean you couldn't make mistakes, or the big, bad world didn't have other plans.

"Come on," Henry said, waving her forward. "She'd want to stay within view of the streets until she could get somewhere where landmarks could guide her. So we'll take the straightest shot we can." He crossed Main Street and then walked through the alley between the post office and the bank.

They crossed the back parking lot, and then into the hardscrabble patch of undeveloped land. The moon shone bright above, the stars doing their graceful waltz around it. It was cool, but summer kept it from being *cold*.

"I did this once," she said before she thought better of it.

"Huh?"

It was an old memory, long forgotten in all the other things that had happened in that year. But doing it again, at night, reminded her. The open sky. The dark. That thrilling feeling of freedom and terror. "My grandmother… I lived with her where Sarabeth and I live now. My mother died when I was a baby, and my father left me with my grandmother. I knew I was a Peterson, and I knew people whispered about them, but I didn't understand… I wanted to see the house. I wanted to figure out… I don't know. What the whole *thing* was."

"Like mother, like daughter, huh?"

"I didn't care about the gold—I didn't even know about it. I was just searching for…" Even now as an adult it was hard to articulate. Some kind of connection. Some kind of root of who she was. She'd loved her grandmother more than anything, but she'd known she'd been a burden to the older woman.

"What is it with this gold?" Henry asked with almost enough disgust to match her own.

"I wish I knew. I wish I understood *any* of it."

He kept walking, farther away from town, deeper into the dark black of night. He seemed to have an inner certainty about where he was going, where his feet would fall.

She would have preferred a flashlight.

"My brothers have horses and four-wheelers. They'll likely get to her first. I've got a walkie on me, so once we get within range, we'll contact them for an update. No doubt she'll have been found. Safe and sound."

Jessie thought about that for a few moments. "So why are we doing this?"

Henry didn't say anything for a long while. She tried to match his stride, step where he stepped so she didn't trip over a bump or fall and twist an ankle on a hole or, God forbid, step on a rattlesnake and—

"Just in case," Henry said. And then she felt his hand on hers. "Come on. I'll lead the way."

He linked his fingers with hers and did just that.

SARABETH WAS TIRED. Her feet hurt, and the backpack suddenly felt like it weighed a hundred million pounds. She wanted to keep going, but her eyes were beginning to droop when she walked. If she took a wrong turn, lost sight of where she was and where she was going, it'd be pretty darn easy to get lost.

Real lost. The kind of lost where bears ate you and nobody ever found you.

She swallowed at her dry throat, her heartbeat picking up a bit at the thought of bears. She had bear spray though. She was prepared. She wasn't dumb.

But boy, was she tired and thirsty.

She shined her little flashlight on her watch. She'd been walking for three hours. She'd wanted to make it to four, but if she set her alarm and got started at sunrise, that would be better than getting lost now.

Sarabeth let the beam of light move around her to determine if this was a good enough place to camp. It was a little bumpy, but she had a tiny backpacking tent that she'd gotten for her birthday after *begging* Mom for it. They liked to camp and did it a lot, but Mom was a restless sleeper and was always moving around, waking Sarabeth up.

She'd wanted her own space. Her own pretend freedom. And now she had it.

Sarabeth looked around at the dark world surrounding her, and though fear wanted to creep in, she only had to look up. The moon was bright and almost full. The stars winked like they were sending her messages of support. Mom said she had a great-grandma up there named Sarabeth who was always looking down on her.

So she didn't need to be afraid. She kneeled on the spot and unzipped her pack. First, she took a long drink. She couldn't help another good look into the dark around her.

She frowned, squinted into the deep night.

There was a flash of light far off in the distance. At first, she thought it might be lightning, but it was too small. Too… methodical. Just a little dot of light, on then off. Blink. Blink. Blink. Rest. Blink. Blink. Blink. Rest.

Was someone sending a message? To her? To someone else?

Sarabeth replaced her water bottle, got back to her feet and secured her pack.

One thing was for sure. She wasn't tired anymore.

Chapter Six

Henry would have moved faster on his own. He tried not to linger too much on that thought or let it frustrate him. It was what it was and after all, they were looking for *her* kid.

Not his problem.

And yet, somehow he was hiking through the Wyoming wilderness in the dark anyway. Holding Jessie's damn hand because God knew she didn't know how to hike through the dark like he did without breaking an ankle.

How *had* he gotten into this mess?

He used his free hand to pull out his walkie. Nothing but static still. They weren't close enough to get an update from his brothers. He switched walkie for cell. Still in the middle of a dead zone.

The only choice was to keep moving forward. Day would break soon. The horizon to the east was already beginning its otherworldly glow. The mountains shadows of darkness to the west—which was where they were headed. It was hard not to feel like it was a bad omen.

But Henry had weathered enough bad omens in his life—it wasn't the omen that was the problem. It was how you dealt with it.

"There's another thing I don't understand about this whole thing." She was a little out of breath and he knew she was struggling to keep pace, but she wasn't about to admit it. He wondered if the attempt at conversation now was to help her keep her mind off sore feet or exhaustion.

"It's a long list."

"Yes. But maybe you can explain this one. Why did Sarabeth come to you specifically? I would have thought she would have gone to Landon."

He could read between the lines. Jessie would much rather be doing this with Landon. Probably thought he wouldn't push her to move so fast or whatever. Well, that was too damn bad, wasn't it? "She said I was the mean one."

"Oh, I'm sure she didn't mean—"

"You think that offends me?"

Jessie laughed a little. "I guess not, but it's hardly accurate. You're not nearly as mean as you think you are."

"You don't know me, Jessie."

"I know you're here. Helping me search for my daughter in the dark. I know you don't particularly like me, but you're doing it anyway, because... Well, I assume because you're good at heart, and because Sarabeth has certainly endeared herself to you and your family by saving Landon."

He had to fight the urge to drop her hand. To distance himself from her physically, as well as all the other stuff jangling around inside him.

"Doing the right thing doesn't make you good at heart."

She made a considering noise, but that was all. Henry had to bite his tongue from continuing to argue. Obviously, this was a stupid argument anyway.

So what if she thought he was a nice guy? She'd be disappointed soon enough.

Because there was a difference between the right thing—something he'd determined he'd always do a long time ago—and being a nice, decent Landon-type guy about it.

The mournful howl of a coyote interrupted the quiet buzz of nightfall, followed by a few yips. He expected Jessie to panic or react in some way, but she didn't so much as tighten her grip on his hand.

Then he remembered she'd said she'd done this herself as a kid. Made this trek. He supposed he could understand if you were running away from something bad—the kind of bad he'd grown up with—but he didn't quite understand it for young women like Jessie and Sarabeth who, it seemed like, had decent enough mothers or grandmothers raising them.

"Sarabeth has bear spray," Jessie said out of nowhere.

Henry supposed she was trying to make herself feel better. "That's a good thing to have." Considering he hadn't thought to bring any. Of course at night, they were more likely to run into coyotes or cougars. Now, that was one animal he didn't want to tangle with. "I figure as long as we don't run into a cougar we'll be just..." He trailed off and winced. Probably shouldn't have brought up cougars to the mother of a little girl wandering about the wilderness on her own.

"I know there are cougars out here, as does Sarabeth." She blew out an audible breath. "Of course *know* and *think about* are two different things." Her hand tightened around his.

He tried to think of something to get her mind off all the dangerous animals around them. "So you grew up here?"

"In Wilde, yes. Until I was thirteen anyway."

"Then what happened?"

"My grandmother died. I had to go live with my father."

"Not a prince, huh?"

Jessie laughed. Bitterly. "You could say that. I wish I'd

made better choices so that Sarabeth would have had a better father than I did, but I was young and stupid."

"She's got you. Trust me. One out of two ain't so bad."

"Why, that almost sounds like a compliment."

"Doubtful."

She chuckled a little, but her following sigh was sad. "I wish I could agree with you. But when a girl has to kill her own father, what's worse?"

"Not doing it, and having your mother die because of it." He hadn't *planned* to say that. It was just a simple truth to him. But he felt the way her hand tensed in his, and realized he'd given away far, far, *far* more than he ever wanted to give away to anyone.

"Henry…"

He hated the way her voice sounded…soft. Like she wanted to soothe him. Probably that decent enough mothering instinct she had going on.

That he wanted no part of.

"In the end, no matter how it messes her up, the other messes you up a lot more. And that is the story of why, I promise you, I *am* a mean asshole, Jessie. Don't forget it."

JESSIE DIDN'T HAVE anything to say to this odd turn of events. She hadn't expected looking for her daughter with Henry would give her some insight into who he was.

He'd laid it all out in very generic terms, but Jessie could read between the lines. She was an expert in weaving her own generic terms that didn't specify what had happened.

His mother had died, at the hand of his father in some way, and he blamed himself for not stepping in and doing something about it.

She supposed it made her soft, but that tragic backstory

sure made it a lot harder to be irritated with the grumpy, abrasive man.

And it was sure a lot better than thinking about cougars and Sarabeth out here alone.

They kept walking, and the world around them got lighter and lighter. Until he was no longer the shadow she was clinging to, but the outline of a man with broad shoulders and confident gait.

God, she wished they could stop. She wished they'd find Sarabeth curled up taking a little nap so they could bundle her up and take her home. And once they did, Jessie was going to...

Oh, she didn't know. But she'd have to get through to Sarabeth somehow. Maybe she'd have to agree to look for the stupid gold. Whatever it took.

Whatever it took to keep her daughter from running off like this.

Henry took out his walkie thing and then his cell phone, one at a time so he could still keep her hand in his grip, grunting disgustedly with each.

"Still nothing," Henry muttered. He surveyed the world around them, bathed in the dim light of dawn. "You need a break."

She shook her head. "I'm not stopping until I've found her."

"You'll drop."

"Then I'll drop."

"And expect me to carry you around?"

"Until *you* drop. If that's what it takes."

"I don't drop," he replied, so certain. She would give him credit and thanks, when this was all over, because that certainty really was helping her keep it together.

"I guess we'll see, then," she replied as loftily as she could manage.

He studied her for a long while, with an intensity that unnerved her. It made her all too aware they were still holding hands, and his was big and callused and scarred. An uncomfortable little flutter centered itself in her stomach.

Oh, no. No flutters with him.

"You're not what you pretend to be, are you?" he asked, still scrutinizing her.

She didn't like that he could see through her, but he'd seen her at her worst too many times. Why wouldn't he? If he helped her find Sarabeth, she couldn't care *what* he saw in her. Sarabeth was all that mattered.

But Jessie was hardly letting him think he had the upper hand here. "Neither are you."

He dropped her hand. Finally. "Not pretending."

"Maybe you don't *think* you're pretending, but you are."

He shrugged as if he didn't care what she thought, but there was something about the way he'd dropped her hand, kind of suddenly. Something about the way he held himself now. He was always tense, but she was beginning to notice there were different *kinds* of tension in him.

This was the kind that wanted any and all attention off him.

"What's this now?" He strode forward, and she assumed he was trying to change the subject, the attention, but when she followed she saw what he was pointing to. It was a tiny little metal link—like the kind that was part of a key chain.

Jessie swallowed. Like the kind of key chains Sarabeth loved to keep on her backpack.

"Henry…" She didn't know what to say. What to do. She was frozen, staring at the little link as Henry picked it up.

He looked around, then began retracing their steps. She

didn't know how he knew where to go, but a few yards away he crouched. "Here."

Jessie came to stand behind him. There was the full key chain. A little plastic pig with a ridiculous grinning face right next to a big rock.

Henry picked it up, then stood and looked around. "She probably stood on this rock to get a better vantage point. Maybe slipped a little—she didn't hurt herself," he was quick to add. "Or she'd still be here or there'd be more indentations around the area. But the key chain probably hit the rock and broke off and she didn't notice."

"Why would she need a vantage point in the dark?"

Henry was quiet for a while, making the nerves already jangling inside her intensify.

"She might have seen a light."

"A light? Out here?" Jessie looked around. She couldn't imagine they were close enough to any of the surrounding ranches to see a light, but she supposed she didn't know that for *sure*.

He studied the ground, holding the key chain in his hand. "This way." He strode into a slightly grassy area, mostly laid flat by the wind that usually blew through this kind of valley. "She came this way."

"But this is a much harder walk. If she planned it out, she'd keep going the way we were."

"But something changed her course. See this?" He pointed to the grass. It just looked like wind-flattened grass to her.

"No."

"There's slight indentations here," he said, pointing to a part of the grass. Then he moved a little bit ahead and pointed again. "And here. Footsteps. And not big enough to be adult ones."

Jessie still didn't see what he was pointing at, but she believed him anyhow. He wasn't going to lead her on a wild goose chase for the fun of it. So she followed him through the grass, watching him as he inspected and seemed to see things there she didn't.

"How do you know all of this?"

"I've tracked a few people in my day."

"Why? I thought you were a rancher."

He paused for a moment, such a short hesitation she almost could believe she was overthinking things.

"Did I say *people*? I meant cows."

He had *not* meant cows, but Jessie didn't feel like pressing him on it. She just wanted him to lead her to Sarabeth. So she followed him. Their pace slowed considerably as Henry was clearly being careful to look for his *indentations*. Eventually, they reached a place where the hardscrabble outcroppings overtook the grass.

"Where are we?" Jessie asked, hoping he hadn't lost her trail. Hoping desperately that this was right.

Henry looked around. "Thompson Ranch is due south. Peterson Ranch west. Town east. We've managed to go a couple miles." He checked his walkie again, but only got static. "It's okay. We've got some footprints here."

Again, he pointed. This time she *sort* of saw what he was pointing at. She never would have noticed those little indents—just in the shape of a crescent moon—but it made sense they were the marks of the heel of Sarabeth's boot.

She swallowed as too many *what-ifs* tried to terrify her to the bone. "You're sure those are Sarabeth's?"

"Key chain, plus size of prints? Yeah, I'm pretty sure."

"Okay," Jessie said, letting her breath out slowly. She'd choose to believe him. To be relieved he knew how to track people—no matter how.

He climbed up the outcropping easily, then held out a hand to her. She frowned at it. "I am a Wyoming girl. I know how to crawl over some rocks," she said. She regretted refusing help almost immediately, because though she *could* climb on her own, her body was bone tired and wanted to give up.

But Henry standing at the top of the rocks motivated her enough to push through.

When she made it, he smiled, and there was that damn flutter again, but the smile softened up some of the hard lines of his face. Made those soft eyes twinkle with something other than his usual flat suspicion.

"She really does take after you," he said, surveying her next to him. "I think I've talked to her twenty whole minutes and she's always correcting me too."

"Well, it sounds like you need to be corrected too much."

His smile didn't die, but he looked out over the other side of the rocks. Wyoming stretched out before them. The rocks, some pasture land, and there in the distance…

Jessie knew that tree. The crooked fence posts, the sagging barbed wire. The scraggly grass. It was an abandoned family cemetery.

Her family.

"Stop," Jessie managed, grabbing Henry before he could start forward. Her throat was dry and it came out more like a croak as her heartbeat panicked against her ribs.

Henry shot her a questioning look.

"This is Peterson land past there."

"So?"

"So if she saw a light, and came here, someone is on the Peterson land. When it's supposed to be deserted. That is not good."

Henry swore.

Chapter Seven

Henry didn't like the jolt of fear that burst through him. "Look, it was just a theory," he offered, hoping Jessie would stop looking so pale and alarmed in the pearly dawn. "We don't know she saw a light." Though he was hard-pressed to come up with another theory for why she'd been standing on that rock.

And he was pretty sure she had been. He'd spent too long tracking people, hiding from people, searching for clues, to miss the story that these clues laid out.

But Jessie didn't need to know that. She might overreact or panic, and that would be the worst thing they could do right now.

Her hand was still clutched on his arm. "If she went toward it…"

"She's a smart girl," Henry said firmly, but his thoughts were right alongside Jessie's. Because Sarabeth *was* a smart girl, but also an impetuous and curious one. She wasn't afraid of danger enough, because she'd gotten some confidence by doing what needed to be done.

A double-edged sword in an eleven-year-old.

"Henry, I know my daughter." She blew out an unsteady breath. "She'd go toward it. She's too… She needs answers and she gets them. But she'd be careful about it. She wouldn't just go charging in."

Henry thought so too, but he was glad Jessie's feelings—calm, no matter how she clutched his arm—aligned with his.

"So let's follow suit." He studied the area around them. This was the eastern edge of Peterson land. They should be getting within walkie range of *someone* soon enough. "We don't know where—if—she saw a light, but she wouldn't go right for it."

Henry walked again to the edge of the rocks and looked back the way they'd come. He studied the rock he thought she'd stood on, the angle of the impression of her fall. He couldn't pinpoint where she'd been looking exactly, but he could rule some directions out.

"The house would be straight through all that," Jessie said. When he returned to her side she was pointing out across the vast expanse before them. "That cemetery—"

"Cemetery?"

"Yes, what that barbed wire is around? It's the old Peterson cemetery."

Henry frowned and looked at the hardscrabble patch of land. There were little markers that he'd figured were just rocks. But they were arranged in a sort of pattern, he supposed. Cemetery made sense.

He suppressed a shudder. He felt Jessie's eyes on him.

"Surely you're not afraid of cemeteries?" she said, sounding faintly surprised.

"I'm not afraid of anything," Henry replied tersely.

"Do you think they're haunted? Are you worried about ghosts?" She seemed far too amused.

It poked at an old…not a *fear* exactly, but just all that pomp and circumstance and grief around cemeteries made for a bit of a discomfort, that was all. Even abandoned, sunken cemeteries that did indeed seem to be the perfect haven for ghosts or spirits.

Because he'd seen real hell and dealt with *real* problems. Ghosts were far more intangible than the reality of what he'd been through.

"I've carried dead bodies out of war zones, Jessie. I'm not worried about ghosts or phantoms or whatever the hell."

She blinked and he inwardly cursed.

"War zones," she echoed. "You were in the military."

He shrugged. Not exactly a secret these days. His brothers were always telling their women about what was supposed to be on the down low. Henry wasn't about to explain it to this woman who meant *nothing* to him.

"Well, that explains some things."

"Huh?"

"You just have that… I don't know. You just make more sense within a military context."

Within a military context. "I don't have the faintest idea what that means."

"Well, I'll figure out a better way of explaining it once we find my daughter." She pointed again. "I don't know the mileage, but I know past the cemetery is a straight shot to the house from that ridge over there. That was the path I took way back when."

Henry looked at the landmarks and tried to orient it all into the map in his mind. He wasn't sure of the mileage either, but it could be a long ways. The Peterson spread was vast. But if Sarabeth had seen a light, it couldn't be clear on the other side of the property, so that was something.

"So if the light came from the area of the house, and if I was Sarabeth, stood there and saw a light and wanted to go toward it, but carefully, I wouldn't take a straight shot," Jessie continued. "But I wouldn't want to get lost."

"We're making a lot of assumptions here," Henry warned. But he was making the same ones in his head, so he couldn't argue with hers. "But if she followed the fence line east, it would take her more toward where that old schoolhouse was. Closer to our ranch. Would she know that?"

Jessie chewed on her lip. "I'm not sure. She spent some time at that old schoolhouse, so probably."

"Well, let's see if I can find some footprints or something." He studied the sharp cliff of the outcropping. It would require some fancy maneuvering. Somehow he could picture Sarabeth crawling down it with ease though. "You need help, Wyoming girl?"

Jessie sniffed. "No."

He tried to bite back a grin. Now *this* Jessie was a lot better than the one pretending to be someone who was too afraid to make eye contact. Not that it mattered what Jessie he dealt with. He was just helping her find her daughter. He didn't need to like her to do that or anything.

He made it to the ground, then looked at her progress. She was being too careful, thinking too hard. What she really needed to do was—

She jumped. A surprisingly graceful and athletic movement. She landed easily, then brushed off her hands. When she looked over at him, it was a kind of snotty *told you so* look, and something low in his gut tightened.

Nope. No way. Not going down that road.

He looked away, down at the task before him. The task that had everything to do with Sarabeth and nothing to do with Jessie.

He started searching for footprints, evidence Sarabeth had taken this route. Had gone west like he hoped she had.

"Is this it?" Jessie asked a little farther out than he'd been looking. She pointed at the ground next to a patch of grass.

Henry studied it. Another little half-moon, not quite as clear as the ones above, but the ground down here was dryer, more susceptible to wind. "Could be." He studied the area around it, trying to find the next one.

But something…trickled down his spine. That old feeling he'd learned to trust—not just as a soldier, but as the son of a man prone to using his fists to make a point. So he stopped looking for footprints and studied the horizon instead. He saw the telltale flash of just enough movement to have his instincts kicking in.

He pulled Jessie to the ground, behind some rocks, and hell, sheltered her body with his. Who knew how well the rocks would act as protection. Might as well add him too.

"What are you doing?" she demanded.

The gunshot exploding through the air answered her question for him.

JESSIE WOULD HAVE screamed if Henry hadn't clamped his hand over her mouth. He had his entire body wrapped around her, pressed against the hard, pointy rock. It was an uncomfortable position. Pointy rock to her back, hard, large man to her front.

But someone had shot a gun. At them, if she had to guess. *Oh, God.*

"Don't start panicking, Jessie. Okay? We're not going to panic."

It was an order, and it kept her tethered to this moment. No panicking. No letting her brain tumble into the possibilities. They weren't shot, and Henry was here with his military background. They were all right. They would be all right.

She wouldn't think about all the Sarabeth what-ifs. She couldn't. She could only focus on… On…

"Take a deep breath," Henry said low in her ear. "Count to three. Then let it out. Same count. You hear me?" Somehow, cocooned inside the protection of him and the rocks, he gave her a little shake.

Another tether. She nodded and he took his hand off her mouth.

"Breathe. One, two, three."

She obeyed. She didn't know what else to do. The counting helped. Focusing on the numbers, something to do, rather than everything she felt. In. Out. She swallowed but her throat was dry.

"Why would anyone shoot at us?" she asked, her voice sounding far more shaken than she preferred.

"No idea. But we're going to find out. Don't move."

Again, she obeyed. He very carefully moved, keeping her pressed to the rock, but some of his body peeled away from hers as he tried to peer around the boulders.

But another shot exploded into the quiet morning, and he ducked back down as Jessie flinched and pressed herself even harder against the rock behind her.

He swore under his breath.

"Henry."

"It's far off. So far they can't get a good shot at us. Which is good. It gives me an idea of the kind of guns they've got, and where we'll be safe."

She wasn't so sure she believed him. If it was so far off why did he duck when the shot went off? Why were they hiding? Why was his body protecting hers?

But she didn't voice any questions. She much preferred his fake story.

He looked down at her. His eyes were dark, his expression grim, but he was clearly in charge. He knew what he was doing. She wasn't used to trusting people, but in this moment he knew how to get them through whatever this was. He'd been in war zones. He knew how to deal with people shooting at them.

And you grew up in the Peterson compound. You know how to handle danger too.

Yes, she wasn't some fainting, screaming dead weight. She could hold her own. Maybe fighting back wasn't her strong suit, but she knew how to avoid danger, didn't she?

"Do you have a gun?" Jessie asked, curling her hands into fists so she didn't feel tempted to grab on to him.

"No, but I have a knife. What about you?"

She shook her head. "Nothing."

He nodded, then reached down and pulled the knife out of his boot and handed it to her.

She didn't take it. "What about you?"

"I can fight with my fists as well as any knife."

Fight. Jessie had never been a fighter. She'd been a hider. A runner. Fighting? She didn't know *how*, and the few times she'd tried, she'd failed.

She couldn't fail Sarabeth.

"Look, we don't know where Sarabeth is. Maybe she's safe and sound at the Thompson Ranch," Henry offered. Another possibility that seemed just as unlikely as far-off guns that couldn't reach them.

"And maybe she's with whoever is shooting at us,"

"Maybe," Henry agreed, and his gaze held hers. "I can handle this. If you want to stay put. Or run. It's not a question for me. I can wade in there and make sure she's not there. You can stay right here, with the walkie or my phone. You can run. All of those are viable options for you."

For you. It shouldn't put her back up. They were clearly very different people. And he was right. "I'm much better at running and hiding than I am at fighting," Jessie said, but how could she do any of those things without Sarabeth beside her? "I can't run away from my daughter, Henry. Not with the possibility she's out there in the middle of this."

Henry studied her. "Sometimes running and hiding are what a person has to do to fight." He took her hand, pressed the sheathed knife to her palm. "But sometimes, like it or not, you have to fight. You follow my lead, you listen to me, you'll fight just fine."

Her fingers curled around the knife. *Fight just fine.* She had her doubts, but Henry sounded so sure. Like he knew exactly what he was doing. She desperately wanted someone to know what they were doing when it came to finding Sarabeth and getting her home safe and sound.

Henry put his hand on her shoulder, gave it a squeeze. "I'm not letting anything happen to you or Sarabeth, okay?"

It hit her too hard, in the middle of *whatever* was going on. No one was ever looking out for them. No one ever cared if anything happened to them. Jessie had been on her own since her grandmother had died. It hadn't felt like an impossible weight until Sarabeth had been born, and even that impossible weight had come with a matching, overwhelming joy and love.

For a brief almost nonexistent second, it looked like panic crossed his face.

"Don't cry on me now," he muttered. "We've got a gunman to take out."

"I'm not going to cry," Jessie managed, though her voice was croaky and she had to dash a tear off her cheek. "I just don't understand why you're doing this."

He laughed, and the sound was bitter. "Yeah, me neither."

Chapter Eight

Henry couldn't concern himself with Jessie's...emotions or whatever. There was a gunman. Shooting at them, and though he hadn't lied when he'd said the shooter was too far away, without a far-range gun, to be a real threat to them, it was only a matter of time before they either advanced, or something escalated.

Henry would really prefer if Jessie stayed here, safe and sound, and he didn't want to analyze *that* at all. But if he could handle whoever was *shooting* at them, maybe Jessie could find Sarabeth. *Or* they could get close enough into walkie range to reach one of his brothers.

Were they close enough for the sound of the gunshot to carry? He didn't know.

And that was the problem here. He didn't *know*.

"What is going on?"

"I don't—"

"No," Henry interrupted. "You're not going to lie, or hedge because it could be a couple different things. We're getting shot at. There's a reason, and you know it. Now I need to know it. Quickly."

She frowned at him, that line digging into her forehead that he was starting to recognize as sheer stubbornness. That they didn't have time for. But before he could tell her that, in not the nicest terms, she sighed. Her shoulders slumped.

"I don't know who's shooting at us, but they're on Peterson land. If it has to do with my family, this ranch, then it's this gold."

"You've got to be kidding me." Henry thought about just leaving her here. Walking right for the gunman and taking his chances. Because he was so tired of nonsense stories about old gold.

"You have no idea how much I wish I was," she said, and she was so serious. Hugging herself like she was cold even as the day warmed. "You have no idea how little I understand it. But my father has dedicated his life to finding that gold. Rob…became obsessed with it after working for my father. If I believed in curses, I'd say just the *idea* of this ridiculous *bounty* cursed people into insanity."

"Jessie."

"And look, I get it. You don't believe me. You think I'm being cryptic because…what? I'm a pain in the ass? I think I can handle it? No, it's because it's *insane*. And no one believes me. Then they wade in thinking that if there is a problem, that it's with some off-his-rocker harmless old man, but my father is a dangerous man. I escaped, and I keep a low profile mostly because he doesn't care about *me*, but if he thought Rob told me or Sarabeth something about that gold, then we'd become his prime target."

"This man is obsessed with gold we don't even know exists?"

"Yes. If anything, it only makes him more dangerous. It's all he cares about. All he's *ever* cared about, and if you live in that compound, it's all *you're* allowed to care about." She stared at him, then rolled her eyes. "I know you don't believe me. The cops wouldn't either, and worse, they'd put Sarabeth's name out there and draw his attention. Bad enough if family services let me keep her, worse if they didn't."

But it wasn't so much a matter of belief. It was more trying to untangle what was happening and line it up with her story.

He'd seen men obsessed with less. Who dedicated their whole life to something—*anything*—just to feel smart or important. Those things didn't have to make sense to anyone but the man feeling them.

"Explain this compound to me."

She looked confused for a second, then looked up at the sky. "I don't think we have time for that."

She wasn't wrong, which irritated him. They needed to deal with the gunman, find Sarabeth and then maybe untangle the whys.

"But know they'll do anything in their pursuit of this. They'll murder you. They'll murder me. They'll..."

She trailed off, but he knew what she'd been trying to say. Sarabeth, too.

He couldn't get his mind around the whole *find gold* thing, but he understood people who wanted to kill. *That* he had far too much experience with.

And they were just indiscriminately shooting at people. They couldn't possibly know what he and Jessie were up to...

Unless they had Sarabeth.

"There's no other reason they could be out here? Shooting at us?"

"None that I know of."

He wished that made him feel better. But gold or some secret reason, someone was shooting at them while Sarabeth was somewhere out here. Henry had to find her—first and foremost.

"Okay, this is what we're going to do. You're going to stay here. I'm going to go find Sarabeth. She can't be far. If she was smart, she'd be hiding at daybreak. We should have caught up to her, generally speaking."

"But—"

"No buts. She's the goal, right? We don't care about gold or your father or whoever is shooting at us. We care that Sarabeth and you are safe. So you'll stay put." He pointed at the knife. "Someone comes, you use that on them, fight like hell, do what you have to. If they end up taking you back to that house, know I'll come get you out."

She looked up at him, eyes wide, but he didn't see what he'd hoped. Agreement. Trust. There was a wariness in there. And something worse than fear. Resignation.

"All that matters is Sarabeth is safe."

"Once she's safe, I'll come get you out. *If* it comes to that." And he had a bad feeling he'd do everything in his power to make sure it didn't.

SARABETH HEARD THE gunshots and froze. She knew what those sounded like now. What they felt like. She knew how to use a gun. She knew how to kill someone.

And still, everything inside her went cold and stiff. Why was someone shooting? *Who* were they shooting at?

She huddled deeper into the little shelter she'd made around a big boulder, an old tree and some fence posts.

Last night she'd kept that blinking light in her line of sight but hadn't gotten anywhere near it. She wanted to know who was out there—on Peterson land—but she'd known better than to get close. She thought whoever had the light was at the house, so she planned on going there once it was dark again.

But as soon as the sun had begun to rise, she'd known

the best thing for her to do was hide. And so she'd been sitting here waiting. Planning. Dozing.

If someone was at the old Peterson place, they had to be looking for the gold. *Had* to be.

But who were they shooting at? Now that it was daylight and she was hidden away, the gunshots were too far away to be about *her*.

Mom.

No, Mom wouldn't be… Sarabeth chewed on the collar of her shirt. Mom would come after her, but she'd ask for help. Henry or Landon or someone. And they knew how to handle men with guns.

Unless Mom *hadn't* asked for help.

Sarabeth squeezed her eyes shut. Everything had gotten all messed up. There weren't supposed to be people here. What should she do now? At night she could handle herself. She was small and careful and could hide. She knew the house now too, since Rob had let her run loose in there when he'd had Mom tied up.

But she didn't know what to do about men shooting in broad daylight, knowing Mom was probably looking for her by now.

Mom had to have asked the Thompson brothers for help. *Had* to have.

But if she hadn't… Well, maybe Sarabeth needed to get to them. When she'd been watching the light last night, she had taken a route that would keep the light in sight while leading her in the direction of the fence line between Thompson and Peterson land. Surely there wouldn't be anyone between her and the Thompsons.

She could make a run for it. Just go as fast as she could and get the first Thompson brother she saw. They could help. They could get Mom out of any trouble.

Unless she's been shot.

Sarabeth wanted to cry at the thought. She nearly jumped to her feet and just started to run. Who cared what happened to her? She just wanted to get to her mom and make sure she was okay.

But she took a deep, gulping breath, because Mom always told her to breathe before she did anything stupid. *A smart woman thinks before she acts.*

Sarabeth had to think. She was smart. She was brave. She took another breath and squeezed her eyes shut so she could think about what to do rather than those two echoing gunshots that had interrupted her nap.

She gathered her things, carefully and quietly. She shrugged into her backpack and thought about where she was and where she wanted to go.

The shooting probably came from the house. She'd have to go closer to the house. Make sure Mom wasn't there. Make sure that was where the people and the lights were.

But…what if she could get the people with the lights *away* from the house? *Away* from Mom, if Mom was out there? She chewed on her bottom lip and then decided that nothing mattered except helping Mom.

She dug in her backpack, came up with the matches, then set about building a fire. She'd make it small, but lots of kindling. She'd do what she could to get it going enough to start a fire signal. Someone would see the smoke and come help.

She used anything she could find—grass, branches, leaves, what splinters of wood she could pull off the old fence posts. She was old hat at building a campfire, but making sure the smoke built and rose was a little trickier than she was expecting.

She was sweating by the time she was satisfied. Still not

certain it was big enough, but it had to be. Had to be. She stepped back to survey the smoke and the fire one last time.

"Keep going," she muttered. She fingered the gold coin in her pocket. "Bring me luck," she whispered.

Then she turned, ready to run for the house. She was far enough away from it and where she thought the shots were coming from that she could run for a little bit without anyone hearing her. Then she'd slow down, take it easy.

If Mom was hurt, she'd get to her. And find a way to help her. Save her. She would do whatever it took.

One more deep breath, and then she took her first step. But something stopped her.

No, not something.

Someone.

Someone had grabbed her backpack, stopping her forward progress. Keeping her still and then nearly lifting her up off her feet.

"Where do you think you're going?"

JESSIE KNEW WHAT it was to wait. In silence. In fear. She had learned in those teenage years to find a center of calm, no matter what threats were leveled against her.

But she could never find that calm when it came to what threats were leveled against her daughter.

Henry had ordered her to stay put. She had the knife he'd given her unsheathed in her hand. She was supposed to fight like hell if anyone came over the ridge of rocks.

If only she knew how.

But if it was for Sarabeth, she would. Whatever it took. And Henry would find Sarabeth. He'd promised, and he'd looked so competent wading out into the open world around them. Like he wasn't afraid of gunshots or imbalanced men with unhealthy obsessions they were willing to kill over.

She didn't really believe promises anymore, but she did believe in Henry's ability. She just kept hearing him say he'd carried men out of war zones. She knew he'd suffered through his father's killing his mother and felt guilty over it.

She knew he understood—in a way so many people couldn't—what the danger really was. Maybe he didn't believe her about the gold. She didn't need him to.

Because he knew what to do with a gunman, and understood Sarabeth was the goal.

It was just hard, because Jessie had never in her life thought to sit tight and wait for someone else to handle something for her. Her entire adolescence at her father's compound had been about hiding, then planning how to get out.

There'd been that brief, stupid moment where she'd thought Rob was the answer, but after she'd escaped *him*, her life had been about keeping Sarabeth away from her family. The gold obsession. The off chance her father might want something from her someday.

Maybe thinking she could make a home in Wilde had been a stupid moment too. She'd just assumed if he didn't *live* in Wilde, didn't spend time looking in Wilde, he didn't really care about it. And whatever gold was still missing— if he believed that—surely was somewhere else.

Anywhere else.

She frowned as she thought over Henry's reaction. Usually people rolled their eyes, scoffed, made fun. Or worse, they agreed with her in that way that suggested they might call a psychiatrist and have her involuntarily committed.

But Henry hadn't done any of those things. He'd considered. She wasn't sure she'd convinced him, but he'd *listened*. And while he'd asked if there was some other reason this could all be going on, he hadn't dismissed her out of hand.

Jessie had to resist the urge to peek out of her little make-shift cover. She wanted to see if those gunmen had come for her. If she could still catch sight of Henry out there. She wanted to…

She heard…something. Something new. The faintest exhale. Maybe a footstep? A rustle. She clutched the knife, positioned her back to the rock and her face to the opening.

She would fight. She could fight.

But when the person appeared, she could only stare. Her fingers went so nerveless she nearly dropped the knife. Catching herself at the last moment. But still, she couldn't fight. She couldn't even speak.

Because the woman standing in front of her looked…*exactly*…like Jessie herself.

Except she had a gun in her hand instead of a knife.

Chapter Nine

Henry held Sarabeth by the straps of her backpack. Once he was sure she wouldn't run or scream, he set her down on her feet.

She must have recognized his voice because she immediately turned and threw herself at him. Her little arms wrapping around him so tightly he could only stand stock-still. Then she began to cry.

Hell.

"Aren't you supposed to be too old for this?" he asked, looking down at her. Her hair had fallen mostly out of its bands and was a bird's nest of reddish tangles. Her hands were clutched in the sides of his coat.

Apparently that was the wrong thing to say because she only cried harder.

"Okay, okay," he muttered. He awkwardly patted the top of her head and looked around helplessly. He'd never been around kids. Granted, he'd been to war and seen grown men cry, but he didn't know what to say or do around a little *girl* crying.

"Mom asked you for help," she said between little hiccupy breaths.

"Well, yeah." The head wasn't working so he tried patting her back instead and peeling one of her hands off his coat.

"She's safe, right?" She looked up at him, her dirt-and dust-covered face streaked with tears. One hand was still clutched in his coat. Her hazel eyes were wet and imploring and something…something seemed to turn over in his chest.

"Yeah, kid." He rested his hand on her shoulder and it didn't feel quite so awkward when she leaned into him. "Let's get back to her, huh?"

She nodded. "But I heard guns."

"Yeah, so did we, but we haven't quite figured out where or why." It was a little bit of a lie, but not a total one. "Come on."

She finally let go of his coat, and he expected her to follow him, but instead, she curled her hand around his. Like it was natural. Normal. Henry didn't have the slightest idea what to do with it.

In the end, all he could do was curl his own fingers around hers and try not to think about how small and vulnerable her hand seemed in his much bigger one. He eyed the horizon and made sure to position himself between Sarabeth and whatever direction the house was. It wasn't foolproof safety, as the gunmen could have moved from the house, but he tried to walk where there was cover.

And he kept on full alert, ready to keep her safe from any gunshots as they walked back to where Jessie was hiding.

"You're really bad at dealing with people crying," she said, using her free arm to wipe her nose.

Henry frowned down at her. He *knew* that, but somehow her saying it rankled. "Yeah, well, people don't usually cry around me. What was I supposed to do?"

"You're supposed to say it's okay. Be encouraging. And the back pat wasn't bad, but a rub is better."

"Well, I'll keep that in mind next time you start the waterworks all over me." God, he hoped this was the one and only time.

"I don't cry very often, but I was worried Mom came and looked for me by herself when I heard those gunshots. That she might be hurt."

"And whose fault would that have been?" He winced. That was a dumb thing to say to a kid.

But she shrugged. "Exactly. But she got you. So everything's going to be okay."

The idea that everything was going to be okay simply because he was here did not sit well with him. At all. He had a lot of confidence in his abilities, but there were a lot of variables here—including this little girl he didn't know what to do with.

He studied his surroundings again. He needed to get Jessie and Sarabeth back to the ranch. Then he and one of his brothers could get to the bottom of the shooting. Maybe even bring in the cops if he got Jessie and Sarabeth out of it. Leave out crazy gold stories and just bring up the gunshots.

It was a plan anyway. And if he focused on that he didn't have to think about the little girl's hand in his. Like she was sure he was going to swoop in and make everything okay for her and her mom.

Like she knew, deep down under all the reasons he told himself this didn't matter to him or have anything to do with him, that was exactly what he wanted.

They didn't walk back the way Henry had come. He took a more careful route, did his best to hide their tracks so no one could track *them* the way he'd tracked Sarabeth.

They hadn't been too off the mark, he and Jessie. Sarabeth hadn't been more than a half mile away, and toward the Thompson Ranch. He looked down at their joined hands, and wanted to keep his mouth shut but…

"You did good, kid. Good job hiding. Good job staying away from the light."

"You saw it too?" she asked, angling her face up toward him. "The blinking light?"

"Blinking?"

"Yeah, three blinks then a break then three blinks. It kept going. Three. Stop. Three."

Henry frowned over that. Blinking lights pointed more to a signal than simply just light to see by. But Sarabeth kept talking.

"I wanted to know what it was, but I figured it'd be better to wait for daytime when I could see. So I just kept it in sight and kept walking. I wanted to be close enough to you guys's place that I could run there. But when the sun came out I figured I'd better hide." She paused, studying him carefully as they walked. "I really did a good job?"

"I mean, running away was stupid. But after that colossal mistake, you made some good choices."

She grinned up at him. Which had that thing turn over in his chest again. Something was seriously wrong with him.

"What were you up to, Sarabeth?"

She chewed on her bottom lip. "Wellll…"

"Might as well spill it now that you've gotten yourself in a heap of trouble."

She sighed, her shoulders slumping. Then she dug her free hand into her pocket and pulled something out. She held it to him so he took it.

A coin. An old…gold coin. Henry swore. "You've got to be kidding me."

"There's more of it. My father was sure of it. And I know Mom's family wants it, and I just thought if I could find it, we wouldn't really be in danger anymore. And it would be ours. Not theirs."

Henry turned the coin over. It was real gold, that was for sure, but he didn't see why all these people were willing to kill over it.

"Can I have it back?" She held out her hand. "It's my good luck charm."

He handed it back to her as they walked. "There ain't no such thing as luck, Sarabeth."

She scrunched up her nose. "I think you're wrong."

Henry shrugged. No point arguing with an eleven-year-old. But she should know… "Look, maybe there's luck. Maybe there's not. But you can't rely on it either way. End of the day, you can only rely on yourself."

She studied the coin, then him. "I can rely on my mom."

It gave him a little pang. What must *that* be like? But he was a grown man. No need to be thinking about old mommy issues when there was a shooter out there, and he needed to get Sarabeth and her mother safe.

They started to approach the place where he'd left Jessie, but Henry slowed. Something was wrong. The sound of…movement. More than the wind. More than an animal.

"Get behind me," he ordered in a quiet whisper.

"But—"

He moved Sarabeth behind him and held her there, and was glad when she had the presence of mind to not say any more. He stayed very still, trying to get a handle on what was wrong.

A voice. Female, so he supposed it could be Jessie talking to herself, but that seemed wrong too. "Stay put," he muttered, arranging Sarabeth so she was seated behind a boulder. "Don't move or make a sound."

She looked at him with a rebellious frown but nodded once. He'd have to take her word for it.

He didn't see anything. Didn't *feel* anything. Though he

sort of suddenly hoped good luck existed and lived within Sarabeth's little coin because none of this made sense.

Another shuffle, the low murmur of voices. Henry crept forward, from the back of the rocks. If he climbed up, he could look down and see what was what. But he had to be careful, and silent.

Luckily he had experience with just that, and though it took longer than he might have wanted he made it to the top without disturbing so much as a pebble. He peered into the little place he'd left Jessie. She was there, and there was some relief that she appeared whole and unharmed.

But she wasn't alone.

He looked back at Sarabeth, who was crouching like he'd told her to, with wide eyes and a worried frown on her face. But she'd listened.

He retraced his steps. Once he was close enough to whisper, he posed his question. "Does your mom have a…twin sister?"

"No," Sarabeth replied.

"Someone who looks just like her?"

Sarabeth shook her head.

Henry looked back at where he'd just been. This didn't make sense. There were two identical women. Henry wasn't even sure he'd have been able to tell them apart.

If one wasn't holding a gun.

EVEN THOUGH A gun was pointed at her, all Jessie could do was stare at the woman's face. Searching for some kind of difference. A scar, a mole, a wrinkle.

It was impossible. Granted, she didn't spend a lot of time *looking* at her own face, but still. It was so darn bizarre she was having trouble paying attention to what the woman was saying.

"Who *are* you?" Jessie finally asked. What else was there to do? She supposed try to get the gun, or fight with the knife still in her hand, but…but… "Why do we look exactly alike?"

The woman didn't seem surprised to find a carbon copy of her hiding out on Peterson land. But there must have been some suspicion and maybe a little confusion in her mind, because she certainly didn't start shooting or ordering Jessie to do anything.

She glanced up at the rocks surrounding them, her suspicious frown smoothing out carefully before she returned her gaze to Jessie. "Are you out here alone?"

Jessie hesitated, which was a mistake. She knew it just by the way the woman looked at her. It reminded her far too much of her father. "More or less."

The woman snorted. "Uh-huh." She seemed to consider, then she stepped to the side. "Come out here."

Jessie swallowed and tightened her grip on the knife. Out there seemed safer—after all, she could run out there. Here she was trapped by rocks and the woman with the gun.

But still. Following orders could be dangerous.

"Now," the woman said, holding the gun just a little tighter.

"I think you should tell me what's going on." But Jessie moved a little forward, and she didn't drop the knife.

Again, the woman snorted. "I'm guessing I don't know much more than you."

"I find that *very* hard to believe."

The woman shrugged, then motioned with the gun. "Come on. Someone's out here. Probably trying to break you out of my evil clutches. If it ain't one of mine, it's one of yours."

"I don't—"

The woman whirled, but she was a second too late. Henry had the gun out of her grasp so quickly Jessie wasn't even sure how it had happened. And then she didn't care, because Sarabeth darted forward and flung her arms around Jessie's waist.

Jessie hugged her back fiercely. For a few precious moments nothing else mattered except her daughter was safe and in her arms. "You're okay?" She pulled her back enough to study her.

Sarabeth nodded. Her eyes were uncharacteristically red-rimmed and Jessie's heart tightened. Sarabeth didn't cry easily. She pulled her back into a tight hug.

"You are in so much trouble," Jessie managed through her tight throat. "So much."

Sarabeth squeezed tighter. "I'm sorry, Mom."

Jessie pulled back again, needing to study Sarabeth's face in more detail. Catalog every freckle, every scratch. "No more doing it on our own, okay? We're in this together. No matter what. Promise?"

Sarabeth's hazel eyes were wide, but she seemed to give it some serious thought. She took a deep breath. "Okay, I promise. If you do."

Jessie hesitated. She was the mother. Didn't that mean sometimes she had to act alone—to protect? Didn't that mean that they weren't always a team of equal partners, even if she wanted Sarabeth to feel like they were?

But that wasn't fair. Jessie wasn't sure how to be *fair* as a mother, though. "We are *always* a team. But sometimes I'm the leader of the team, and make decisions for the both of us, okay?"

Sarabeth wrinkled her nose, but before she could agree or argue, Henry cleared his throat, and everything else came crashing down.

Right. This wasn't over. Jessie stood.

Henry was holding the identical woman's hands behind her back. She looked…bored, rather than scared or irritated. And she looked a little too hard at Sarabeth.

Jessie stood between them. "Why don't you tell us who you are?"

The woman seemed to give this some thought. In fact, everything about the woman wasn't so much bored as… calculating. "Quinn."

"Quinn Peterson?"

"How very observant."

Jessie frowned. "What are you doing here? Why do you look like me?"

"And what are you after?" Henry added.

"That's a *lot* of questions, guys."

"Were you the one shooting?" Sarabeth asked, her head peeking around Jessie's body.

"Now, that is a good question," Henry said. "Answer that one first."

"Today? No, I wasn't the one shooting."

"Then who was?" Henry demanded.

"How about this? You get me out of here without any more people shooting at us—or at least without me getting *shot*—I'll tell you everything you want to know."

Henry's gaze flicked to Jessie's. He was leaving it up to her.

"Why do you need to get out of here?" Jessie asked.

The woman rolled her eyes. "God, the questions with you people. Isn't it obvious? Shooting? Bad guys hiding in falling-down houses. Et cetera."

It didn't add up, Jessie knew. Why would this woman need help getting out of here if she was wandering around on her own with a gun? A gun she was more than willing to point at Jessie before Henry had gotten ahold of it.

But she likely had answers. And clearly Henry could handle the woman. She gave Henry a little nod.

"All right. You two, get behind me. Our friend here will lead the way."

Sarabeth scurried to do as Henry instructed, but Jessie… hesitated. This all felt like Peterson and gold nonsense and it felt wrong to get Henry wrapped up in that. He might not believe it, but anything that connected to her father was dangerous. Maybe Henry could handle it, but it didn't—

"Jessie." She looked up at him. His dark eyes were serious, but not…angry. And when he spoke, she couldn't puzzle out his tone, but it wasn't demanding or commanding. "Go on now." There was a softness to it, and to him, in the way he nodded at Sarabeth.

Or she was losing her mind from exhaustion. But still, she didn't know what else to do but move behind Henry.

He let go of the woman's—*Quinn's*—hands. He patted her down like she'd seen police officers do on television shows.

"At least buy me a drink first," Quinn quipped.

Henry ignored her, finished the pat down, then stepped back toward Jessie and Sarabeth. He pointed the gun at her. With Jessie and Sarabeth behind him, he gestured at the horizon. "You'll walk in front of us. Straight ahead till I tell you otherwise. Make a wrong move, I can't promise I won't be the one shooting at you."

She grinned at Henry. Flirtatiously. "Don't make promises you can't keep, big guy."

Something…acidic curled in Jessie's chest, so odd and foreign she didn't know what it was. So she simply took Sarabeth's hand in hers.

"Go on now. Straight ahead," Henry said.

Quinn shrugged and began to walk. So Henry began to follow, and then Jessie and Sarabeth. When he wanted Quinn to move in a different direction, he told her right or left or to walk toward a tree. Jessie watched him more than the woman. He was alert, watching every single space around them. His frown only seemed to deepen the closer they got to Thompson land.

"You sure she wasn't the one shooting at us?" Henry asked, his voice low enough and close enough only she could hear.

And she should not have a bodily reaction to that, but she *did*. Annoyingly. "Sure? No. I'm not sure about any-thing." *Anything*.

He nodded. "Well, we'll get to the bottom of it back at the ranch."

"Are you sure you want to take her there?"

"Six military men against one question mark? Yeah, I'm sure."

"Six…" She looked up at him and he had an odd expression on his face like he wasn't supposed to say that. "You're *all* former military?"

"Runs in the family," he muttered. "Like apparently looks do in yours," he said, pointing to Quinn, who seemed as re-laxed as anyone taking a casual stroll.

Quinn hadn't confirmed that they were sisters. She hadn't even fully confirmed she was a Peterson, but Jessie didn't know any other reason for looking that much alike. It was so strange. To watch someone who looked so much like her move and speak differently. To *be* a different person.

"Is there a way to give your brothers some kind of heads-up?"

"Already sent a text. It'll go through once we're in range."

"And then what?"

"Then we figure out what your twin is up to."

Chapter Ten

Henry kept the gun trained on this Quinn woman's back as they walked. He kept waiting for an ambush. A surprise. But nothing happened. Something was off, and it was irritating the hell out of him he couldn't pick up on what.

They crossed the fence line back to Thompson property. His brothers should have gotten his text by now and were hopefully all reconvening at the house like he'd asked.

He gave a quick glance back at Jessie and Sarabeth.

They were both fading. Shadows under their eyes, feet dragging a little. Jessie had Sarabeth's hand clutched in hers and somehow that made something clutch inside him. They were both too stubborn for their own good. They needed a tender, for heaven's sake. Well, they'd get tended at the ranch. Not by him, of course. Hazeleigh or Kate or somebody'd probably flutter about them.

Frustrated with his line of thinking, Henry turned his attention back to Quinn. Presumably Peterson. She looked exactly like Jessie, but it was easy enough to tell them apart when they moved. Jessie was all efficient movements, most of them designed to keep attention *off* her. Quinn moved with a certain kind of swagger, like she was used to wading into the center of attention.

Which made the space between his shoulder blades itch.

She didn't need help. She didn't need to escape whatever she'd been a part of. So why was she acting like she did?

He scanned the horizon again. He kept waiting for some-one—something—because this Quinn woman was *not* on the up and up.

But the stables to his own ranch came into view. He could see Landon cleaning a horse—but not in the normal spot they brushed and washed down the horses. He was the lookout. He'd send the message on to the other brothers that they were here.

Henry hadn't been lying when he'd told Jessie, stupidly, that he trusted his military brothers to take care of whatever threat this Quinn woman posed. They could handle what-ever nonsense was going on about gold—or anything else.

What he worried about more, again stupidly, was how it would affect Jessie and Sarabeth. Whatever *it* was. Because this wasn't just weird obsessions with gold anymore. It was a twin sister—surely they had to be sisters, no matter how few questions Quinn had answered.

Family junk, and boy, he knew about some family junk.

They reached Landon and he didn't say anything, just moved to stand next to Henry while he told Quinn to keep walking to the house.

"So. This is a turn of events." He looked over his shoul-der. "You could stop running away at *any* point, kiddo."

Sarabeth wrinkled her nose at him.

"Hazeleigh coming back?" Henry asked.

"Yeah. She locked up back at the apartment. Listen." Landon lowered his voice, so only Henry could hear. "She said a truck drove by a couple times this morning. Never stopped. Never slowed. Non-descript enough she normally wouldn't have thought anything of it, but knowing Jessie was worried about going to the cops, Hazeleigh figured it was worth noting."

Henry did not like that. At all. "For sure. She get a plate?"

"Yeah, she's got it in her phone. I'll search it once I get to my computer, but I was out on my horse looking around when you texted. From where I was looking around the house, there's definitely someone camped out at the Peterson place, but I didn't want to get too close until we knew more."

"Get an idea of how many?"

"Not exactly, but definitely a small group. They weren't being too careful either. Footprints. Tents. Cal says ten at the most, three at the least."

That was still a broad range of people. He studied Quinn's back. "You think she was one of them?"

Landon joined his study. "Could be. Problem is I saw the evidence of people, but no actual people. Jake and Zara were up on the other side. Maybe they saw something else."

They reached the front porch and the door opened. Cal stood there. Looking disapproving as always. "I guess we're doing this inside?"

"Sarabeth and Jessie need some food, water and rest."

"I wouldn't mind a little of that," Quinn said, and he could tell by the way Cal's expression hardened that she was grinning at him.

Henry decided to ignore her. "She doesn't have any other weapons. I searched her."

"Was it good for you too?" she asked with a smirk over her shoulder.

He didn't find her brand of humor very funny. Particularly in front of Sarabeth. *Yeah, that's who you're worried about.*

"Go on in and sit on the couch, Quinn."

"The hospitality is overwhelming." But she did as she

was told. Of course, he had a gun, and while he wouldn't shoot her—he could likely take her down without use of the gun—she didn't need to know that.

"You guys keep an eye on her. I'm going to get Jessie and Sarabeth settled."

"You don't have to—"

"Come on now," he said over Jessie's argument. He handed Quinn's shotgun to Cal and then strode for the stairway, and was gratified when Sarabeth followed him, because it gave Jessie no other choice but to follow as well.

He led them up to his room. It just seemed the most reasonable option. He had a big bed they could share. It was across from the bathroom where they could clean themselves up.

He refused to look any further into it. He stepped into the room, and in a quick movement took his gun off his dresser and stuffed it into the back of his pants. He made sure his sweatshirt covered it as Jessie and Sarabeth stepped inside.

"Make yourselves comfortable. I'll have somebody bring you up something to eat, and one of the women to get you guys some clothes and towels and stuff so you can take a shower."

"You're just going to question this woman who's identical to me without me being in the room?" Jessie asked.

"You've had a rough night. Take a rest."

"No. Sarabeth can take a rest and I—"

"Mom, you said we were a team," Sarabeth interrupted.

Jessie's mouth firmed. "Sarabeth, we *are*, but you've been up all night. I have only been up half the night. And—"

"Take a rest, Jessie. I promise if we get anything out of her—which I'm not so sure we will—I will tell you all about it. And you'll be in a much better frame of mind to wade through whatever information we get if you've eaten something and taken a nap. I know you're probably not used to someone taking care of things, but you're going to have to deal."

She looked stricken enough he figured he hit the nail on the head there. She felt like she had to handle everything, and that was honorable enough. Probably even a necessity for most of her life, but in the here and now there was a whole group of people ready to take care of some things.

Kate appeared with a tray of food. "Hey, I bet you guys are hungry."

Sarabeth practically leaped for the food, and Henry took the distraction to slip away. Because he was going to get to the bottom of this Quinn woman and make sure she didn't pose a threat to Jessie or Sarabeth.

JESSIE DIDN'T KNOW what to do. She was being *fussed* over. By Hazeleigh and Kate. They brought food. Clothes. They practically forced her into the shower after Sarabeth's bath. And when she got out of the shower, with plans to check to make sure Sarabeth was asleep and then go downstairs to confront Quinn herself, Zara was waiting for her.

"Sarabeth is asleep, but Henry's got a big bed. You can crawl in there with her to catch a few hours."

Henry's bed. Oh, dear.

"I don't—"

"So far all that Quinn woman has done is flirt outrageously with all six men. She's not cracking, at least not for a while. Get some sleep. I know it feels like the guys are sweeping in and taking over, but I promise, they might try, but we women are on your side. And they can't stand up to us."

"Even Henry?" Jessie asked dubiously.

Zara seemed to consider. "Believe it or not, I think Henry's got quite the soft spot for Sarabeth." Then she tilted her head. "Well, or you."

"I'm sure it's Sarabeth," Jessie replied, trying to ignore… everything about how any of this made her feel. What did it matter? This was about what was going on. Not Henry and his soft spots. "She does have that kind of effect."

Zara shrugged. "Suit yourself. Just take care of yourself a little bit. I promise you won't miss a thing."

Jessie didn't know why she believed Zara. After all, they weren't friends. Zara was engaged to one of Henry's brothers. She had no reason to keep Jessie up-to-date on anything.

But God, Jessie was tired, and when Zara gently nudged her into the room and closed the door in her face, Jessie turned to see Sarabeth curled up on the bed. Fast asleep.

She didn't even remember sliding into bed next to Sarabeth.

But what felt like moments later, she opened her eyes, curled up in a ball in Henry's bed. The room around her was dark.

And Sarabeth was gone.

Please not again.

Jessie jumped from the bed and rushed to the door, but a Post-it on the doorknob stopped her. She pulled her hand back and held the now crumpled piece of paper up to the shaft of moonlight slanting through the window.

You were out cold. SB down with us.

She knew anyone in the house could have written it, but something about the nearly illegible masculine handwriting made her think it was Henry.

She didn't understand her reaction to him. Oh sure, she was mature enough to admit he was *attractive*. That the flutters could be boiled down to simple physical attraction. It meant no more or less than watching a movie with a good-looking actor in it.

What complicated things was the way he handled her daughter—not perfectly, but honestly. There was the way he'd said *because help is what we do*—and then proceeded to prove that, over and over again.

What was she supposed to do with *that*?

Jessie took a deep breath and settled herself. Henry might be involved in everything that was going on—somehow, someway—but he wasn't her primary concern. Sarabeth was. The mysterious Quinn was.

But she still checked her reflection in the bathroom mirror before she headed downstairs. Because she'd gone to bed with wet hair and no one needed to see the disaster it had become. She pulled it back as best she could with a rubber band she'd found underneath the sink. It didn't need to look good, it just needed to not look like Medusa.

Satisfied—well, not really, more like resigned—she went downstairs to find her daughter. The house was old but had been kept up well. There was some peeling paint here, or chipped baseboards there, but the wood was lovingly polished. Windows were scrubbed clean to let in the moonlight and starlight tonight—sun during the day.

It was nice. Homey.

And her heart stopped in her chest when she turned from the end of the stairs to enter the living room.

Henry and Sarabeth were facing each other, Sarabeth sitting on the floor, Henry lying on his side, a chessboard between them. Sarabeth was giggling like a loon, and Henry was grinning at her—somehow looking both big and imposing and perfectly comfortable sprawled out on the floor.

Her heartbeat started again, but the throbbing inside her chest was anything but calm or regular.

Oh dear.

Henry's eyes lifted, meeting her own. If he understood the look on her face—some mix of startled panic and a mushy feeling that did *not* belong in this scenario—he didn't act like it.

Thank *God*.

Though that easy-going grin that she'd never once seen on his face seemed to…tense. Firm. Still a smile, but not the same warmth.

She should *not* feel disappointment at that.

"I'm beating Henry at chess," Sarabeth announced.

"You can't beat someone at chess until you've won," Henry replied.

Jessie had to clear her throat to speak calmly and clearly. "When did you learn how to play chess?"

"Just now," Sarabeth replied, frowning at the board. "I was bored so Henry told me he'd teach me."

"That was very kind."

Henry shrugged and said nothing.

Jessie didn't know why she felt *nervous*, except she was in a strange house doing… Wait. Where was Quinn? "Where—"

A little cheer went up from the kitchen area and Jessie shifted so she could see. Quinn was in there with Cal and Dunne and Landon and they appeared to be doing…shots.

"What on earth."

"She challenged Cal to a drinking contest," Henry said, moving a piece on the chessboard after Sarabeth did. "For some inexplicable reason, Cal agreed to it."

"With the strange woman we know nothing about?"

"Don't worry. Dunne's playing guard."

"I feel like I've woken up in an alternate reality. What time is it?"

"Nine."

"Well, thank you for everything. Really, I don't even know how to express my gratitude, but Sarabeth and I should be getting out of your way and getting home."

Henry got to his feet, a strangely graceful movement for such a big man. Like some sort of predatory cat. "I'm afraid that's not going to be an option just yet," he said in that closed off, foreboding way that irritated her even before the words penetrated.

Jessie frowned at him. "What?"

He looked down at Sarabeth, then up at Jessie again. She could tell he wanted to say something, but not in front of Sarabeth. Jessie could send Sarabeth to her—Henry's, someone's—room, but that would only pique Sarabeth's curiosity. Besides, they needed to go *home*.

Someone swept in. It wasn't Hazeleigh or Zara, so it had to be the other woman. Kate, Jessie thought. They'd been in a class together in elementary school…maybe. She couldn't quite remember.

"Hey, guys. I'm going to feed the barn kittens we've got out on the summer porch. I thought you might want to help, Sarabeth."

Sarabeth's eyes widened. "Kittens?"

Kate nodded. "They're all holed up underneath the porch furniture, but they'll come out and play if we bring them some cream."

Sarabeth looked up at Jessie. It was a distraction, and it would allow Henry to talk freely. Jessie managed a smile and nodded. "Sure."

Sarabeth scrambled after Kate. She wore an adult size T-shirt that went down to her calves. It was definitely a man's shirt and Jessie felt something very strange over her daughter possibly wearing one of Henry's T-shirts.

When he put his hand on her elbow she nearly jumped a foot. "Let's talk on the front porch."

"Right. Sure. Yes." She felt like she'd been electrocuted. Surely the way-too-long nap she'd taken had dulled her senses. Some fresh air would help. She needed to get her brain in gear.

She stepped out into the cool summer evening. The stars and moon were shining, most of the world dark except the last hints of day to the western horizon. It was beautiful out here.

And her life was a mess.

"I figured telling Sarabeth to scram wasn't the way to be able to talk to you alone. I texted Kate once you were up," Henry said. He stood, leaning against the porch post, studying her.

Jessie's heart jangled in her chest. "That's very…perceptive."

"Yeah, well, listen, when Hazeleigh was at your place in case Sarabeth came back, she saw someone casing the place."

"Casing?"

"Driving past. Looking for something. Someone's looking for you guys, Jessie."

It wasn't a surprise. Not now. Not after being shot at and finding a woman who looked just like her. Nothing was a surprise. "Henry, I don't think this is just about the gold anymore."

"No, it seems unlikely."

"But I genuinely don't know *what* it's about."

Henry nodded. He was just a dark shadow out here, and it should make her nervous. He should look scary and dangerous, like a ghost. But she found his presence, his calm demeanor, reassuring.

Whatever this was, they'd figure out how to handle it.

They? Since when were you ever a they *beyond Sarabeth? You need to figure this out on your own.*

"I realize people looking for us is a problem." God, it was a problem. "But Sarabeth and I can't just…stay here. If someone really is looking for me, they'll find me. At the apartment. Here." She thought about Quinn, her identical *twin*. "Maybe they already have."

"Well, until we figure that out, you should stay here."

She narrowed her eyes at him, because that wasn't an invitation. "Should or will?"

Henry seemed to mull that over. "I get the feeling telling you what to do would go over about as well as telling Sarabeth what to do."

"So you're going to pretend like there's a choice, even though you don't plan on giving me one?"

"I told you a while back, I'm not letting anything happen to you two. So no, there's no choice. The smart, sensible thing is to stay here till we sort out Quinn and whatever else is going on."

"I have a job," Jessie said, feeling tears sting her eyes. Because she knew she was safer here than in town, but that didn't mean she and Sarabeth were completely safe. It just meant she had to leave. No Wilde roots for Sarabeth. Maybe they should go back to Florida. Or somewhere new. Iowa or Kansas. Disappear, the way she'd done once before. "Sarabeth starts school in a few weeks." She'd have to get somewhere she could safely enroll her. "You have a full house as it is. We can't just…"

"That gives us a few weeks then, doesn't it? And if you can't take time off work, that's fine. One of us will just go with you. We don't know what's going on, so no, we can't just hide here and hope it all goes away. But that doesn't mean I'm about to let you go gallivanting around waiting to get kidnapped again."

"Gallivanting?" Temper spurted, and she recognized it as something not *only* because of his high-handed, obnoxious attitude, but boy, was it a nice place to land.

"I'm trying to put things nicely, but it's not my forte."

She snorted. "No kidding." But she supposed beneath the anger she appreciated the fact if nothing else she wasn't getting any lies from Henry. "Don't be nice. Just be honest."

"That I can promise."

"Henry, we can't stay. You have to know that."

There was a long, fraught silence where he was only a shadow. A disapproving one. Then he stepped forward, into the little swath of moonlight. Too close—and she was too stubborn to back away.

Or too caught up in the way the moonlight softened that hard face and hardened those soft eyes.

"So you're going to run?"

"I *have* to run. I told you it's all I'm any good at."

"You could face it. Get to the bottom of it. We're going to help you, Jessie. Why would you run away from that?"

"You don't owe us anything. I know you have some warped guilt over what happened with your mother—"

"Excuse *me*?" he said, deadly calm dripping from both words. The kind of deadly calm that made a smart woman shut up and rethink.

"You don't think I understand? I know you don't talk much, and you rarely speak kindly when you do, but I can read between the lines. Your mother died, and you felt responsible. You joined the army—or whatever military branch—to assuage your guilt. It didn't work, so you got out. You and your brothers started this, away from war or whatever horrible things you must have seen. But you're still out here, helping whoever you can, trying to make that guilt go away. How right am I?"

His face was inscrutable. "Maybe fifty percent. Tops."

"But the fifty percent is the fifty percent that matters, isn't it? I don't want your parental guilt."

"Even if it meant Sarabeth could stay here, where you know she wants to stay? Be safe. Put down roots. Getting to the bottom of it means you could give her what I know you want to give her—because you might argue with me or fake skittishness with me, but I can read between the lines, too, Jessie. You wanted to build a life for her here. Why would you give up on that so easily? When help is being offered."

It hurt. In so many little ways she couldn't catalog them all. Of course she wanted to give Sarabeth all those things. But… "I was offered help once. To get out. To escape. But it was just a slightly different version of the same prison."

"This isn't escape. And it isn't prison. Trust me. I've got no use caging you or your little girl. I'm offering you a solution."

"I don't know if I can believe that." But God, she wanted to. She wanted to give in and hand it over to him. To believe these people she barely knew would sweep in and find a *solution*. So she could give Sarabeth everything he'd outlined.

She didn't want to run again. The very thought filled her with exhaustion and dread. She wanted to lean, just a little. And Henry, so big and sturdy and certain, seemed a perfectly safe place to lean.

He even stepped a little closer, close enough it wouldn't take much at all to rest her cheek on his chest. But she stopped herself. Looked up at him instead.

"I know you don't have any reason to trust me, or any

of us really. But why don't you give us a chance? Running is always an answer if you figure you don't like how it's going. For now you don't even have to trust me. You just have to stay put."

But the problem was she did trust him. Far too much.

Chapter Eleven

Jessie looked like a silvery Western fairy out in the moonlight, and Henry realized far too late that standing this close…posed a problem. He could smell her shampoo, and it didn't matter that it had to be the same one Kate or Zara used. On her it smelled different. Enticing.

In the dark everything about her seemed soft. Oh, even now he knew it hid an inner strength she kept well covered, but her hair looked like it would feel like velvet if he reached out and ran his fingers through it.

And why the hell was he thinking about touching her hair?

He might have stepped back. For very inexplicable reasons he felt scalded, but he knew enough to realize if he broke the moment she'd run now. When she needed to stay put. Running would only put her and Sarabeth in continued danger.

He needed… No. This wasn't about what he needed. It was about what was smart. She wanted to run? He wouldn't stop her. But if she could suck it up and stay, they could get to the bottom of it. So they could both stay put. Both build a life he knew they each so desperately wanted.

She could run. He could let her. But it would be smarter to stay.

He had to curl his hands into fists at the thought of actually letting her run. It made him want to grab her in the here and now. Shake some sense into her. Or something else. Something far more dangerous. Because who was he kidding?

If she tried to run, he'd stop her in a heartbeat.

Over and over. He didn't know why. Didn't want to analyze why. It was the right thing to do and a long time ago he'd promised himself he'd always do the right thing. Even if it was hard. Even if it hurt.

Why did all of this crawl inside him and *hurt*, when neither Jessie nor Sarabeth should mean anything to him?

Should being the operative word.

She inhaled a long, shaky breath even as her eyes continued to hold his. He should back off. Away. *Now.*

The door opened. Henry held himself very still. He wasn't about to let anyone make this look like more than it was. No matter how close he was currently standing to Jessie.

Who jumped like a rabbit caught in a predator's clutches.

Henry flicked what he hoped was a cool, unfeeling glance at Dunne standing there in the doorway.

"Said she's ready to talk."

Henry nodded. "We'll be in in a minute."

Dunne nodded. Said nothing. His expression gave nothing away. And *still*, Henry stiffened. He looked down at the woman who had him tied up in knots. He should go inside.

But he couldn't quite help himself.

"Don't run, Jessie. Please." Then he stepped inside where he could leave all that…weird, uncomfortable emotion outside.

Quinn, looking identical to Jessie down to the way the stray hair from her band seemed to curl around her face, helped ice it out.

He didn't trust this woman, and no matter how much she looked like Jessie, there was a cold, calculating glint to her eyes. And he didn't like her here.

But here she was. While the living room was mostly empty, his brothers were spread out around the house strategically. Cal still at the kitchen table—likely not as inebriated as he pretended to be when he was having a drinking contest with the woman.

Dunne at the entrance to the kitchen taking his job as guard seriously. Henry couldn't see the rest of them, but no doubt Brody was out with Kate and Sarabeth and the kittens. Jake guarding the back door so they didn't come in without warning. Landon, hopefully, on his computer trying to come up with something on Quinn or the truck that was driving by Jessie's apartment.

"So?"

She shrugged. "So what?"

"What have you got to say?" Henry replied.

"What do you want to know?"

Henry struggled not to groan. "Who are you? Why are you here? Who are you here with? Who's casing Jessie and Sarabeth's place?"

The last question seemed to surprise her. There was just the slightest flicker in her expression, like she had to rethink some things.

"Let's start with who you are," Jessie said. She'd quietly followed him in. And whatever breathy uncertainty had been on display outside was gone.

It gave Henry the uncomfortable realization that he shouldn't lead this questioning. That Jessie needed to wade in there and ask her own questions, handle this as much as she could. For her own peace of mind.

It was hard—way too hard—to step back. To give Jessie the floor.

But he knew he had to.

JESSIE SWALLOWED AS Henry stepped back. At first, she thought he was going to take over, or worse, leave her alone to handle it.

But he did neither. He simply gave her the space to face off against this identical woman. Stayed close, right next to her really, but made it clear she…was in charge for the time being.

He hadn't just told her to stay. He'd said *please*.

But that was not what was important right now. Getting to the bottom of her mysterious twin was.

"Who are you and why do we look so much alike?"

Quinn shrugged. "We've got the same parents."

"We're twins?"

"I mean, I assume. It's not like I remember you when we were fetuses. I didn't exactly know I had an identical twin out there looking just like me."

"The word *exactly* makes me think you had more of an idea than Jessie did."

Quinn flicked a glance at Henry and considered. "Yeah, looks like. I always knew I had a sister, and that my mom had decided to take her when she left."

Left. But that wasn't right. "My mother died in childbirth."

Quinn seemed unfazed by that. "Not the story I got."

"But it makes more sense. That she would have died, complications to having twins, than that she just took one of us."

"Maybe she could only get away with one of us."

That had an uncomfortable pit of…sadness…grow in Jessie's gut. She couldn't imagine having to leave a daughter behind, but she also knew how desperate she had once been to escape that compound. A compound… Quinn should have been at. "But I lived at my father's compound for over five years. I never saw you. No one ever mentioned you."

"Yeah, for a reason. *Obviously*."

"How is any of this obvious?"

"I really don't get how you could have been a part of it for five years and not picked up on any of it, but okay, let's lay it all on the table here. You don't know about the person who looks just like you? It's because one of you is meant to replace the other."

"Explain," Henry ordered, in that voice that likely would have prompted her to fall all over herself to explain if he'd been talking to her.

But he wasn't, so she could probably stop *fluttering* over that dark, intimidating way he'd said that one word.

"Look, I'm not a part of it," Quinn said, spreading her hands wide. "Whatever dear old Dad's got going on is always his business. I'm a pawn. You're probably a pawn. I don't know for what. Gold, sure, but there's more now that Rob's dead. Dad knows I'm a bit of a flight risk, and not totally on his side, my bad, but I'm willing to wager he thinks the kid knows something."

Jessie's entire body went cold. "Knows something?"

"About the gold. Again, *obviously*."

None of this seemed obvious to Jessie, and the idea Sarabeth was on her father's radar was…beyond terrifying. The cold froze her. She had no words. No thoughts. Just *fear*.

And then she felt a hand on her back. Warm and firm.

"But it's more than the gold," Henry said. His tone was low and controlled like maybe the world wasn't ending. "If anything is obvious, it's that."

Quinn tilted her head, seemed to study the space between Jessie and Henry—what little there was of it, because he'd come closer. Put his hand on her back. A reassuring gesture that something…something could be done to protect Sarabeth. Had to be done.

"Got yourself quite the bodyguard. Not bad." Quinn looked over at Dunne in the doorway between kitchen and living room. "Or should I say bodyguard*s*. Must be nice."

"Nothing about this is nice." Because her daughter might be in danger. Because Henry thought she should stay and fight and Jessie felt like all these unanswered questions only added up to one thing: run.

Quinn got to her feet. "You know what? Let's cut the crap, huh?" She moved past Henry and Jessie and walked over to where Dunne was blocking the way to the kitchen. She swayed a little, like she wasn't steady on her feet. "Move, would ya?"

He looked over his shoulder at Cal, and decidedly didn't move.

"That's real cute." She looked back at Henry. "You guys are a real band of brothers, huh? And you!" She pointed to Cal over Dunne's shoulder. "You're the leader. So why don't you tell your little soldier to move the hell out of my way?"

"Pass," Cal replied dispassionately.

She pushed at Dunne's chest. Dunne rolled his eyes. "You're not half as drunk as you'd like me to believe."

And then Jessie watched the way the act all fell away. No more stumbles. No more vaguely slurred words. Quinn's eyes, the same exact shade as Jessie's own, narrowed. She reached out to punch him, but it was a fake. When Dunne grabbed that hand to stop the blow, shifted his weight away from her lifted knee, she used her other hand to punch his leg.

Jessie knew Dunne limped, and by the way the blow landed on an awkward part of his leg, she figured Quinn had deduced where the injury was and hit exactly that spot. Because Dunne let out a whiff of breath and she pushed by him.

Jessie hurried after her, Henry right behind her. But Cal stopped Quinn before she got much farther than the kitchen table, not that it mattered.

"Hey, kid?" Quinn yelled in the direction of the screen door. Sarabeth was with Kate and some kittens on the other side of that screen. "When are you going to tell your mom what you know?"

SARABETH PRETENDED LIKE she didn't hear the lady who looked like Mom but had…something different. It wasn't looking at her that Sarabeth felt it. It was when she talked. It was something…uncomfortable.

She let Kate distract her with a cat, as the adults scuffled and argued inside. After a few minutes, Zara suggested they go upstairs. When Sarabeth had asked to take one of the kittens, Zara and Kate had looked at each other with matching eyes of worry and uncertainty.

But they'd let her take the kitten as they'd gone with her back to the bedroom upstairs. In the kitchen, she didn't see anyone. All the way upstairs she didn't see or hear anyone.

Her heart beat hard against her chest. But no one asked her what she knew. No one poked at her. They left her alone in the room.

She held on to the cat for dear life, and then curled up on the big bed. She rested her chin on the headboard and looked out at the window it was shoved underneath.

Things were bad. She'd thought coming to the Thompson Ranch would mean they were safe, but the lady who looked like Mom wasn't safe. Sarabeth wasn't sure she was *bad*, but she wasn't good.

When the door squeaked open, Sarabeth assumed it would be Mom. Coming to ask her what she was hiding.

But it was Henry.

Sarabeth held the cat tighter. She wasn't scared of Henry, but something about his expression made her stomach cramp into knots. "Where's Mom?"

"Hazeleigh convinced her to sit down and eat something before she came to bed, so I said I'd come check on you."

"I'm okay. Can I name your cat?"

"Not my cat."

"I think he looks like a Henry."

"I think *she* looks like a Henrietta."

"Oh." Sarabeth thought the cat looked like a boy, but she hadn't checked to make sure her feelings were accurate.

"Sarabeth."

She didn't like the way he said her name. It came out like…like Mom. Like she was both in trouble but not in trouble. Like she did something wrong, but she wasn't going to get punished. She was just going to feel yucky about it. So she didn't look at him. She looked at the little black fuzzball squirming in her arms.

She felt the bed dip a little, and she had to look over at Henry. He'd sat down on the bed, but on the very edge of the other side. His eyes were on her. He didn't look mad or mean or that confused way he'd looked when she'd cried. He looked like…

She'd thought about what it would be like to have a father. She'd had dreams of what he might be like—not her real, biological one, but someone who wanted to be her *dad*.

Lately, they tended to all look and sound like Henry.

"Why would you keep something from her?" he asked.

Soft, almost hurt, not the usual grumpiness or meanness she'd wanted. Nothing she could fight against.

Sarabeth stared hard out the window. Outside everything was dark or silver. Shadows or moonlight. Tears threatened, but she wasn't about to cry in front of Henry again. He hadn't handled it *so* badly, and at least she hadn't upset him like she did when she cried in front of Mom, but still. Mom always said a woman had her pride, and Sarabeth supposed this was hers.

"I'm not really keeping anything from Mom. I mean, she doesn't know about the gold coin I have."

"Does someone else?"

"No!"

"Then why do you look guilty?"

Sarabeth frowned down at Henrietta—Henry might have said that as a joke, but she liked it. So there. She wasn't guilty. She wasn't keeping anything from anyone.

Mostly.

But why would that lady know… Why would that lady…

"Sarabeth." And again, Henry's voice was gentle. Not that gruff ordering thing he did so often. "You've got something in that brain of yours none of us have. Maybe you're scared, or you don't want to get in trouble, or whatever. I get it, but honey, you've got to be honest with me, at the very least. What are we missing?"

Sarabeth swallowed at the lump in her throat. She didn't know what to do with him calling her *honey*. She wanted to crawl into his lap, cry on his shoulder and pretend he was her dad and would take care of everything.

But he wasn't. She'd killed her father. She'd taken care of things.

Or thought she had.

Which was so much of why she hadn't wanted to tell

Mom. She thought she'd handle it herself. Save Mom the worry, and maybe, Sarabeth had wanted to stay in Wilde more than she'd cared about being safe.

"Mom will want to go away if I tell you," she managed in a croaky whisper. "I don't want to leave Wilde. I like it here."

Henry thought that over for a moment, the kind of pause where she knew an adult was actually listening to her. Not just trying to figure out a way to get what they wanted.

"You might be right. Your mom wants to protect you more than anything, but I know if she felt safe here, she'd want to stay here. Why don't you tell me, and I can make sure it's safe for you guys to stay here."

She looked up at him, studied his face. He had nice eyes. No matter what he was doing—even when he was yelling or swearing—he had nice eyes, and he'd never even acted like he *might* hit her. Henry had always done exactly what he'd said he'd do, and he was always gentle with her and Mom, even when he was mean.

She believed he *could* make it safe for them here, but she also knew he wasn't in charge of where she went. Mom was. Which meant…she needed more than *could*.

"Do you promise?"

Henry's eyebrows drew together and he continued to study her as Henrietta escaped her grasp and tried to take a leap off the bed. Henry caught her easily, then handed her back to Sarabeth.

"I promise," he said as he passed the cat back to her.

He held her gaze when he said it, and he sounded like… he didn't really want to promise. She knew from experience with Mom that was usually when she was the best at keeping promises. Because if she broke one she made even though she didn't want to, she'd feel extra guilty.

Sarabeth didn't understand that part of adults, but whatever worked.

So she told him. She wasn't sure it was what that Quinn lady meant, or even what Henry expected, but it was the only thing she knew.

"When… Rob had my mom tied up, and he let me go… It was because I was small and could crawl into some spaces he wanted to look for the gold."

"Okay."

"He had it all planned out. For me. And when it wasn't where he thought, when I didn't get him what he wanted, he didn't have any use for me."

Henry got very, very still. She wasn't sure he took a breath. "He wanted you. Not her."

Sarabeth chewed on her bottom lip. "I don't know that," she replied. Because it wasn't like Rob had said it. It wasn't like anyone had ever come out and said she'd been the real target of Rob taking them.

It was just…a feeling she'd gotten. There was something about *her* Rob had focused on in the beginning of all that horrible stuff. And at first she'd thought…

Sarabeth had to fight back the tears again, because it was embarrassing and awful and bad. She knew it was bad. Mom had been taken and tied up and she shouldn't have hoped that her father wanted something to do with *her*. She should have just hated him.

But she hadn't. And she couldn't ever tell Mom that. She couldn't tell anyone that.

She felt the bed move, and then Henry came to sit next to her. He put his hand on her back, rubbed up and down once. Just like she'd told him to do back when she'd cried the first time.

"Let it out, kid. You'll feel better."

She didn't want to—let it out *or* feel better—but she couldn't swallow down the lump or blink back the tears when he was rubbing her back like Mom did when she was upset. She couldn't fight it back when she knew she was the bad guy and nobody understood.

She didn't want anybody to understand.

But that only made the tears fall, her breathing hitch. And she couldn't seem to do anything else but what he said—let it out. She pressed her forehead into his shoulder and cried while he rubbed her back and told her it would be okay.

Chapter Twelve

When Jessie finally stepped into *Henry's* room, which she preferred to think of as *the room they were staying in*, she expected to find Sarabeth curled up in bed. Hopefully asleep. Maybe someone in the room with her, watching her, but certainly not her daughter crying on a big man's shoulder while he rubbed a hand up and down her back.

She could tell Henry wasn't comfortable by the grimace on his face, but he soothed Sarabeth anyway.

Jessie just froze there in the doorway. While her daughter cried, and Henry handled it. She knew she should have rushed forward, but she couldn't seem to get her feet to work.

Surely it was natural for any woman to feel a little fluttery over a guy who was good with her daughter...when said guy looked like *that*. It certainly didn't mean she was developing actual feelings for him. She was smarter than that.

She really needed to be smarter than that.

Henry turned as if he sensed her there. Their gazes met. She let out a shaky breath, needing to get a handle on herself. On everything.

He gave her a kind of *please, God, take over* look and she stepped into the room, still feeling far too shaky for her own good.

But with an ease that felt more like years of partnership than a few days, Henry exchanged places with her and she wrapped her arms around Sarabeth. "Baby. What's wrong?"

Sarabeth shook her head and burrowed in deeper. Jessie soothed, sang an old lullaby she rarely got to pull out these days because Sarabeth usually rolled her eyes and said she was too old for baby stuff. But she let her sing. Let her tuck her into bed.

And when Sarabeth slid off to sleep in just a few minutes, when usually she tossed and turned and fought sleep with everything she was, Jessie knew she was exhausted. Hopefully that was an explanation for the uncharacteristic crying.

Yes, not at all killing her father, running away and now dealing with a mysterious twin sister for her mother.

Jessie squeezed her eyes shut for a moment, her hand still rubbing circles on Sarabeth's sleeping back. Guilt was trying to win, but Jessie knew guilt didn't solve problems. If she'd gotten Sarabeth into all these messes, it was only her job to stop the pattern. Fix the problem.

Maybe Henry had been right back there. She couldn't run. Running didn't work. Eventually everything you were running from caught up with you.

And her daughter was paying the price.

She felt something more than heard it and looked up.

Henry was still there. He was in the doorway, but she didn't get the impression he'd ever left. He'd just stood there. Watching. It wasn't exactly embarrassing. It was just…he'd watched a private moment.

Of course, she'd watched him comfort Sarabeth. But Sarabeth was *hers* and…

Maybe she was exhausted, too. Though she didn't feel it. She felt uneasy and revved and…other things that it didn't do to think about.

Henry jerked his chin toward the hallway. Jessie steeled herself for…whatever and got up and followed him outside. He left the door open, but he spoke quietly, as if he wasn't sure Sarabeth was really asleep.

"She knows more than she's letting on." Henry looked back at the room. "She feels guilty about something."

"Guilty?"

"I might not get the myriad of eleven-year-old girl feelings, but what I saw in there? Guilt. I'm sure of it. Not just about her father."

Jessie rubbed at her chest. Everything seemed to contract there, a hard, painful knot.

"Look, I can only take one crying person a day. It's like a rule."

She laughed, in spite of all that pressure and pain, and sure, guilt. "I'll do my best."

"I'm going to talk to Quinn. That woman *also* knows more than she's letting on, and I'd rather yell it out of a grown obnoxious woman than a little girl."

"I want to be there." She looked back into the darkened room. She didn't want to leave Sarabeth alone. It was silly. She was in a house full of people, and Jessie knew she'd made herself at home here.

"I can get someone to come sit with her."

Jessie chewed on her bottom lip. "I feel like I'm pawning her off."

"You can't have it all ways, Jess. No one can."

She wondered if he noticed he'd shortened her name. Then she wondered why *she'd* noticed. It certainly didn't matter. It was probably just faster.

What did matter, sadly, was that he was right. She couldn't have it all the ways. That was like the single mom motto. "Yeah, isn't that the truth. Can't have it all ways. Can't have it any good way."

Henry stood there, frowning at her. She was about to apologize—no one needed to listen to her pity party, her guilt, but before she could, he put his hand on her arm. Why did it have to be so *big*? So *warm*? Why did she have to feel settled by his fingers curling around her biceps?

"Surely you don't need me to tell you you're doing a good job."

"At what?"

"The whole mom thing," he said gruffly.

"Ha, well, it doesn't feel like it. My daughter is guilty and crying herself to sleep and running away and was forced to *kill* her father so he wouldn't kill anyone else."

His grip on her tightened, just a little. Just enough to have her gaze rising to his. And his dark eyes were solemn. Serious. Enough to have her heart shuddering in her chest.

"Jessie, trust me, bad moms don't care. They don't have guilt. They give up. On their kids. On themselves. They do *not* beat themselves up. They do *not* worry—at least not about the kid."

"Well." She had to clear her throat to say the rest. She wished it were emotion that was clogged there, but it was something else too, and it had to do with the way her body reacted when he touched her. She tried for a casual smile. "Who knew you could give a decent enough pep talk."

"Yeah, who knew," he muttered.

He didn't let go of her arm. He just stared at her with his eyebrows drawn together, and his *who knew* seemed to take on a different meaning. Like who knew there could be this? Who knew...?

His gaze dropped to her mouth, and her heart jumped. Just *jumped*. She was probably hallucinating, but...

THERE WERE TOO many things circling around in his brain. That was what Henry would blame this on. Too many thoughts. Too many feelings. Comforting Sarabeth had messed with him somehow. Messed with everything.

And now Jessie was standing here and he could see it on her face. The guilt and the worry and that little hitch of… clearly not feeling good enough. When he'd watched her. Hug her daughter, ease her into bed, sing songs and just shower her with love.

She hadn't demanded answers, and he knew she wanted them. She hadn't scolded or tried to do anything but *comfort*.

He couldn't stand the thought she might not know *that* was the mark of a mother. Care and comfort over her own wants. That she would let guilt and everything that had happened that wasn't Jessie's fault cloud the very basic fact she was a good mom. The best mom.

And it shouldn't feel *good* that she'd said he gave a good pep talk. It shouldn't feel *good*, her arm under his hands. Strong and tough, but still soft. He shouldn't want to or need to comfort her or touch her or talk to her.

He shouldn't notice her mouth, study it. He shouldn't want to…

He released her. Probably abruptly. "I'll go grab Landon or Hazeleigh." And then he escaped. Like a *coward*.

But what the hell was wrong with him anyway?

Thinking about kissing her in the middle of all this. He was an idiot. Warped. Yeah, he knew that. He'd always known that. Usually he left vulnerable moms and their good kids out of it.

Clearly there was something about helping a woman that made a guy think there was something romantic there when, *ha ha ha*, like romantic was something he'd ever been involved in. He wasn't Jake or Landon or even Brody. Somehow they'd turned these types of situations into something...

Domestic. Jake and Zara were getting married. Hazeleigh and Landon had settled into that little cabin and lived together like an old married couple. Brody and Kate took care of everyone in the house like they were the parents of the group.

All because they'd been thrown into some danger together. Like that just...forged some kind of bond. Like a few bullets flying made love sprout into existence.

He wished he didn't believe his brothers were in love, whatever that meant. But he saw them all. The way they were with each other. It wasn't all lovey-dovey looks and touches. It was arguments and makeups. It was casual gestures. The way Jake would slide his hand down Zara's ponytail—the way she'd waited on him when he'd been recovering from his gunshot wound when he was pretty sure Zara Hart waited on no one *ever*.

It was the way Brody and Kate made meals together like it was a dance, and Landon and Hazeleigh looked at each other with knowing smiles like they could read each other's thoughts.

And none of this had to do with him and Jessie because wanting to kiss her was just...basic chemistry. Liking the kid was just... She was a good kid. Watching Jessie sing and tuck Sarabeth into *his* bed in *his* room and feeling like...it was kind of nice. The kind of thing he wouldn't mind seeing over and over again.

He stopped at the bottom of the stairs and shook his head like a dog trying to shake off water from its fur.

This was *insane*. He had to get his head on straight. Because this was bad. This was lethal. Someone had shot at them. That Quinn woman—a near identical copy of Jessie—was nothing but trouble, clearly. Sarabeth was in *danger*.

That was what he needed to be thinking about.

Landon came around the corner, stopped and studied Henry. "You good?"

"Sure. Where's Quinn?"

"Oh, Dunne and Cal are keeping an eye on her in Dunne's room. She doesn't act like she's going to bolt. I think she likes the attention."

"I think she's a damn threat."

"Maybe, but we can handle that, can't we?"

"Yeah. *We* can. Listen, Jessie and I are going to talk to Quinn. Jess wants someone up there with the kid. Sarabeth is asleep, but you know, just in case."

Landon nodded. "I'll do it."

"Great," Henry replied, feeling decidedly *not* great. Especially as Landon continued to study him.

"You're sure wrapped up in this."

Henry scowled. "So what? You think I'm following the danger-love pattern here? Because I don't think so." And he'd really proven his point bringing up *love* of all damn things.

"Well, truth be told, I kind of had a thing for Hazeleigh before all that danger. Jake for Zara, too. It wasn't like danger *led* to love. It was just the situation to act on already-there feelings, I guess."

Why did that not make him feel *any* better? He'd much rather blame all this…whatever on danger mixing stuff up. "I don't have feelings," Henry muttered.

"Oh, buddy, you got a whole boatload of them. You just don't know what to do with them." He gave Henry a hard slap on the back. "I'll send Jessie down." Then he disappeared up the stairs.

A boatload seemed like a conservative estimate right about now, particularly when Jessie came down the stairs in clothes that weren't her own. Her hair had dried curlier than it usually was after her shower.

"Have you slept at all? I slept the day away and didn't think to ask. You were up—"

"I'm fine," he replied. "Do I not look it?"

She stared at him and, oddly enough, a faint pink stained her cheeks. "Sure, you look fine."

Why did that make him want to smile? *Because you're warped, remember*? Right. "She's in Dunne's room. Follow me."

He led her through the house. Dunne had the biggest room—what had once been the parlor. It wasn't in the best of shape, but since Dunne did any necessary medical administering, he got the extra space. Besides, his injured leg made the stairs too hard for him.

Henry knocked once, then entered. Cal stood by the window, looking out into the dark with a scowl on his face. Dunne was stretched out on his bed reading a book. Quinn sat on a chair in the middle of the room, pretending to gaze at the ceiling.

Henry was pretty sure she was studying the men in the room with her, just as they were studying her without looking like it.

"Give us a few alone with her," Henry said.

Dunne looked at Cal, Cal at Henry. He nodded and they both left.

"Spooky, the six of you," Quinn said, pretending to shudder. "Like you can read each other's minds."

"Maybe we can," Henry replied.

Quinn grinned at him. "You don't seem like the type to believe in mind reading."

He didn't respond to that, just pulled another chair over so Jessie could sit across from Quinn. So identical even *he* thought it was eerie.

Quinn studied them both—Jessie sitting, him standing behind her. There was a lot going on there, and Henry hated admitting he didn't know what. He *knew* she posed a threat—there had been gunshots, then her. She'd pointed a gun at Jessie. But she sure didn't act like she was going to run or hurt them.

Maybe she was waiting for backup. Henry considered it the most plausible possibility, but she also didn't act like she was waiting. So maybe it was far off. Maybe she was a good actor.

No matter what, though, whatever she was waiting for, whoever she was, she wasn't going to hurt Jessie and Sarabeth.

He was going to make sure of it.

Chapter Thirteen

Jessie couldn't stop studying Quinn, trying to find differences. But they were *so* identical. Sure, Jessie would never sit in a chair that way—all languid like she didn't have a care in the world. And yes, Jessie had a freckle on her earlobe that Quinn didn't have. But that seemed to be the only things: attitude and a *freckle*.

Who would notice that?

"So. Aren't you going to interrogate me?" Quinn asked, her gaze flicking from Henry to Jessie and then back to Henry again. She grinned at Henry with a kind of brash flirtatiousness Jessie could never imagine having herself.

Jessie frowned a little at that. It was clear it was all this kind of...bravado act, but Jessie didn't really like it being geared toward Henry. No matter how stupid that was—or how brick-wall-like he responded.

And hardly the point. Hardly important. Jessie sighed, overwhelmed. So many feelings. So many questions. "I don't even know where to begin."

"The beginning is a good place," Henry said firmly, making her glad he was here. She didn't want him to take the lead, per se. She just needed...someone to help her focus. "You're twin sisters. Identical twin sisters."

"I guess," Quinn said. "I mean, that's what I was always

told. But I've been lied to a lot. Maybe it's a coincidence we look the same."

"Yes, that's *so* likely."

Quinn grinned.

But Jessie couldn't find the situation humorous. "How? How can we be identical twins? Are you telling me our mother *didn't* die in childbirth? That she had two identical babies and then took me to her mother and left you behind?"

"Don't really know. I don't remember her. The story I got was the ditched-me thing. They used that one pretty hard against me for a while, so died in childbirth seems just as likely. Though not sure how we would have been split up if so. Still, most stuff they tried to shove down my throat I've learned probably isn't real, even if it's true."

"Explain," Henry said in that focused, demanding way he had that usually irritated Jessie when it was geared at her. In this situation, she was grateful for it.

Quinn rolled her eyes. "You guys and your one-word commands," she muttered. Some of that languid relaxation in the chair tensed, and she didn't look quite so *at ease.* "I grew up in that compound, so at first you kind of have to take it all for truth. Like, oh, your mom didn't care about you, but she cared about the other one. The other one got everything and you got nothing. Don't you want revenge? Worked for a while."

"Then what?"

"Then she came to the compound," Quinn said, nodding her head toward Jessie. "I was thirteen. We were thirteen, I guess. And *I* had to go away. Couldn't have her knowing about me. Maybe the first couple years I resented it. All that *wilderness survival* training got a little old. But eventually, I got old enough and wise enough to the Peterson way of doing things. They brought me back and I realized I was just a tool. Tools don't matter. They're replaceable. So if I was—she was. But unlike her, I didn't have anywhere to go. That compound was all I'd ever had. So when I was supposed to slide into her place, I did."

Slide into her place. A cold bolt of unease trickled up Jessie's spine. She was always in her own place, so how could… "What do you mean?"

Quinn's dark eyes, the same deep brown as Jessie's own, locked with her. "Why do you think Rob didn't come after you for, like, ten years?"

Jessie froze—from the inside out. Like a ton of ice just encased her. "I hid," she managed to croak.

Quinn snorted. "No. *I* slid into place."

Jessie couldn't absorb it. Couldn't imagine… All those years of hiding and being careful so he'd never know Sarabeth existed and… Rob had thought she was still there, by his side?

"You're telling me she bailed, you *slid into place* and the guy didn't notice?" Henry returned, clearly not believing Quinn's story.

"Why would he notice? We're identical, mostly. He wanted her for her connection to the Petersons, for what she might know *or* what he might be able to use to get out of her—*our*—father. She was a tool. Someone replaces a tool with an identical copy, hard to notice."

"I can't believe this," Jessie said, shaking her head back and forth. "I can't." But the tool thing… Oh, she understood the tool thing.

Quinn shrugged, unbothered. "Guess you don't have to."

"Who wanted you to do it?"

Quinn flicked her gaze to Henry. There was a slight hesitation. "Daddy dearest."

Shot in the Dark

"So why were you still doing his dirty work? Out here. Pointing a gun at Jessie."

"Didn't have a way out yet. I've got no ID. There's no record of me existing, far as I can tell. I have no money. No way to make it on my own. Oh, I was planning some things, but I hadn't gotten there yet. Then you came along, took the gun out of my hands and oops. I got caught. What better way to escape than that?"

"You aren't afraid of them?" Jessie asked, carefully. Quietly. "Tracking you down?"

Again, Quinn's dark gaze met her own and Jessie felt…a wave of sympathy for this woman. Maybe it was misplaced. Maybe this was all a lie. But something about all this…made it hard to think she wasn't telling the truth.

"I'm afraid of them when I'm on the inside, so what's the difference if I'm afraid of them on the outside? At least I have a chance out here. At least I call the shots out here." She glanced at Henry. "Or will."

Jessie understood that. All too well and to the letter. She slid a glance at Henry. He was frowning at Quinn, but it wasn't all disbelief. Maybe some disapproval. Definitely suspicion, but he was considering her words. Weighing them against what he knew.

But this wasn't all about Quinn, or even Jessie herself. "What do you think my daughter knows that she isn't telling me?"

Quinn's eyebrows rose. "She didn't tell you?"

"She was exhausted. Overwrought. I'm not going to press her."

"But you'll press your sister?"

"The grown adult sitting here that I barely know? Yes."

Quinn took some time to consider that, then with another

one of her careless shrugs, settled back into her chair. "There was a little showdown between Rob and our father. Couple months back. I don't know what happened exactly, but when Rob came home he knew I wasn't you. He'd figured out he had a kid. He knew there were ways to use the kid."

"Use Sarabeth? He didn't care about Sarabeth."

"Care? No. Use? Yes. I mean, surely you know *you* don't matter to our dad, or you'd have been dead or back at the compound a decade ago. Wasn't any different for Rob and the kid. She was just a means to an end, a tool like you and me, but she was a new shiny one. And one he didn't think our father would pay much attention to. So he set out to get her."

It all made a terrible kind of sense. She'd thought it was about her. *Her* Peterson connection, but all Rob had done was tie her up in that basement. Been ready to kill her at the drop of a hat. But he'd let Sarabeth run. Explore.

Get caught up in stories of gold.

Jessie's stomach roiled so violently she was afraid she would be sick. She knew she needed to keep her cool. To work through this. But the idea Rob had been after Sarabeth... All this time she'd been so focused on herself. On *her* connections to the Petersons. Or Sarabeth's connection *through* her. She'd never considered it hadn't been about her at all.

She really was going to be sick. "I think I've heard enough." She got up and she bolted.

HENRY WANTED TO rush after Jessie, but he wasn't about to leave this woman alone. He believed Quinn, weirdly. But that didn't mean he trusted her.

"You're telling the truth," he said, hoping one of his brothers would return soon so he could check on Jessie.

Quinn shrugged. "Why wouldn't I be?"

"I'm sure there are as many reasons for that as there are for telling the truth." He studied her for another minute. "If you keep telling the truth, keep helping your *sister*, we'll help you, you know."

"Who's this mysterious *we*?"

"All of us here. If you're honest, and on the up and up, and don't put anyone here in danger, we'll do whatever it takes to keep you away from the people who want to hurt you."

"Sure you will, cowboy."

"It's a promise, Quinn. You don't have to believe it, but it's a promise nonetheless."

She said nothing to that, and Dunne returned. Henry was eager to go find Jessie, but then Landon grabbed him with information about the truck that had been driving past Jessie's apartment. By the time they were done poring over that material, the sun was rising and Henry didn't have a clue as to where Jessie was.

It bothered him, not because he figured she'd run off or done anything stupid, but because…

Because.

Frustrated with himself, he stalked through the house. Kate was up and making breakfast. When he passed Zara in the living room, she informed him Jessie was out in the stables, helping with some chores, but before he could go find her, he heard a clattering on the stairs.

Sarabeth bounded into the room, all bright eyes and energy. Her hair was tousled, but she was back in her clothes from yesterday—clearly, someone had washed them for her and given them back to her. She stopped when she saw him.

"Morning," she offered cheerfully. But she hesitated, like she didn't know what to do now that she'd seen him. Like she remembered this wasn't her house. Like she remembered they were in some kind of danger.

He didn't want her thinking about it. He wanted her having as much normal as possible, so he figured he'd have to act normal, too.

"Breakfast is on. Then you can earn your keep out in the stables."

Her eyes brightened. "Really? I can work with the horses?"

"Yeah, and it's work, so you better be ready."

She gave him a quick squeeze as she passed. "Thanks, Henry," she said, then she scurried into the kitchen.

Like she hadn't just killed him dead. They both did, mother and daughter, and it didn't matter what he told himself about it, all the excuses he tried to make. It wasn't about danger, about helping. It was about them.

Damn it.

Grumpy now, or even more so, he went to find Jessie in the stables. Jake was outside washing the truck—an unnecessary chore, which told Henry that everyone was making sure someone always had an eye on Jessie without making it too obvious.

Because it was the right thing to do. To help Jessie and Sarabeth as best they could—because they could.

Henry walked past Jake, trying not to think too hard about all these jangling emotions not shuffling into place—or away—like he could usually make them.

"I've got it from here," he said to Jake.

"I just bet you do." Jake grinned. "I'll finish all the same."

Henry grunted, his attitude not getting any better at Jake's cheerfulness. Still, he stepped into the stables. And all that irritation and anger just sort of leaked out. Because Jessie looked miserable. And beautiful, standing there stroking her hands down the horse's mane.

"Hey." Why did his voice sound so damn *affected*?

"Hi." She smiled or tried to. "Sorry I ditched you in there with Quinn." She sighed heavily. "I needed to get a handle on myself. I threw up." She closed her eyes and groaned. "I don't know why I told you that."

"I can handle a little puke."

It made her laugh, and it was…some kind of amazing he could make her do that. In the here and now. At all. When he was not exactly known for his humor.

"I just needed some…alone time to work it all out." She gestured helplessly at the horse.

"Yeah, I get that."

He looked at him with a wry smile. "I'm not sure you do until you have a child and are constantly surrounded."

"I have five brothers living on the same ranch. Isn't that the same thing?"

She laughed again and something in his chest expanded.

"Maybe." She sucked in a breath and let it out. She stood on nearly the opposite side of the stables. There was a strange kind of awkwardness in the silence that stretched out.

Even stranger, Henry didn't really know what to do about it.

Jessie cleared her throat and began to walk for the doors. "I should go check on Sarabeth."

"She's up. Eating breakfast." For a reason he could not explain to himself, he stopped her forward progress by stepping in her way. "We'll put her on light chore duty this morning, make her feel useful."

Jessie stopped walking, a good few yards in front of him, but she smiled. "She'll like that."

"What would you like?" he asked, taking a few steps forward.

Some of that bravado faded and her shoulders slumped. "For my daughter not to be at the center of all this. I can't stand the thought they're after *her*." Her voice broke, but she kept going. "That it isn't just protecting her from the fallout, but the actual...*thing*. About gold? But it's the reality. I have to figure out a way to deal with it." She looked up at him, and there were tears in her eyes. "And somehow thank you all for...doing all this when you didn't have to do."

It grated—not in an irritating way. Her thanks just scraped against him like... Like, he didn't know. "You don't have to thank me."

She nodded, but he could see she was going to lose the battle. The tears were going to win and though he grimaced a little, he also knew he couldn't just...stand there. He had to reach out. To pull her to him. He thought of what Sarabeth had told him back when he'd found her hiding out. Back rub. Say it's going to be okay. He could do that.

And Jessie didn't fight him on it. She leaned in. Relaxed. Cried. She smelled like horses and...her, and she seemed to fit right here, tucked up against him. She was so strong, held so much on her shoulders, but everyone needed a little...release sometimes.

He tended to choose things like lifting weights and chopping wood, but probably not the best suggestion. So he let her cry, and rubbed her back.

And he told her it was going to be okay, because he'd find a way to make sure it could be. Somehow.

She sniffled and began to pull away. "Well, you're not so bad at the comforting thing," she managed, wiping at her cheeks.

He had to fight the urge to wipe the tears himself, so he chose to simply not let her go. "You can thank your daughter for that."

She looked up at him quizzically. His hands still on her shoulders.

"When I found her out there, she cried a bit. Then told me I did a terrible job with crying people and I should rub a back and say comforting things."

Jessie laughed through the tears. "That girl."

And she didn't step away, and he didn't let his hands fall. They just stood there in this weird world. Where he could comfort someone. Where he wanted to. Where he wanted to make everything right—familiar enough—but he didn't want to let go while he did it.

He didn't have a clue what was going on in her head, but she didn't back away. She held his gaze. And when he pulled her just a hair closer, when he tilted his head just so—

"Are you guys going to kiss?" Sarabeth's voice interrupted, making them both jump apart like guilty teenagers.

Sarabeth just stood there at the opening to the stables, looking at them both—not accusingly, but with a kind of innocent interest. "It looks like you are."

"Sarabeth," Jessie said firmly, but seemed at a loss as to what else to say.

"You can kiss him if you want, Mom."

Jessie closed her eyes. "Thank you for your permission," she muttered dryly. "But I think I'll go inside and get some breakfast."

And she moved—not a scurry exactly, but a very careful move that put a lot of distance between them—out of the stables, leaving him with Sarabeth. Who studied him carefully.

"You should definitely kiss her," Sarabeth said after a

while, nodding as if she'd come to the conclusion after thinking it over.

"You are something else, kid," he muttered.

"Why does everyone keep saying that?" she wondered aloud.

SARABETH DIDN'T SAY anything more about Henry kissing her mom while he showed her what to do with the horses, but she thought about it.

She wasn't dumb. She knew that if she got Henry to kiss Mom it wasn't like they'd magically get married and he'd be her dad and everything would be perfect. There was that lady who looked like Mom and someone shooting and the gold and all sorts of things that would complicate that.

But Sarabeth figured it didn't hurt to plan. *If* they did kiss, they might want to get married at *some* point. And if they *did* get married, Henry would be her stepdad, and maybe they could even live here with the horses.

And Henry would always protect them, and Mom wouldn't have to worry so much. And Sarabeth could keep Henrietta the cat and get a dog and…

Well, she couldn't get too excited about that yet. First, she had to work out a plan. Step by step. And the first step was Mom and Henry kissing.

Henry gave her a little carrot to feed the horse and she squealed in delight when the horse ate it. "Horses are so cool."

"Well, as long as you're staying here, you'll be helping with them. It's called earning your keep."

"What does my mom have to do to earn her keep?"

Henry made a strangled kind of noise, though Sarabeth couldn't figure out why. "Whatever needs doing, I suppose," he finally said. "Lots of people equal lots of chores."

"I like the lots of people. *And* horses," Sarabeth said.

"And cats and dogs and ranches." She looked up at him through her lashes. "And you."

"Thought I was mean," he said in that rumbly voice Sarabeth was beginning to recognize as discomfort.

"You can be. I like that, too. I'm mean sometimes. Mom says it's okay, as long as it's geared toward the right people, and if you end up being mean and wrong you apologize."

"Guess she's right."

"She's right a lot," Sarabeth replied. Then wondered if that was something Henry would like. Maybe *he* liked being right a lot? She frowned a little and rubbed the horse while Henry moved to a different stable.

He came back with two shovels, one big, one a little smaller. He handed her the smaller one. "Poop duty."

Sarabeth wrinkled her nose. "Gross."

"Yeah, it is. Lots of things that are cool come with gross parts. You gotta be willing to handle the hard, gross stuff if you want the good parts."

Sarabeth wasn't sure she agreed with that, but she let Henry teach her how to shovel up the poop and put it in the bucket. It was smelly, but she tried to think of it like she was helping out Sammy the horse.

"You know, it's a good life lesson," Henry said after a while. "Gross parts and good parts are a part of life."

"Okay."

Henry sighed, then he took the shovel from her when they were done. He put his hand on her shoulder.

She liked when he did that. It was like when Mom ran her hand over her hair. It felt…like care.

Then he crouched and got eye to eye with her. He looked serious and Sarabeth's heartbeat got a little fast in her chest.

"You're going to have to tell your mom the whole truth. All of it."

Panic started to creep in. "What do you mean?"

"I mean whatever it is. You've been keeping stuff hidden. I know you don't want to get in trouble, but…" He trailed off, his eyebrows scrunching together, and he studied her hard enough she wanted to run away. Hide. "You're not afraid of getting in trouble. You're trying to protect her." He seemed…surprised by that.

Sarabeth tried to use that surprise and bolt, but Henry held her firm. Not hard like her father had, but *firm*. Gentle. But she still couldn't wriggle away.

"Running's not solving this problem, Sarabeth. Face it. You've got guts, kid. Use them."

Guts. She liked to think she was brave. Strong. *Guts*. But she didn't want Mom to be worried. She didn't want Mom to know… But Henry… He knew. He didn't *know* know, but he kind of knew. And she wanted him to protect them, didn't she? Wasn't that why she came to him in the first place?

His other hand rested on her shoulder, and his eyes were… Well, they were more like Mom's. He was waiting for her answer, not shouting. He wanted something from her, but not just that and then he'd turn around and disappear.

"Sarabeth."

"I don't want her to be scared. I don't want her to cry." And she didn't want to cry herself.

"I get that. And I can't promise she won't be scared. I can't promise she won't cry, but, Sarabeth, if you tell us all the truth—all of us—we can figure out how you *and* your mom don't have to be scared anymore. You came to me because you thought I could handle this, right?"

She nodded, not trusting herself to speak.

"Then I need you to let me handle it by telling me everything, but your mom has to be there, okay? She has to know, too."

Chapter Fourteen

Jessie felt more herself after she ate something, and then helped Kate with the breakfast dishes. She still felt...on edge, but more equipped to handle it.

She wasn't going to dwell on what had happened in the stables—not the *moment*, and certainly not her daughter suggesting she could kiss Henry.

Kiss him! Ha! What a disaster that would be.

Probably an enjoyable disaster, but still a disaster. She wasn't a young, dumb teenager trying to escape any longer. She wasn't going to let a man sweep in and save her and kiss her and...

Jessie squeezed her eyes shut for a moment as she washed down the kitchen table. Henry wasn't Rob, and it wasn't fair to compare them. She wasn't even the same Jessie she'd been all those years ago.

But she was not kissing Henry. Certainly not before this whole daughter-in-danger, identical twin, gold thing was sorted.

After...

Well, there was no point even considering *after* now when they were still so in the dark.

She heard the front door squeak open, the low sounds of conversation, and then Sarabeth trudged into the kitchen.

She no longer looked excited about horses or kissing. She looked...upset.

Jessie left the washcloth on the table and crossed to her. "What's wrong, baby?"

Before Sarabeth could answer, Henry entered. Sarabeth looked up at him, and Jessie almost jumped to accuse him of upsetting her daughter, but his expression stopped her.

Underneath that careful veneer of stoic military man, there was this tightness around his mouth. Worry.

"Sarabeth, I'm going to give you the choice, okay?" Henry began. "You can tell your mom everything just the two of you. But she's going to need to fill me in. Or you can tell both of us. But I'm going to have to tell everyone what's going on. So the last alternative is telling everyone yourself. It's up to you what you want to do."

Jessie didn't have a clue as to what was going on, but she pulled Sarabeth close. "You don't have to do anything in front of anyone, sweetheart. Let's—"

"I want to tell everyone."

"Sarabe—"

"Mom. It's the right thing to do." She sounded so adult. So sure. It was like getting a flash of the woman she'd become someday. Jessie didn't know how to argue with it. "I don't really have answers, just stuff Rob told me. Stuff I heard Rob say. I knew it would upset you, so let's tell everyone. Everyone here wants to help."

Jessie looked up at Henry. She wanted to...blame him, somehow, for how much Sarabeth was taking on her shoulders. But that was hardly Henry's fault. Henry hadn't put them in this situation. In fact, he'd been dragged into it by the both of them.

"Can I go get Henrietta first?" Sarabeth asked, looking up at Henry.

"Uh, where *is* Henrietta?"

Sarabeth's expression went sheepish. "Wellll…"

"In my room wreaking havoc, no doubt. All right, go get her. Maybe clean up the worst of it? We'll get everyone together in the living room in about fifteen."

Sarabeth nodded, but before she scurried off she looked at Jessie. Her expression went firm. Determined. "It's going to be okay, Mom." Then she dashed off, no doubt excited about cat wrangling.

Jessie slowly stood, trying to get her bearings. Trying to figure out the right thing to say.

But Henry spoke first. "We'll gather everyone up in the living room. She can say her piece. No one will pressure her. I promise you that, and if she needs to stop to take a break, just take her upstairs."

Jessie nodded. It was strange. All these years of being a single mom, she'd never really believed anyone else had Sarabeth's best interests at heart. She'd never let anyone close enough for that to happen.

But she believed in the Thompson brothers. Henry in particular. She just wished she could wash away the heavy cloud of guilt. "It kills me to know she's been keeping something from me. That she's standing there measuring *me* when it should be the other way around.

"You've done plenty of reassuring and it shows. She's a tough kid. And she loves you. She wants to protect you."

"It's not supposed to be that way, though."

"I think it is. I think that's the way love is always supposed to be."

It felt very strange to be discussing love, but she knew he was talking about mothers and children. Not *love*.

"Maybe we should take this private moment to discuss what happened in the stables."

Jessie was surprised. Shocked, actually, that he'd bring it up, not let it go. She cleared her throat. "Ah, what would that be?"

"Sarabeth suggesting I kiss you."

"Oh, that. Well." She was otherwise speechless. What was she supposed to say? *You're welcome to?* Because she was…too curious, but also this was so not the time and…

"I just want to make it clear, if I ever do kiss you, it won't be because your daughter brought it up. It'll be because I think about you too damn much."

Jessie opened her mouth, but no words came out. Maybe because every coherent thought just…melted out of her.

I think about you too damn much.

Wow.

Luckily, she didn't have to think of anything to say. Jake came in through the kitchen door, already talking. "Zara won't be long. Hazeleigh's at the fort, but Landon thought he could fill her in later. Not sure about Cal."

Dunne and Quinn appeared from the door to his quarters. "Cal's coming. Finishing up some research." Dunne frowned at Quinn behind him. "Should she really be a part of this?" Dunne asked.

"Should *you*?" Quinn returned, looking pointedly at his bad leg.

"Living room," Henry ordered. "Everyone," he said. A clear response to Dunne's initial question.

Jessie wondered as well if Quinn should be part of it, but… Well, Quinn was *part* of this. Maybe they couldn't trust her yet, but maybe it would turn out she had information they needed. Maybe it would turn out she actually had…a sister.

She watched Quinn follow Dunne out, then Jake. Everyone talked. Joked. Touched. And when she reached Henry, he put his hand on the small of her back. Like he was some-how…hers.

She looked up at him, and his gaze lowered to hers.

"Too damn much," he muttered, looking back ahead, where his family had arranged themselves to deal with *her* problem. What Sarabeth knew. What danger they were all in.

And it didn't matter who was the reason, she realized. No one blamed anyone. They saw a problem, and they came together to fix it.

Jessie found…that was the kind of group she wanted to be a part of. Wanted her daughter to learn from. Not guilt. Not worry.

Teamwork.

THE FAMILY HAD GATHERED. Henry studied them all. Sara-beth playing with the kitten, curled up next to Jessie in the oversize chair. Hazeleigh and Zara sandwiching Jake on the couch, while Landon sat on the arm next to Hazeleigh, who'd come back from the fort. Cal had dragged in chairs from the kitchen table, and he, Quinn and Dunne had settled into those. Kate sat crosslegged on the floor, Brody stand-ing next to her, leaning against the wall.

Henry stood in front of them all. He'd called the "meet-ing" so to speak, so it was up to him to move it along. But there was something about the moment—they weren't a biological family, but something about the ways they'd all come together had created…this. Maybe Jessie, Sarabeth and Quinn weren't a part of it, but they seemed to slot right in.

Every part had its function, and now they needed to work together to solve the problem.

But the eleven-year-old girl snuggling the cat within an

inch of its life was going to have to explain the problem to them first.

"We're all mostly up to speed on what's been going down the last few days, and even some of the backstory for everybody, but Sarabeth has some information that might help us make sure everyone's safe," Henry began. "That's the goal here. Everyone can go about their normal lives without worrying about any threats."

"No one's interested in the gold?" Quinn asked, studying her nails with fake disinterest. Henry could tell she read the room very carefully, and Henry couldn't decide if that was a comfort or suspicious.

Dunne muttered darkly. Landon and Hazeleigh gave an emphatic *no* simultaneously. The only one who seemed the least bit interested in gold was Sarabeth herself.

As Jessie had said in the stables: *that girl.*

Henry gave her a disapproving look, and she wrinkled her nose in return.

"This gold seems to be the cause of a lot of problems, and an answer to absolutely none. Men have been murdered. Lives have been threatened. But it's bigger than that, isn't it, Sarabeth?"

"Sort of," Sarabeth agreed. She sat there with the kitten, then decided to come stand by Henry. She faced down all the adults in the room. She didn't crumple with everyone's eyes on her. Much like that night when she'd faced down the police, she held herself very still. And she focused on her mother.

Henry knew that was where she got her strength.

"There's supposed to be a whole house," Sarabeth said.

"A house?" Jessie replied, clearly hearing this for the first time.

"Full of stuff. Gold and money and some kind of jewelry

thing. Some guy was a robber, back a long time ago, and he kept all this stuff in one house. Hidden away. And the story is his kids thought it was cursed or something, so when he died they just left it there."

Henry could feel Cal's gaze cut to him, and Cal didn't need to say anything for Henry to know what he was thinking.

You can't be serious.

"But some people had clues, I guess, and joined clubs to find it or something. And some of the groups tried to make it look like it didn't exist so no one would look for it, and some of the groups fought and hurt each other until there was basically only one left."

"Led by my father," Jessie said, sounding shaken, but certain.

Sarabeth shrugged. "Rob complained a lot about *them*, but he didn't say anyone specifically. Just said they were dumb or angry, but he was smart. There's clues somewhere, I guess, but they've never been able to find where. Rob was looking for a map. That's why he killed the museum guy. He thought he had it. He didn't, but he had pictures that led them to some of the gold, but not the house with the other stuff."

"You sure know a lot, kid," Quinn said. Her gaze was sharp on Sarabeth, and it wasn't kind, but considering.

Henry angled his body to put a buffer between Quinn and Sarabeth.

"So a bunch of men are after a house full of—" Henry searched for a word that wasn't *treasure*, because he was pretty sure that would send Cal off the deep end "—valuable stuff."

Sarabeth nodded. "They have a bunch of plans when they

get the money. Like bombs and stuff. I didn't understand it exactly, but they don't like the government."

"Now *that* makes some sense," Cal replied. "A group of antigovernment militia types, living in a compound, dreaming up fake riches."

"But they aren't fake," Sarabeth said. "The gold was real."

Cal didn't say anything to that.

"The gold was real," Henry agreed to keep Sarabeth from getting insulted enough to stop talking. "And it doesn't matter if the rest is real. If they *think* it is, that's all that matters. They'll keep looking for it."

"Because it's *real*," Sarabeth insisted. "It has to be."

Henry knew Cal wanted to argue with her, and he watched the way Quinn very carefully watched her. He didn't like that. Not at all. So he mentioned something about feeding the other kittens and convinced Kate to take Sarabeth out to do just that.

And keep her out of earshot.

"So we've got a houseful of treasure somewhere," Cal said, sounding derisive.

But Jessie was chewing on her bottom lip, that clear sign she was worrying over something. "A map," she said, her eyebrows drawing together. "Sarabeth said he was looking for a map."

"What, like you know where it is?" Quinn demanded.

"I'm not sure."

Henry was gratified that Jessie studied Quinn with a careful kind of suspicion. Quinn seemed to realize her enthusiasm *was* suspicious.

"What do you know about the map?" Henry asked Quinn.

Quinn scowled, crossing her arms over her chest. "That they think it exists, and is the great, majestic answer to all their problems. The kid's right. Mostly. Antigovernment.

Militia. That sort of thing keeps them focused, but at the end of the day, it's the treasure hunt. They want to find it—they can claim these grand plans once they do, but they're obsessed with the hunt. And beating each other to it."

"Each other? There's more than Rob going against our father?"

Quinn's gaze on Jessie was cool. Henry knew he could be reading into things, but he saw a kind of…resentment in the identical dark eyes. "Every now and again. Different factions of the same messed up whatever. Work together when it's them against the world, but it happens that they sometimes want the whole piece of the pie and go off alone."

"I don't follow," Dunne muttered.

"*You* wouldn't," Quinn returned.

"That the whole truth, Quinn?" Henry asked.

She turned that cool gaze on him. And kept it there. He'd give her points for that. "Nothing is the whole truth when it comes to the Petersons."

"I'm not talking about the Petersons. I'm talking about you."

She flicked a gaze to Jessie, but then turned it back to him. She seemed to consider things. "We've got George in one camp. We've got Gene in the other."

Jessie frowned. "Who's Gene?"

"Our father's brother. Less group, more recluse, but he's always one step ahead of George, and George hates it. But neither of them have found the jackpot. Both are on the hunt for the map. Rob thought it was here. George was following some cockamamie old story about it being in Oregon. Gene… Well, no one quite knows what Gene thinks, no matter how George tries to smoke him out."

"This sounds like a bunch of family insanity to me," Cal said. "*Your* family insanity. Not mine."

"Then feel free to butt out," Quinn replied, faking a sweet smile.

"People are in danger," Henry said, keeping his tone cool and calm rather than reactionary. "We'll help them get out of danger, no matter whose family is involved."

Cal sent him a sharp, disapproving look, but said nothing.

"So what's the next step?" Dunne asked.

"I think we need to find out who's casing Jessie's house." He nodded at Landon.

Landon stood to address the group. "We did some digging on the truck Hazeleigh saw driving by the apartment the day Sarabeth ran away. The license is stolen, the truck isn't registered anywhere I can find, and with the blacked-out windows we couldn't get an idea of who was driving. There's still a few more avenues I want to prod, but the bottom line is I think we can be assured this isn't a coincidence. That truck is looking for Jessie. Or Sarabeth."

"We want to find out who's driving. And why," Henry reiterated. "I think we should go into town. You have a stagecoach shift this afternoon, right, Jessie?"

"Yes," she replied. She looked like she wanted to say something else, but bit her lip instead.

Henry would prod on that later.

"Good. I'll go with Jessie on that. We'll look out for followers. And to make things interesting, we'll bring in the twin."

"Huh?" Quinn replied.

"One of you will go with Quinn to Jessie's apartment," Henry said to his brothers. "We'll see where we get a follow. And if we can circle around and get something out of them."

"Why should I agree to that?" Quinn demanded.

"Why shouldn't you?" Dunne returned.

Quinn scowled at him. "Fine. Whatever. Just not with these two dour Dans." She pointed at Landon. "You look fun."

Hazeleigh frowned a little, but that wasn't why Henry wanted a different option. "Landon's on computer duty with whatever we might find. Sorry, you're going to have to pick one of the dour Dans."

"Ugh," Quinn said, but she didn't argue.

Chapter Fifteen

The morning went by in a blur. Jessie kept trying to get Henry alone, but it was a no-go with so many people around, making arrangements. The men seemed to talk in a military code that wasn't so much incomprehensible as confusing.

Sarabeth clung close. Even knowing she'd be well watched over, Jessie wasn't looking forward to leaving her behind when she went into town. But it had to be done.

Especially with what Jessie had to tell Henry.

She just needed him alone. She couldn't say what needed to be said in front of Quinn. Not until she knew for sure Quinn would protect Sarabeth above herself.

Jessie changed back into her own clothes, since someone had been kind enough to wash hers and put them in Henry's room. Sarabeth sat cross-legged in the middle of the bed with Henrietta—and Jessie knew that once all this danger was over, Sarabeth would be begging to take the kitten home with them.

"Are you and Henry going to be alone?" Sarabeth asked, looking down at the cat who purred in her lap.

Jessie thought about the stables, this morning, Sarabeth asking if they were going to kiss. Embarrassment and something else shifted through her, but she tried to push it away. "Sarabeth…"

"It's just, I didn't say something I maybe should have. Henry wanted me to be honest, and I was. Mostly. But…"

Embarrassment forgotten, Jessie turned to stare at her daughter, worry and panic sprouting anew. "But what?"

"The real thing I didn't tell you wasn't the house. I mean, I didn't tell you that because I knew you wouldn't really believe it."

Jessie opened her mouth to argue, but then shut it. She wouldn't have. She barely believed in this gold and she'd seen it with her own eyes.

"Okay, so what's the real thing?" Jessie asked, trying to remain calm. Trying to find her equilibrium in this constant whirl of change and confusion.

"I didn't want to say in front of Quinn. I kind of like her, and lots of what she said is the truth as I know it." Sarabeth frowned deeper. "But I don't know if she'd keep me safe, like I know everyone else would."

Jessie couldn't fault her for that. Jessie had the same kinds of concerns. "Okay, what else?"

"Rob talked to somebody on the phone. A lot. Somebody who told him what to do. I don't know who it was, but Rob told him about me. I think that might be who's looking at the apartment."

Jessie had to stand very still and work very hard to breathe normally. This wasn't new information per se. This was just…more of Sarabeth being the target. It gave more context. It wasn't new.

And they were handling it. But still… "Sarabeth, why would you run away knowing someone might be after you?"

"So he'd stay away from you." Her voice pitched and she sat up on her knees. "So you'd know Henry had to help!" She slumped back down, chin to chest. "So maybe

I could find the stuff and then nobody could hurt anybody," she muttered.

Jessie sighed. "And this is it? All you know?"

Sarabeth looked up, her eyes a little shiny, but Jessie knew she wasn't going to cry. "Yes. I promise. I *promise*."

Jessie swallowed down all the fear and worry. She wanted Sarabeth to look at her and see certainty. Know she'd be protected and everything would be okay.

It had to be okay. For her daughter. "All right. Henry and I will discuss that." Plus what Jessie had to tell him. "We'll get to the bottom of this, and we'll make sure everyone's safe."

"Even Quinn?"

Torn, Jessie sat down on the corner of the bed. She took Sarabeth's hand in hers and met her daughter's worried gaze. "I don't know. There's still a lot we don't know about Quinn."

Before she could say more, Henry appeared at the doorway. "Ready?"

Jessie managed a thin smile and a nod. No, she wasn't ready, but a lot had to be dealt with. "Now, Sarabeth, while we're gone you need to be on your best behavior."

Sarabeth nodded, studying them both.

"Jake and Zara have some horse chores for you, if you're up to it," Henry offered.

Sarabeth nodded emphatically, but she held Henrietta to her chest. "Can she come with?"

Henry eyed the kitten. "Best to keep her out of the way of the horses. Maybe let her play with her brothers and sisters for a bit."

Sarabeth considered, then sighed. "Okay, I guess."

They went downstairs together, and Jessie wasn't sure why that felt...odd. Maybe because it felt cozy. Like a normal… Well, not family, since they weren't one, but unit? Something.

They met Cal and Quinn at the bottom of the stairs. Jake and Zara were there too, all ready to sweep Sarabeth away to do something. Keep her mind occupied. Keep her safe.

Jessie didn't know how she'd gotten so lucky to have all… *this*. Sure, none of the gold, Peterson, daughter-in-danger stuff was lucky, but it had almost always been her life. Help and protection had *never* been a part of it.

She said her goodbyes to Sarabeth, warning her once more to be on her best behavior. Then she followed Henry, Cal and Quinn outside. Cal and Quinn got into a truck, and Jessie followed Henry to his.

"The chores, the animals, giving her something to do so she feels productive. You're good with her. I didn't see that one coming," Jessie said.

"She's not so bad."

Jessie didn't have the slightest clue why that charmed her. Something about the gruff, uncomfortable way he said it.

They got in the car and she hadn't even clicked on her seat belt when he asked her a question that surprised her. "Did she tell you whatever else?"

"How did you know there was whatever else?"

"I saw the way she looked at Quinn, then stuck close to you. She had something else on her mind, but she didn't want to say it in front of the question mark."

"Perceptive. Someone knows about Sarabeth."

"I figured."

"She heard Rob talk to someone. She made it sound like someone was telling Rob what to do. I always figured him for the ringleader, but it seems not."

"Makes sense. He had a fake wife for ten years. He definitely wasn't fully in charge."

Jessie shuddered at the thought. "I don't trust her. I can't. But I feel for her."

"Yeah, well, I don't trust her, either."

"And you don't feel for her?"

Henry flicked a glance at her. "I feel for people I care about. So no. Not at the moment."

Jessie knew she shouldn't wonder if she was one of those people he cared about. If Sarabeth was. It didn't matter. Whether he felt for them or not, he'd protect them. And that was all that mattered.

"Landon will be at the computer," he explained. "Anything we see, or Cal and Quinn see, we text to him and he'll do his thing. Mostly, we're just feeling out who's looking for you and Sarabeth. No action. Just information gathering. So all you have to do is drive the stagecoach thing and keep your eyes peeled."

"Okay, but… Henry, there's something else."

He muttered what sounded like a curse under his breath. "Is there ever not going to be?"

"This is a new something else. Something Sarabeth and Quinn said that made me remember. I hadn't thought much about it—I'd been so concerned about Sarabeth and what she'd done to Rob and all that, but when they said *map*, I remembered." Jessie inhaled. She'd considered keeping this to herself. Handling it herself, but maybe she'd learned that wouldn't do.

Maybe Henry had no reason to help her, but he wanted to. Or needed to. Or something. And God knew she needed help. "There was just this…odd map. In my grandmother's belongings that I got after she died." Jessie swallowed. "I never knew what it was. But I…" She looked at Henry's harsh profile. "Henry, Sarabeth mentioned a map, and obviously I don't have a clue if it's *the* map, but… I didn't take it with me after Grandma died. I just knew… I knew if I was going to my father's family, I didn't want to bring her things. I didn't want… I just knew it wouldn't be mine."

"So what did you do with it?"

"It's kind of weird."

Henry laughed, and she'd always considered that laugh bitter, but maybe it wasn't so much bitter as fatalistic.

"What about this isn't weird?" he returned.

Fair enough. "So my grandmother used to visit my grandfather's grave every week. And her parents'. She brought them flowers, tidied up, that kind of thing, and she showed me how her father had this thing in his stone. It was put in there to hide alcohol during prohibition. You unscrew this part and people would hide booze in there, but obviously it wasn't used anymore so I… I put the stuff in there. A necklace, her rings and the papers I didn't understand."

"This map, that they've been looking for for decades, is hidden in a gravestone."

"I don't know for sure. My grandmother wasn't a Peterson. She shouldn't be connected to this. It was a map that made no sense to me at thirteen. Maybe it's nothing."

"And maybe it's everything."

HENRY HAD TO figure out how to proceed. He had no interest in finding some treasure—whether it was real or fake—but maybe finding it ended the nonsense surrounding it.

He doubted it, but it was a step anyway. For the time being, Jessie had work to do. They had a stalker of some kind to suss out. All before they could go find a *map* hidden in a *gravestone*.

And he'd thought being in a secret military group to take down terrorist organizations had been complicated.

"If it's a map that leads us to this…house of treasure or

whatever we want to call it, that groups of people have been after for decades far as I can tell, what do we do?" she asked, staring out the window.

That *was* the question. "I think we need to make sure it's there first. And that no one's following us when we do." But how to make that happen. Whoever was after Sarabeth knew Jessie had a twin, likely had an inkling said twin had been "taken" by those helping Jessie.

He drove into town, keeping his eye on anything that might appear out of the ordinary. He drove past where Cal and Quinn had parked in front of the hardware store.

Henry didn't slow. He trusted Cal to handle whoever might be after Quinn. His job was to keep Jessie safe. So he drove her out to the stagecoach main offices and stables, between Wilde and Bent.

When he parked, Jessie hesitated. "They want Sarabeth. They think she knows something. And I'm going to go to work?"

"Just remember, we've got seven people at that ranch keeping an eye on her. Out of everyone, she's the safest."

"But if they think she knows and Quinn and I don't—" She looked up at him, desperate for some assurances.

"I think Quinn knows quite a bit, and they know it. They'd assume Sarabeth told you anything. They might want her, but that doesn't make you disposable. I think that means any one of you could be a target."

Jessie sighed. "I don't know how this got so out of hand."

"Probably around the time someone decided, 'I know, I'm going to dedicate my life to finding some 1800s bank robber's cache.'"

Jessie managed a smile at that. She got out of the truck, but stopped when he started to do the same. "Stay here. I have to check in and talk to the manager and a few other things. They'll think it's strange if you're hulking around me the whole time."

"I don't hulk, and you aren't going anywhere alone."

"Maybe *hulk* was the wrong word, but it's weird to have someone following me around, particularly a large, intimidating man. So actually, hulking was apt. It arouses suspicion, doesn't it? You following me *everywhere*. And shouldn't we avoid that?"

Henry scowled. He didn't want her going anywhere on her own.

"Unless they're lying in wait here, at the stagecoach company, you'll be able to see if anyone suspicious comes in. You can step in then. But for the time being, I need to be able to do this normally. Not just for looks, but for myself. I can handle some things myself. I *have* to be able to call some of the shots myself. In order to come out on the other side of this, I need that, okay? I don't need a protector."

Henry couldn't look at her, so he stared straight ahead. He understood what she was saying. He even agreed with her. The problem wasn't her or that, it was this…thing inside him. This desperate need.

And it wasn't about the way he'd failed his mother— at least not fully. Though he knew that was what Jessie thought. Maybe he should let her think that. But…

"No, you probably don't need one, but I need you to let me protect you and Sarabeth anyway."

"I've tried to tell you I don't want to be some stand-in for the things you think you did wrong."

"Not that," Henry muttered. "Not all."

"Then what?"

It was a wonder the steering wheel didn't bend under the strength of his grip. He kept staring straight ahead, still seated in the driver's seat. If he didn't hold on to the wheel, he might grab on to her.

And something about that made the truth seem...necessary. He was a man who prided himself on facing the realities of the situation, and whether or not he liked it, the reality was simple. "I care about the both of you."

There was a sharp inhale at that, but he wasn't about to look over and see what kind of expression was on her face. It was a fact. Didn't mean he had to deal with the aftermath of the facts. "Aren't you going to be late?"

"Are you going to stay here?"

"Yeah. Unless I see something."

"Good." She began to walk toward the building, and he stayed in the driver's seat. But he watched her. She took four steps and then stopped, turned. Met his gaze as she walked back to the truck.

"Something about the way you say you care about us like it's the worst possible thing just... I don't know." She fisted a hand at her heart. "Makes it mean more."

He frowned at her. "That's messed up."

She laughed. "Probably."

But he supposed that was the thing. What would he do with not messed up? He wouldn't have a clue.

"I think we're both a little messed up," she continued, and her gaze was earnest. Studying. He didn't know why they were having this conversation here. Now.

"Guess most people are," he returned, rather than stopping it. Telling her to go inside. Telling her to get back in the truck so he could tuck her away and handle it himself. Alone. Like he should.

But he didn't. Because she needed to be part of it. She needed to stand on her own two feet, and he understood that better than anything else.

No one could fight your demons for you.

"I guess so." But before she turned and left, she leaned in and brushed her lips across his cheek. "Thank you," she said.

He was too puzzled—by the chaste kiss and the genuine thanks—to simply let it go. "For what?"

"Protecting. Caring." She smiled a little and backed away from the car. "Being good with Sarabeth when so many people, men especially, have hurt her. She needs that. I need that for her. I'll be right back."

She turned and strode for the office building. Henry watched her go. He didn't know what to make of any of that, and there wasn't yet time to figure it out. He supposed there would be.

He'd make sure there would be. Which meant getting to the end of this mystery and danger.

Chapter Sixteen

Jessie wasn't as on edge as she had been. It was likely stupidity on her part, but the idea Henry *needed* to act as some kind of protector, because he cared about both her and Sarabeth, had settled…something.

Aside from all that emotional stuff, there was the fact it was hard to feel like a target when a large, former military man sat next to you, scanning the world around you with a steely-eyed concentration she trusted meant he saw anything and everything.

He cared. *Cared.* And she wasn't foolish enough to think that it didn't have anything to do with his past failures at protecting people, which probably weren't even failures. Just felt like them. But she also knew a man like Henry didn't grumpily admit care if it wasn't there.

And she felt the same. She was scared of it. Unsure about what it meant for the future. It complicated…so many things.

But it was there.

Before they could deal with that, though, they had to figure out a way to make sure Sarabeth was safe.

She smiled at those who handed their tickets to Henry. Answered questions. Led the horses around the stagecoach trail. She could almost pretend this was just a normal day.

Almost.

She dropped the last ticket holders off at their requested stop closer to Wilde than Bent. She still had about an hour left on her shift, and she'd just ride the circuit unless she got word that more tickets had been bought.

"Stop," Henry said, one of those gruff orders that had her obeying before she fully thought it through.

She frowned at him. They were basically in the middle of nowhere, between two of the stagecoach stops, between the two main towns. "What?"

"That the cemetery your grandfather is buried at?" he asked, pointing at the hill. Gravestones dotted the roll of green grass. This was the back side and her grandfather was buried at the front side that faced Wilde—you could see almost the entire town from the top of that hill.

"Yes."

"We've taken all the tickets, right? Dropped everyone off. Why not go look now? We'll just do it really quick before your shift is up."

"It's off the path."

Henry gave her a *seriously?* kind of look.

"I'm not supposed to take the coach off the path." She watched impatience pass over his face before he schooled it away.

"All right."

That was just another thing about him. He could be bossy and pushy, but it was about the right things. He picked his battles. Carefully.

"Although, sometimes we're allowed to go off path if it's a particular customer request." She gave him a sheepish smile. "And they pay."

"Fine. Consider it a request and I'll pony up at the office after."

"I'll pay you back once I—"

"No, you won't. Come on now. Before your shift is over."

She frowned at his steamroll. She'd pay him back. One way or another. But for now she turned the horses. There was an old, overgrown path here into the back of the cemetery. She let the horses up as far as she could before the path got too narrow for the coach. She could tie the horses to the bench there, and they'd be able to keep horses and coach in view as they walked over to the other side of the hill.

Henry got down, and she gripped the reins and followed suit. But Henry was there by the time her feet hit the ground.

He took the reins from her and secured them to the bench. "We won't go too far. We'll get a lay of the land, and if it looks safe, we'll get the map. If not, we'll come back."

Jessie nodded. He paused for a second, then took her hand in his. Sort of like the other night when they'd been out looking for Sarabeth. But this was more…casual. Friendly. *Care.*

They began to walk up the hill. The cemetery was mostly older gravestones, some tilted or sinking with age. Some even broken so that large grass grew around the pieces as the mower likely couldn't get close enough easily.

The breeze was cool, the sun was warm and Henry's hand was firm and rough. She looked up at him, almost haloed by all that golden sun. He didn't have pretty words. He didn't offer promises of some grand future together. Rob had done both those things.

Henry simply offered his gruff protection. Because it was the right thing to do, and what had shaped him as a child meant he felt compelled to follow right. Because her daughter had climbed under all those angry defenses to the softhearted man underneath.

But why did he care about *her* when she'd done nothing but cause him trouble?

Her thoughts came to an abrupt halt and she stopped when she heard voices. Henry stopped, too. She shaded her eyes against the sun. As they reached the top she saw a little group of people. They appeared to be doing something… maybe cleaning the graves?

"Should we just turn back?" she said to Henry, even as a few heads turned toward them.

"Don't want to be suspicious. We'll come back and do what we need to later," Henry said. "For now we'll keep going and you can pretend to give me some kind of historical lecture."

"I don't know any historical lectures."

"Just try to think of stuff your grandmother told you. Think quick, though. Here comes Mrs. Caruthers."

Mrs. Caruthers. Jessie frowned at that. Why would she be out here when she should be at her store?

"Well, hello, Jessie. Now, where have you and your girl disappeared to? And who's this?" She narrowed her eyes at Henry. "One of those Thompson brothers, aren't you?"

Henry smiled, and it was dangerously close to being a *charming* smile. Who knew he could fake charm?

"Yes, ma'am."

"Well, that's interesting. What are two young people doing holding hands walking through the cemetery? Unless you were hoping to find some alone time."

"Jessie was just offering me some historical background of the town."

Mrs. Caruthers smiled at that and beamed at Jessie. "Your grandmother would be proud. Nothing more important than history. Family. Connection." She nodded emphatically then turned her attention back to Henry. "You watch after this one. Her grandmother was a dear, dear friend of mine."

Which wasn't true. Grandma hadn't cared much for Mrs. Caruthers at all. She'd called her a harmless gossip, when she was being generous. But Jessie could see why Mrs. Caruthers might not remember it that way—Mrs. Caruthers often thought people liked her because she had gossip to spread. Not that they just tolerated her *for* the gossip.

"What is all this?" Henry asked, still with that pleasant, nonthreatening smile. It was almost like he made himself seem smaller. Not at all lethal, when Jessie knew he most certainly was.

"Oh, I'm part of the Wilde Historical Society. Hazeleigh suggested we do some work cleaning up the cemetery a few months back. She saw something online about that sort of thing." Mrs. Caruthers rolled her eyes. "We finally got around to doing it. You've got some people buried here, don't you, Jessie?"

"Uh, yes. Yes, I do." Grandma. The grandfather she'd never known. Great-grandparents and likely Petersons as far back as the gravestones went. She'd never thought of it as *having people*.

Maybe she should have, but she'd always felt so disconnected from "family" unless it was her grandmother.

"Why don't you point them out? We'll clean them up for you."

Jessie tried to fix on a smile. "Oh, no. Just follow whatever plan you had. I'm not one for cemeteries, really. I haven't even visited my grandmother's grave since I've been back."

"A shame," Mrs. Caruthers said, sounding disapproving. "But then, why are you here?"

"Ah, my fault. Jessie mentioned history and this place and I drug her along."

"I thought you lived with two historian types. But you chose Jessie?"

Henry smiled again, then leaned forward in an almost conspiratorial manner. "Well, I may have had ulterior motives."

Mrs. Caruthers laughed and patted Henry's arm. She left her hand there and blushed a little. "My, ranch work does wonders for a body, doesn't it? Never did for my Al, but…" She patted his arm a few more times. Then laughed a little breathlessly. "Well, anyway. I won't keep you any longer. You two have your walk or what have you." She winked and then made her way back to her group.

"We'll walk around a bit more then head back," Henry said, his voice quiet.

"Let's avoid my great-grandparents' graves. I don't want her getting it into her head to clean them."

Henry nodded and they walked the perimeter of the cemetery as much as they could while also keeping the horses in view.

"We'll come back after dark, when we're sure they're done cleaning," Henry said.

Jessie tried not to think about the cemetery at dark. She glanced back over her shoulder as they walked toward the stagecoach. Mrs. Caruthers was still standing there, watching them.

It made sense. She was a busybody. She was probably curious about how she could tell the town one of the Thompson brothers was escorting her around a cemetery. She wanted to find it amusing, but…

"I don't trust that woman," she muttered.

"Mrs. Caruthers?"

"Yes, it's probably silly, but she's always given me a gut

bad feeling." She climbed into the coach and Henry did the same.

"We'll have Landon look into her. Never dismiss a gut feeling, Jess. Never."

THEY RETURNED TO the ranch. Cal decided to stay in town with Quinn at least until nightfall on the off chance the truck casing the apartment went by again.

They related what they'd seen, asked Landon to add Mrs. Caruthers to his list of people to look into, ate, then napped.

When they woke, they played a card game with Sarabeth and listened to her relate stories of Henrietta's antics.

It almost felt like a normal day for Henry, except instead of his usual hiding at the fringes, or grumbling at the fringes, he was in the middle of it all. Laughing with Sarabeth and Jessie like they were some kind of...

Well, it didn't do to think about.

They waited for nightfall. Henry wanted to find a way to convince Jessie to stay behind, but he knew it was likely a losing battle. He wasn't about to broach the topic unless he knew he had a foolproof argument.

Night was quickly falling and no such luck. Still, Landon talked with them a little about what he'd found.

"I looked into this Edith Caruthers. I didn't really find anything to raise suspicion, at least on the basics. One thing I did think was a little...weird, let's say, is her maiden name is Chinelly."

Jessie looked blankly at Landon. "Does that mean something?"

"It might not, but Rob had a connection to a guy named Ham Chinelly. A guy who helped him out when he was trying to get information from Hazeleigh. They were related by marriage, I believe."

"Well, I don't like that."

"Edith and Ham aren't siblings. I haven't found the actual familial connection besides the name, but it's not a common one. And in a small town like Wilde, it seems unlikely there's *no* connection."

"A connection to one person involved doesn't necessarily mean anything," Jessie replied. "I'm pretty sure half the town has some connection to a Peterson."

"But not Rob," Henry pointed out.

"Cal says still no sign of whoever Hazeleigh saw," Landon continued. "I don't like that, either. They might be laying low because they know someone caught on. Or they might be laying low because they have something planned. But they're laying low, one way or another."

Henry took that as his chance. He pinned Jessie with a serious look. "You could stay here with Sarabeth. You don't need to put yourself directly in harm's way."

"Neither do you," she said stubbornly.

"I don't have a kid counting on me, Jess."

She sighed. "I know. I know. But sitting here waiting?" She looked up at Landon, then back at Henry. "It doesn't make sense. I know too much. If you have trouble opening up the compartment on the stone, if you find something odd. I can make too many connections based on what might be on that map—if it's even *the* map. It makes the most sense for me to go."

"I could argue that," Henry returned darkly.

"You could, and I could argue that I don't need you, but you asked me to let you protect us, Henry. That's what I'm doing."

Henry didn't look at Landon, though he felt considering eyes on him from that direction. Still, he focused on Jessie. There was no good way to talk her out of this, so he had to protect her.

"We'll take my truck. We'll park at the back of the cemetery again. Avoid lights as much as we can. We'll get the map from the gravestone," Henry said. If he outlined the plan enough times, hopefully nothing went wrong. "We'll alert everyone we've got it. We'll head directly back to the ranch."

"Should Quinn and Cal stay at my apartment?"

"I'm thinking so. Just in case they see someone. Something." He looked up at Landon for agreement. And got it.

"And if Quinn acts squirrelly, Cal can warn us all," Henry continued.

"Maybe we should put one more person on the apartment," Landon suggested. "Without Quinn necessarily knowing."

"I like it. Dunne?"

Landon nodded. "I'll talk to him."

Landon went off to do just that and Henry went over the plan a few more times with Jessie. She went to put Sarabeth to bed and Henry stood on the back porch watching the sun fully set.

Landon came to stand next to him. "Dunne's on his way out. Cal and Quinn will stay put till he gets the signal."

Henry nodded, staring at the last glowing beams of light to the west. "Someone needs to be on any possible exit here. I don't think Sarabeth will run again, but that girl has a mind of her own."

"That she does. Weird owing your life to an eleven-year-old."

Henry slid a glance at Landon. He didn't seem bothered by it, exactly. Henry supposed it was just a kind of weird weight of feeling like you owed somebody. "Yeah, well."

Landon turned and grinned at him, waggled his eyebrows. "You're crazy about the both of them."

No point in arguing. It'd just prove Landon's point. So Henry grunted and looked back out at the fading sun.

"Nothing wrong with that, you know."

Henry couldn't help the bitter laugh. "Sure."

"I get the kid might be a complication."

"Sarabeth isn't a complication," Henry said firmly, and he knew it gave away too much, but it was just flat-out wrong to call her that. "And we don't need to have this conversation."

"I think we do," Landon said good-naturedly. "The thing is we all joined the military, and then Team Breaker, because we came from something that made us want to be more, right? Do something. Mean something. We wanted to prove it—to ourselves, and I imagine some of us to the people we came from. That we weren't as worthless as they made us feel."

"I didn't sign up to be psychoanalyzed by you, Landon."

"No," Landon said, clapping him on the shoulder. "You didn't even sign up to be my brother and a cowboy, but here you are. Because life isn't about signing up. The military was. But life isn't."

"That supposed to mean something?"

"Nothing wrong with letting the soldier go, the messed up kid go, and build a life—a real life."

"Well, that's all well and good for you and Hazeleigh." Henry could have been his normal mean and nasty self if he wanted to, but the words stuck in his throat. "Looks good on you."

Landon grinned. "Yeah. I imagine it does. Feels good. But you know, I was here for the great Jake and Brody fall too, so I know what it's like to look at it from the outside and think they must be built a little different. That somehow they're ready or good at it and you just wouldn't be."

"Trust me."

Landon shook his head. "But that's the thing. It's not magic or miracles or personality. Hazeleigh and I have our problems. Our hang-ups. Neither of us came from anything too great. But we decided to deal with them, work through them. Be honest about them. It's not rocket science. It's just…making a decision and sticking to it. You've always been damn good at that, Henry. Don't know why making a family would be any different."

"Families suck."

"The ones we were given? Sure. But the ones we choose?" Landon gestured at the ranch around them. "Not so much."

Choose seemed to be the operative word in this annoying little conversation. Chosen family. Choose to stick. *Choose, choose, choose.* "What about when you can't make the right one?" he managed to say, though he didn't care for the way his voice sounded rough and far too affected.

Landon took a moment. When he spoke, his voice was equally grave. "When push comes to shove, Henry, you tend to make the right ones. I know you wish you could have saved your mom. Or stopped that bomb back in that village, or been quick enough to get to the suicide bomber before Jefferson. I know what events haunt you, but those weren't choices, were they? Because if you'd had the choice, you'd likely have done it. And been dead in the process. So consider me one of the many who are glad you didn't *have* the choice in those scenarios."

Henry frowned at that. It made a strange, twisted kind of sense. He'd always blamed himself for not being able to stop his father but… If he waded through the emotions of that time, the pain of it, he could almost accept the truth that all the years he'd thought he should have done something, saved his mother in some way, the fact of the matter was he'd been eight. He'd been asleep in his bed. There was no way, at that age, at that time, he'd have been able to change the course of what happened.

No matter how much he wanted to. If there'd been a choice, he'd have made it. Maybe that was the true thing that had always haunted him.

No matter how much he wanted to save people, to make things right, sometimes the world just...didn't let you.

"Uh, well, howdy, Jessie," Landon said.

Henry didn't turn. He merely stood where he was and tried not to wince.

"I'm just...going to go do some more computer work."

Silence stretched out after Landon escaped inside and Henry figured it was cowardly to pretend like she wasn't there. Particularly when they had things to do. He turned slowly. Jessie stood at the threshold, hands clasped together. The porch light illuminated her face, but he couldn't read her expression.

But his heart kicked in his chest, something strange and foreign twisting deep in his gut. She was just...beautiful. And stronger than he'd given her credit for. A good mother, even with everything life had dealt her.

All those choices she hadn't had, but she had to face anyway because she wanted her daughter to be safe.

Henry would do anything, *anything*, to keep them both safe.

"I guess I should apologize," she said finally after the silence had stretched on too long.

"For what?" he muttered.

Jessie hesitated. "I listened to more of that than I should have without announcing my presence."

Henry didn't know what to say to that. He could hardly interrogate her on what parts she'd heard. Besides, he might have been vague, but she knew the stuff about his mother. Knew he'd been in the military. She knew...things he'd sworn no one would ever know outside his brothers.

He should be more...something. But it just didn't settle like he'd thought it would. It felt more like a relief.

He didn't have to say it himself. He didn't have to put her off himself. Now she knew and she'd—

She crossed the space between them, dark eyes never leaving his. He was afraid to read the emotion in them, but he couldn't seem to come up with the words to stop...whatever this was.

Because she didn't stop. She came right up to him, looked up at him and brought her hands up to his cheeks and held him there. Gently. Then she pressed her mouth to his.

Nothing could have undone him more, as he wasn't sure anyone in his entire life had treated him with gentleness. Certainly not a gentleness with this undercurrent of care. It should have scared him. Brought back that old anger as a wall against all the things fighting for purchase inside him.

But he only sank into it, felt somehow washed new.

She eased back and blew out a long, shaky breath, but when she opened her eyes, they were clear. Certain. "Let's go end this."

Henry didn't have any words, not after that, so he simply nodded.

Chapter Seventeen

They didn't speak the entire ride to the cemetery. Jessie didn't mind. It helped her work through exactly what had happened. What she felt.

And if she thought about the kiss, and the way Henry Thompson of all people had softened around her, she didn't have to think about gravestones and maps.

At least for a little while.

Henry slowed to a stop about the same place they'd parked the stagecoach earlier in the day. He pulled the keys out of the ignition, then handed them to her. "If you need to run, run."

"Henry—"

"No arguments. That's the rule. If you need to run, you trust me to take care of myself. I've survived war zones, Jessie. And I know you've survived on your own, but if there's trouble, I want you to get back to Sarabeth. That's all that matters."

Sarabeth was her primary worry. The number one on the list of what mattered. But she was hardly the only thing on that list.

"You matter. To me. To her. To your brothers."

"I don't plan on sacrificing myself," he said gruffly.

She understood what he was very carefully *not* saying. "But you would if you had to."

He sat there, staring straight ahead, but after a few moments of silence he finally turned to face her. "I would. That's just…who I am. I can't change it. I'd need to. I'd need you to let me."

She swallowed, because it wasn't just his normal fierceness, but a plea in his eyes. For her to understand. This wasn't about being noble for the sake of it. Protecting her because she couldn't protect herself.

It was simply who he was. Who he'd made himself out to be. Landon had spoken to Henry about choices, and Jessie knew from being a mother that some choices didn't feel like choices. "Okay," she managed, though her throat was tight with emotion. She took the keys he'd pressed into her palm.

If they ran into trouble, she'd run. To get help. To get backup. Henry had said it himself. Running could be okay. Fighting could be okay. She'd do whatever the situation warranted.

They got out of the truck. It was summer, but it felt a bit like Halloween with wispy clouds shading the moon, a cool breeze and hint of rain in the air.

She moved around to the front of the truck and Henry took her hand. Firm. Sure.

"Lead the way," he said.

She moved forward. It was dark, but the path was right here. There could be little ruts in it, but they should be able to follow it even in the dark. Henry had a flashlight in his pocket if they needed it, but they'd both agreed to do without light as much as they could.

"We're not going to run into any trouble," she said firmly.

"Way to jinx it," Henry muttered.

"You don't honestly believe in jinxes."

"I believe in all manner of things. Because I've seen all manner of unexplainable things."

"Don't tell me you believe in ghosts."

"Okay, I won't tell you."

Jessie was honestly shocked a man as…grumpy and cynical and smart and capable as Henry could believe in ghosts. She didn't.

Or hadn't, until she'd been walking through a cemetery in the dark with a man who did. The air twisted around them like it was spirits, not weather. Shadows flickered, moved, morphed.

She leaned into Henry and gripped his hand harder.

"Don't tell me *you* believe in ghosts," he whispered with just a hint of humor.

"Your fault," she muttered. They followed the path up the hill, then back down. She'd need a little light now, just to be sure she had the right stone. "You have the penlight?"

Henry handed it to her. She flicked it on and noted the gravestone in front of them, then thought about all the times she'd visited with Grandma. Then the one time after Grandma had passed.

"A few more to the left, then into the rows."

They moved. She turned on the light again to get her bearings, then hid it when she thought she could move without illumination. When she finally shone it on the obelisk that was her grandparents' grave, she let out a breath that was all nerves. To the right were her great-grandparents, and the monument with a removable nameplate where hopefully her grandmother's belongings still lay.

She moved over, ran her hands over the cold stone and didn't think about what lay beneath her feet. She handed the penlight to Henry. "Here. Hold it pointed right…there."

He did as he was instructed and she tried to undo the

bolts. Age or disuse had fused them and she could no longer do it with simply her fingers. Brody had been the one who'd pointed out the possibility, so they'd thought to bring tools, thank goodness.

But it added time to the whole process, and it made nerves kick in. Henry pulled a little wrench out of his pocket and Jessie had to work in the small, dim light of the penlight to adjust it to fit the bolts on the nameplate.

It was still difficult to get the bolts to turn, especially when her fingers felt nerveless and fumbled.

She finally succeeded and let out a breath of relief. She tried to hurry, but Henry's free hand patted her shoulder.

"Take it easy. Take a breath. We've got time."

Time. *Time.* Why did that make her want to laugh? What *time* did they have? She'd lived under this shadow ever since she'd turned thirteen and now all she wanted wasn't time, but a conclusion.

Still, she took a breath so she didn't drop the bolt when it finally came loose. She worked methodically on the other three bolts. By the time she got them all off, she was breathing hard.

She handed the wrench and bolts to Henry so she could use both hands to pull the plaque off the stone. She had to get her nails in there and really wiggle it to get it to come off. The sound the metal made against the stone creaked loudly in the quiet night.

But Jessie couldn't think about that. Henry shone the light into the little crevice. Everything she'd put there when she'd been just a little older than Sarabeth was still in place. The pearl necklace, her grandmother's wedding rings, the little diary and…the rolled up map.

Swallowing against an odd swell of nerves, Jessie reached in and pulled the map out. For now she'd leave the rest.

Come back when she knew… When she knew everything would be safe.

In fraught silence, she began to replace the plaque, map secured under her arm. But curiosity got the better of her and she didn't bother to tighten the bolts. She took the map and began to unroll the paper, to examine if it really was some kind of treasure map, but the penlight clicked off. Before she could protest, Henry's arm came around her shoulders, holding her still.

"Shh," he murmured.

She fell silent and stood as still as her racing heart would let her. Henry slid the paper from her fingers. Nerves jangled, but Jessie managed to breathe in time with Henry rather than hyperventilate.

Someone had to be here. Jessie closed her eyes, focused not on the possibility of danger but on the fact she was here with Henry. They would work together to avoid the danger.

She felt the slide of something against her back pocket and realized Henry was slipping the map into her pocket. Out of sight.

Part of her wondered if they shouldn't just give up the map. Hand it over and run. Let whoever find the damn treasure and leave them out of it. But she supposed that didn't really make them safe. Knowing about it made them probably as much of a target as anyone.

"We're going to move for the truck in the dark. Hold on to me. Step where I step. No light. No noise. Just move," Henry said, his voice barely a whisper. Barely anything above the whir of summer insects and nocturnal wildlife all around.

She didn't speak—she knew she wouldn't be able to keep her voice that even and quiet. So she nodded against his shoulder.

He took her hand and began to lead her forward. She

trusted his lead. But she stopped and turned when she heard someth—

Pain exploded across her skull and she cried out. So surprised by it, confused by it, she didn't think. Simply let go of Henry's hand to fight off whoever had grabbed her by the hair. But in the dark she couldn't make out the shadow she was grappling with, and every punch or kick seemed to meet with air until a strong arm banded around her, keeping her almost completely still.

She wriggled, she fought, but it was no use. Someone had her.

A light appeared. Henry's. Not the tiny penlight, but a stronger flashlight that nearly blinded her. She blinked against it when she heard Henry's voice cut through the quiet.

"I'd let her go if I were you," he said, low and dangerous.

"I'd give me the map if I were you." The hand in her hair tightened and she tried not to react, but then she felt something at her throat. Her knees wobbled. A knife.

Nothing on Henry's face changed, but everything about him was still. So still. It scared her almost as much as the knife at her throat, and the fact she recognized the voice.

Her father.

Henry's gaze flicked from the man holding her to her. Something in his expression flashed in all that stillness, but she wasn't quite sure what it was.

"I've got the map," Henry said. Which Jessie knew wasn't true. She was tempted to say that, so Henry would be left alone. But he'd asked her to let him protect her and she knew this was his version of that.

She also knew if her father knew she had the map he'd likely take it and slit her throat without a second thought.

"Let me go and he'll give it to you," Jessie said, managing to keep her voice even. She looked pointedly at Henry. *"Dad."*

Henry gave an almost imperceptible nod. "Remember what I told you in the truck?" he asked as if her father wasn't there, holding a knife to her throat.

Her mind raced with everything they'd said in the truck. He'd given her the keys. He wanted her to run.

"Shut up and hand over the map," her father said and she felt the knife dig a little into her skin. A sharp slice of pain.

But she couldn't let Henry know that. She had to be calm. She had to handle this. "I remember," she managed to say.

Henry nodded once, and then there was a blur of movement and her father's knife clattered to the ground.

When Henry told her to run, she did.

HENRY HAD NO doubt he could take down one lone knife-wielding man. The problem wasn't that. It wasn't even getting Jessie free without a scratch. He knew how to handle all of that easily enough.

It was the fact he doubted very much the man was truly alone. Which meant he'd just sent Jessie to run...possibly into someone else's clutches.

He didn't let himself dwell on that. There were immediate threats and *what-if* threats and thinking about *what-if* threats was likely to get a person killed by the immediate ones.

He'd had to drop the flashlight and though it was still on it was pointed in the opposite direction, so he fought the man—Jessie's *father*—in the dark. He dodged the knife the man had picked back up out of instinct and feel rather than being able to see it swinging toward him.

He landed an elbow to the gut that had the man doubling over, but Henry stumbled over a flat gravestone he hadn't seen and didn't manage to land the follow-up blow.

He jumped back. The man's knife scraped against his jaw, but the cut would be shallow at best.

Unfortunately, the jerk away had him stumbling over another damn stone. A good reason not to have a fight in a cemetery, Henry thought wryly as he landed hard on his back against another stone.

He didn't groan in pain, but *damn*, that hurt.

The attacker stepped over the stone he'd tripped on. He was nothing but an approaching shadow, but Henry took the moment to catch his breath. The guy clearly didn't have a gun, so he had time.

"Don't know what you're getting yourself into," the man said, looming over Henry.

"And neither do you." Henry managed a kick that sent the man flying and gave Henry the precious seconds needed to get back to his feet.

Henry charged the man, but the attacker used gravestones as a kind of morbid obstacle course. Still, Henry knew he couldn't let him get away. This was Jessie's father. The ringleader. He had to bring him down.

Just as he managed to get a grip on the man, a gunshot rang out, loud and fatal against the quiet night, but Henry didn't feel the expected burn of bullet exploding through flesh—he knew just what that felt like. The man he was grappling with jerked, stumbled, fell.

Henry grabbed the flashlight, keeping low and behind gravestones as best he could. He pointed the beam at the man. He'd been shot in the stomach. It was a bad spot, but it wouldn't necessarily kill him if he got quick enough medical care. Henry scanned the area. Based on where they'd been, where the wound was, he had to assume the shooter was to the northeast. Maybe behind the big tree there.

There was no way to get to the shot man without exposing himself. He texted his brothers to pass the information on to an ambulance, the cops if need be. Jessie was out there somewhere running. Hopefully, she'd gotten in the truck and driven away, but unless he'd been too busy fighting to hear the sound, he'd heard no engines turn over.

Frustrated at the lack of options, Henry got as low as he could. No more gunshots rang out, but he didn't let that put him at ease. Carefully and quickly, he reached out an arm and began to drag Jessie's dad toward him. Where there'd be cover.

Another gunshot echoed through the night, but the sound of stone exploding wasn't as close as it had been.

"Not one of mine." The man laughed, actually laughed, as the blood spurted from his stomach.

Henry shrugged off his jacket and stripped off his sweatshirt. He rolled it up, pressed it against the man's wound. Then worked to get his coat back on, switching arms to keep pressure on the wound.

Sirens sounded far off, but they'd get here soon enough. Henry just had to keep himself from getting shot, too.

The man just kept laughing, even as he writhed in pain. "The ghost is going to get you. The ghost gets everyone eventually. Even me."

"I don't believe in ghosts," Henry lied.

"You're going to believe in this one."

Chapter Eighteen

Jessie didn't run to the truck. It would have been faster, sure, but if her father was out here, he wasn't alone. He never worked alone. Not ever. Which meant he had men out here, and likely had someone stationed at the truck.

How had he known about the map? The cemetery? Was he following them?

She had a hard time believing Henry had missed that, but maybe she was giving him far too much credit.

Except he'd handled that back there. Gotten her out of knifepoint, all so she could escape with this ridiculous map. She had half a mind to burn it and watch them all go insane.

But that was stupid. If she could get to the cops, she could hand over the map. Maybe they still wouldn't believe her, but she'd have evidence. They'd have to look into it.

And if they didn't, wouldn't, well, then she'd know she had to get back to Sarabeth and leave. Get out of here, off the grid again. It wasn't the childhood she wanted for her daughter, but alive was better than dead. Alive and on their own, even off the grid, was better than living in that compound.

Once she got far enough away, safe enough to risk the light of her phone, she'd text Cal and have him come help Henry. Text all of them to help Henry.

She had to believe Henry could hold his own until she was in a safer spot. He'd want her in a safer spot.

A loud *pop* echoed out across the night. Jessie had been running and breathing hard enough she could almost convince herself it was…nothing. Something else. Surely not…a gunshot.

She slowed, willed her breathing to even so she could listen. She got out her phone. She wasn't about to risk Henry this way. If it gave her away, so be it. She typed in a quick text to Cal.

Father at cemetery. I ran. Henry there. Have map. Help. ASAP.

She hit Send and then she heard it again.

Pop.

A gunshot.

She fought back her first instinct—to run toward it. Her father hadn't had a gun. If he had, he would have held that to her head rather than a knife to her neck. Had Henry brought a gun? She hadn't thought to ask. Not when they'd just been going to the cemetery to retrieve the map.

What now? She could run for the truck, for town, for safety. Or she could run back and make sure Henry was okay.

Henry wanted to protect her. Not because she needed it, but because he needed to do that. She understood—how could a mother not? Love was a complex motivator.

Love. Boy, did she not have time for that thought.

Another gunshot rang out and she flinched and crouched, as if that would somehow make a bullet miss her. But who could be shooting? There was no light. Only darkness. Even the wispy clouds had strengthened and covered the moon.

If someone was shooting it was either close range, or…

She swallowed. Well, she'd find out. Because she couldn't leave Henry here without access to the truck.

She pulled out the knife Henry had given her. It wouldn't save her from a gunshot, but if one of her father's men jumped out and grabbed her she could try to fight them off.

She thought of her own father holding a knife to her throat. So consumed by all this. It didn't make any sense.

No more gunshots rang out so she gave herself a moment to breathe, to orient herself, and to really decide if she wanted to go for truck or gravestone.

She thought she heard something… Not a footstep. Not a whisper. She wasn't sure what it was. Almost like a squeak.

Away from it or toward it? Shadows moved around her, but were they real? Were they friend or enemy? Was Henry still in there? Was he okay? She'd have to get to the other side of the cemetery to make sure.

She couldn't look at her phone now. Not when the light could draw unwanted attention.

She'd just get to the truck. Once she got into the truck…

Well, she'd turn it on. And if there was someone out there shooting, she'd drive away. If there wasn't, she'd wait for Henry to come.

She stepped forward, being careful to make a straight shot walking. When she thought she should be getting close to the truck, taking careful steps to test the ground, her foot nudged against something solid.

Warm.

Something—no, someone groaned. Jessie jumped back out of instinct. She couldn't make out what exactly was on the ground, but clearly it was a person. And though she'd never heard Henry groan, she didn't think it was him. The pitch was too…high. The body she'd accidentally nudged with her foot too soft.

Maybe it was whoever her father had assigned to watch the truck. Maybe Henry had gone through and disabled the entire group. He was capable. She was sure he was capable of that kind of thing.

But she had to be sure. Swallowing, she crouched and carefully pulled her phone out of her pocket. She hid the light with her body as much as she could, and leaned closer to the man on the ground.

Blond hair. Not Henry. Eyes closed. Pale face. Very bloody arm. And leg.

Jessie was rendered frozen for a moment. She didn't know what to do with someone hurt this way.

She looked at the screen of her phone. Cal had responded to her text. Nothing informative. Just: ok.

Jessie heard a noise and hurriedly shoved her phone into her pocket. But another light popped on, along with the creaking sound of a door opening. The interior light on the truck. Her own face was outlined by the dim light.

No, not her face. Not *her*.

"Quinn." Jessie knew she should be scared. Terrified, really, but she was…hurt.

Quinn wasn't here to help. Not with a gun in her hand. Not looking at her like *that*.

Jessie's heart sank, and no matter how soft and silly it was, she felt…heartbroken. Quinn had never had a chance. Jessie had been given her—*their*—grandmother. A sense of normalcy before it had all been taken away.

Quinn had only had that compound and lies. So even with Quinn holding the gun, even knowing she might shoot, Jessie simply felt sorry for her. For them.

"Do you have the map?" Quinn asked. Her voice was

very…blank. None of that bravado or pointed laziness. It was like she was a completely different person than she'd been the past few days.

And Jessie understood, as much as she didn't want to, that this was probably the real Quinn. Not funny and shocking and hard to read. Cold and calculating and here for the only thing everyone in her family cared about. Gold and treasure.

"Do you have the map, Jessie?" Quinn repeated. She didn't point the gun at Jessie, but Jessie was under no illusions she wouldn't use it on her if she saw fit.

She could lie. Just like she'd lied before. Tell her Henry had it. That would be the smart thing to do.

But her heart wouldn't let her. She took the map out of her back pocket and held it up even as the sound of sirens could be heard in the distance. Maybe they'd get here fast enough. Maybe they wouldn't.

But there was no use pretending. "If this is really the map, I've got it."

THE SHOOTING HAD STOPPED. Henry could see the flashing lights now. He wasn't sure what had happened, and that sat all wrong.

There were clearly players in this he didn't know about. It couldn't just be Jessie's father and his goons, or why was the dad the one who'd gone alarmingly still and silent?

Henry could see the lights of the ambulance parked at the front entrance to the cemetery. He could wave them down, but he thought it'd be safer for them if he carried the unconscious man himself.

He supposed Jessie's father didn't deserve the courtesy, but life or death would be up to the hospital workers. Not him.

And should the man live to see tomorrow, Henry would

make sure he paid for everything he'd done to hurt Jessie and Sarabeth. Dying was just a little too easy.

"You might wish you had died," Henry muttered, picking the man up. He groaned, moved a little and then went back to dead weight.

With the lights of the ambulance, Henry could make out the gravestones enough to avoid them as he carried the man to the medics who hopped out.

"Shot. Shooter is still out there as far as I know," he said to the EMT who quickly worked to get a stretcher. Henry put the man down on it and the medics began to work.

They asked him questions, and cops arrived to ask him more. He answered them with enough information to make them aware of the dangerous situation they found themselves in, to maybe find the person shooting, or even Jessie.

But not enough to catch who he was or why he was here. He answered each question with an eye out to how to escape before they pinned him down or got a good look at him.

In the dark, in the confusion, with the skills he'd spent his adult life building, it was easy to slip away.

He started making his way toward the back of the cemetery and the truck. He didn't have the keys, but he was almost sure he hadn't heard it drive away. So Jessie was either waiting for him or...

It didn't do to think about the *or*.

As he reached the gate out the back side, he heard the telltale whistle from one of his brothers. He stopped, waited for them to materialize.

Cal appeared next to him.

"Where's Jessie?" Henry demanded.

"Not sure. Got a text all wasn't well, but she didn't say where she was and hasn't texted back. Listen—"

Henry swore. He had to get to Jessie before the gunman did. He started moving forward, toward where the truck was.

But Cal followed, and made it worse. "Quinn gave us the slip. Quite a while ago. She might be out here, too."

Henry stopped cold. "She got away from you guys?" He didn't have to see in the dark to know Cal's face would be cold fury.

"Used the bathroom window, climbed out the back. Dunne heard her, but he couldn't keep up with the leg. Apparently she can run like the devil."

"Apparently she *is* the devil," Henry growled. He reached the truck. It was unlocked, but there was no sign of anyone. He swore, viciously.

"Uh-oh," Dunne said. Apparently he'd been hiding in the shadows too, and Henry had been so focused on finding Jessie he hadn't noticed.

He needed to get his head on straight. For all of them.

"Got a man's body here," Dunne said. "Still breathing, but he might need one of those ambulances."

Another man shot. The bad guys, presumably. It didn't add up and they didn't have time to do a thorough search with the cops and medics crawling around.

He had to find Jessie before Quinn did. Before the gunman did.

Assuming they weren't one and the same.

Chapter Nineteen

"Give it to me, then," Quinn instructed.

She still didn't point the gun *at* Jessie, but it was right there and her finger was definitely on the trigger.

Jessie didn't care about the map in the grand scheme of things. She cared about the safety of her daughter. If she ran just to save the map and got shot, wasn't she just as bad as her family obsessed with this ridiculous "treasure"?

Jessie stepped forward slowly and carefully. Clearly, Quinn didn't *want* her dead, or she'd be shot already. Maybe if she went along with Quinn for a little bit, they could all get out of this in one piece.

Sirens were louder, their lights flashing not far off now. Were they coming here? Should she bolt?

"Quinn—"

"Don't say anything," Quinn hissed, grabbing the map and shoving it into her pocket as she scanned the world around them. She closed the truck door, but Jessie noted she did it soundlessly.

It was dark again. Jessie could run. Maybe she *should* make noise. Yell and scream.

Sirens were coming. If they were coming here because of her text to Cal, they'd go to the entrance likely. Not this back part. She should make a run for it.

Quinn's hand closed around her arm. "Not a word," she hissed. "Unless you want to end up dead."

Jessie swallowed at the nerves as Quinn grabbed her arm and dragged her through the cemetery, unerringly leading them around stones and fences and walkways.

Jessie didn't know how to handle Quinn, but she couldn't help but think she might be able to get through to her. Somehow. Maybe?

They were sisters. Identical *twins*. Even if they hadn't grown up together, even if Jessie hadn't known about her, surely there was some way to…to…something.

"Where are we going?"

"Shh! You want to die?"

It was strange the way she said that. Not like a threat. More like they were in this together. Though Quinn's grip on Jessie's arm was rough and authoritative as she pulled her along.

Jessie wondered if she pulled out of Quinn's grasp, would Quinn shoot her?

Quinn had led her out of the cemetery, in the opposite direction of the flashing lights.

"If you're taking me to our father—"

"You think our dad is the problem?" Quinn said, still in that hushed whisper. "You really don't pick up on anything, do you?"

Confused, Jessie pulled at her arm a little bit. Quinn heaved out a sigh and stopped. She brought her face close to Jessie's and spoke in a rushed, desperate whisper.

"Oh, he's mean and he's sneaky, but if he was half as smart as he thought he was, this would all be over. Instead, it's all family feuds and one-upmanship and… Look, I'll save you the details. You want to survive? Just follow me."

Maybe it was foolish to believe Quinn, to trust her. Maybe it was leading with an emotion the other woman didn't have.

But Jessie didn't have any better options. She didn't just *want* to survive. She needed to. For Sarabeth. For herself. For Henry even. She didn't want him heaping any more guilt on himself for things that were beyond his control.

So she let Quinn lead her deeper and deeper into the dark. She didn't say anything more. They moved through the evening shadows, quickly but cautiously. The sounds of whirring insects and the occasional hoot of an owl gave everything another echoing layer of tension.

Quinn stopped, pulling Jessie behind a tree with her. She didn't let go, but when she lifted the gun she pointed it outward. To the night around them.

"What about Cal and Dunne?"

"What about them?" Quinn returned irritably. Though she couldn't see in the dark, between shadow and the noise, she had the impression of Quinn turning her head toward her. "What? You think I shot them and left them for dead?"

Quinn sounded almost offended, which made very little sense to Jessie. But none of this did. "No. I just don't know how you got away from them. They're pretty…"

"Military guys are all the same. It's all *I know everything*. And *I'm big and strong and oh, so smart*. But you put on the waterworks, excuse yourself to the bathroom, they don't expect you to jump out of a window. Idiots."

Jessie blinked. "You…faked crying, and then jumped out my bathroom window?"

"More of a climb down than a jump." Quinn did her patented shrug. "Didn't count on Dunne being there, but I knew I could outrun him. A little surprised he didn't shoot, but eh. Maybe he's a bad shot."

"I can assure you, he's not."

"Whatever. Look, we need to be quiet again. I think I picked off most of what we have to worry about, but you never know. Follow me. Don't make a sound. Got it?"

It finally, fully dawned on Jessie what was happening. "You're helping me."

"What else would I be doing?"

Jessie didn't answer that. Didn't figure she needed to since Quinn knew very well what else she might be doing.

She let Quinn take her arm again, but then thought better of it. She pulled Quinn's hand off her arm and clasped it in her own. Just like Henry had done, leading her through the dark, hand in hand.

Then they moved. Through the dark. Quick, purposeful strides. Jessie worked hard to follow Quinn's every move so she didn't stumble. She got the sense Quinn was adjusting her pace to accommodate Jessie's slower strides.

Because she was *helping*.

This wasn't a mistake to trust her sister. They were looking out for each other. They were going to get out of this together.

There was a noise, and then a splash of light that had Jessie flinching and squeezing her eyes shut. Quinn came up short, and Jessie bumped into her. But she kept her hand in Quinn's—both of them squeezing onto each other.

When Jessie could blink her eyes open, she realized Quinn had angled her body as if she was protecting Jessie from the light in front of them.

But Jessie could still see. She knew the man standing there with a powerful lamplight. Her heart sank. "Dad." If he was here, he'd somehow bested Henry. He'd somehow...

"No," Quinn said, and her voice was as flat as it had been back when she'd asked about the map. "I shot our father back in the cemetery," Quinn whispered. "Remember when I said George had a brother? Sadly, identical twins beget identical twins. That's our uncle. Gene. And now we're as good as dead."

THEY MOVED THROUGH the dark, a unit. Sticking to the shadows, avoiding cops and flashing lights. Cal thought he'd picked up a kind of trail at the truck, and Henry trusted him to catch the small cues.

He had to trust Cal, or the panic might overtake him completely. "Where would she have gone if not the truck?"

Cal came up short and looked around. They'd left the cemetery, and now that they were still, Henry realized they were far enough away not to hear the commotion of voices, see the flashes of lights.

Cal flicked on a flashlight. The beam was pointed at the ground. "Two sets of footprints," he said grimly.

Henry crouched to study them. "Awfully similar." It took an incredible force of will to sound calm when he posed his question. "You think Quinn got to her already?"

"Yes, but two sets of footprints moving means she's alive and well," Dunne offered.

"And being taken somewhere."

"Where? The father got shot."

"Maybe the father was the patsy all along and Quinn's the one who wants the treasure."

"She doesn't need Jessie for the treasure," Henry returned, and they began following the prints with Cal's light on. Slowly, quietly, so they could hear if they came up against something. "Jessie has the map."

"Maybe she didn't tell Quinn that."

"I think Quinn would have figured it out if she's behind this. If she's the mastermind."

"She's not," Dunne said. "She could have shot me."

"What?" Henry replied, turning to look back at Dunne before he remembered in the dark he wouldn't be able to make out Dunne's expression.

"She had a gun. I couldn't catch up, sure, but she could have shot me."

"Are you defending her?" Cal demanded.

"No, I'm pointing out there might be something else going on. That we need to be careful. Quinn might be in cahoots with the Peterson family nonsense, but we have to be careful not to make her out to be the only villain. She could have shot me, stopped me from telling you or anyone else what was wrong as quickly as I did."

"I'm pretty sure I would have heard the *gunshot*, Dunne."

"But I wouldn't have been able to tell you what happened."

"You could have shot *her*," Cal continued. Not willing to let the point go, clearly.

"I'm not about to shoot a scared, running woman. You really think we were *all* wrong and she's evil? Complicated? Sure. Evil? I don't see it."

"Maybe something's clouding your vision."

Dunne didn't respond in kind. He spoke calmly and completely unperturbed. "Or something's clouding yours. I'm suggesting we make sure to weigh all the facts rather than run off half-cocked. Something you're usually on board with."

Cal didn't have anything to say to that, and Henry didn't either, as they made their way through the dark night, following two women's footprints.

Not having a clue who to be on the lookout for.

SARABETH SAT CURLED up in the window seat in the living room. She knew the adults wanted her to go to sleep, but

Mom and Henry were out there. She could lie in bed and stare at the ceiling, or she could sit here with Henrietta and watch for them to come back.

They had to come back.

Sarabeth sighed and leaned her forehead against the window. This was worse than last month. Just sitting here. Just waiting. Last month was scary, but she'd been able to do something about it. She'd had something to *do*.

She frowned a little at the dark outside. Something had... moved out there in the side yard. Her heart leaped to her throat. Mom?

But...no. Mom wouldn't lurk. She wouldn't hide. Neither would Henry.

Sarabeth scrambled from the window seat.

"What is it?" Hazeleigh asked from her spot on the couch where she'd been working on her laptop.

"I saw someone outside."

Hazeleigh set the laptop aside. "Okay, come on. Come here, away from the window." She held out her arms. "Landon?" she called.

"Someone is out there. This is bad. Someone..."

Landon came into the room, eyebrows drawn together. "What is it?"

"Sarabeth said she saw someone outside."

Landon frowned, but nodded. "All right. Let's—"

The window crashed and splintering glass went everywhere. Landon pushed her and Hazeleigh to the floor, covering them with his body.

Someone had shot it, Sarabeth realized. They shot the window where she'd just been sitting.

"They want me. They want to get me. I know they do." She tried to stand, but Hazeleigh held her in the corner.

The rest of the adults were now in the living room, moving around. Jake and Brody had guns. Landon got to his feet.

"You stay here with Kate and Hazeleigh, okay?" he said, not looking at her, but taking a gun from Jake. "Jake, Brody, Zara and I will take care of it."

"But they want me. They'll hurt you to get to me."

Landon crouched down in front of her, put his hand on her shoulder, just like Henry always did. He looked her right in the eye.

"What happened last month?"

"I… Well, I saved you."

"Exactly. Now it's our turn to save you."

Chapter Twenty

The man—Jessie's *uncle* apparently, another identical twin in this insane family who liked to keep them hidden away—demanded the guns and their phones and everything else. Jessie handed it all over, as did Quinn.

She did not hand over the map, and somehow, even when the uncle searched her pockets, he didn't come up with the piece of paper. When the man turned his head a little to talk to another man with him, Quinn sent Jessie a wink.

Jessie wished she could laugh or find some kind of comfort from that outrageous gesture, but some part of this would need to make sense. And it just flat out didn't.

"Get in."

Jessie didn't know what to make of *any* of this, but Quinn pulled her toward the car the man—her *uncle*—pointed at. Quinn all but pushed her into the back seat and then followed herself.

She leaned close to Jessie's ear. "Whatever you do, don't mention the map."

Jessie didn't have time to respond. The man got into the driver's seat. Another man got into the passenger seat. He pointed a gun at them. The uncle started to drive, no words exchanged.

She tried to get a handle on where they were driving. It

was dark, but the headlights cut through the night. Gravel roads. Dirt roads.

Some started to look familiar. Or she was delirious. It was really hard to say. Closer to Wilde. Away from Wilde.

Why had she let Quinn push her into the car? They could go anywhere. They could be taken back to that compound, separated from Sarabeth. Henry could be…

But Quinn had shot their father, so Henry had to be okay, right? Somewhere out there, looking for her. Would he be able to find her?

The car pulled to a stop next to a truck. The driver got out, but the gunman stayed put. Still pointing the gun at them.

Quinn looked out the window, then turned to the gunman. She grinned at him, that languid laziness from the past few days back. "You can't honestly want to keep playing second fiddle to Gene."

The gunman rolled his eyes. "You can't honestly think I'd play second fiddle to *you*."

"I know something you don't," she returned in a singsong kind of voice.

The man narrowed his eyes. "We only need one of you, and I don't think it's you, Quinn."

Jessie's heart jumped at that. Quinn kept that antagonizing grin on her face, and Jessie realized… It was another form of protection. Quinn was trying to keep the attention, the threats on *her*. Not Jessie.

And Jessie just couldn't let her do it.

"But are you sure *she's* Quinn?" Jessie adopted the same pose of lazy disinterest. She cocked her head the same way Quinn did when she was trying to irritate people. "Seems like a gamble, bud."

He flicked a glance at Jessie, then at Quinn. Sneered.

"It doesn't matter who's who. You'll both be disposable soon enough."

Jessie had to work very hard not to react to that. To keep a Quinn kind of facade above all her fear. They shouldn't have gotten in this car. They should just hand over the map and maybe…

Well, no, disposable meant dead. She wasn't that naive. Maybe there was no good way to deal. Maybe they were only going along until she had a chance to escape.

She'd thought that with Rob, too. And it had taken Landon, Hazeleigh and Sarabeth to make escape happen.

But she was alive. Sarabeth was alive and safe inside the Thompson ranch house far away. Even if the danger had come to that doorstep, Jessie knew everyone in that house would do everything they could to protect Sarabeth.

It filled her with a kind of strength. She would do everything to survive this for her daughter, but she also knew her daughter was in good hands.

Gene got back in the car and they began to drive again. It didn't take much longer for Jessie to recognize where they were going.

The Thompson Ranch.

Jessie's blood ran cold. "No."

Quinn reached over and gripped her hand, squeezing it. Reassuringly almost. Jessie tried to be reassured, but the car moved up the gravel drive and the house came into view.

Jake and Zara stood on the front porch, rifles pointed. Sarabeth, thank God, was nowhere to be seen. But she was here. In there.

They were here for Sarabeth.

The car came to a stop and the man with the gun pointed it at Jessie. "Get out."

"No," Jessie replied. He couldn't make her get out, and

if he got out first, hopefully Jake or Zara would shoot first and ask questions later.

The man jerked the gun at her again. "I said get out."

"And I said *no*."

Her uncle sighed. Heavily. He pulled out a gun and reached back to point it directly at Quinn's forehead. "Get out of the car or I'll kill her in five, four, three—"

Quinn tried to hold on to her hand. "Don't listen to him—"

But Jessie pulled her hand free and scrambled out of the car. She had no doubt this could end in them both dead. If she got out of the car, she at least had a chance. She couldn't let Quinn die here.

Now she just had to find a way to get Quinn out of the car.

The passenger got out, the gun trained on her head the entire time. Quinn exited the car next, their uncle behind her.

Quinn and Jessie were human shields. But Jessie had to trust the Thompson brothers and the women who'd helped her. And not just because Sarabeth had saved one of their own, but because it was...the right thing to do.

They wanted to do the right thing. The good thing.

"I suggest you lower those guns," Jake said from the porch. "It's not going to end well for you."

Her uncle laughed. "They'll both die before you even pull the trigger. Now, give us the girl."

HENRY WASN'T SURE how much longer he could bite back his frustration. The prints they'd followed ended at car tracks.

Cal pulled out his phone, checked on the texts and swore. "Landon says someone's at the house. Shot out the bay window."

Henry wanted to pound something to dust. Sarabeth was

there, and though his brothers could handle any threat, he hated he wasn't there to handle it. "Quickest way there?"

Cal was consulting his phone. He pulled a face. "Cops back at the cemetery."

Henry swore. Again and again. "Wait. Either of you got the phone number for the one who's Zara and Hazeleigh's cousin?"

"I do," Cal said. Because of course he did.

"Was he up there?"

"I'm pretty sure I saw him," Dunne confirmed.

"Give him a call. Tell him to meet us at the highway. No sirens. No headlights if he can help it. I'm running."

Dunne took the phone from Cal. "You both run. I'll call."

Henry hesitated. You didn't leave a man behind.

But Dunne shook his head. "Go."

Henry didn't need a second urging. He took off west, knowing he'd meet the main highway that would take them out to the Thompson Ranch. Cal kept pace, but Henry doubted the same panic beat through him. The same blinding terror.

They made it to the highway, but there was no sign of the cop car. Henry wanted to scream in frustration, but instead, he took a deep breath and kept running. It wasn't as fast as a car, but he'd be damned if he was going to—

"There," Cal said, gripping his shoulder to slow him down.

Henry turned. No sirens. No lights—not even headlights, but the sound of an engine. It slowed and came to a stop. The passenger door popped open, the light illuminating Thomas Hart, Bent County Deputy, and Zara and Hazeleigh's cousin.

"Get in," he said.

Henry didn't need to be told twice. They both got into the car and Thomas took off, no lights, but plenty of speed.

"Thank God for cops who know the backroads, huh?" Cal offered.

"What's the situation?" Thomas replied.

Henry explained as best he could, best he knew. There were still a lot of question marks. But Thomas was able to fill in some.

"Someone picked off about four men in the cemetery. No IDs on the men yet, but there was some chatter they were part of the Peterson family."

"You should talk to Edith Caruthers," Cal pointed out. "She might know something."

"Why? Because she's a busybody?"

"No," Henry returned. "Because I think she tipped off whoever it was that Jessie and I would be at the cemetery looking for something in the future. Slow down," Henry ordered as they approached the Thompson entry gate.

Thomas did as he was told, which moderately surprised Henry. "We should approach on foot. A surprise."

"Agreed," Cal returned.

"I'll radio someone to talk to Edith. Just give me a second."

"You can stay here and—"

"My cousins are here. This is my county. I'm a part of this. I'm law enforcement. I'm going in with you, whether you like it or not."

Henry didn't have time to argue with him. And besides, three was better than two.

"Okay. I'll come in straight ahead. Cal, you're west. Thomas, you're east once you radio it in. Meet at the house. The most important thing is whoever is shooting at the house they're after that little girl, and we're not going to let them lay a finger on her."

"What about the map?" Cal asked skeptically.

"Screw the damn map. Keep…" He stopped himself from specifying. For whatever reason. "Keep the civilians safe." Then he got out of the car and moved. He ran at first, keeping his footfall quiet against the gravel. He didn't think about Cal or Thomas. He focused on the target.

The front porch lights were on—he could tell that before anything else. He slowed his progress, made sure to be absolutely silent as he moved forward. He could hear the low murmur of voices, and paused behind a parked tractor.

He skirted around it, trying to get an idea of what was going on.

A car, not any of theirs, sat in the middle of the front yard with all its doors open. In front of it, two identical women being held at gunpoint by two men—one who looked oddly enough like George Peterson.

Jake and Zara were holding their own guns on the front porch. Henry didn't see anyone else, which meant Landon and Brody were likely guarding other exits, and Hazeleigh and Kate were keeping Sarabeth safe.

God, he hoped.

He couldn't tell which of the women was Jessie. Not in the dim light. Not when they stood still and didn't speak.

He supposed it didn't matter which one was Jessie. He needed to save them both, because he agreed with Dunne. Whatever Quinn might have done, it wasn't straight up evil, and she had a gun to her head at the moment.

The gunmen were using Quinn and Jessie as shields. They didn't expect anyone to come from the back. Henry wouldn't be able to pick them off with a shot—too close to the women, and he didn't have a quick enough gun to take them both out before the other might shoot the woman in front of him.

If he could communicate with Jake, they could do it in

tandem, but Henry wasn't sure how he could do that without raising suspicion.

"Bring me the girl!" a man shouted. "I'm counting down and then they're both dead."

No, not on his watch.

"What about the map?" He heard Jessie say, and he finally knew which was which, because that statement was all Jessie. All about protecting her daughter. And the look Quinn sent her was *not* kind.

But it certainly got the attention of the man who was demanding Sarabeth.

"What map?"

Quinn sighed and reached into her shirt, pulling a folded piece of paper out of her, well, bra. "This one, geniuses."

But Henry couldn't watch what happened next. He saw something out of the corner of his eye. The flash of something. A shadow. Over by the stables. A small shadow.

Terror iced his veins. Was Sarabeth out here? No doubt she'd do something stupid to try and save her mother. Torn between the reality of Jessie being held at gunpoint and the potential of Sarabeth putting herself in danger, Henry didn't know who to go after.

Except, Jessie would never survive it if something happened to Sarabeth. She just…wouldn't.

He moved quickly through the shadows. Toward the stables. Toward the movement.

He stopped abruptly at an odd sound.

The *snick* of a match lighting. It illuminated the shadow. A *boy* held a match. Just a boy, but not one he recognized. He knelt down and…

Fire blazed suddenly, and the smell of gasoline burned his nostrils. He moved for the boy, but he realized the line of fire went straight for the stables. Where the horses were. Where Sarabeth's precious cats were.

Sarabeth.

He didn't know for a fact she was in there, but it would be a smart place to hide. Which meant Kate and Hazeleigh were likely in there, too. He ran for the door. Fire blazed in front of it, starting to lick up the sides, and with that illumination he could see that someone had tied the doors shut with a zip tie.

He heard Cal swear behind him. "What the hell."

"I think Sarabeth is in there."

Henry didn't have to say anything else. They moved as a team immediately. "I gave Jessie my knife."

Cal produced a small pocketknife and immediately began to saw at the plastic of the zip tie while Henry tried to beat back the flames with his coat.

"Gas," Cal said grimly.

Henry said nothing. He was about to yank the knife out of Cal's hands when the plastic finally fell to the ground. They each pulled a side of the door open, but a gust of wind sent the flames blazing higher and deeper into the stables.

"Sarabeth?"

"We're in here," he heard Hazeleigh say. She was very calm. Thank *God*. But there was nothing but fire. No way to get to them. "The horses were already gone when we got here, then someone locked us in."

"I'll go around to the other side. Get an ax or something," Cal said.

"No, wait," Kate replied before he could dash off. "We soaked the horses' blankets in the drinking water. We can get across if we can get out on that side."

"Good. One of you come through with Sarabeth. Then Cal will help the other."

There was no discussion. Hazeleigh and Kate worked as a team, too. Wrapped in the sopping blankets, Kate and Sarabeth appeared. Sarabeth practically leaped for him.

"The bad men came for me," she said, crying into Henry's chest. "Where's Mom? Where's my mom? My arm hurts. I can't breathe."

Henry had to swallow against his own aching throat—not because of the smoke, but because she was hurt. He carried her with one arm, helped Kate with his other. Cal and Hazeleigh weren't far behind. They'd likely all have burns, smoke inhalation, so he had to get them outside. Away from the smoke.

Sarabeth cried into his shoulder. "I want my mom. I want my mom."

Once they were in fresh air, he squeezed her once, pressed a kiss to her hair and then handed her over to Cal. "Stay with Cal, baby. I'm going to go get her."

Chapter Twenty-One

Jessie could have hugged Quinn. It was clear Quinn didn't want to give up the map, but she was doing it. Jessie supposed she'd forced her into it, but Quinn didn't have to produce the map.

"That's not it," Gene said dismissively.

"Why don't you come find out?"

"I should have killed you when your father sent you," he said with a sneer.

"Yeah, you probably should have. Or one of you should have realized I don't have allegiance to either of you."

Jessie remembered what Quinn had said about where she'd gone when Jessie had arrived at the compound. She'd been vague. But she'd gone to live with the uncle. And likely was used as a pawn—her father trying to get information from the uncle, the uncle trying to trick their father.

"Only out for yourself, Quinn?" the other man said—the man who had a gun on Jessie.

"Shut up, Kirk. Daddy doesn't like mouthy little minions."

This Kirk guy lifted his hand like he was going to try to hit Quinn, but Gene stopped him, and Jessie realized...he was his son. This was her cousin.

"Keep the gun on that one," Gene said, clearly disgusted with how easy it was to get a rise out of his son.

This was her family. Her uncle. Her cousin. Her identical sister. All brought to blows over some old gold.

"Hand it over," Gene said to Quinn.

With great reluctance, Quinn did. Jessie knew this wouldn't be it. It might keep their attention off Sarabeth, but it wouldn't *stop* anything. She glanced at Jake and Zara, still carefully holding guns. Like they were just waiting for their moment. Patient. Not risking anyone.

Then she saw…a shadow. Two shadows. Grappling. She could tell it wasn't Henry. A shade too tall, a shade too lean. But it was one of the Thompson brothers, grappling with another man.

It wasn't just Gene and Kirk. It was more.

Jessie swallowed at the grip of fear. She turned her gaze back to her uncle. Gene unfolded the paper, tilted it presumably to see it in the porch light. "Well. Look at you, Quinn. You might be useful after all."

Jessie didn't like this. She didn't… No, something bad was about to happen. They couldn't stand here being patient anymore. She had to act.

Gene nodded at his son. "Kill them."

Jessie lunged. She didn't think, just acted. She used the full force of her body to shove into Gene. It knocked him over, the gun clattering out of his hand before he could shoot.

And then it was chaos.

A gunshot. The thuds of bodies hitting the ground. The new smell of smoke so acrid it made her eyes water, but she couldn't pay any attention to that. There was only keeping her uncle from shooting anyone.

She stayed on top of him. She couldn't see his gun, but she knew he likely still had it on him. She tried to pin his hands down, but one escaped and grabbed her by the throat, squeezing the breath from her. Still, she didn't get up. She used all her weight to keep him down, to keep him from bucking her off.

She couldn't risk looking around, seeing if she had help. She had to get the man's gun off him. But she couldn't breathe with his grip on her neck. She tried to pull away, but he was so strong. She wasn't winning anymore.

He was.

"I'm going to kill you, and then I'm going to take your daughter," her uncle said, though his breathing was labored as they struggled. "Not to kill her. No, that would be too easy. I'm going to make her mine in every way that counts."

The ball of fury was so big and so bright, it took over every rational thought. She couldn't breathe to scream, but a noise came from within her and she lunged forward, clawed his face. She used her elbows, her knees She paid attention to nothing but inflicting harm on this *evil* man who would dare threaten her daughter.

His grip on her neck loosened. He landed blows of his own, but she could barely feel them between gasping for air and biting, scratching, kneeing.

Until he stopped moving. Until there was only the odd gurgling noise coming from his throat. She slowed her blows, saw the glint of his gun and reached for it.

"Jessie!" Quinn's voice. She looked toward it. Just as Kirk turned his gun on her.

She was going to die.

It was the only thought in her head as the gunshot rang out.

HENRY WAS ONE second too late.

But Quinn wasn't.

She stepped in front of Jessie and as the gun went off,

she fell almost simultaneously as *another* gunshot rang out. The shooter jerked back, stumbled and fell to the ground.

Henry rushed forward, along with just about everyone. Jake and Zara from the porch, Thomas from wherever he'd been, Brody from the back.

Jessie knelt next to Quinn, while Jake barked out orders, making sure all men were disarmed and taken care of and everyone was accounted for.

But Henry could only move next to Jessie. "Jessie—"

Jessie was touching Quinn's face as Thomas was working to find a way to stave off the blood seeping from Quinn's leg.

"She saved me. I thought… I thought it was her, but then she helped and protected me and saved me."

"You're okay?"

Jessie nodded, her eyes on Quinn. "She has to be okay."

"She will be." God, he wished Dunne were here so he could know whether he was lying or not.

"Ambulance is on its way," Thomas said. "Sent a call out the minute I saw that fire go up. Cops will be here, too."

"Move aside."

Henry looked up to see Dunne stride through the chaos.

"Landon's bringing my supplies. You've got an ambulance on the way?"

Thomas nodded. "You a doctor?"

Dunne gave Henry a look. Henry knew exactly what it meant. Would they give more of themselves away here?

Henry nodded.

"Combat medic," Dunne answered. "I can get her stabilized while we wait."

"Is she going to be okay?" Jessie asked.

Dunne knelt next to Quinn's very still body. "We'll do everything we can, Jessie. Why don't you step out of the fray?"

Henry gently pulled her back. She resisted, but he knew what buttons to push. "Sarabeth wants you."

Jessie nodded. "She... Quinn stepped in front of a bullet for me."

"You're sisters."

Jessie shook her head and leaned into him as he led her to the house. "But..." She didn't seem to have anything to say about that. She seemed to realize... She took his hand. "You... You're burnt. What happened?" She looked around, gasped at the stables.

"Little fire. It'll be all right. No one was hurt too much. Come on now. Sarabeth—"

The little girl ran out the door and into her mother's arms. They cried all over each other and Henry just...stood there. Maybe he should give them privacy, but his relief was too great. He just wanted them in his sight. He wanted to...

Jessie reached out an arm. He took it and she pulled him in. Like a three-person hug. Though they were hurt and smoky and both women were still crying, they were holding on to him. Bringing him into the fold.

So he wrapped his arms around them and indulged in a breath of relief. They were safe. They were okay.

The sirens sounded, and lights flashed. The ambulance would get here and Quinn would be okay... It would all be okay.

It had to be.

Over the next few hours, Quinn was taken to the hospital. Everyone got checked out by a medic. Cops took the injured men away. Landon, Brody and Cal surveyed the fire damage, while Dunne lectured anyone with burns how to handle their wounds. Sarabeth dozed in Jessie's lap in the living room, and Henry knew that was the only thing keeping Jessie from racing to the hospital.

He'd take her there himself later, but Quinn was in surgery and Jessie needed some rest herself. She already had bruising on her throat, and her hands were scraped and bandaged from attacking her uncle. It hurt Henry just to look at her, but he also couldn't look away.

She was okay. Here. Okay. Both of them.

When Thomas entered with Landon and Brody, everyone quieted. And sat down in the living room. Henry stopped pacing and settled in next to Jessie.

Thomas's face was as soot covered as the rest of them and he thanked Hazeleigh when she brought him a glass of water.

He cleared his throat, then with a look at the sleeping Sarabeth, spoke carefully and quietly. "Well, we've got a ways to go to work through the whole mess, but there are some things I can tell you. Edith Caruthers talked. She gave one of our deputies a list of names of those involved in this treasure map scheme, as she called it. She wasn't involved, she claims, but giving the names will help her case if it goes to trial. Four of the names matched the shooting victims at the cemetery. I imagine we'll find the same goes for the men we rounded up here, but we're still working on IDs."

"Is Gene still alive?" Jessie asked, her voice low and controlled. Henry knew in part to keep from waking Sarabeth, but in part because she didn't know how to feel about it.

"He is. You did quite a number on him, but he'll make it. We talked to the police in Idaho and both Gene and George are wanted on a lot of charges, so we've posted cops at the hospital to make sure there's no funny business. Idaho sounded like they'd bring the feds in, so it seems unlikely you'll have to worry about any of them once they've healed. They'll likely head straight to jail."

Jessie closed her eyes, and Henry could feel her absolute

relief. But it was only for a moment or two. "Deputy Hart… What on earth do we do about this treasure?"

Thomas scratched a hand through his hair. "Well. I'm not sure. Old treasure isn't my area of expertise. We'll check on that and get back to you."

Jessie nodded and smiled wanly. "Thank you, Deputy Hart. Really."

He answered a few more questions, promised to be in touch and then he left. No one got up right away. Everyone just kind of sat there.

It was Jessie who finally broke the silence. "I can't begin to thank…" Her voice broke and she pressed fingertips to her eyes. She cleared her throat and tried again. "I am so sorr—"

"No," Henry said firmly. He would *not* let her apologize.

"Henry, I brought all of this on your doorste—"

"No," he repeated. "You needed help. We offered it. It was the right thing to do. I don't have any regrets."

"But…" She looked around at all the other faces in the room.

For the first time in a long time, Henry took stock of the people in his life. The men he trusted, who'd become his brothers. All who assured this woman that she wasn't to blame. That help was help.

He'd been a grumpy SOB for a few years now. Sarabeth had been right when she'd come to him. He was the mean one. It was a role he'd leaned into after their military careers had ended.

But he didn't want to be that anymore.

Epilogue

A month later

Sarabeth Peterson was eleven years old, but tomorrow she would be twelve. She was excited about her birthday, but she was more excited about today. Because she was finally, *finally*, going to be able to see the treasure.

Her treasure.

She knew Mom didn't like the idea that they owned the treasure—she and Aunt Quinn—but Sarabeth *loved* the idea, and now that all the people who needed to sort those things out had, and Aunt Quinn had come home from the hospital, they could go look.

No one had told her to call Quinn *Aunt*, but she was Mom's sister, so that made her Sarabeth's aunt.

Sarabeth was pretty sure Aunt Quinn was the only one who was as excited about the treasure as she was.

"Are we there yet?"

Henry looked at her in the rearview mirror. "Does it look like we're there yet, kid?"

She didn't like it when anyone called her *kid*. Except Henry. She liked it a lot when he said it. She liked it even more when he said it and then gave her mom a look afterward. It was kind of a...lovey look, she'd decided. Not that she'd tell them that.

Or that she watched those lovey looks closely, hoping it might mean they could stay at the ranch.

They hadn't had to go back to the apartment yet. Mom didn't want to live above Mrs. Caruthers, who'd gotten in some trouble but not enough to put her in jail. She also didn't want to live in a place with tall stairs because Aunt Quinn wasn't fully healed yet and Mom was determined to look after her.

So Henry had convinced her to stay at the ranch, but Mom was always saying how it wasn't permanent.

Sarabeth was going to see about that. The way she saw it, they *all* belonged at the ranch. Even Aunt Quinn. It worked. Everything was great.

Mom hadn't *thanked* her for asking Henry for help all those weeks ago, but the way Sarabeth saw it she probably should.

She sighed heavily and then looked over at Aunt Quinn. She still didn't look so good. Even Sarabeth could tell. But she kind of thought that was why Mom was even letting them go look at the treasure, to cheer Quinn up.

Henry pulled to a stop in front of a kind of...barn. Only it was round. And old-looking, but it had a lot of odd windows and rusty metal.

The nice police officer was there and he smiled warmly at all of them when they got out. "You all look a lot better than the last time I saw you."

"Where is it?" Sarabeth demanded.

When all the adults chuckled, she scowled. She *hated* when adults laughed at her. Still, the police officer led them forward and undid a padlock and gestured them inside.

It was like a fairy tale. There were tables of things. Gold

things and silver things. Jewelry and things Sarabeth didn't even know *what* they were.

"Jackpot," she heard Aunt Quinn whisper.

JESSIE LET SARABETH and Quinn move to look at everything. She…wanted nothing to do with it, truth be told.

"We worked with the feds and they confiscated some things that could be returned, but most of it's too old to go back to original owners," Thomas explained. "Since you're both on the deed for the land, it's technically all yours."

"Deed for the land," Jessie echoed. "I don't own any land here."

"Uh, that's not what the records say. They say you and Quinn were deeded it on your grandmother's passing."

"Grandmother…" She'd had the map. And the deed to the land. "But she wasn't a Peterson."

"That's a mystery I can't solve for you," Thomas said with a kind smile. His phone beeped and he looked at the readout. "Excuse me for a second."

He left the round barn. Jessie looked up at Henry. "It doesn't make sense."

"I'm sure you and Quinn will figure out a way to make it make sense. Besides, you're basically loaded now. You can hire a private investigator. You can do all sorts of things."

All sorts of things. Jessie frowned. At him. At the treasure. "I just have the terrible feeling this is all…cursed." Jessie watched Sarabeth bound around, Quinn hobbling behind her. They were both clearly so pleased, but Jessie couldn't get there.

"A woman who doesn't believe in ghosts can't believe in curses," Henry said, but he smiled at her.

She tried to keep a straight face, but couldn't manage. "And a man who believes in ghosts can't *not* believe in curses."

He grinned at her now. "Sure he can." She reached up and put her palm to his rough cheek. He grinned more and more now. Smiled. Laughed. *Enjoyed.*

She didn't care about this treasure. Hers was right here. With him. With Sarabeth. With her sister.

She had a family now. A real one she'd made.

Henry nuzzled into her palm. "I don't believe in curses, because we've both beat maybe not curses, but quite a few odds to stand here, alive and well. Take the treasure, Jess. You *survived.* You've got safety and a future now. To do whatever you want with."

She looked up at this man, who'd helped her simply because it had been the right thing to do. Who'd saved her daughter, time and time again. Who hadn't left her side as they'd sorted through weeks of aftermath.

He'd even brought her flowers.

He still scowled and grunted when the mood struck, but she knew he'd lightened up quite a bit. He laughed with Sarabeth, with his brothers. He…enjoyed the life and family around him.

It was still a strange concept that her life was her own. All the old threats were gone and she well and truly could build a life for Sarabeth here in Wilde without fear. With her sister, her identical twin.

And with the man she loved.

"What about you?"

"What about me?"

"What do you want to do with your life?"

HENRY LOOKED DOWN at the woman who'd changed that life. He'd been through a lot of changes. Most of them bad. A few good.

She and her daughter were by far the best.

"I don't want you to leave the ranch."

"That's an *I don't want*, not an *I want*."

Henry grunted, his smile dying a little. "Fine, I want you and Sarabeth to stay."

"Why?"

He looked at her, really looked. Soaked it in. How lucky he'd gotten, after such a rotten start. Her, too, after a rotten middle. And here they were.

So no, he didn't believe in curses. He believed in something else entirely.

"Because I love you and your daughter. And I want to be with you and build a life with you."

"Well." She cleared her throat, leaned into him and furiously blinked back tears. "I guess it's lucky that's what I want, too."

He leaned his mouth to hers. "Why?"

She laughed, her eyes alight with amusement and emotion. "Because I love you, Henry. And Sarabeth loves you."

Because treasure didn't matter. Changes could be good and bad. Life was life, always plowing on, but you could choose to focus on the good over the bad, or as much as the bad. You could change the course of your life.

Because curses weren't real.

But love was.

* * * * *

TEXAS BODYGUARD: BRAX

BRAX

JANIE CROUCH

Since this book is about family, it's dedicated to Kiddo #2.

Watching you on the court has always been one of my favourite things in the world. Second only to seeing the man you've become.

Prologue

Brax smiled at the couple sitting across from him in the San Antonio Child Protective Services office. They were talking with the social worker about him coming to stay with them.

They seemed nice enough. Older than dirt—at least forty or something. But the guy—Clinton—kept a protective arm around his wife, Sheila. He spoke respectfully to both her and the social worker, whose name Brax couldn't remember.

Of course, Brax knew Clinton could be completely fake. That under all that respect and protectiveness could be a guy who liked to hit, or worse, *touch*. But Brax was twelve now. He could outrun these old people no problem if he needed to. Get back out to the streets.

He'd lived on the streets last year, running from one of the care workers at a group home who had liked to touch. But being on the streets hadn't been as great as Brax thought it would be. Hiding from almost all adults, finding places to sleep where it was safe, having to figure out where he was going to get food…he hadn't liked any of it.

He'd survived, but there had been a little bit of relief when the cops had finally caught him and brought him back into this very office. It had been a different social worker then. Brax couldn't remember her name either.

They hadn't made him go back to the group home he'd

run away from, so that was good. And now the people in front of him were talking about him living with them on a permanent basis.

Clinton answered something the social worker asked and Sheila looked over at Brax, returning his smile.

"Would you like to come and live with us?" she asked. Clinton and the social worker stopped talking and stared at Brax too.

Brax played it cool. "Do you have your own kids?"

Clinton shook his head. "No. We weren't able to have biological children. Plus, we've always wanted to adopt."

"Why do you want me? Why don't you want to get a baby like everyone else?" Brax kept the smile on his face as he asked it.

Any kid who lived in the system learned their defense mechanisms. For most it was a scowl or pretending to be tough and ready to fight. Brax had discovered that he could joke and charm his way out of a lot of bad situations. Or at least smile big enough that whoever was giving him a problem would let down their guard and he could run.

Big smile, fast legs. That's how Brax had survived since going into the system when he was nine, and it was how he would survive after Clinton and Sheila got tired of him.

"We're not really 'baby' people," Sheila responded. "We already have one adopted son. He's about your age."

Clinton nodded. "His name is Weston. We think you would like him."

Brax nodded, but didn't give the other kid much thought. He'd deal with that problem later if it was needed. Right now he wanted to get the question out that had been bugging him since he'd seen the couple walk in.

"Do you want me because I'm what your bio kid would look like if you could have one?"

Clinton was Black, Sheila was Latina. Their kids would be biracial like Brax, although Brax's mother had been Black and his father was white, not Latina. Maybe they wanted him as some sort of trophy or something. Brax wouldn't even mind that so much, but he wanted to know what situation he was getting himself into.

"My goodness, Brax, that's quite rude…" Ms. Social Worker sputtered.

Clinton held out a hand toward her. "No, it's okay." He turned to Brax. "It's very observant of you to even put that together so quickly. But no, we're not interested in you because you're biracial. Weston is Black. Luke, another boy your age who has stayed with us, is white. Race isn't what's important to us."

"What is important to you?"

Ms. Social Worker started sputtering again, but Clinton and Sheila ignored her.

"We are very blessed," Sheila said. "We have a big house where you can have your own room. We have money to be able to support a big family. And most importantly, we have love."

Clinton grabbed Sheila's hand, but kept his eyes on Brax. "And if you're interested, we'd like for you to give us a try. If it doesn't work, the group home or another foster family is always an option."

Brax stared at them for a long moment before giving them another smile and a nod. What did he have to lose? If he needed to take off, he knew how to do that. Knew how to survive. But for now he would give Clinton and Sheila and their little rainbow family a try.

It probably wouldn't last long. Good things usually didn't—Brax had found that out early.

Either way, he would survive.

Chapter One

At age eleven, Brax Patterson had endured seven weeks living on the streets by himself, hoping things would get better when he grew up. *If* he grew up.

Whatever he'd imagined during those long nights ignoring the hunger, trying to keep himself warm and alive, it hadn't been *this*.

A security company with his three brothers—none of whom had the same color skin as him, but who all had each other's backs and everyone knew they could count on the others no matter what.

They'd built a business where they could take the skills they'd learned from their pasts in the military, on the San Antonio Police Force, and even from being tossed around by the foster care system when they were younger, and use those skills to help protect others. San Antonio Security was on its way to becoming one of the most trusted firms in the San Antonio area. Although they did quite a bit of investigation, they specialized in protection—both bodyguarding and developing holistic systems to keep people safe.

Their office was rarely a quiet place, but that suited Brax just fine. Unlike his brothers, he thrived on the buzz of being around people.

On the whole, if all of them were in the office at once,

that meant things were good. They were working, they were together, they were safe for the time being. Brax could smile to himself in relief when this was the situation.

Normally, anyway.

"If you would just leave my things alone, we wouldn't keep having this argument!"

Brax stepped into the hallway of their office, planning to get a drink from the fridge in the break room down the hall, but paused as he passed his brother Chance's office. Chance was running his hands over his head, lacing his fingers at the back of his neck. Brax had seen that move before. It was what his brother did whenever he needed to keep his hands still for fear of hurting something.

Or somebody.

In this case, it was somebody, though Brax knew Chance would never lay hands on a woman. None of them would—at least not in anger.

Maci Ford, their petite office manager, stood on the opposite side of Chance's desk, arms folded. "I told you. I wrote down everything you scrawled on that board before washing it off. I even took photos of it to keep the information for you."

"But why would you do that?" Chance's arms looked as if they'd jerk out of their sockets as he gestured emphatically toward the sparklingly clean whiteboard, which yesterday had been covered in a rainbow of words, arrows and circles—admittedly nearly impossible for anyone else to decipher.

"Because what happens if somebody walks in here and sees what you've written down? If they could read that chicken scratch of yours, that is. You never know what could happen. What if there was a break-in?"

Chance snorted. "Unlikely."

"Which isn't the same as impossible. Do you want somebody seeing the plans you're working on for this client's new security system? It's completely possible, and it's my job to make sure this office is run smoothly."

"By sending out invoices and tracking payment," Chance snapped. "Not by interfering with my work."

"Good morning." Brax smiled from the doorway, deciding to step in before the two killed each other. "If you keep going back and forth like this, you'll give me a sore neck. It's like watching a tennis match."

Maci jumped a little like he'd surprised her. She'd been too busy glaring at his brother to notice they had an audience.

"Sorry. I'll be going back to my desk." That didn't mean she couldn't throw one last exasperated look at Chance, who rolled his eyes at her and jammed his fists into his pockets.

Those two needed to get a room already.

Brax waited until they were more or less alone to jerk his head in her direction. "You'd better play nice. You know Luke says the office can't survive without her."

Chance rolled his eyes again. "Luke can't survive without her because of the filing he refuses to do on his own." Then, he smiled a little. "And we all know Luke loves everything right now."

"I guess that'll happen when a man gets engaged." It still felt strange, imagining any of them getting married. A bunch of confirmed bachelors—at least, that was what they'd been before the love of Luke's life had walked in one day a few months ago needing help to stay alive.

Claire had been more than worth the effort they'd put into protecting her, and not only because Luke loved her. She was a wonderful woman, brave and smart. And good for Luke.

Luke was in his office working on a case. Even when he was busy, there was a smile on his face. Brax wanted to joke about it but had decided to let the matter rest. It wasn't like Brax didn't have more than enough work to do himself. The exponential growth of San Antonio Security over the past year was a double-edged sword.

Weston passed his office around lunchtime and knocked on the open door. "How's that witness statement on the cartel case coming along?"

"Still need to finish writing it," Brax admitted, gesturing to what was in front of him. "I figured since the cartel trial isn't until later in the month, I should concentrate on wrapping up my current case and putting it to bed."

His latest case had involved a well-off woman who'd suspected her husband was guilty of cheating—among other things. She'd been right, of course, and right to believe she'd needed somebody watching her back at all times. Her husband had hired men to take her out so he could collect on her life insurance to cover his extensive, secret debts.

Brax had wrapped up the case, but not before his client had made a pass at him. More than one pass, in fact. He'd left her disappointed. The Patterson men were better than that. Professional.

And not stupid enough to get involved with married women trying to get back at their criminal husbands.

After tackling part of the mound of paperwork, Brax headed to the gym to work out the kinks he'd earned hunched over his desk all day. All four brothers kept themselves in top shape. It was one of the reasons a security business fit them all so well—it required engagement of both their minds and their bodies. They were all willing to endure both.

By the time he finished his workout, ate dinner and

stopped back by the office to finish a little more of the never-ending paperwork, it was getting late. Time to head home. He enjoyed spending time with his brothers, but didn't mind being by himself. A little peace and quiet at the end of the day. Privacy. One thing he'd never had much of as a kid in one foster home after another.

Which was the reason he'd chosen to live in a house in the middle of nowhere with no neighbors close by. The most he heard at night was an owl's hoot or a cricket's song. He welcomed the nightly symphony as he dragged himself up the stairs toward his bedroom.

The ring of the doorbell brought him up short, tension coursing through him. He didn't get many visitors, especially at this time of night. His gun was already in the safe.

Another ring. He crept down the stairs, eyeing the door, grabbing a second weapon he kept hidden in a top kitchen cabinet.

Of course, if it was somebody coming to stir up trouble, they wouldn't ring the bell. They'd barge right in.

Still, it was worth caution.

Caution that didn't diminish when he heard the voice coming from the porch. "Brax? Let me in, man. I need you."

Brax muttered a curse. Of all the people to show up in the middle of the night, his half brother, Robert, would be the one. He put the SIG Sauer back in its hiding place.

He could ignore the bell, something he wouldn't consider for a split second if the man on the other side of that door was a Patterson. Luke, Chance and Weston were his real brothers. Much more than Robert, though he and Robert shared blood by means of having the same father.

Brax opened the door before Robert started shouting. "What are you doing here?"

"Hi to you too." Robert flashed his typical, greasy smile.

Under the porch light, Brax could see Robert's sweaty forehead, dark circles under his eyes, his skin paler than usual and oily black hair that looked as if he'd run his fingers through it over and over.

Robert glanced nervously over his shoulder, then back at Brax. "You going to let me in?"

"Do I have a choice?" Brax stepped aside, noting his brother's nonstop fidgeting. Hands he rubbed together, a twitchy jaw. Was he high on something? It wouldn't come as a surprise.

Robert hadn't exactly lived an honest life.

Brax and Robert looked almost nothing alike, something Robert had been quick to point out countless times in the five years since they'd known of each other's existence. Robert had also made it obvious he looked down on Brax's mixed race through little comments and slight aggressions against him and all of Brax's adopted brothers.

Funny how he showed up when he wanted something, though. Usually cash.

"What do you want?"

"There's been an emergency."

Again, no surprise. There was always trouble. It was difficult for Brax to muster interest. "What sort of emergency?"

Robert shrugged his thin shoulders and surveyed the room. Anything to avoid eye contact. "It's a long story. I've got a friend who owes me money. It's important that I get this money right away."

"I'm sure it is. But I don't see why you had to come to me about it. Do you need protection? Help in some other way?"

"Yeah. Some other way." Robert held up a finger and went to the door, pausing with one hand on the knob. "Will you help me, bro?"

Bro? That made Brax's teeth clench.

The only reason he nodded his agreement was he knew Robert would never leave him alone otherwise. Besides, Brax was curious. He wanted to see how this would play out.

Whatever he had been expecting, it wasn't what Robert carried in one hand when he came back from his car. Not even close. "You're kidding me."

Robert looked down at the baby in the infant car seat. "Meet your nephew."

"My nephew? Since when do you have a kid?" Then, another thought, one that would've made him shout the house down if it hadn't been for the sleeping baby. "Are you alone otherwise?"

"Yeah."

"You left the baby alone in the car? What's wrong with you?"

Robert snorted. "He wasn't going to run away, you know." He dropped a diaper bag on the floor by his feet.

Brax blinked hard. Had he gone to bed, after all? Was this all a mixed-up dream? "You're going to need to explain a few things to me. When did you have a baby? Where is his mother? Why are you bringing him here to me? Where do I come in?"

"Wow. Where should I start?" Robert placed the car seat on the coffee table. The baby stirred slightly but didn't make a sound. "His name is Walker. He's…uh…like four-and-a-half months old now or something."

Robert a father? It would've made Brax laugh in any other circumstance. "Okay. Why is he here?"

"I need you to watch him for a few days while I do what I have to do."

He was so cool about it. Like it was nothing. Like it

wasn't the biggest favor one estranged half brother could ask another.

If this had come from any of his other brothers, it would've been one thing—a big thing, considering Brax had no experience with babies—but Robert?

"Are you out of your mind? I don't know the first thing about babies. You think you can show up here at this time of night after not speaking for, what, at least a year? And drop your son on my doorstep? What about his mother?"

"His mother's dead."

That took a little of the wind out of Brax's sails. "Oh. I'm sorry to hear that."

"Don't worry about it." Robert lifted a shoulder. "I never liked her that much."

Brax scrubbed a hand down his face. What could he possibly say to that?

Robert pointed to the diaper bag on the floor. "Everything you'll need for a few days is in there. Diapers, formula, all that stuff. He's a good baby. Everybody who's ever been around him says so. He doesn't cry all that much. When he's hungry, when he needs a change. Otherwise, he just sorta lays there."

Brax bit his tongue against what threatened to come out, knowing if he raised his voice it might wake the kid. *Maybe you leave him lying there because you're a terrible parent who probably doesn't care about him—or why else would you leave him with me?*

"I've got to go. I can't wait around while you keep telling me you can't do it. I'm in a hurry." Robert wiped fresh sweat off his brow. He wasn't pretending. The man was really and truly scared half out of his mind over something.

The reason he needed that money in such a hurry, no doubt.

The baby stirred again. This time, he let out a soft sigh in his sleep. It was the sigh that got Brax. Softened his heart.

"Okay." Brax held out his hands to try to get Robert to think this through. "Let's compromise. Why don't you stay here for a few days? I'll do everything I can to help you. I have resources through my company. You won't be in any danger here. Nobody would even think to look for you."

Robert, he noticed, didn't bother pretending there wouldn't be anyone looking for him. He ran his hands through his sweaty hair, jaw twitching, nostrils flaring. Not meeting Brax's eyes.

His answer came as a surprise. "Yeah, okay. We'll both stay here. Thank you."

Brax had expected another few minutes of argument, at least. He decided to take what he could get without questioning it. "I'll give you the spare room on the other side of the house. You look like you could use the sleep." Robert carried the baby and the bag upstairs and practically collapsed into bed, confirming Brax's suspicions. The man was exhausted. No telling how long he'd been on the run.

The baby seemed content in the carrier next to Robert on the bed, so Brax backed out, closing the door behind him. He headed back to his own bedroom.

He stared up at the ceiling for a long time. It took a while for him to finally stop thinking about the situation, wondering exactly what happened. About his brother, the baby, the dead mother. And what had brought Robert to his doorstep.

The sound of Walker's cries woke Brax in the morning. At first, he thought it was a dream. But then it all came back at once. He covered his head with a pillow in hopes of muffling the incessant noise.

"Robert!" he yelled. "The kid's crying his head off! Try taking care of him!"

He received no response. Not even the slamming of a door. The crying continued, getting louder.

A sick certainty took root in Brax's gut and started to grow. He got out of bed and walked down the hall, almost positive what he'd find before he even opened the bedroom door.

One baby, still in a car seat. The room stank of whatever mixture was starting to soak through the kid's diaper and the little outfit he wore over top.

No Robert.

A note sat on the pillow. *I'll be back before you're out of diapers. I promise.*

Brax crumpled the note in his fist. He'd stopped believing in empty promises a long time ago.

Chapter Two

How did anybody survive a baby?

Three days. It had been three days since Brax had slept more than a few minutes at a time. Three days since he'd gone more than an hour without hearing a baby cry.

No. Not cry. *Wail*. The kid wailed until Brax's ears rang.

He kept expecting Robert to come back. That was the wildest part of all, waiting on somebody who'd been unreliable all his life to come back. To keep his word as the supply of diapers in the bag got lower and lower.

Diapers Brax had only figured out how to change by watching videos. Sad but true.

His brothers would've laughed themselves sick if they'd known. He could've told them, but it was smarter to stay quiet. Odds were whatever Robert was involved in wasn't exactly on the up and up. He was a father now, and there was no telling what would happen to Walker if Robert went to prison.

But three days was the breaking point. There was nothing Brax could say to explain why he hadn't been to the office the past few days. None of his brothers would accept another excuse. They would come out to the house soon, and then he'd have a lot more explaining to do.

It was better to come clean and get the whole thing over with.

Which was what led him to strap the car seat into the back seat—again with the help of online videos—and drive to the office.

"What is *that*?" Chance's jaw nearly hit the floor when Brax entered, seat in hand, diaper bag slung over his shoulder.

Brax held a finger to his lips, but it was no use. The ride had calmed Walker, but the respite was too brief. Maci hurried over from behind her desk, hands over her mouth, when the baby started up again.

Weston darted out from his office at the sound of Walker's wails. "Where'd that come from?" He pointed to the baby, who Maci had taken from the carrier and held against her shoulder.

"Meet Robert's son, Walker." Brax sank into one of the chairs they kept out in the reception area and rested his head against the wall. "He likes to cry."

"Robert? Your bio brother, Robert?" Weston looked like he was having a hard time keeping up. "Where is he?"

"I'm not sure."

Chance followed Maci with his eyes as she walked up and down the length of the reception space with the baby, sort of bouncing him gently and patting his bottom with one hand. "So Robert showed up and left his baby with you?"

"Pretty much, though I barely remember. I don't think I've slept two hours over the past three days."

"I can take him to your office and try to get him calm," Maci offered. Brax thanked her and meant it with all his heart. At least the closed door muffled the sound.

Weston's confusion was clear in his dark eyes. "Did he tell you why he was doing it?"

"How long does he expect you to take care of the kid?" Chance asked, always logical and tactical. "Did he give you what you needed? Are you running low on supplies? Don't babies need a lot of supplies?"

Brax held up both hands in a silent plea. "One thing at a time. Robert said he needed to get money from a friend who owed it to him. That was all he'd tell me, and it's been three days without a word. He spent the night, but all that was left in the morning was Walker and a note saying Robert would be back before the diapers ran out. He gave me formula and clothes too."

"What about the mother?" Weston asked.

Brax ran a hand over his eyes. "Dead."

Weston and Chance both muttered a curse. None of them wanted to think of a baby growing up without a mother, although they all were testament that a woman giving birth to you didn't necessarily mean she would be your mother beyond the word *biological*.

"Okay. Let's run it down, see if we can find out anything about Robert." Chance was already on the way to his computer by the time he'd finished speaking. Brax forced himself out of the chair and followed along with Weston. Walker was still crying, though somewhat softer than before.

"How did you figure out how to take care of him for the past couple days?" Weston asked while Chance ran Robert's name through their system.

"Internet. Thank goodness." Brax tried to muster a smile.

"You know you could've come to us for help."

"What do you two know about babies?"

Weston shrugged. "Nothing, but you didn't have to do this on your own."

"Here we go." Chance leaned in closer to his screen, eyes

moving back and forth. "Big surprise. The last time he used his credit card was in Eagle Pass."

"Gambling," Weston muttered.

"Most of the activity on these cards the past few months has come from either there or Vegas," Chance confirmed. "He seems to be bouncing back and forth."

"Damn it." Brax rubbed his temples against an approaching headache. "I figured this was all about him owing somebody money, not the other way around. I doubt there's a friend involved. He has to run around trying to scratch together what he can now."

"Yeah, and getting out of town means avoiding whoever it is he owes." Weston shook his head. "Typical."

"Here's something interesting." Chance pointed to a couple of lines, which Brax read over his shoulder.

"We're not the only ones looking for him." Somebody else had put out feelers on Robert's card activity over the past few days. There was no way of knowing who without the digging getting much more complicated. The confirmation that someone else was after Robert was enough for the time being.

"What are you going to do about Walker?" Weston scratched his chin. "I think you should take him to Mom and Dad. You know how thrilled Mom would be to hold a baby, no matter whose it was."

It wasn't a bad idea. Not at all. Still… "I'd rather have him with me when Robert comes back. The fewer opportunities for Robert to slip away, the better."

Weston's scowl and Chance's sudden silence spoke to their disagreement. They were smart enough to stay quiet, at least. As tired as he was, he might've said something he'd end up regretting.

The crying grew louder when Maci left Brax's office. He turned in time to find her going through the diaper bag with one hand while holding Walker in the other arm. "What's up?" he asked.

"I was looking for a pacifier. His diaper's dry. When's the last time he was fed?"

"Right before I left the house with him. Burped him too," he added in case she was wondering. "I had to change my shirt thanks to his spit up."

"Daddy didn't pack any burping cloths?" Maci sighed, shaking her head. "Unprepared."

Brax wasn't about to ask what she was talking about, not with the kid wailing like he was. They nearly shouted just to be heard over the noise.

Maci handed Walker over and practically stuck her head in the bag to look through. "What's this?" She nudged aside a few more diapers and undershirts, pulling a tag attached to the bag's lining.

There was a phone number written on it. "That's not Robert's number."

Maci looked at him. "Whose do you think it could be?"

"I don't know but I'm going to give it a try." He handed Walker back to Maci and pulled out his phone, dialing the number while she took Walker back to his office and closed the door.

"Hello?"

A woman's voice. She sounded troubled, concerned. Then again, he was calling from a random number. And how was he supposed to explain this?

"Uh, hi. This is going to sound strange. My name is Brax Patterson. Do you know a baby named Walker?"

She went quiet long enough to make Brax nervous. "Why are you calling me?" she finally asked.

He heard the suspicion in her voice and was about to try to ease it when Walker let loose with an ear-splitting scream. Even through the closed door, it rang out loud and clear.

"What's wrong with him?" She sounded as frantic as Brax felt.

"I don't know. That's why I'm calling. I found your number in his diaper bag and figured it was worth a shot. I'm his uncle. His father is my half brother. He left him with me for a few days, but I can't get him to stop crying."

"Have you tried swaddling him?"

"What's that?"

She let out a sigh. "I'll take that as a no. Swaddling is when you wrap the baby in a blanket. Do you have a blanket around?"

"Yeah, there's one in the bag."

"Okay. Here's how you do it. Think of it as a baby burrito." She walked him through the steps, making sure Brax knew to leave room for Walker's legs to move around. "He likes to be snug like that."

It worked. The second Walker was wrapped up tight, he calmed down.

"You're a miracle worker." Brax sighed into the phone, not caring that he probably sounded half out of his mind. "I can't thank you enough."

"He's always liked being swaddled. It calms him right away. It's a shame his father didn't know that."

Even if he had, Robert hadn't stuck around long enough to explain it. "How do you know what Walker likes? What's your name?"

She was quiet again, which raised his suspicions. Why was she so hesitant? "I took care of him for a little while. My name's Tessa."

She was a babysitter or nanny or something. That made sense.

"Thank you. You've pretty much saved my sanity. Not to mention Walker's lungs."

"I'm glad I could help."

As a last-second thought, he asked, "Have you heard from Robert?"

Another pause. "No, not any time recently. Is he in trouble or something?"

Brax decided to keep the specifics to himself. No telling who this Tessa was or who she knew. While his brother's protection didn't mean much to Brax, protecting Walker's father meant a great deal.

"No. Just waiting to hear from him. Would you do me a favor and take down my number in case he does contact you?"

Tessa read off the number as it appeared on her phone, and he confirmed it. "Can I have your address, just in case?" she asked. He didn't see any problem with that and, still feeling grateful for her help, recited the office address.

Finally, there was somebody from Walker's life on his side.

"Thank you, Tessa. You don't know how you've helped."

"I've heard him holler. I know how I've helped. Please, just take care of him." She sounded almost desperate.

"I will. I promise." She disconnected the call before he could say anything else.

"You can leave him in the car seat for now," he told Maci. "I'll keep him next to my desk. Maybe I'll be able to get some work done now that he's quiet."

Wishful thinking. While Walker didn't interrupt him, fatigue did. It took no more than fifteen minutes before Brax started nodding off. Maci was kind enough to bring him a cup of coffee, which helped some. But not for long.

He woke with a start at the sound of the doorbell out front. His gaze immediately darted over to the baby, but he'd finally fallen asleep and didn't seem ready to stir.

"Brax Patterson."

Brax shot out of his chair like he'd been fired from a gun. Had Robert finally come back? For the first time in his life, had he stood by his word?

No. It was a courier holding a thick manila envelope. "I'll need you to sign for these documents, Mr. Patterson."

Brax exchanged a confused look with Maci before accepting the courier's tablet and scribbling his name with the stylus. That earned him the envelope and its contents.

"Were you expecting something?" Maci asked.

"No." He opened it and withdrew a sheaf of legal documents. He spread the documents on Maci's desk, eager to find out what this was all about.

This had to be a mistake. He blinked hard, but that didn't change anything. "Robert has given me custody of the baby. I'm Walker's legal guardian."

Chapter Three

Tessa Mahoney could barely breathe as she ended her call with Brax Patterson. She folded the napkin on which she'd written his address with shaky hands and slipped it into her back pocket.

She couldn't afford to lose any of her jobs and had irritated her boss at the diner something awful when she'd taken the call, but it had been worth the risk. Even if she got fired.

"Good night!" she called out to the evening crew, waving as she stepped through the door and into the late-afternoon sunshine.

But it wasn't sunshine or fresh air that hit her awareness. It was the sense of being watched. A prickly feeling on the back of her neck.

Again.

This was the third or fourth day she'd felt it. The certainty that unseen eyes tracked her every move. Unnerving, especially since there was nothing she could do about it.

Including showing awareness. Her brown eyes darted back and forth as she hurried to the corner in hopes of catching the bus to her tiny apartment. At least she'd be indoors, away from the gaze of whoever currently watched her hustle down the street.

She couldn't let them know she knew. Nobody had to tell her that. It was instinct.

Ignoring her exhaustion, she sprinted toward the corner, waving her arms and begging the last person waiting to board to hold the bus for her.

The driver couldn't leave without her. She wouldn't be able to tolerate sitting on a bench out in the open feeling like someone was watching her as she waited for the next bus. She'd go out of her mind.

If she wasn't already insane.

"Thank you," she panted after leaping aboard, waving to the person who'd held the bus for her. She sank into a seat and closed her arms around herself in hopes of calming her trembling body.

This was all Robert's fault. All of it. She knew they were looking for him, which was why they were watching her.

Hilarious. As if he'd come to *her*. As if she'd let him.

And she was definitely the last person on the planet he'd share his plans with.

That didn't stop him from ruining her life from a distance, though. He didn't have many talents, but ruining lives was right up there at the top of the list.

She jumped with a strangled gasp as somebody behind her dropped their keys. Her nerves had reached their breaking point. She was losing it.

Breathe. There were times over the nightmare of the past three months when she'd had to consciously remind herself of that. *Breathe. In. Out. Repeat.*

She would survive this. She'd survived the unimaginable already. If there was anything she'd learned, it was how strong she was. How much she could withstand without breaking. She'd get through this too.

Eventually, the people watching her would clue in to the fact she had no idea what Robert was doing or where he was.

At least the guy on the phone hadn't sounded bad—Robert's half brother, Brax Patterson. Different last name than Robert and Robert had never mentioned having a brother, but that wasn't a surprise. He had never exactly been forthcoming.

Brax had sounded like he was truly concerned about Walker—had swaddled him and gotten him to stop crying. That was good, right? But why wouldn't Brax know how to contact his brother if he was taking care of Walker? There were too many questions pounding inside her already aching head.

Arriving at her stop didn't provide much comfort. It meant exposing herself again since, if it was like the last few days, somebody was probably already watching. Waiting.

Or was she imagining things? Truly going out of her mind?

All questions vanished when Tessa reached her half-open front door. The door she knew she'd locked before leaving for her shift. A cold sweat covered her body, chilling her to the bone. Her stomach turned, threatening to give up everything she'd eaten for lunch.

Should she go inside? What if somebody was still in there? No, they probably would've closed the door to trick her into a false sense of security.

She nudged the door open with her foot, then stepped back. Her heart hammered in her chest as she expected somebody to jump out at her, to yank her inside the apartment.

The reality was just as bad. Someone had destroyed her apartment.

Broken dishes. Her plants thrown to the floor, dirt everywhere. The couch cushions and pillows strewn around, slashed open. Drawers emptied. Her clothes torn out of the closet and ripped to shreds. Her mattress on the floor.

Her apartment wasn't much—barely a living room and bedroom, a kitchenette and a closet-sized bathroom. But it was a place to rest her head, where she could feel safe. Or it had been. Every bit of safety she'd ever felt dissolved as she struggled with the sense of violation attacking from all sides.

Who would do this? And why?

"Oh no!" Terror flooded her system as she raced to the nightstand drawer where she kept her money.

Every dollar she'd sacrificed to save was gone. They had taken all of it. She sank to her knees, tears streaming down her cheeks.

The ringing of the phone jarred her. She didn't recognize the number but answered anyway. "Hello?"

"Do you like the redecorating job we did for you?" a cold, nasty voice asked.

Her eyes went wide, her heart hammering wildly against her ribs. Whoever had done this took pleasure in the pain and panic they had to know they'd caused.

"Why?" She hated the shaky whisper, hated knowing she was powerless against them, hated knowing there was nothing she could do.

"You know why. All you've got to do is tell us where Robert is."

She didn't whisper this time. She yelled. "I don't know!"

"Well, maybe it's a matter of jogging your memory. What about that? I wonder if somebody comes over to talk to you in person, you'll remember better."

She bit back a gasp before ending the call.

That wasn't an idle threat. She knew that much. People

capable of breaking into her apartment, ransacking it and stealing her money were capable of anything.

Whatever Robert had done, she was paying for it. And she'd keep paying if she stayed here.

That realization forced her to her feet. Made her grab the bag thrown across the room at random, dig up the few pieces of clothing still whole and worth wearing and toss them inside.

Her knees threatened to give out, but she pushed herself forward, through the living room and out the door.

Someone rounded the corner of the stairs at the far end of the hall. A tall, hulking sort of man with a neck as thick as his head.

A wave of adrenaline crashed through her system. She darted back into the apartment and closed the door then wedged a chair under the door knob. Not that it would do much good. At best, it would buy her a few extra seconds, but she'd take them. She headed for the fire escape, praying that no one was waiting at the back of the building. The man in the hall hadn't seen her and wasn't hurrying so maybe she had a chance.

She moved as fast as her shaky legs would allow, nearly tumbling down the steep, rusted steps. When she reached the ladder, she looked up. Her window was still closed.

But it wouldn't be for long.

Sacrificing stealth for speed, she clambered down the ladder and into the alley behind the building. Which way should she go? It wouldn't take Thick Neck long to realize she had escaped and call his friends. She had to figure out a way to hide until they stopped looking.

Think, Tessa, think!

People. She needed a crowd to blend into. Would the pharmacy at the end of the block work? It had to, because there was no other option. She ran down the alley, not daring to waste precious seconds looking over her shoulder. If Thick Neck was following her, she would've heard him lumbering down the ladder, but all she heard was the traffic at the end of the alley.

She skidded to a stop and poked her head out just enough to check the sidewalk. All clear. She jogged out of the alley, rounded the corner and ducked inside the pharmacy, where it was hopefully safe.

With her head down, Tessa made her way to the back of the store, grabbed a magazine from the rack, and wedged herself into the corner across from the dome security mirror. Keeping her eyes glued to the mirror, she ran through her options.

Every nickel she had was in her pocket—the tips from her shift at the diner. The few clothes that had survived the "redecorating" were on her back or in the bag slung over her shoulder.

How far could she possibly hope to go?

She jumped when the phone in her pocket rang. It was the same number as before. Her palms were slick, making it hard to keep a hold on the device. There was no way she was going to answer. She powered it down. At least they wouldn't be able to track her using it if she left it off.

She needed a plan. There had to be something she could do. Somewhere she could go.

Like a gift from the guardian angel she probably didn't have, inspiration struck. The folded napkin still in her pocket, holding the address of an office building in San Antonio. That was only a couple hours from here.

A man who had called her needing advice about swaddling a baby… How bad could he be? And maybe he would find Robert and all of this hell could be over with.

Not all. Tessa rubbed her tired eyes. Even if Robert showed up again, her hell wouldn't be finished. She'd have to worry about that later.

She headed for the bus station with just enough cash to get her to San Antonio, hoping she wasn't making the worst mistake of her life.

Chapter Four

Thank heaven for swaddling.

Last night's fractured sleep was far from his usual state of unconsciousness, but it had been better than the few stolen minutes he'd been able to snatch the other nights since Walker had come into his life.

Brax was functional, but barely. And he wasn't ready for this. Any of it. He'd never planned to have a kid in the first place—even if he had, didn't a person usually have a little time to prepare themselves? To learn, to adjust their mentality?

A man didn't normally have a baby dropped into his life with no warning and no way out of the arrangement.

"What about calling a nanny service?" Maci bounced Walker slightly as she walked back and forth. Though Chance saw Maci as an annoyance and was grateful to have her preoccupied with a baby, Brax saw her as a saint.

"That's not a bad idea," Weston agreed.

Brax blew out a long sigh. "I don't know the first thing about choosing a nanny. I don't know anything about any of this."

"That's the point of calling a service. They do the vetting for you. All you have to do is say yes or no once you meet the nanny they send." Maci shrugged. "It's an idea, anyway."

"It's a good idea." And when Weston decided something, that was that.

"Sure. Whatever." Brax leaned back into his chair, eyes closing. "If it means that I can get some sleep every once in a while and come to work without lugging the baby and all the stuff that comes with him, count me in. This can't go on forever."

Weston perched on the edge of Brax's desk, holding the paperwork. "I looked into this."

"And?"

"No big surprise, it's a mess." He pointed at the signature next to Brax's printed name. "Obviously a forgery."

"Yeah. Robert got a little creative there, didn't he?"

"And this Raymond Volver, the judge who signed it without even setting eyes on you? Very shady."

"That's Robert's cousin through his mom, and the only reason my half brother isn't in prison, I guarantee it. Ray cleans up after Robert all the time."

"I'm fairly confident an impartial judge will overturn this."

Brax nodded slowly, staring at the wall. "Yeah. But we all know what happens when guardianship is revoked. Walker goes into the system."

Weston put a brotherly hand on Brax's shoulder, a silent affirmation that no one wanted that to happen. "We'll track down Robert, figure it out. For your sake and for Walker's."

Brax put his hand on Weston's. Walker's soft noises floated in from the reception area where Maci paced with him.

And it was sweet. Fatigue and frustration weren't enough to keep him from smiling.

Walker was the only living blood relative Brax had besides Robert. Not that he felt alone. He hadn't for years, ever since his mom and dad had taken him in at twelve and shown him what family could mean.

Walker was his blood. Brax couldn't willingly, knowingly dump the kid into the foster care system. Not with his personal history.

By late morning, it was clear everybody had needed a break. Luke was still off in his personal happy place with his fiancée and would be in later. Chance was out shopping for baby supplies. Weston was following a lead for a client, though Brax knew leaving the office hadn't been necessary. Maci had volunteered to pick up lunch.

Brax was alone with Walker.

At least the baby was sleeping, swaddled up in his car seat. He was so much cuter that way. Was it wrong to think that?

A soft, female voice floated over from the reception area. "Hello?"

He was up in a flash, if only to keep whoever was out there from waking Walker. "Yes? Can I help you?" he asked as he closed his door behind him.

She was beautiful. That struck him first. Petite with delicate features. Brown hair pulled back into a ponytail. A full mouth that tugged downward at the corners, and dark brown eyes that met his and held his gaze without flinching.

She looked confused. Tired. Troubled.

Instantly, something tightened in his chest. He wanted to help her. He *needed* to.

She opened her mouth, then closed it. Her brows lifted before drawing together. "Uh, yes. I think so?"

He waited, watching her. She carried a cheap fake-leather bag over one shoulder. A jittery hand plucked at the strap; her teeth dug into her bottom lip.

Nervous. His senses sharpened, tuned in to her every

move, her every breath. The image of a wounded bird formed in his mind.

If he pushed too hard or came on too strong, the bird would fly away. "Would you like to sit down? Can I get you something to drink?"

"Um, I guess? Water?"

Was it a question? Why was she so uncertain?

He was about to ask that very question when a familiar noise started up from inside his office.

"Is that Walker?" she asked, eyes leaving Brax's face for the first time since they'd met.

Brax tensed. Just when he'd thought his protective instincts couldn't rev any higher. "Who are you? How do you know the baby's name?"

It was rare for anybody to relax in his presence once he'd barked at them that way, but she did. "I'm Tessa. We spoke on the phone yesterday. 'Swaddling'?"

He relaxed. Maci must've called the agency she was talking about, and they'd probably reached out to Tessa since she'd taken care of Walker before. "Of course. Sorry for sounding suspicious. It's been a long few days."

"I understand." She pointed to his office, brows lifting in silent question, and he nodded.

She hurried toward the baby. "Hey, Walker!" Her sweet voice was soft as she unlatched the straps holding Walker in place. "How's my buddy? How come you're crying, huh?"

It was magic. The second the baby was in her arms, he quieted down. "There he is," she whispered, stroking his downy cheek with one finger and smiling down at him. "Missed you, buddy."

"You're incredible with him," Brax murmured. "He likes you."

She couldn't have been older than her early twenties, yet

she handled the baby like she'd been caring for children for decades. Some people had the magic touch, he guessed, and thank heaven, again, Tessa had found her way to him.

By the time the guys showed up and Maci arrived with lunch, Tessa had fed and changed Walker and was rocking him to sleep in her arms.

"All right. Hold on." Luke stopped in front of Brax's office. "I heard there was a baby, but for some reason I still imagined it was a joke."

"Wow, that agency was quick," Weston muttered to Brax while Luke and Chance introduced themselves to Tessa.

"I know. Barely quick enough, though." Brax rolled his head back and forth, rubbing his neck. Why did his neck hurt? The damage a baby could do.

"Let's get you set up in the conference room," Weston offered. "If you don't mind working out of the office, that is."

"Not at all." Tessa looked at Brax with a smile. "This is unexpected. All this attention."

"Yeah. My brothers are always ready to jump in and help. It's just that we have to work, of course, and Robert dropped Walker on me without warning."

Tessa tilted her face away, but not in time to hide the way she grimaced at Robert's name.

Brax could understand that. It was obvious from the way she'd lit up when she'd seen the baby that she cared about Walker and couldn't believe Robert would do something as stupid as walking away from his child.

That was something they agreed on.

He left her in the conference room, softly singing to the baby in hopes of getting him to sleep. There was something so sweet and perfect about Tessa and Walker together that he couldn't stop looking over his shoulder at them. He forced his feet toward his office knowing the rest of him wanted to stay.

Chapter Five

Tessa finally had her son back in her arms.

It was all she could do to not break down sobbing, but with all the Patterson men watching, she knew that wasn't an option. They would ask too many questions.

Questions she didn't have answers for.

Tessa nuzzled Walker's downy, fuzzy cheek, breathing in his baby scent. Soaking it in. Drowning in it.

He'd grown so much bigger than she had imagined he'd be by now—and she had imagined it so many times. All day, every day. Every time she'd seen a baby in the street, in the diner or at the dry cleaner's, or in any of the houses she'd cleaned. No matter where she'd been working at the time, the sight or the sound or the evidence of a baby's existence had left her arms aching and her eyes stinging with tears.

He was so beautiful. He had her eyes, dark and deep. She had no doubt they held the secrets of the universe. All the wisdom in the world.

He'd shed the fine, wispy hair he'd been born with. What grew in now was her shade of brown, touched with a tiny bit of red that brought her mother to mind.

She kissed his forehead and closed her eyes and thanked God. She had her son in her arms again.

"I've missed you," she whispered, her mouth close to

his ear. "I love you so much. Did you know that? I do. I do. Mama loves you."

This was an unimaginable gift. Worth the bus ride from Eagle Pass. Worth sleeping at the bus station. All so she could be with her baby for the first time in three months.

The longest three months of her life.

Two of the Pattersons were talking not far from the conference room. She looked up from Walker, frowning as she considered them. What was their story? What was this Brax person all about?

He'd called Robert his brother, but then he'd called the other Pattersons his brothers too. Did that mean Robert was related to all of them? Not only had Robert never talked about brothers, but the Pattersons were all of different races. Who was biologically related to whom?

Which one of them could potentially take her son away if they proved to a judge that Walker was related to them?

Who could she trust?

If Brax and Robert did share blood, there were more differences than similarities. Not only physically, though those differences had jumped out at Tessa the second she'd laid eyes on Walker's uncle. Brax had a commanding presence, tall and broad-shouldered, built like he took his body seriously and worked hard to stay muscular. He had a penetrating gaze that she guessed could inspire fear or confidence, depending on what he intended.

It seemed as if he didn't know she was Walker's mother. He thought somebody had sent her there—she'd overheard him saying something to one of the other men about an agency. That was fine for now, since she had no idea whether Robert had mentioned her.

Or what he might've said if he had.

No, there was no question about what he'd say. He

would've told Brax what he'd told the judge. That she was a drug addict, an unfit mother.

And once again, he'd leave out the part where he'd drugged her and paid other people to call her unfit.

She held Walker a little tighter. There had been so many times when she'd feared she'd never have this opportunity again.

Why would that vindictive pig go to all that trouble to get custody if he was just going to run off and leave the baby with Brax?

Walker fussed like he felt the direction her thoughts had taken. How her blood started boiling the second she thought about that awful time. The powerlessness. The helplessness. It made her sick.

What had been Robert's plan when he'd destroyed her life and taken away the one good, pure thing that had ever been hers? His cruelty made no sense.

Walker whimpered. "It's okay, sweetheart," she whispered. Just looking down at him was enough to make her forget everything that had ever hurt her. Everything that had ever made her angry.

Now, she had to find a way to keep him. She wouldn't let go of him again. She couldn't.

Maci stopped in not long after Tessa had settled Walker down. The woman gave Tessa a good feeling, like she had an ally in this new world.

"How is he?" Maci whispered with a smile.

"Fine. Calm now." Tessa stopped short of thanking Maci for taking care of him. That would be a dead giveaway. Ally or not, Tessa had no way of knowing how much she could get away with.

"Good. He's a sweetheart. Just unhappy, I think. But he's happier now that you're here."

"I'm glad that's true." Tessa nodded past Maci. "What's the story here? Who are these men? It seems like they care a lot about a strange baby."

Maci smiled fondly as she took a seat across the table. "Brax's brother Robert gave him legal custody of Walker."

Tessa swallowed her fury. Why would Robert take Walker from her, then leave him with his brother?

"They're good men," Maci continued. "Private investigators. I think all of them were born with stronger protective instincts than most people. The work comes naturally to them."

That would partly explain why they took Walker's well-being to heart. But were they trustworthy?

"They're brothers?" she asked.

"Adopted, yes. All of them." Maci leaned in, whispering more softly now. "They were all foster kids, lost in the system until the Pattersons took them in."

That explained things, while somehow boosting Tessa's opinion of them. Was that why they wanted to take care of her baby? So he wouldn't get lost too?

Maci muttered a mild curse as she hustled to her desk to answer the phone, but Tessa was glad to be alone again so she could think.

They did security and private investigations. That meant the odds of her getting away with Walker were slim to none. They'd track her down without breaking a sweat, especially since she had no money and no friends in San Antonio.

Or anywhere.

"Hey."

Her head snapped toward the sound. Brax. Her cheeks flushed, though there was no way he knew what she'd been thinking. Guilt prickled under her skin, which made no sense. Walker was her son. Why should she feel guilty about wanting to keep him?

"Hi." She forced a smile. "I don't want to put him down. He might wake up."

He grinned. "Yeah, I understand. My arms are still sore from carrying him." He stretched them, bending at the elbows.

I seriously doubt arms that size could tire so easily.

What a weird thought to have.

"Where'd you go just then?"

The question stirred her from the strange, oddly aroused thoughts Brax's body stirred in her subconscious. "Hmm? Nowhere. I'm just…"

He came into the room and sat across from her. His body language was easy, friendly. One of the skills she'd learned waiting tables was how to read a customer's body language. Whether a guy was feeling particularly handsy that day, whether it would be better to put a little extra space between her body and his if she wanted to avoid having her rear end pinched.

Or worse.

Brax wasn't suspicious of her, which struck her as both touching and painfully naive. He didn't know who she was. He'd assumed. And every second she held her son, she was taking advantage of that assumption.

"Are you okay?" he asked, lowering his brows over his brilliant, penetrating eyes that seemed to look right through her. Was that a tingle running down her spine? Or a flash of guilt?

She shifted Walker to her shoulder. "Sure."

"It's just that when you first walked in earlier, I had the feeling you were in trouble somehow. Call it a professional habit, but I tend to pick up on those things. I honestly figured you for a client."

She nodded slowly, though her brain moved at top speed. Trying to figure out whether he was for real or if he was taunting her the way Robert had. Torturing her like a cat that had cornered a mouse.

Brax would never believe it if she told him what his brother had done to her. After all, she was a nobody. A stranger.

And if he knew she wasn't a nanny, he'd take Walker away from her. She couldn't let that happen. She had to do whatever she could to keep Walker in her arms.

So she lied. "I was thinking about my parents, I guess. They've been on my mind lately. I was feeling sort of sad. Missing them."

"I guess being with Walker is only stirring that up more," he mused.

Was he playing around? She didn't think so—or maybe she didn't want to think so. It was all too confusing, and she was so tired.

"Yes. I guess so." She wanted to snuggle the baby closer but knew that might give her away.

"Well, I have nothing but good things to say about how he's responded to you so far. Between you and me, you're a godsend."

"Thanks."

This was it. The point where he'd drop the *but* on her. *You're great with him, but I don't need you. You're a godsend, but we'd better not see you sneaking around here anymore.*

"Are you free tomorrow?"

Her eyes popped open wide before good sense told her to cool her surprise. "Yes. I am."

"What about the rest of the week?" He offered a sheepish smile. Charming, even. "You see how busy we are around here. I've been scrambling for days trying to take care of him while getting my work done."

"Absolutely." She would've agreed to just about anything as long as it meant being with her son. "Whatever you need."

It was almost a dream day. They'd even given her half of a sandwich and a cup of soup left over from lunch.

This was the safest and happiest she'd felt since Robert had taken their son from her.

But all good things came to an end. By six o'clock, the guys were preparing to leave for the night. She'd have to go too, even though she had nowhere to stay. She couldn't hide in the ladies' room until they locked up or camp under the conference room table.

"Good night. And thanks again for everything." Brax waved one last time before he walked off toward a car parked close to the building. Tessa walked slowly away from the front door, and with a glance over her shoulder to check if he was watching, slipped into the shadows of the alley between the buildings.

He didn't know she was watching. It was the best way to see how he treated Walker.

There was nothing to worry about. He was gentle with the baby, secured his seat in the car and spoke quietly to him. She couldn't make out exactly what he was saying, but the specifics didn't matter. He wasn't harsh or cold.

She breathed a sigh of relief before retreating deeper into the alley so he wouldn't see her when he drove past.

Where was she supposed to go now? She knew without counting there wasn't enough left from yesterday's tips to afford a hotel room, which was why she'd spent the night at the bus station.

She couldn't go back there. The cops might pick her up this time.

That left the alley. It was secluded enough. Clean enough. There weren't any rats, and it didn't reek of urine.

It would do for now.

She set her bag down along the wall and settled in with it against her back, guarding what little she had against potential thieves. Her brain hummed with the joy of having held her son again, the memories from the day replaying over and over.

She fell asleep with a smile, sitting upright in a narrow alley.

Chapter Six

It had been a dream week. A week spent soaking in everything about her son. Playing with him. Cuddling him. Singing songs to make him smile. Studying every inch of him as he slept.

Taking every second she could get.

She'd also spent the week sleeping in the alley and freshening up in gas station bathrooms. Washing her hair in the sink of one had been…an interesting challenge. But it had been worth it because she had her baby. She would live the rest of her life in an alley if it meant spending time with Walker. Watching him grow. Loving him.

Maci was always the first to arrive at the office, usually carrying donuts or bagels when she did. Tessa would follow her inside, answering questions about her night with made-up stories before quickly turning the tables and asking the office manager about her night.

Maci was thoughtful and friendly. And organized, considering how she kept four men in line. The Patterson brothers didn't seem like they'd be easy to wrangle.

Tessa had overheard Chance joking with Brax about how their mom would flip out if she knew there was a baby around and nobody had told her. Whoever she was, their mom had to be a special lady. Adopting four kids out of the foster care system wasn't for the faint of heart.

Tessa had moved into the break room. It was better than the conference room, more comfortable in there for both Tessa and Walker.

The fridge was right there, so was the microwave when it came time to warm bottles. She didn't love the idea of using a microwave and thought it would be healthier to warm his formula in a pan of simmering water, but people did what they had to do in tough times.

Like sponge bathing in gas station bathrooms.

At least her baby was eating and she was the one feeding him. That was what mattered most. She may have preferred taking care of Walker at a house, but she couldn't blame Brax for not trusting her alone with him.

The break room made it possible for her to get to know all the men as they wandered in and out. They each seemed caring and genuinely curious about Walker.

Weston had confirmed what Maci had already shared. "It means a lot to us that he has a stable upbringing," he'd confessed while nuking a cup of coffee. "We got lucky. Lots of kids don't. Not everybody gets adopted by loving people with the patience to undo years of damage."

Knowing they'd gone through so much hurt her heart.

But look how they'd turned out. They could've taken those years of damage and turned against the whole world. They could've taken their pain out on the people around them. Instead, they helped people. Protected them. It was their mission in life.

And it had made them hyperaware of what might happen to Walker if Brax didn't maintain guardianship.

Brax. Every time she thought about him, she fought back a tiny smile. What was it about him that made her react that way? Was it his voice? So distinctive she could home in on it even if she hadn't heard it for a few days. Or maybe his cologne? Her stomach tightened every time she caught a whiff.

All of her senses were focused on him at all times. Waiting for him to poke his head into the break room. Hoping to pass him in the hall.

He was easygoing, and he obviously took good care of Walker. That had to be why she was so tuned into him.

Easygoing or not, Brax would kick her out in a heartbeat if he ever learned who she really was.

It was clear he didn't like Robert very much. Whenever she mentioned Walker's daddy, Brax got a pinched look on his face like he'd just tasted something bitter. Did he know he reacted that way? Probably not. He'd never said much about his brother, but his body language spoke for him.

That didn't mean Brax would hear her out if she tried to explain what Robert had done to her. Walker's best interests would always come first, which would mean kicking out the supposed junkie mom.

Tessa could respect Robert for putting her son's well-being above all else. Even if everything he said about her had been an outright lie.

Tessa scooched closer to Walker and bent to rub his back. He hated tummy time, but all of the articles she'd read said it was vital for his muscle development. Her body instinctively straightened as the intoxicating scent of Brax's cologne wafted her way.

"Come on, buddy," she urged Walker. "You can do it. Push yourself up on those arms of yours."

Brax leaned against the doorjamb and chuckled at the sight of his nephew fighting to push himself up off the floor. "That's right, little man. Work those biceps." Her heart skipped a beat when he flexed his own considerable biceps.

The best—or worst—part was he seemed oblivious. He wasn't trying to grab her attention. He wasn't deliberately showing off or flirting. He just happened to possess more charm than anybody should be allowed to.

And a body to match.

Robert had been charming at first, back when he'd been trying to get her into bed. He'd even made her believe he'd cared about her. Until proving how much he didn't.

That memory was like a bucket of ice water dumped over her head. She had to be smarter this time.

Brax's expression turned serious. Did he know what she was thinking? Of course not—he couldn't.

That didn't keep her stomach from turning into a sea of acid when he looked at her that way. Didn't stop her mind from spinning out in a thousand directions, trying to come up with a plan to get away with her son before Brax figured out who she was.

"I need to know how to pay you."

Oh, was that all? She almost laughed in relief but stopped herself in time. Laughter wouldn't be an appropriate reaction. "It's been such a joy spending time with this guy again, I almost forgot about that."

His frown deepened. "But you do have to get paid."

"Of course."

"I haven't received any paperwork from the agency, though. Nobody got in contact with me. I don't know how to set this up."

Right. The nonexistent agency.

"Well, I'm new in town." She shrugged. Did she look and sound confident in her lies? She had to. He was sharp. He'd see through lies. "Maybe my bank account hasn't finished getting set up yet. Why don't you pay me, then the agency will bill me for their cut?"

He would never go for it. Not when she'd only come up with that idea on the fly. No way.

"Sure. Would cash be okay this week, since your account isn't set up?"

Whoa. He was either deeply distracted or his powers of perception didn't extend very far. And she didn't care which.

"Sure, that would be great." It might mean buying a little food, some fresh clothes.

"Good. Tomorrow we'll settle up for the week?"

"That sounds good." Better than good. Could it be this easy?

He turned away, then pivoted to face her. "I don't even know where to contact you if I ever need you."

It was all she could do not to plant her face in her hands. She couldn't exactly give him the address of the alley. *I'm easy to find. Make a right out the front door, then another right when you get to the alley. Third trash can on the left.*

He had her phone number, though she'd taken pains to leave the phone off ever since that last day in Eagle Pass. But what about an address?

She scribbled down the first thing that came to mind, completely made up. Was there a Pine Street in San Antonio? Who knew? It was a risk she had to take.

"Great. Thanks." He slipped the paper into his pocket before running a distracted hand over his head. "Sorry. My mind's in so many directions right now. Word came in yesterday morning that a low-level drug dealer we helped put away jumped bail. We're trying to track him down before he gets too far away."

"Wow. That's intense."

He nodded, his jaw twitching. "Yeah. It's one of those things where we don't want the police involved since this isn't exactly a dangerous man. Drug dealer? Absolutely. But he's not a violent criminal. It'll be easier if we track him down first and bring him in. Once guns are involved..."

"I understand." Not only did it give her a clearer picture of the Patterson brothers, but knowing they were distracted by an important case gave her a little breathing room. No wonder he was willing to accept the first excuse about the agency that came to mind.

When closing time rolled around, Tessa prepared herself for another night in the alley. After Brax took Walker out in his car seat, she slid two bottles of water into her bag and followed him. Now that she knew there was pay coming her way, it was easier to let go of what little cash she had left. Maybe later tonight, she'd use the rest of her money to buy bread and peanut butter at the closest grocery store.

"Good night, buddy." She bit her tongue against the rest of what wanted to come out. *I love you. Mama loves you so much.* Words she whispered to him whenever they were alone.

But knowing she would lose sight of him for an entire fifteen hours made her want to say them anyway. Just in case.

"You need a ride?" Brax was all smiles, his usual charming self. So charming she wished she could say yes, that she wanted him to drive her home.

Only she couldn't because her address didn't exist.

"Oh, uh, no, thank you." As if someone had flipped a switch, her palms went sweaty. She licked her dry lips and hoped he couldn't read body language as well as she could. Because if he could, he'd know there was a problem.

"No, thank you," she repeated. "I like the fresh air. I think I'll walk."

"Oh, so you're not that far from here?"

"Nope." Did that sound as casual as she'd intended? Her

blood froze in her veins when he frowned a little, like he was starting to put the pieces of something together in his head.

"Would you mind if I call you in early tomorrow morning?" he finally asked. "I don't know exactly how early. This case has us on our toes. There's no telling when or where we'll find this guy."

Her blood thawed. "Sure. I understand."

"So that's okay with you? I can pay double for the extra time."

Extra time with Walker and extra money? Like she would ever turn that down.

"No problem. I'll, um, keep my phone close by." But when he called, she'd have to be sure not to stay on the phone long enough for the men hunting Robert to use it to find her.

"Thanks." He granted her one wide, relieved smile before waving and turning toward his car. Her own smile stayed on her face long after he was gone, blood thawing even more.

THERE WAS NO such thing as getting decent sleep in an alley. Even if the alley didn't reek of urine and was fairly secluded. It was still dark without so much as a hint of light in the sky when Tessa's phone rang. Adrenaline sent her bolt upright, her heart pounding hard enough to make her sick.

When she finally found her phone, it told her two things: it was two in the morning, and it was Brax who had awakened her from not-so-deep sleep.

"Hello?" She could barely push the word out of her mouth. If she didn't get a grip, he might figure out something was wrong.

"Tessa, I'm so sorry to wake you up like this, but things just broke with this case, and we think we know where to find our guy. It's something we all need to be there for. Can

I come and pick you up at your place? I could drop you off at the office with Walker."

"No, no, it's okay. I'll meet you at the office in fifteen minutes." She put a hand over the phone when a car passed at the end of the alley.

"I'll be there in five."

She looked at the phone to confirm he'd already ended the call, ignoring all the messages from the diner wondering where she was.

She looked around in a panic before shoving her things into her bag: what was left of the bread and peanut butter and half a bottle of water. She couldn't let him see her makeshift home.

It happened so fast. She only realized she'd lost her grip on her phone when the thing hit the ground hard enough to break the screen.

"No!" Hot, frustrated tears welled in her eyes. She couldn't afford to be without a phone. How would Brax get ahold of her if he needed her?

She had barely reached the front door before he pulled up in front of the building.

He hurried around to open the back door and unstrap the car seat. "Thank you, thank you, thank you. You have no idea how much you're helping," he muttered. His arm brushed against her as he hustled to enter the code that unlocked the door.

"You have to do what you have to do."

If he thought it was strange that she'd made it to the office so quickly, he didn't mention it. "I'll be back as soon as I can. I promise. Thank you again for this."

"You're welcome." She took the car seat with a sleeping Walker inside.

Before he ran out the door, Brax pressed a kiss against her forehead. He didn't say anything, just left.

She reeled from the suddenness. And from how much she liked it. How could blood go from frozen to boiling so quickly?

She watched Brax peel away, staring into the darkness long after his taillights had faded. Mechanically, she turned out the lights, her head still spinning from Brax's kiss. It was innocent. Pure. So why had it hit her like a freight train? Why did it linger? She could've sworn she still felt his lips against her skin.

It had been so long since she'd had adult human contact. Even something that simple and quick. Robert hadn't exactly been big on affection or tenderness. Once he'd gotten her into bed there hadn't been a reason to pretend to be romantic.

He had even taken away her son. She'd been alone for months. Without a friend, without anybody.

Now she had her Walker, and in a simple, friendly way, she had Brax. Things were looking up.

The footsteps rang out a moment before a face appeared at the front window.

Tessa strangled a gasp and eased into the shadows, praying Walker wouldn't pick this moment to wake up. She studied the face she didn't know. Didn't want to know. It chilled her, those cold, hard eyes staring into the office.

Another man pushed him aside and tried to open the door. He pulled hard, but it didn't budge. Thank goodness Brax had taken the time to lock them inside. Thank goodness she'd turned out the lights. Thank goodness Walker slumbered peacefully.

She plastered herself against the wall, pushing deeper into the shadows, holding her breath like the men outside might be able to hear. Who were they? Not friends of the Pattersons—she would've bet good money on that if she'd had more than eighteen cents left to her name.

"I followed the signal," the one at the door growled. "You positive it died?"

"Yeah." The man at the window nodded, throwing a filthy look inside the building like his frustration was the building's fault. "Maybe there was something wrong with the equipment. Why would she be here in the middle of the night?"

Tessa's stomach flipped. They were there for her, probably having traced her phone in the short time she'd used it. Wanting to be available for her son, available for Brax, had led them to her. It hadn't felt like it at the time, but her smashed phone had been a blessing in disguise. What if she had left the phone on?

She gasped softly as Walker stirred in his car seat. With one eye on the men outside, she lowered the seat to the floor, unlatched the straps, and clutched him to her chest. "Shh, baby," she whispered, holding him close, hoping her heartbeat and contact with him would keep him quiet.

Holding her breath, holding her baby, she watched the men. She was afraid to move or even breathe. One of them tried the door again and examined the lock before pulling hard.

Finally, they muttered a few vile words and stalked toward a nondescript car. Just as she had with Brax, she watched the taillights disappear into the night and she was able to breathe easily again. "Thank you," she whispered into the otherwise silent room.

Her knees wobbled as she made her way to the break

room. There were no windows there. They would be safe. Nobody would be able to find her here. Nobody would be able to take her son away.

Chapter Seven

What had he been thinking, kissing Tessa like that?

That was hardly what Brax needed to be worried about on the way to the trailer where Nick Lomax's girlfriend lived with their three-year-old son.

No, Brax should have been thinking about the case. About surrounding the trailer and getting Nick to go with them before anything hit the fan.

Especially with a woman involved. Not to mention a little kid.

Yet kissing Tessa was all he could think about as he'd sped out of town toward the rendezvous point. He tried to tell himself he'd been distracted, in a hurry to meet up with the guys. That it was important that Nick didn't feel threatened, and Brax was always best in situations like this.

But the lips that were supposed to coax Nick out of the trailer still burned from the sweet, innocent kiss he'd pressed to Tessa's forehead like any dutiful husband leaving his wife and child at home before heading to work. That should bother him. So why didn't it?

He ran a frustrated hand through his hair. How was he supposed to concentrate on helping Nick out of this situation without his family getting hurt if he couldn't stop thinking about Tessa?

What if she quit because of this? He'd stepped over the line. Not too far, but far enough. Assuming a sort of intimacy they didn't share.

He wouldn't have blamed her if she wanted out of their arrangement. Like it wasn't bad enough he'd called her at two in the morning and pulled her out of bed. Like he wasn't already making her life difficult.

He made it to the meeting spot roughly a half mile from the trailer park.

"About time you showed up." Weston gave him no time to defend himself before gesturing to the tablet Chance held. "We were discussing how we plan to surround the place."

"I'll take point," Brax decided. "If I'm going to be the one to talk him out of there, that's where I need to be."

"I'll flank on the right, Luke on the left," Weston announced. "Chance, you take the rear in case he decides to escape through a window. Keep eyes on the structure— some of them have doors in the floor. He could slip out and try to make a run for it while we're all focused on the front."

"Everything okay?" Luke caught Brax's eye before hitting him in the face with the beam of his flashlight.

"I was okay before you blinded me." Brax held up a hand in front of his face. "I'm fine. I had to take care of things with Walker first."

"Right. Of course." Weston sounded apologetic, at least, though he didn't offer any true apology for his remark. Not that Brax expected one.

It was nearly a quarter to three by the time they rolled to a stop and exited their vehicles alongside the fence that defined the trailer park's boundaries. Keeping his flashlight low, Brax kept an eye on the windows as they approached their target.

"We don't know whether the girlfriend and kid are inside," Chance reminded them through the comm system as he took his place behind the trailer.

Brax would've bet on it. There were toys in front of the trailer. An inflatable kiddie pool. And a car parked close by. The entire family was probably in there.

He kept this in mind as he crept to the door, waiting for visual confirmation that his brothers were in place before banging his fist against the metal. "Nick Lomax. Come on out."

It was important to keep his voice strong, firm, but low enough not to shock or startle Nick—or the neighbors, who if they chose to get involved could complicate things.

A light went on in the rear. The sounds of tight, frantic whispering filtered out through the screened window.

"Nick, we're not here to hurt you or your family. But you can't keep running. You know you'll get caught, and it'll be that much worse for you when you do. Don't put your family in harm's way like this."

There was movement inside. A lot of it. Things getting pushed around, doors opening and closing. The man wasn't exactly skilled at making a silent getaway.

"Nick." He rapped harder on the trailer. "This doesn't have to end badly. Come in with us, and we'll get it worked out in your favor without having to involve the cops."

Weston gestured to the window where Nick was visible. His voice rang out in the night air. "I ain't going back. I'll shoot you dead before I let anybody take me back."

Brax's throat tightened, and he fought to control the tension ratcheting up inside him. One of them had to remain calm and in control.

"It doesn't have to be that way," he assured the man. "Notice how we didn't bring bounty hunters or cops with us. We don't want to put Darlene or your son in danger."

"They didn't do nothing wrong!"

"We know that. Which is why we're only here to bring you back in. You missed your appearance and a warrant will be issued for your arrest. You know that. We have the trailer surrounded. It's for the best that you come out now without putting up a fight."

The baby cried. Not a baby, not anymore, but young enough to instantly bring Walker to mind. What would he do if he were trapped in a trailer with Walker, knowing there were armed men outside? Whatever it took to ensure the kid's safety, without a doubt.

But how could he say goodbye to him? What if the entire reason he'd run was to be with his child, who he'd now be torn away from?

"Nick, I know you want to be with your family. I get that. But you have to keep them in mind. You're right. They didn't do anything wrong. They're innocent in all this. But you're dragging them into it now. Don't you see that?"

Darlene's crying mixed with the kid's twisted the knife in Brax's chest. "You've got to do what's best for them right now, Nick. Which means coming with us. Not putting up a fight. We don't want any gunfire with a woman and child in the house. And we don't want to see you get hurt. If you serve your time, you'll be with your boy in a few years. You try to run and you risk much worse."

"Bathroom window opened," Chance whispered in his earpiece. "Looks like he's going to make a run."

Weston went around back to prepare for it.

Brax muttered a curse. This was not the way things were supposed to go. "Nick, I need you to talk to me. Where are you? Come on, man. For your son."

"Please. Don't shoot him." That was Darlene near the front door. Her voice was thick with emotion.

"We have no intention of opening fire. I promise you that. But I need him to come out without a weapon. We will defend ourselves if it comes to it."

"She'll convince him," Luke predicted.

Brax wasn't so sure. The man didn't want to go to prison. Anybody could understand that.

"For your boy," he nearly begged. "Let him grow up knowing he has a daddy who loved him enough that he didn't do anything stupid at a crucial moment. Let him look forward to seeing you again, Nick. You can put this behind you someday. But you have to be smart now."

His weapon was at the ready, in case their man came out shooting.

The lock flipped. "I'm coming out. I'm unarmed. Don't hurt my family."

Brax could've collapsed with relief. "We won't hurt any of you." Then, more quietly for the sake of his brothers, "He's coming out through the front."

Chance and Weston joined him and Luke in time for the door to swing open. "Hey, Nick," Brax offered. "It's good to see you."

By the time he had Nick back in custody and awaiting his rescheduled court appearance, it was nearly dawn. Would Tessa be worried? He hoped she'd managed to get some sleep—the sofa in the reception area was comfortable enough.

Yet she wasn't out there when he arrived at the office. He entered the code to unlock the door and turn off the alarm, his gaze sweeping the floor as he did. Where was she?

For the briefest moment, just a flash in the back of his mind, Brax imagined Tessa taking Walker and running. Disappearing into the night while he'd been miles away talking a bail jumper out of doing anything stupid.

But no. If she'd left, he would've gotten an alert that the alarm had been tripped. Knowing she had to be around somewhere, he could breathe easier as he walked from one room to another looking for her.

He found them in the break room on a pile of blankets on the floor. Tessa slept curled around Walker like she was protecting him.

Brax crouched beside them, content to observe for a moment or two. Walker slept peacefully, his mouth curved into a little bow. What did babies dream about? Diaper rash? No, not if they looked as sweet and comfortable as his nephew did.

Tessa didn't look so peaceful. Her delicate brows were drawn together, her forehead pinched like she was in pain. What was she dreaming about? Nothing good, that much was clear, especially when she whimpered like a wounded puppy.

It would've been mean to leave her that way any longer. Being awake had to be better than whatever was happening in her dream.

"Tessa?" He hesitated to touch her after the stupid kiss earlier, but she wasn't budging. With a hand on her shoulder, he whispered her name again.

Her eyes flew open, and her body jumped. "What? Huh?"

"Shh, it's just me. It's Brax. Everything's okay." He stopped short of taking her into his arms to calm her down—barely, since that was all he wanted to do. To hold her and calm her and let her know everything was okay.

She blinked hard, holding a hand to her forehead. "Brax? Oh, I'm sorry."

"No, I'm sorry. I startled you."

"It's just that I got a little freaked out, I guess." She offered a weak little laugh. "All alone here, middle of the night, that sort of thing."

"I'm sorry. I didn't think about that when I asked you to spend the night here. It must've been creepy." He was careful to speak quietly, and not only for the baby's sake. Tessa was still spooked.

"At first," she admitted with a shaky sigh. "But things turned around. And he was an angel the whole time."

"I'm glad to hear that—though I'm sorry you slept here on the floor. It couldn't have been comfortable."

She shrugged. "It was fine. And it's only been a few hours. Not all that long."

Before he could dispute this or apologize yet again, she asked, "Did everything turn out okay?"

It took a second for him to understand what she was talking about. "Oh, yeah. It went as well as it could. We took the guy in before anything went wrong."

"That's a relief." She ran a hand over her face, yawning. "What a night for both of us, I guess."

What would he have done without her? "I can't thank you enough. I wish I could tell you this sort of thing will never happen again, but I don't like making promises I can't keep."

"I understand. You have an unpredictable job. And I like spending time with this one." She rubbed Walker's back with a gentle hand, smiling softly.

The question was out of his mouth before he could even consider thinking twice. "Would you like to make this a full-time arrangement?"

She gulped. "Full-time?"

Now that he'd gotten started, he couldn't stop. It was like somebody had pulled the plug from a drain.

"You could move into my house—it has three bedrooms, with two on the other side of the house from mine. No strings attached. You're free to say no. And I hope you know I would never dream of doing anything to make you—"

"Yes." She touched his knee with a shy smile, cutting off the flow of words pouring from him. "Yes, I would love to do that. Thank you."

That one touch lit up his insides and convinced him he'd made the right choice.

As long as he could learn to live with a woman and a baby in the house without driving them both insane.

Chapter Eight

"Happy birthday, dear Walker…" Tessa leaned over to kiss her son's forehead. "Happy birthday to you."

She snuggled him a little closer, laughing at herself for even thinking of singing Happy Birthday to a five-month-old.

"It's your five-month birthday," she whispered with another kiss before putting him in his highchair. It was brand new, one of many things Brax had purchased over the past two weeks. "You're getting to be such a big boy now."

Walker waved his fists, smiling from ear to ear. Even if he couldn't understand what she was saying, she could tell he liked the sound of her voice.

So she talked to him all day long. Anything to make him happy. It didn't hurt that it made her happy too. When she wasn't talking to the baby, she was singing. Every song she knew, one after the other.

Not only because he enjoyed it, but because she did too. It had been so long since she'd sang or had any reason to sing. Being with Walker gave her that reason.

More than that. It was feeling safe in a beautiful home set on lots of land without a neighbor in sight. Plenty of trees, tons of sunshine. Room inside to move around. No sense of claustrophobia, no sounds and smells from neighbors on five sides of her apartment.

This was exactly the sort of home she'd always wanted. It was like living in a happy dream. Waking up, caring for her son, loving him openly.

And Brax. He was great too.

Not that she loved him. Not even close. But being around him was wonderful. There was somebody to look forward to seeing at the end of the day. To say good-night to before heading to bed. Somebody to share Walker's latest super-human achievement with.

Because they'd agreed early on that Walker was the smartest and most talented child who had ever existed in the history of the world.

The thought made her smile as she fixed herself breakfast. Brax had left earlier than usual—she liked to at least have coffee with him in the morning to go over Walker's schedule. When she should expect him home, whether he should pick up anything at the store along the way.

The simplest, most mundane conversations. Yet they meant the world to her.

"I was lonely for a long time, buddy." She glanced over at Walker, who was in the process of trying to eat his fist. "I didn't know how lonely until now, since I'm not lonely anymore. Now I can see."

She could also see why it had been so easy for Robert to get her into bed. He'd probably spotted a big old target in the middle of her forehead when they'd met. No challenge whatsoever.

It had been that way since the accident. Losing one parent would have been rough enough, she guessed, but both at once? At the age of twenty? She'd been thrust into a new life overnight.

No more comfortable house. No more family dinners. No more security. No more love.

Walker banged his fists on his tray, happy with himself. The noise shook her from dark thoughts. "You're into making noise lately, aren't you?"

He banged on the tray again like he was answering her. "You know, your timing is uncanny sometimes."

The phone rang after lunch. Brax's landline, so old-fashioned in a way, but helpful since she'd broken her phone. He checked in at least once a day to see if everything was okay.

She realized on answering that she had even come to look forward to these little calls.

"Hi." There was no wiping away her goofy smile. Good thing he couldn't see her.

"Hey." His deep, rich voice held a touch of laughter in it. He was almost always in a good mood. Charming, funny. Pretty much the polar opposite of Robert. "How's it going there?"

"The usual. Plenty of peace and quiet now that Super Walker is down for a nap. He'll be an excellent drummer someday, I think. Great rhythm when he's banging things together."

"Remind me to never pick up a drum set."

She giggled. "Pots and pans. Wooden spoons. You do the math."

"I was never much good at math." They shared a laugh. "Hey, I meant to tell you. I took your phone over to a guy who runs a shop a few blocks from here. He said it should be fine in a couple of days."

"He'll fix it for me?"

"Well, for me," he chuckled. "We've done a little security work for him in the past. He said he sees phones like that all the time and can almost always fix them up."

"Wow. It was so sweet of you to go to the trouble."

"No trouble at all. Just think, you'll be able to take some time away from the house now since you'll have a phone you can use to get in touch if you need anything."

Right. Because that was her excuse to stick close to Walker. Not having a car was one thing—Brax had already offered to lend her his car if she wanted it.

Not having a phone was another. There weren't pay phones on every block like there'd been in the old days.

Brax, being the protective man he was, hated the idea of her going out without a way to call if the car broke down or some catastrophe occurred.

Being the absolute sweetheart he was, he thought about her comfort and happiness all the time. As if they truly mattered. And he was dead set on her taking time for herself, not knowing she had nowhere to go and no one to see.

"Thanks," she said, though her heart wasn't quite in it. The fact that she was afraid to be out of Walker's presence for even a little while didn't lessen the kind gesture, so she injected a little sunshine into her voice. "I'll owe you a special dinner tonight to make up for it."

He groaned. "You're speaking my language, though I don't see how you have the energy after taking care of the baby and the house."

She was used to being on her feet all day, waiting tables and cleaning houses and doing anything else she could to make ends meet. Walker was still at the stage where he slept a lot, giving her time to check off her daily tasks without a problem.

"So, what's for dinner?" he asked.

"It's a surprise," she teased. "So don't be late."

"I love surprises. See you at six fifteen on the dot," he promised before hanging up.

She clutched the handset to her chest with a grin as she remembered how surprised Brax had been that first night she'd scrounged around the kitchen looking for dinner ingredients, hoping for inspiration. He'd gotten used to a lot of frozen meals and takeout, evidenced by the number of packages in the freezer and containers in the fridge. The aroma of a home-cooked dinner had practically sent him drooling.

It was a pleasure for her to watch him as he enjoyed her cooking. She knew she was a good cook thanks to the time in the kitchen bonding with her mother once she was tall enough to reach the stove. It felt good knowing she could provide a little something for him after he'd given her so much.

He would never know how much he'd given her. He *couldn't* know.

The knowledge that this wasn't real always sat at the back of her mind. He could find out about her at any time. It was why her heart leapt every time the phone mounted on the kitchen wall rang.

He could be calling to say hello, or he could be calling to say goodbye, to tell her to get her things together and get out.

As it was, he'd been suspicious when she'd suggested he pay her in cash every week. "I don't like paying the check and direct deposit fees at the bank." She'd shrugged. "Every penny counts."

He'd let it go without questions, though it had been clear from his frown that he thought it was strange. How many more strange things could she say or do without him demanding answers? Soon he would want to know why he hadn't heard anything from the agency about paperwork.

Which was why she'd keep her head down and save every cent she could. Eventually, she'd have enough money to hire somebody who could clear her name—ironically, San Antonio Security was exactly the sort of business to do something like that.

It was impossible. She couldn't even hint at needing their help. They would take Walker away. She couldn't lose him again.

But she couldn't fool Brax forever. The sooner she had enough money saved, the better. What if Robert decided to come back all of a sudden? That would be the end of everything.

And it could happen at any time. The sense of an anvil hanging over her head followed her wherever she went. It could drop whenever, wherever.

Walker's soft cries from his crib filtered through the monitor. It was like he felt her thoughts sometimes. He had a way of breaking in before she went really dark and depressed herself.

After changing him, she picked up a blanket and walked him downstairs. "Let's go outside and get some fresh air and sunshine." That was what she needed, a way of recharging her spirits.

It was their late afternoon ritual. He'd wake up from his nap, and they'd lie out on the blanket for a while basking in the sunshine. It was the only sort of life she wanted to live. Lazy afternoons with her son enjoying the last of the sun's rays before getting dinner started.

And saying hello to the man of the house when he got home.

Tessa flinched when the hair along the back of her neck stood straight up. She raised a hand to the area, rubbing like that would help ward off the sudden chill.

Walker continued gazing up at the clouds and babbling while she sat up, her head on a swivel. There was nobody out there. No neighbors near enough to make out their houses in the distance. No passing or parked cars.

Why did it feel like there was somebody watching her?

She hadn't felt this way since Eagle Pass. Her instincts had been dead-on then, and those same instincts were screaming at her now. But Eagle Pass was more than two weeks behind her. There hadn't been any trouble since the night she'd spent at the office when those two men had come looking for her.

"I'm letting my imagination run away with me," she murmured to Walker, still scanning the horizon in all directions. "Come on. Let's go back into the house."

Even if it was nothing more than her overactive imagination—and it had to be—she rushed Walker inside and locked the door behind them.

Chapter Nine

"Nothing all day. Movement and shadows mostly but nothing verifiable. Nobody in or out."

Brax groaned, rolling his head around on his stiff neck. "I never knew sitting still and watching an apartment could leave me aching the way it does."

"You don't get up and move around enough. I warned you about that." Weston would know, having performed his fair share of stakeouts when he'd been with the police department.

"I can't shake the feeling that the second I look away for anything more than an emergency, I'll miss something important."

"I get it." Weston took a seat where Brax had spent the day in the apartment they'd rented across from that of a suspect they suspected in a string of home invasions. When the San Antonio PD had thrown up their hands in despair after a dozen invasions left them with no evidence and no real suspects, one of the victims had hired the Patterson brothers to look into it.

Within two weeks, they'd found their prime suspect and had been staking out his apartment ever since, keeping track of his movements and of any visitors.

"I guess you'll be on your way home now." There was a

hint of a smile tugging Weston's lips as he looked Brax up and down. "A hot, hearty meal waiting for you. A woman to serve it. You've got it made, brother."

Brax waved off Weston's obvious joking. "Please. She has time on her hands, and she likes to cook. I'm not getting any ideas about it."

"Why not?"

"Because she works for me. Enough of the devil's advocate." He cleared his throat before changing the topic. "Anything new about Robert?"

"Nothing we didn't find before. Though truth be told, we've been busy."

"Yeah, and I've been doing all right with Tessa—and Walker," Brax added, but it was too late. The spark in Weston's eyes said everything.

"Doing all right with the nanny. I wonder what Mom would think about that."

"Okay, enough." Brax held up his hands in mock surrender. "Fact is Tessa is twenty-two years old. A nine-year age difference is sort of substantial."

"I'll grant you that. But don't pretend you don't look forward to getting home and seeing her. You smile almost as much as Luke does nowadays. Honestly, I don't recognize either of you."

"Funny guy. You know, Walker might have something to do with that."

He did. Now that those early days were over and there was no more panic, Brax had been able to relax and get to know his nephew. The kid was adorable when he wasn't screaming. Tessa was good with him.

It cracked him up to no end to see the baby watching as the two of them held a conversation. He was so serious, studying their mouths with his little face scrunched up in concentration. He'd be a smart kid, no doubt.

Unlike his father.

"So? Have you spied on her while she's alone with the kid?"

Brax bristled at this, though there was a slight amount of embarrassment behind it. "How'd you guess?"

"I'd wonder about you if you didn't. Where did you hide the cameras?"

"One in the kitchen, one in Walker's room."

"And?"

"And she was great with him the entire time. I only did it for the first couple of days. Just to satisfy myself that she was as good to him in private as she was in front of me."

"Of course."

He didn't tell Weston about her singing. About the endless games of peekaboo. How she talked and talked to the baby—the audio went in and out depending on her volume and the room she was in at the time, but her facial expressions said it all.

She loved Walker, and it showed.

If anything, that only helped him like her more. They had something they loved in common. Something they worked together to nurture. Something that made them laugh at the dinner table with his comical facial expressions and sudden outbursts.

Those evenings with Tessa had become the highlight of his day.

Which meant he had to get moving if he was going to enjoy another one. "I'd better go. She might worry if I'm late."

"She's got you following orders already."

"Watch it," Brax warned, and he was only half kidding. There were limits to joking around.

"Can I offer you a little brotherly advice before you go? In all seriousness." When Brax nodded, Weston continued. "You have a lot to think over. Plans to make. Decisions to come to."

"I know I do. And once my testimony against the cartel is delivered, I'll have the emotional bandwidth to consider the rest of my life. I'll start making those plans once that's all wrapped up."

"Do you think Tessa might fit into those plans?"

He only shrugged a shoulder and grinned before saying goodbye. There was only one word to answer that.

Yes.

With each passing day, she had worked her way deeper into his heart.

He already regretted his original attitude toward Walker, who now gave him reasons to smile, to relax and enjoy life. His heart had already changed.

What about having a woman to come home to? His woman. Not a nanny or babysitter. Somebody whose face lit up when he walked through the door.

The way Tessa's did.

"No way," he warned himself. Hadn't he promised there wouldn't be any funny business? The last thing that poor, haunted woman needed was to feel pressured. Like she had to sleep with him if she wanted to keep her job.

There were times when he wanted nothing more than to wrap her in his arms and beg her to tell him what was wrong. What she hid about herself. Why she sometimes averted her eyes when they touched on the topic of Robert or her life before meeting Brax.

Whenever that happened, he recalled the wounded bird

who'd first walked into the office and given him the sense of somebody needing help. Protection. Safety.

His cell rang, the sound echoing through the car's sound system. He imagined it was Tessa calling from the house asking him to pick up something on the way.

It wasn't. The call came from a very different number. "District Attorney Morgan. I just mentioned the cartel case to my brother a few minutes ago. Your ears must be burning."

He could normally charm just about any woman with little to no effort. It was a talent he chose to use for good instead of evil.

Janice Morgan didn't so much as snicker, which was how he knew they had a problem even before her voice rang out. "Remember that shopkeeper? The main witness we have lined up for the trial?"

"Of course. Older guy, right?"

"Mr. Henderson is in his fifties, yes. And he just had a heart attack. I got word from the ICU just a few minutes ago."

Brax muttered a curse under his breath. Of all the things...

"Did they give you an indication of an expected outcome?"

"No." She sighed. "But I don't think it matters much either way as far as the case is concerned. He's set to testify in ten days, and he's in the ICU this very minute. No way is he going to be strong enough for court. You don't face down Prince Riviera and his entire gang when you're at half strength."

Prince Riviera. The name still made Brax roll his eyes, even knowing the sort of filth and degradation the man and his gang were capable of. The Riviera cartel practically owned the border between west Texas and Mexico and had since before any of the Patterson brothers had been born.

"Honest question—do you think the cartel is capable of this?"

"Giving the man a heart attack to keep him from testifying?" She sighed heavily, the sound of a woman completely run down by work. "I'll just say I wouldn't put it past them to inject him with something and leave it there. Let's keep in mind that our witness is at an age when heart attacks are more common."

"True." It felt hollow, but what else was there to say?

"What about you? Are you still set on testifying?"

"Absolutely."

"Even though it's obvious you suspect the heart attack was cartel related?"

"Let me tell you something. The things I saw those scumbags do are seared into my memory. I want to take them down."

The women in the box truck being herded like cattle into waiting vans. Filthy, covered in bruises, looking like they hadn't eaten a decent meal in weeks. Chained together at the waist, one after another.

Not to mention the other items removed from the truck. Crates, one of which was opened to reveal plastic-wrapped bricks of white powder.

Brax had hidden himself in the shadows outside the warehouse—he'd been searching the riverbank for the presence of skid marks after a sketchy, staged car accident and happened to be around when the truck came through. Nobody had seen him in passing, and they hadn't noticed his presence outside the loading bay.

"They don't know who I am," he reminded the district attorney. "But I know who they are. I know who Prince

Riviera is, and I've seen what he's capable of. No way I'm going to let this guy back out on the street. We both know he's the entire backbone of that organization. With him behind bars, they lose all their clout and protection. They'll go down in flames."

"You don't know how relieved I am to hear that. I was afraid the news would scare you off."

"I don't scare that easily, ma'am."

She chuckled this time, though it was short-lived. "Still, I want you to watch your back. There's no telling what these scumbags know. Let's not underestimate them."

Brax turned off the main road and onto the smaller, two-lane dirt road leading to his house. There it was, lit up inside, with two people waiting to welcome him home after a long day.

Now was not the time to underestimate anybody.

Chapter Ten

It had taken three days for Brax's friend to fix Tessa's phone. When Brax had come home Wednesday night, he'd presented it like a great treasure. "Here you go. Your key to freedom."

She couldn't help beaming at how happy it made him to provide her with a phone, even if she didn't quite understand the connection between it and her freedom.

Still, she'd accepted the gesture and thanked him profusely. "Not to be picky, but this isn't a car," she'd reminded him. "I'm not exactly free."

"Sure, you are. Don't I keep telling you to use my car? In fact…" His charming grin had widened, making him almost irresistible. "I took tomorrow off so you can go out. Do whatever it is you want to do."

Ice had formed in her stomach. "I can't do that. It's—"

"It's only fair to you," he'd insisted, kind but firm. He had that way about him. A gentleness that didn't seem to mix with his physical size and line of work. "You've been working so hard. Two weeks without a break."

"It's nothing."

His brow had lowered. "Tessa, we both know I know what you go through with him. You might have more experience, but still. It's no cakewalk. Now that you have your phone back, we can both breathe a little easier. I know you didn't want to leave the house on your own without a phone handy."

"And you weren't crazy about the idea either."

"That's true." His smile had softened along with his voice. "Go out. Take care of yourself. Just for a day. You deserve it."

Which was what had led her to a mall in San Antonio. Even that morning, she'd resisted leaving the house until Brax had teased her, calling her "mother hen" since she was so worried about leaving Walker.

Mother. The thought that he might know something had carried her out of the house in a blink. While he didn't seem like the type to play games, there was no telling. After all, Brax was related to Robert, the king of game players. She couldn't put anything past him.

For all her worrying, though, it felt good to walk through the mall. How long had it been since she'd taken the time to window shop? She couldn't remember the last time.

When she was a kid, the mall had been the place to hang out. Even then, however, older kids and her parents had talked about the way things used to be. Back before online and big box store shopping had chipped away at mall culture.

There were a couple of groups of kids there in the late afternoon, long after school would've let out for the day. Otherwise, the only shoppers were older people. Some of them looked like they were getting exercise rather than paying any attention to store windows.

She paused at a baby store and smiled at a sweet nursery set, then studied a bouncy swing and wondered if it would be right for Walker. Granted, she didn't have the money for it—all of her money was stashed in her purse, every penny

Brax had paid her up to this point minus the cost of a few necessities—but she might be able to talk him into it. Walker needed to build up his legs.

She knew Brax would deny him nothing. If he had his way, her son would grow up spoiled beyond all reason.

That didn't do anything to loosen the smile from her face. She caught sight of her reflection. She looked so happy.

All things considered, she didn't have any reason to be unhappy.

So what if she carried all her money around with her in case she needed to make a run for it?

So what if she still entertained the idea of running away with her baby from time to time? In the dark of night, lying in bed in Brax's guest room, sometimes that idea would sneak up on her. She couldn't get rid of it.

She stopped in front of a boutique to admire the mannequins in their spangly cocktail dresses. What would it be like to live the sort of life where she needed a dress like this? To get all fancied up and go out on the town?

On Brax's arm?

Another dangerous train of thought that also tended to visit her in the night.

She turned away from the window and checked her phone for the millionth time since leaving the house. No calls from Brax. Walker didn't need her.

She couldn't be separated from him again. Even a trip to the mall was too much time spent apart from her baby. Especially after what Robert had done.

Brax wasn't expecting her for at least another hour or two, but that didn't matter. She couldn't bear to be away from Walker for another minute.

It was getting dark by then. Time had slipped by while she'd wandered the mall. Was it possible for Walker to be afraid she'd left him—again? No, he was too young, wasn't he?

She wandered through a nearly empty parking lot and silently cursed herself for not parking under a light. Relieved to finally open the car door, something slammed into her from behind and sent her sprawling across the driver's side of Brax's car.

Not something. Someone.

Someone yanked her out of the car by her hair, pushed her against the door and pressed a gun against her back. "Quiet," a man rasped close to her ear, "or I'll blow a hole through you. You've already been more trouble than you're worth."

Bile rose in her throat. There was nobody to help her. Not a soul anywhere nearby.

"Where is Robert?"

"I don't know." She could barely hear herself, so she tried again. "I don't know where he is. I swear it."

"Where've you been for almost three weeks now? Is he out here? Is that why you came all this way?"

"I'm telling you. I don't have the first idea where he is. You're wasting your time."

That only earned her a jab in the back as he pressed the gun harder. "Where's the kid? You hiding him too?"

She swallowed against her rising horror, then gritted her teeth. How dare he even speak of her son?

"I have no idea what you're talking about. I don't know any kid." She turned her head just slightly, enough to make out part of the man's pockmarked face. "I'm telling you. Robert didn't exactly leave things on good terms between us. I might kill him myself if I ever see him again."

At least that part was true.

"Then who are you out here with? You ain't got no family. We know that much about you."

But they didn't know whether or not she was the mother of Robert's baby or where Walker was. They weren't as smart as they thought.

And they didn't know about Brax either. Otherwise, this thug would've mentioned him, if not by name, at least by description.

"It's none of your business. I already knew I made a mistake hooking up with Robert. I didn't know that mistake would haunt me this long." Also not a lie.

"Listen up." His body pressed her tighter against the car—the keys, wedged between her body and the door, dug into her ribs, but she didn't dare shift her weight or even breathe too deeply. "You better find out where Robert is and fast. We'll be watching you from now on, and we won't be so gentle next time."

He had her purse before she could think to react, shoving her against the car one last time. Her ribs screamed in protest as the breath left her lungs in a single rush and the world went slightly gray.

The squealing tires weren't loud enough to drown out the rush of blood in her ears.

Her purse. Her phone. All that money she'd been carrying around in case she needed to make a getaway. Everything she had in the world. Gone. Again.

But she was alive. And she had the car keys in her fist.

Once she was sure the other car was out of the lot, she opened the door and slid behind the wheel as gingerly as she could. Her ribs would hurt for a day or two, but that was fine compared to what might've happened.

"Breathe," she whispered, doing everything she could to drive normally. To not attract attention. It wouldn't do her any good to get pulled over when she'd just lost her license to a thug with a gun.

Somehow, she made it to the house without anyone following her there. With such light traffic, it would be difficult for anyone to follow her without being noticed. Another pair of headlights would stick out like a sore thumb, and no way could anybody drive that dirt road in the dark without flipping on their lights.

Her legs shook hard enough to send her tumbling into the house. Brax was by her side in an instant. "What's wrong? What happened?"

Was he holding her up? Yes, he was. She was in his arms, and he was holding her against him, and that was good. That was what she needed.

"My...my purse got stolen by some kids in the parking lot at the mall." Lies slid so easily out of her mouth nowadays.

"Are you okay? Did they hurt you?"

"Not really. One of them knocked me against the car, and I was dazed for a second. But that was it."

"How many were there? How old were they? Male, female?"

"Brax, please." She touched her forehead to his chest. "Let me breathe."

"Of course. I'm sorry." He held the back of her head in one hand, cradling it while his other arm held her close. "I'm so sorry that happened to you. You're safe now."

Safe. She barely managed to hold back a panicky laugh. There was no such thing as safe, not now. Maybe there never had been.

How could he keep her safe when she couldn't tell him the truth?

"I'll call some of my contacts with the San Antonio PD."

"No." She lifted her head. "Don't do that."

"Why not? They stole your purse, the little—"

"They're kids. I don't think what they did was okay, but

let's face it. I doubt I'll ever get anything back at this point. I should've parked closer to the mall. I shouldn't have stayed so late when there was hardly anybody there."

"This isn't your fault. Don't blame yourself." He touched her cheek with the backs of his fingers, letting them glide down to her jaw. The tenderness of this gesture both eased her and stirred something deep inside her to life. "You're positive you aren't hurt?"

"I'm not hurt—and that's another reason to let this go. It isn't worth the time it would take for me to go to the station and fill out a report. I'll never see my purse again."

"You're still shaking." He guided her to the couch. "Sit. Rest. You've been through a lot."

He had no idea.

What would happen if they found her? Watched her? Saw her with Walker?

What about Brax? What would they do to him if he tried to help her?

"It's been a stressful evening so far." She slid the elastic from her hair and shook it out over her shoulders, scrubbing her fingers into her scalp. What was she supposed to do now? She didn't even have her escape money. Nothing to support Walker with.

"It's been a stressful couple of weeks." Brax sat beside her, close enough for their legs to touch. She would normally have moved away out of reflex, but not now. Not when she needed the comfort of his nearness.

"It has, I guess. But I love it," she insisted, looking at him in mixed earnestness and panic. What was he leading up to? "I love being with Walker. I'm happy here."

"You need to step back, though. I've put too much in your hands. You're here alone all day. It would get to anybody."

It was a sick joke. Here he was, concerned for her and

completely missing the mark. This sweet, caring, generous man.

And all she could do was lie.

"Tomorrow's Friday," he mused. "Why don't you take the weekend off? I don't have anything pressing to manage. I could take Walker to meet my parents, and you can have the whole weekend to yourself. Think of it as a mini-vacation. Treat yourself. Go stay with some friends."

She bit back a hysterical laugh. *What friends*?

"I'll borrow one of my brothers' cars for the weekend, and you can take mine. If you get ticketed for driving without a license, call me and I'll use one of the favors the San Antonio PD owes me to get you out of it." He stood, smiling like it was all settled. "I should finish making dinner. I'm not half the cook you are, but you've inspired me to break out the pots and pans."

How was she supposed to say no? She had no legitimate reason to. He didn't know she'd lost every cent she had to her name—he thought she had a bank account, for heaven's sake, and that she'd been depositing the generous amounts of cash he paid.

There was no fighting it. She had no reason to say no unless she felt like confessing the entire truth. That wasn't going to happen.

"Okay." She shrugged with a sinking heart. "Sounds great."

Chapter Eleven

"You sure I can't get you something to eat?"

Tessa felt sorry for the waitress. The poor woman was only trying to earn a decent tip, or at least to turn over the table in hopes that the next customer to sit there would order a meal and leave a few bucks.

She offered an apologetic smile. "Just coffee for me. Thank you." The waitress frowned before walking away.

Tessa wanted to spill her guts, to put it all out there. How hungry she was. How the aroma of fried food and juicy burgers made her mouth water and her empty stomach clench up tight.

How almost every cent she had in the world was going to this endless cup of coffee, which at least she could get free refills on. It helped curb her appetite, though not by much.

And being inside the diner gave her someplace warm, dry and safe to while away the hours.

What a fun Friday night she was having.

Looking around, she was reminded of the world still turning. There were people whose lives made sense. People who went out on a Friday night, had fun and went to the diner for a plate of fries or a stack of pancakes to soak up the alcohol they'd just drank. People who got together with friends and talked about their week before comparing weekend plans.

Life went on for these people. They didn't know what it meant to live one lie after another. What it was like to feel her desperation. Forced to spend endless hours alone with nowhere to go, all so she could be with her baby. So his guardian wouldn't know about the lies Robert had concocted.

She wasn't the first person to deal with this, and she knew it. Being homeless, having no money.

Which was probably the only thing that kept her going. Knowing other people also dealt with challenges.

She chuckled at the sight of the purse sitting next to her in the booth. Brax had been so happy when he'd gotten the call that morning from her cell—somebody had turned it in at the police station after finding it in the mall parking lot. It hadn't gotten far after all.

Even her phone and wallet were still inside. Her driver's license, all of it.

Except for the money.

Just another cruel joke. Having to pretend to be happy her purse had been found. Brax didn't know she'd carried all of her money inside. And there was no way of telling him without revealing a whole lot more.

So even though she'd been terrified at the thought of losing Walker for the weekend and distraught at knowing she had no money, she'd marveled over how smart it had been for the officer to call the most recent contact in her cell and ask if they knew her. How lucky she was to have her wallet and phone back.

Right. Lucky.

It was easy to fall into despair, especially when she had the prospect of spending the night in the back seat of Brax's car to look forward to. Though all things considered, it was better than an alley.

A flash of light reflecting off metal caught her eye, made her look out the window. Pure reflex, nothing more than that.

Reflex fast enough that she was able to catch sight of a pockmarked face staring out from inside a car passing slowly outside.

She knew that face. She'd never forget it. Just like she'd never forget the sound of his voice as he'd warned her to find Robert.

What was she supposed to do? She was trapped, cornered, her heart thudding. The car rounded the block but would be back. She knew it in her bones.

Her hands shook as she dug around for the loose change she'd collected—she wouldn't stiff her waitress, even now.

The sight of her phone sitting there in the bag froze her in place.

Her phone. This confirmed that was how they kept finding her. Whenever she left it on, somebody came sniffing around. It was how they'd tracked her to the office building, how her attacker had found her at the mall.

Now, how he'd found her at the diner.

She dropped a handful of quarters on the table before ducking into the ladies' room, careful to keep her head down, her face turned away from the window in case the car came around again. She fought the impulse to run, struggled to remain calm, to act as if nothing out of the ordinary was going on.

Once she was inside with the door locked, she looked around. No, the windows were too narrow. No escape through there.

With a deep breath and a silent prayer, she erased the contacts in her phone—she couldn't leave Brax vulnerable—before leaving it lying on the counter and ducking out of the room.

It wasn't easy, cutting her last tie to the rest of the world, and it would be hard to explain how she lost it again. But whatever it took to make Brax believe her, she would do.

She kept her head down, taking the exit closest to the restroom rather than the main door out front. It was dark, almost eleven o'clock, with plenty of cars in the lot to hide behind.

The car pulled up near the door she'd just come out of. An older model, a little banged up. Professional villainy must not pay much, she guessed.

A few panic-filled minutes later, the passenger went inside. She could barely see over the hood of the car she'd hidden behind, crouching in weeds and broken glass. The pockmarked driver stayed behind the wheel, peering out over the lot.

She hardly dared breathe, much less move. Could he see her? Did he know she was there?

After a few minutes, the man came out from the diner and muttered something to the driver before getting back into the car and slamming the door. He was angry. They both were. Their voices carried her way, faint but audible. Plenty of unsavory words were thrown around.

Brax's car was only four down from the car she hid behind. The only real shot she had of getting away was putting as much distance between those two buffoons and herself as possible. As soon as they left, she'd have to get out of there.

She moved slowly, carefully, one eye always on her pursuers. They were arguing over what to do next, she guessed, too busy to notice any movement up ahead.

Or to notice Brax's car parked right in front of them. It was the same car she'd used at the mall, so one would think they'd stake it out until she appeared. They must not have considered it. Too busy wondering why they couldn't pin her down.

The driver pulled away—slowly, cautiously, like he was waiting for her to pop out from the shadows at any second. He wasn't a complete idiot. But he couldn't stay there all night, idling in the lot and blocking cars from leaving or entering.

She crept alongside the door and opened it just enough to slide inside, closing it quickly to kill the interior light. Her pursuers were gone. There was nobody to see.

That didn't mean she was out of danger, and she knew it.

Seatbelt fastened, hands at the perfect ten and two on the wheel—which she was practically crushing with her grip— she eased out of the lot and started driving.

But where could she go?

She certainly couldn't spend the entire night driving. There was only so much gas in the tank, and she had no money to refill it.

A deep, head-splitting yawn answered any further questions. She'd been up since five with Walker, and it was now half past eleven. Even a gallon of coffee couldn't combat her deep fatigue.

She eyed the parking lot of a supermarket. Would it be a good place to pull into and go to sleep?

Before she could make a decision, a flash of headlights in the mirror almost blinded her. She turned her head away, blinking hard. Some people were such jerks. There was no reason to follow so—

Her already cramping hands gripped the wheel harder as that familiar tingling sensation prickled at the back of her neck.

A sudden right turn pointed her in the direction of downtown. The car behind her took a right too.

He'd only gone around the block again.

Tears threatened to spill onto her cheeks. She couldn't let them. Wouldn't. It would mean she was beaten, but she hadn't been beaten yet.

The cars and cabs and pedestrians of a downtown Friday night were just what she needed. Not that she expected to blend in, but tailing her would be more of a challenge with so many obstacles to get around. As it was, groups of people crossed in the middle of the street, not bothering to walk to the corner. Cars double-parked to drop off and pick up. It took time just to creep from one light to the next.

Tessa steered around one of those double-parked cars and was glad to see the double-parker pulled out before her pursuers could get past. The pockmarked man leaned on the horn, shouting something that blended in with the noise of the street.

She took advantage of this and made a sharp left at the next corner, barely missing a couple who'd started to cross without seeing her. She winced, waving in apology before flooring the gas pedal, then took another left at the next corner.

Right, left. Doubling back on herself. Always checking in the mirror. She'd thought she'd caught a glimpse of her tail now and then, but never for long. There were too many people in the way, too many cars suddenly pulling out of spaces and blocking the view.

After an hour of playing cat and mouse with Robert's *friends*, Tessa was fairly confident she'd lost them for good. Her vision was starting to blur, and real, true exhaustion set in once the adrenaline rush calmed down.

She pulled in behind a dark strip mall. Another alley. She sensed a pattern, but at least nobody would come looking for her behind the row of stores.

And if they did, she mused as she stretched out along the back seat, she was too tired to make another successful getaway.

"WHAT ARE YOU doing up?"

Brax stopped walking halfway down the stairs at the sound of his mother's voice. She wasn't the only person in the kitchen. Both Sheila and Clinton Patterson were up and around at four in the morning.

He found them sitting at the table, both reading a newspaper that had to still be hot off the press. Coffee was brewing in a pot.

"Well?" Sheila asked, eyeing him from over the top of a page.

"I couldn't sleep." He pointed from one of them to the other. "And you two? Is this the norm?"

"We're both early birds, you know that." Clinton set down the section he'd been reading and picked up another.

"But four o'clock?"

They exchanged a look. "Well, we were hoping to be up when the baby wakes. You said he gets up before dawn."

"I should've known." Brax snickered, taking a seat at the table. "You're incorrigible."

But it meant the world to him. Watching his parents fall in love with his nephew. They'd taken the news in stride—neither of them had a great opinion of Robert, so the news of him skipping town and handing guardianship over hadn't shocked them much.

It only made sense for him to bring Walker to meet them. After all, they were the people who'd taught Brax what it meant to be part of a family.

"What kept you from sleeping?" Sheila leaned in with a

motherly expression, otherwise known as *scrutiny*. "I don't like those circles under your eyes."

"Thanks." He leaned back in his chair with a shrug and remembered being a kid. New to the entire concept of family. Resenting the questions his foster mother asked.

He wasn't that kid anymore.

Which was what made him sit up straight. "I kept worrying about the woman who takes care of Walker while I'm at work."

"Tessa, right?" Clinton asked, lowering the paper. "You mentioned her."

"Right. She's young, and she strikes me as being… wounded somehow. I wish I could explain it. She's troubled. Jumpy sometimes. She never offers any information about herself other than having taken care of Walker for a little while back in Eagle Pass. I gave her the weekend off to take care of herself since she's been with Walker twenty-four seven for two weeks straight. She deserved it."

"You said she stays with you?" his dad asked.

"Yes."

"So she's at the house now? Why not call her?"

"For one thing, it's not even dawn yet. She's probably asleep. For another, no, she's not at the house. I don't know where she went. She didn't share her plans."

Sheila cocked her head to the side. Brax knew that move. It meant he was in trouble.

"When did you give her this gift of free time?"

"Thursday night. I told her I'd taken the weekend off and she should do the same."

"And you forced her out of the house? Two weeks after forcing her to move in with you?"

"I didn't force her to do anything, Mom."

Clinton cleared his throat. "What your mother is trying

to say is, you gave that poor girl nowhere to go. What if she didn't have much money saved up? Not everybody can book a hotel room at the last minute. No wonder you're worried about her. Your subconscious is nagging you."

"You said she's secretive and jumpy," Sheila added. "What if you're her only means of safety right now? She couldn't have been living a safe, steady sort of life if she was able to pick up and move into your spare bedroom at a moment's notice. You could be the godsend she was waiting for."

"Oh, no." He held his head in his hands. Why hadn't he seen it sooner? "I should've thought about that. It's obvious she's been hiding something. She looked so fragile and alone when I first met her."

"Give her a call," Clinton suggested. "If you're worried enough about her that it kept you up all night, call her."

"It's too early."

"Call her anyway. You can ease your worries, and she'll know you were thinking about her. You can't lose."

Strange. It was like he'd been waiting for permission. The second he knew his parents thought it would be okay for him to call, he was up from the table and going out to the living room for a little privacy.

Tessa would forgive him for waking her up, wouldn't she?

"Where are you, bitch?"

Like he'd been slapped, Brax's head snapped back at the sound of the snarl that greeted him.

"What, you calling to see if we found your phone? Well, we did, you sneaky—"

"Who is this?" Brax barked, cutting the man off before he could insult Tessa again.

There was silence. Then, "Who's this?"

"I asked first. Who has this phone? Who are you? Where

are you?" From the corner of his eye, he caught sight of his parents entering the room. His mom held her hands over her mouth.

More silence. Then a beep to signal the call's end.

"What was that about?" Clinton asked.

"I have no idea. But some foul-mouthed bully has Tessa's phone." He called the number again, but this time it rang endlessly with no answer.

Memories of Thursday night hit him from all sides.

She'd been so shaken up—maybe too shaky for her purse to have been stolen by kids.

Did this have to do with whoever had mugged her at the mall?

He ran up to his room without further explanation and went straight to the laptop he'd left on the nightstand. Tessa was driving his car while he'd borrowed Chance's Jeep. All of their cars had GPS installed so they could track mileage as a tax deduction.

"Oh, you've got to be kidding me." The sight of Tessa's erratic driving patterns from just a few short hours ago made his stomach churn. Why had she been going up and down one street after another in the downtown section? Why had she spent a solid hour doubling back over herself?

And why was the car now parked at some strip mall?

Who was she meeting?

Or, worse, who'd stolen the car? What had happened to her?

One thing was clear: Tessa was in trouble.

He pulled on his clothes and headed downstairs again, where his parents waited. "Can you keep watch over Walker for a little while? I have to find her. There's trouble."

"Of course. Help her," Sheila urged.

He intended to do just that.

Chapter Twelve

Brax cursed himself the entire way to the location where Tessa had parked his car.

What had he been thinking? Had he thought at all?

It didn't seem that way, looking at the situation through new eyes. Now that his mom had set him straight, he couldn't believe he'd thought he was being the good guy by practically forcing Tessa out of the house for the weekend.

He didn't know the first thing about her. Not really. Nothing substantial. Only that she loved Walker. At least they agreed about that.

Otherwise? He'd imagined her going to a hotel, maybe getting a manicure or whatever young women did when they wanted to pamper themselves. A facial, a haircut. It wasn't like he knew a lot about those things.

Now, he tried to imagine the situation through the eyes of a woman with nowhere else to go.

But why didn't she have any other options? That was the question. He had nothing but questions about her.

She was behind a strip mall. He rounded the corner of the store on the end and instantly made out the shape of his car parked in the shadows of a line of trees behind the loading area.

And the sight of another car swinging into view at the

opposite end of the mall, headlights washing over the glass-strewn concrete. It was barely dawn. What were they doing there?

It was clear soon enough as the car stopped and two men jumped out and headed straight for his car, marching with fisted hands swinging at their sides.

Brax acted before he thought, flooring the gas pedal, tires squealing as he raced their way. His approach startled them both into stopping.

"What are you doing?" he demanded on rushing out of the Jeep. "Get out of here."

One of them snorted. "Get lost, boy scout."

"I don't know who you're looking at, but I'm well past the age of being a boy scout." When the second man continued toward the car, even trying to open one of the doors, he shouted, "I said, leave it alone."

"Who the hell are you?"

"I'm the guy whose car you're touching, and you might want to take your hands off it right damn now." Brax didn't raise his voice.

Suddenly, so suddenly all three of them jumped in surprise, the door swung open and out popped Tessa.

Brax didn't have time to figure out the implications of this—Had she slept in the car? Why?—before he caught sight of what she held in one hand.

The bat he'd forgotten he'd left in the back seat.

"Get in the Jeep!" he shouted, moving forward to put himself between Tessa and the men now stalking toward her.

One of the men shoved him, or tried to, and was visibly surprised when Brax didn't budge. And even more surprised when Brax's fist crashed into his jaw and sent him falling back.

Tessa grunted. Brax turned to her, ready to kill whoever

had put their hands on her, but found that she'd grunted in the act of swinging the bat and it connecting with the second man.

"He was going to jump you from behind," she gasped, looking down at the man who'd collapsed with both hands against his lower back.

Brax didn't waste time waiting for the guys to recover. He took her hand, running for the Jeep. She jumped inside and within moments, they'd fled the lot.

"They'll follow us." She sounded so confident. And so flat. Matter-of-fact.

"I trust they will." It was the Riviera cartel. It had to be. They'd been searching for his car.

And he might've gotten her killed.

She turned in the seat, peering behind them. "Yeah, I see a car coming out of the parking lot. Turn as soon as you can. They might not see us yet, especially if they're both dazed."

"They'll be dazed and furious," he grunted, knowing the lengths men like that would go to make somebody pay for hurting them. He took a quick right, tires squealing, and thanked his lucky stars there weren't many cars on the road at this time of the morning.

She faced forward again. "Maybe that little side street," she suggested, pointing up ahead. How was she still so calm? Was she in shock?

She should've been screaming. Demanding answers. If he hadn't gotten there when he had…

He turned onto the side street and cruised a little more slowly. They were now in a residential area. The last thing he wanted was to strike an innocent bystander out for their morning jog.

Tessa looked behind them again. "I think they just turned

onto the street three blocks back. I can't really make out the car."

"Okay." He took a left, then another quick left, before making a right, which led back to the commercial area. There was a road ahead that he knew led out of town.

"How did you know where to find me?" she asked, still looking behind them.

"I wasn't sure I'd find you there. I was looking for my car."

"Why?"

Guilt raced through him. She'd really flip her lid now. Bracing himself, he explained, "I was worried, so I tracked the car's GPS. I tried calling you earlier, but a man picked up and shouted at me. Did you lose your phone?"

"I left it at a diner."

He waited for more explanation. She didn't offer one.

"Okay." He drew out the word. What was she trying to get at? Why would she leave her phone behind?

That choice of words too. She'd left it. She didn't lose it. She didn't forget it. She'd performed a deliberate act. And it didn't seem to come as a shock that he'd tracked her. Like she didn't care.

Why?

"Wait." She clutched his shoulder. Now he was in for it. This was where she'd lose it on him. "Where's Walker?"

"He's fine. He's with my parents." She let out a sigh that sounded a lot like relief before letting go of him. Was that all she cared about?

Not the fact that two men had almost attacked her?

"I'm so sorry." He checked the mirror for signs of them on his tail. "This is all my fault. I've put you in danger. It's unforgivable."

She didn't reply. It had to be shock. No wonder. She'd been through something that had probably traumatized her.

He had done this to her.

After an hour of driving aimlessly, erratic turns and more than a few blown stoplights, Brax was positive they'd lost their tail. Tessa sat upright, unable or unwilling to relax.

"I think we're safe. Let's go back to my parents' house for now. We'll figure out what to do when we get there."

"Okay."

He glanced over and found her checking the mirrors. Still watching.

Seeing her like that was the final nail in the coffin. He knew what he had to do. There was no excuse for dragging her into his problems, for ruining her life, for putting her through this.

"Tessa, I have to tell you this. You can't work for me anymore." It was one of the hardest things he'd ever forced himself to say.

He didn't want it this way. In fact, now that he'd said it, he knew just how much he wanted the opposite. For her to stay. To be part of his life. But she didn't deserve to be hunted and attacked. Having her in his life was too risky. Her safety mattered more than his feelings for her.

She made a sound that seemed almost like a wounded animal. "No, please. I can't… I can't…"

"I'm sorry. You can't understand how much I hate this."

"But…no. Please. I need…"

He scrubbed a hand down his face. She was scared of losing her income. "Hey, don't worry. I'll give you another two weeks' salary to hold you over until you find another job. Can you find a place to stay? I'll help you with that too."

He glanced over at her. She was shaking, wrapping her arms around her middle like she might fly apart. Her eyes were darting around the Jeep. "What did I do wrong? Why are you sending me away?"

He recognized a panic attack when he saw one and sped up. "Tessa, you have to breathe. We'll get you through this. Don't panic."

"Don't panic?" She laughed—bitter, jagged—then sucked in a breath. "I can't leave you and Walker! Don't make me, please. I'll do whatever you want, I swear. Don't make me leave."

"This is for your safety."

Her arms wrapped tighter around herself. She was rocking back and forth. "Please let me stay. Please."

By the time he pulled up in front of his parents' house, she was almost hysterical, shaking from the force of her emotions. Some of this had to be residual from this morning, but he couldn't add to it.

"Hey." He reached out, touching her shoulder. "Hey, it's going to be okay. If you really want to stay, you can."

She nodded over and over. "I do. Thank you."

She was thanking *him*? He was just hoping he wasn't about to put her in danger again.

He offered her a smile that started out forced but became genuine once he saw her palpable relief. And he couldn't deny the relief he felt in turn. He hadn't wanted Tessa to leave, even if it was for her own safety.

Now all that was left was figuring out how to move forward.

Chapter Thirteen

Tessa opened her eyes slowly. Why were they so heavy? It would be better to go back to sleep. She was so comfortable...

It all rushed back at once before sleep could overtake her again.

The fight in the parking lot. The zigzagging around trying to lose the men following them. Doing the same thing by herself, terrified, unable to call anybody for help.

Her eyes opened fully, and she looked around. Where was she?

The hazy memory of Brax leading her into the house came back in pieces. Only once she'd seen Walker for herself did she let Brax put her to bed. Everything was blank after that.

She'd had a breakdown. The memory made her wince in embarrassment. He had to think she was off her rocker. She couldn't help it, though, not when he'd told her she had to go. The idea of being kept away from Walker again was too much.

It had broken her. Combined with the fear and exhaustion, she had lost her grip. There'd been nothing left in her.

Now, she had to find a way to look him in the eye. It was humiliating.

He would have questions. Although for some reason, it was as if he blamed himself for those goons coming after her. Why would he think that? Now that she could think clearly, it was obvious he'd told her to look for another job because he thought it was for the best. Hadn't he mentioned her safety?

Or was that just an excuse to get rid of her?

Judging by the amber light coming through the window, she'd slept most of the day away. Great, now his entire family would think she was a crackpot or a druggie like Robert had claimed.

Humiliating or not, she had to get out of bed and face the consequences of her actions.

After freshening up in the hall bathroom, she crept downstairs. There were voices in the kitchen, one of which was Brax's. Would he hate her? Or—and this was somehow worse—pity her?

"Hey, look who's up," Brax greeted her with a smile. He slid out the chair next to him at the long table. "How are you feeling?"

"Better now that I've slept, thanks."

What mattered more than anything, what her eyes kept darting over to look at, was her son. He was in the arms of a beautiful woman with a warm smile. Even when Walker took a fistful of her dark hair and pulled, she only laughed indulgently.

"Tessa? I'm Clinton Patterson." Brax's dad. His large hand engulfed hers. "And this is my wife, Sheila."

"I'm glad to meet you. Thank you for letting me sleep here for a little while. I was—"

"Think nothing of it." There wasn't so much as a hint of anything but pure kindness in Sheila's voice, in her expression. "I'm glad to see you looking better. We were worried about you when you first got here. You looked worn out."

That was an understatement.

Walker burst out with a string of very forceful babble, making them all laugh. "This one's going to have a lot to say once he learns to talk, isn't he?" Clinton leaned over him, making funny faces, and Walker giggled before taking one of the man's fingers in his fist.

"What a grip!" Clinton gasped in mock surprise, which made Walker giggle again.

They were sweet people, but then she'd figured that out already. The sort of people with room in their hearts for children in need of love. Watching them take to Walker the way they did was a beautiful thing.

Though pretending she didn't ache to hold him wasn't exactly easy.

Clinton turned to Brax. "While I have you here, can you help me move some boxes in the garage?"

"Sure." Brax glanced at Tessa like he was wary of leaving her alone with his mom. She did her best not to look too nervous.

It helped that Walker seemed so happy. Sheila bounced him on her hip with a grin that almost touched her ears. "He's such a sweetheart."

"He is," Tessa agreed. She folded her arms across her chest to keep from reaching for him. It was torture not being able to hold him after everything she'd gone through in the past twenty-four hours.

"I'm about to get dinner started." Sheila appeared to study Tessa, arching an eyebrow. "Can you hold him for me while I cook?"

"Yes, of course." It was nothing less than a gift. She held

out her arms and gratefully accepted her baby, hugging him tight and kissing his forehead. "Hey, buddy. I missed you."

"It's nice to have a baby around." Sheila got to work chopping vegetables. "So, tell me about yourself. Brax says you've been a miracle. I guess you can understand how unprepared he was."

She sensed Walker's honorary grandmother was giving her the third degree, but at least Sheila was kind and gentle about it.

"There isn't much to tell," Tessa admitted. "My parents died in a car accident two years ago. I've been on my own since then."

"Oh, I'm so sorry." It wasn't mere lip service. Sincerity poured from her.

"It sort of derailed my plans," she continued. "You know, college and all that. I had to focus on supporting myself."

"Naturally." Sheila glanced up from the cutting board. "So, you're a nanny now?"

"Right. I love it. I love being around kids." One in particular, whose head she kissed again.

"I know the feeling. It's part of the reason my husband and I decided to adopt. That, and we shared a desire to provide what children were missing. Like Brax, for example."

Tessa listened harder. She couldn't help it.

"He's a charmer, my son," Sheila chuckled before blowing a whistle between pursed lips. "He could charm the birds from the trees, that one. Always quick with a smile or a joke. Very clever too. Many's the time I wished he wasn't half so clever."

Tessa grinned. "I bet."

"But it could've turned out much differently." Sheila wasn't joking anymore. Her brows drew together. "He was alone for most of his childhood. Neglected. Very poor. It seems to me he remembers that experience and the memories are what make him determined to help others. He's protective of people in similar situations. All alone, fending for themselves."

"I see."

"I would hate to see anybody take advantage of that."

They exchanged a look that spoke volumes, said more than words ever could. "I would hate that too," Tessa murmured.

"I thought you would." Sheila wiped her hands on her apron before going to the fridge. "He was a tough nut to crack, even though it might be hard to imagine now. It took a while to get through to him. He held a lot of secrets he wasn't ready to share. That's a heavy burden for anyone to carry."

The woman's back was to her, half-bent while looking through the fridge, so Tessa couldn't see her face. How much did she know? Why was she conveniently talking about secrets?

What had Brax told her?

It couldn't have been anything too bad, since Sheila was smiling when she turned back toward Tessa and Walker. "It's important to trust people, I think. Good people. Brax is a good man—all of my sons are. They've helped so many. It seems they have a limitless capacity for compassion and service."

"And they have you to thank for that."

"I can't take all the credit. My husband had a hand in it too."

"Hey." Brax joined them a moment later, looking between the women like he was trying to decide if everything was okay. "How's it going in here?"

"Oh, you know. Just chatting while Walker does his

darndest to understand what we're saying." Sheila beamed at Walker, who waved his fists.

Brax touched Tessa's back. "We'd better get moving."

Sheila sighed. "I was fixing dinner for you!"

"Sorry. I need to talk to the others about what happened this morning and I have to pick up my car. Chance would probably like his Jeep back at some point." He looked to Tessa with a sheepish shrug. "I'm sorry."

"You don't owe me an apology." They got Walker's things together and said goodbye to the Pattersons.

"I expect to see you both again, and soon." Sheila hugged Tessa before letting her out the door, then kissed Walker's chubby cheeks. "I could just eat him up."

"Not if I do it first." They laughed together before Tessa followed Brax to the Jeep.

Inside the Jeep was a different story. There was no laughter.

In fact, Brax looked downright murderous. "I have to tell you something I should've told you way before now. I never imagined it would seep into my personal life."

"What is it?"

"I'm testifying in a few days against the Riviera cartel. I don't know if you've ever heard of them."

"I'd have to be living under a rock to never hear the name."

"Yeah, well, it looks like they already put one of the two witnesses out of commission. I don't know whether the heart attack he had was natural or induced. Either way, it looks like they're coming after me now. I was so confident they didn't know who I was, but what other explanation is there?"

Silence hung heavy between them as Tessa struggled to process this. "You...think what happened this morning was related to the cartel trouble?"

"They found my car. Why else would they be looking for it? That's why I wanted to let you go. I didn't want you to suffer over this again. You've been through enough because of me."

On one hand, her heart swelled at the thought of him caring that much about her. Wanting to keep her out of harm's way.

On the other hand, she just about wanted to melt away under the weight of her guilt. He thought he was the reason she was being stalked.

Sheila's comment about the burden of secrets rang out in Tessa's memory. That was no random piece of wisdom—she'd known it at the time too. Sheila Patterson was a mother through and through, dropping little bits of advice without coming right out with the unvarnished facts.

There was nothing left to do but tell the truth. She owed it to Brax.

She owed it to her son.

What if he takes Walker away? The question made her shiver. The fact was, unless they played it safe from now on, one of the goons looking for Robert might kidnap Walker to get to him. More than likely Robert wouldn't care. He'd be too concerned about his own life to worry about his son's.

But those creeps wouldn't know that, would they?

Walker's safety meant more than anything.

So much, in fact, that Tessa cleared her throat. "There's something you need to know. I should've told you from the beginning, but I was too afraid."

"Afraid? Of what?" He didn't sound surprised, she noticed. He'd always treated her like he was waiting for her to come clean about something or other. Like he would accept her explanations even if he didn't actually believe them.

The phone rang before she could continue. Brax touched a button on the steering wheel to answer. "Hello?"

"It's Weston." He didn't sound happy. "Is Tessa with you?"

"Yeah, she's right here." Brax glanced her way.

She couldn't breathe.

"I'm sorry to tell you this," Weston continued, "but she isn't who she says she is. You need to be careful."

Chapter Fourteen

"Weston? I think you should know you're on speaker." Brax looked to Tessa for some sign. Some surprise or shock. Something.

She sat still, staring straight ahead. The only thing to give away the strain she was under was the way she clenched her fists in her lap.

"Do you want me to call back later? When you're alone?"

"Don't bother." Tessa's voice was heavy with…defeat? Fatigue? "Go ahead."

"What's going on?" Brax demanded. It didn't matter which of them thought the question was directed their way.

Weston sighed heavily. "I found Walker's birth certificate. According to this, his mother's name is Theresa Mahoney."

It was a good thing Brax was pulling down the road, just in front of the house. He might've gotten them in an accident otherwise. As it was, he felt like he'd just been run over by an eighteen-wheeler.

Walker's mother wasn't dead. *Tessa* was his mother.

He pulled to a stop and put the Jeep into Park but didn't bother opening the door. Neither did she. Walker slept in the back, blissfully unaware.

"Tessa's parental rights were stripped," Weston continued. "Due to drug use. And, of course, she's never worked for a nanny service. She tricked us."

It got worse with every passing second.

Brax looked to her for something, anything. Explanation. Anger. Instead, there she was, slumped against the door like she wanted to melt into it. If that wasn't an admission of guilt, he didn't know what was.

"I'm sorry to break it to you like this. But I thought you needed to know."

It took a second for Brax to find his voice. "Thanks. I'll call you later."

The silence was unbearable. Heavy, thick, making it hard to breathe. For someone who'd been able to come up with quick responses and charming phrases all his life, being left with nothing to say was a new experience.

"Is there a reason I didn't hear about this from you?" he finally asked.

"I didn't know if you'd want to listen." She ran a hand under both eyes.

"You'd better believe I want to hear your side of this after you've lied all these weeks."

"What was I supposed to do?" She whirled on him. Instead of screaming, her voice fell into a hissing whisper, which was somehow more effective than the shrillest shriek.

"Yes, I'm Walker's mother. And the reason I came to you was because I had nowhere else to go. The day you called about Walker, that first day, I got home from work and found my apartment ransacked. They stole my money and threatened to beat me up. All because they were looking for Robert and figured I knew where to find him."

"Did you?"

"He took our son away from me because he's a spiteful, hateful monster. Why would he tell me anything about his plans?" She snorted. "He dropped me the minute he got what he wanted."

So far that sounded like Robert.

She looked into the back seat, and her gaze softened a little. "I had nowhere else to go. I didn't even know you had Walker until you called. Robert took him away."

"You had nothing to do with that?"

Her head snapped around again, and he wished he hadn't said it. "You know your brother. Do you think he's beyond setting me up?"

"Did he?"

She raised an eyebrow. "I've lived with you for more than two weeks. Have I ever given you even the slightest indication I had a drug problem?"

"You could've gotten yourself clean by now."

He had never seen so much disdain packed into a single eye roll. "Fine. But it isn't true. What Robert said isn't true at all. He set me up, lied about me and he took Walker away. Why he would do that when he was only going to hand him over to you, I have no idea. I've never been able to understand him."

That made two of them.

"How did you get involved with him in the first place?"

She shrugged with a sigh. "I was a cocktail waitress at a casino in Eagle Pass. He was in there a lot. Charming. Handsome. I had just lost my parents not long before that and was on my own. Lonely." Another quick hand under her eyes.

Brax bit back his sympathy in favor of letting her talk. Hadn't he wanted to know the truth about her all this time?

"Maybe a week after we slept together, Robert stopped calling. Looking back, I realize I shouldn't have been surprised. He didn't care about me. But I was hurt and angry. Then I found out I was pregnant. I managed to get hold of him. He told me the baby couldn't be his because he'd used protection. So I was on my own again."

"I have to ask." Damn it. This was a hard question. "Are you sure Walker is his—"

"He was the only one," she snapped.

"Okay."

"If he wasn't going to help me I decided I would make it on my own. I worked hard. Took extra shifts. Started cleaning houses on the side to make extra money."

"While pregnant?"

"I had to support the baby somehow, didn't I? But it was okay. I guess it felt like I had a purpose again. A direction. Without my parents, I'd lost my way. Nothing bad, but I was drifting. I stopped taking my college classes, stopped seeing friends. With the baby to work for, there was a reason to get out of bed every morning."

She looked down at her hands. "Robert showed up at the hospital when Walker was born. Said he was sorry and that he wanted to be part of our lives. I was stupid enough to believe him. He even stuck around my apartment for the first two weeks. I told myself he wasn't as helpful as he could've been because he didn't know anything about babies. But there were other things that weren't so easy to explain away. Like the way he kept peeking out the window from behind the curtains."

"I have a feeling I know where this is going."

"He got a call after two weeks. I don't know who it was from, but it was enough to get him to pack up his things and tell me he was only using me and Walker as a way to hide out. He didn't really want to be a father. I shouldn't expect to see him again."

Brax winced. He could almost see it playing out in his head.

"It was okay, though. There was another single mom in my building who worked during the day shift. I watched her little girl along with Walker while she was working, and she watched Walker for me at night so I could work."

"You must've been exhausted."

"Yeah." She sighed. "But we were making it. I could pay the rent, keep him in diapers and get formula and clothes, feed myself. It was hard, but it was good. He was worth it."

Another heavy sigh. "Robert came back when Walker was almost two months old, and said he wanted to be part of our lives again. This time I told him to get lost."

"Good for you."

"It wasn't good enough for him, though. I know that now. A couple of days later, I was leaving the casino when a man bumped into me. That's all I remember. He bumped into me, and everything got blurry. Somehow I made it home, but I was fuzzy and my coordination was all off. When CPS showed up, I was completely unable to pull it together."

Her breathing picked up speed. "They took Walker away. Pulled him out of my arms. He was screaming. I knew in my head that I had to do something, but I couldn't understand anything coming out of my mouth no matter how hard I tried to make sense. All I remember is them saying somebody reported me for neglect and drug use. It was a nightmare. The sort of thing you see in a movie. It kept getting worse. Robert made it look like the whole 'being on drugs' thing was the norm. I know now that whoever bumped into me must've injected something, but I couldn't prove it. I couldn't prove I was a good mother. He got a judge to permanently revoke my parental rights."

She snorted. "I didn't have any money or any way to prove I was innocent. I didn't know what to do."

Walker stirred and fussed. It gave Brax an excuse to get

out of the car. Sitting there wondering what to believe—whether it was right or wrong to take what he knew about Robert and allow himself to believe his brother would go that far—would drive him crazy before long.

He unstrapped Walker and held him against his shoulder. Tessa got out on her side. "Do you believe me or not?"

"I don't know."

She shook her head, color bleeding from her face. "You think I'd make up something like this?"

Brax faced her in front of the Jeep. "Do I think Robert would stoop to anything? Yes. Do I believe he'd completely make up something like this? It's hard. Why would he even want a baby?"

Tessa's eyes filled with tears. And he realized how unbelievably stupid it was not to believe her. Playing it smart and exercising caution were one thing. But this was a woman with nothing to lose because she'd already lost everything.

And she loved Walker. *That* Brax could have zero doubt about.

"I don't think you'd make this up," he had to admit. "I believe Robert would sink to any level to get what he wanted. I couldn't have guessed he would ever stoop this low, though. I'm sorry he did that to you."

"Thank you."

"That doesn't mean I'm not furious with you for lying the way you did. For weeks. Every time I asked you about yourself. Every time I commented on how good you were with him. You pretended to be a nanny. You—"

"I didn't know how you would react." Her tears spilled over. She didn't brush them away this time. "I figured you would take Walker away just like CPS did. Like Robert did. I couldn't lose him again."

She wrung her hands together as her eyes met her son's,

and the tears fell faster than ever. "I... I can't lose him. When you told me I couldn't work for you anymore, it felt like my heart was literally breaking. There was pain in my chest, I swear. I don't think I could take it if I couldn't be with him."

Walker whimpered.

"Mama loves you," she said to the baby, but didn't reach for him.

He felt like a monster. "Here. Take him." Brax handed Walker over rather than torture Tessa any longer.

"Thank you, thank you." She closed her eyes, kissing the baby's cheeks and forehead.

Anyone with eyes could see she adored her son. Brax's heart softened. If he had been in her position, what would he have done? How many people would he have lied to if he felt powerless to do anything else?

She opened her eyes. "The people looking for Robert are the ones who took my purse at the mall. They were using my phone to track me. They don't know about you and Robert being brothers, and they don't know the baby is here. I made sure of that."

That was enough for him. She could've told those thugs about him to get them to leave her alone. Instead, she'd chosen to protect him.

He folded his arms. "No more secrets."

She shook her head. "No more secrets."

"Okay." When he draped an arm over her shoulders and led her to the house, she didn't shrug away from his touch. "We'll work this out together."

Chapter Fifteen

Telling the truth hadn't been easy. Putting it out there and hoping Brax would understand. Leaving her life in his hands.

Tessa kissed Walker for the fiftieth time since Brax had handed him to her. Coming clean had been worth the fear. And this was her reward.

"Come on, buddy," she whispered, guiding the bottle to Walker's mouth. "Let's have our dinner so you can go to bed."

Brax was on the phone, pacing the kitchen. She could hear him down there from the nursery, though there was no making out exactly what he said.

It was enough to know he believed her. And she'd believed him when he'd told her so. This wasn't a game to lure her into trusting him.

"There I was," she whispered to Walker with a smile, "thinking he'd call the cops before I even finished, you know? I just knew he wouldn't believe me. That he would take you away. But he surprised me."

Brax's deep voice reverberated from downstairs.

"He's a surprising man," she concluded as Walker finished his bottle.

She burped and changed him before putting him down

to sleep. His fine hair was so soft under her fingers as she stroked his head. "I love you so much. Nobody's going to take you away again. You know how I know? Because your uncle Brax is on it now."

He was in the process of wrapping things up on the phone when she went downstairs. "We'll touch base on that first thing in the morning. For now, let's look up the paperwork involved in the custody case and follow up with CPS about the reports."

He turned to her when she reached the doorway leading from the dining room. "They're on it. And once my brothers decide to get to the bottom of something, consider it done."

"I can't thank you enough. For everything."

He cocked an eyebrow, eyes twinkling. "What did I do?"

"Are you kidding? Or is this your way of getting me to list everything you've done for me so far?" She held up a hand, counting off on her fingers. "You gave me somewhere to live when I had literally nowhere to go. You believed me when you could've easily called the cops and turned your back on me. You called your brothers and got them on the case. And this won't be the end of it. You'll find ways to keep amazing me."

It was gratifying, the way his charming smile slid into sheepishness. "Don't worry about it. I know Robert, and I'm so very sorry he hurt you."

There was no way to answer that, so she shrugged it off. "I'm starving. I can get something together for us."

"Don't bother with that." He placed his hands on her shoulders and steered her to the table. "Take a seat. I'll handle dinner."

"You don't have to do that."

"You deserve to have somebody take care of you after everything you've been through. It's the least I can do." He bent, looking through the fridge. "Though I can't guarantee it'll be gourmet cuisine. We're a little low on supplies. I didn't plan on coming back until tomorrow."

"I don't need anything gourmet." She rested her head on her palm, watching him. There was something to be said for a man who knew his way around the kitchen.

Especially when the man in question looked like Brax.

He eyed her while opening a jar of spaghetti sauce. "You had a little time to talk with Mom today. Did she scare you off?"

Tessa laughed softly, since the opposite was true. "I doubt she could scare anybody off."

"Think again. But you're not a teenager with an attitude, so it's probably different for you."

"I guess she had to be pretty tough to keep you guys in line."

"We didn't always make it easy on her." He poured the sauce into a pan and covered it, setting it aside while a larger pot filled with water in the sink. "But somehow, she and Dad made it work. And let me tell you, I never imagined I'd look at my brothers as anything but strangers. Now? They're more my brothers than Robert will ever be."

She frowned at the sound of his name. It was sort of a habit. "How the two of you could share DNA is beyond me."

"I think being half brothers helps—and the fact that we weren't raised together. We didn't even know about each other until I did one of those genetic test things a few years back."

"Oh, really?"

"Yeah, one of those late-night impulse decisions. Ordering the test, spitting into a tube." He lifted a shoulder like it didn't matter, but Tessa noticed the way he averted his eyes. It had obviously mattered, finding his blood relatives.

"So you share a..."

"Father. He was an affair my mom had. Or rather, my father was already married to Robert's mother."

She winced. "I see."

"He never acknowledged me. I was nine when my mother died. Without a father willing to claim me and no other family, I went into foster care."

"I'm really sorry."

Another shrug. He salted the pasta water before turning to the pantry. "I had a hard time. I thought I was a pretty tough kid by the time Mom and Dad took me in. The Pattersons, I mean. Two years on the streets and in some sketchy foster homes had hardened me, and life hadn't exactly been easy before then."

"But you came around."

"I did. It wasn't easy for anybody, of course, but I got there. I was one of the lucky ones."

He turned to her with a sigh, concern etched on his handsome face. Even more handsome now that he knew about her past and hadn't turned her away.

Before now, she couldn't have imagined him being more attractive than he already was, since he'd been heart-stopping the second she'd laid eyes on him.

"To be honest, that's one of the reasons we all want to help Walker. He told me you were dead. It never occurred to me to fact check that info. And if I refused to take custody or accused Robert of dropping him on me and lying about our arrangement, Walker would've gone into foster care. Nobody wanted that."

She shivered at the thought. "Thank you again, then. For taking care of my son."

"Hey, he's a cute kid. And just about as smart as his uncle, but not quite."

"Considering he's barely more than five months old, I don't know what that says about you."

It was good to hear Brax laugh, and it felt good to laugh along with him. If it wasn't for the whole Robert-on-the-run situation, they might be any other couple in the world enjoying a quiet night together.

Wow. Had she just thought of them as a couple?

"Like I said, nothing fancy." Brax brought a steaming bowl of spaghetti to the table to go with the salad he'd already prepared and freshly warmed rolls.

"Nothing fancy? I lived on cereal and instant noodles for way longer than I feel comfortable admitting. This is a feast."

Tessa attacked her food. It wasn't until then that she realized that she hadn't had much of an appetite for a long time. The weight of secrets and fear had been heavy.

"I have to ask you something." He rested his elbows on the table, and she didn't think it would be right to correct him. "What attracted you to Robert? I know you said he was charming."

Yes, he used to be, and now that Tessa understood the specifics of his relationship to Brax, she knew their father must've been a real handsome devil of a man. He'd passed those looks on to both of his sons, along with his charm.

"What else did I need?" She shrugged. "Like I said, I was lonely. He must've seen that in me. Some people know how to home in on that and take advantage."

"He's the type, of that I have no doubt." Brax shook his head in disgust as he took his plate to the sink.

Funny how his father had passed on his selfishness to Robert but not to Brax.

Brax was good. Honest. Decent. Even after being hit

with some of the worst life had to offer, he hadn't become hard and cold.

"At least let me help with the dishes," she offered, bringing her plate to the sink. "How about you dry? I'll wash up."

"You won't get an argument out of me." He grinned. "I hate washing dishes. I'll cook all day, but I'd have to use disposable plates."

She only shook her head with a smile. "Let me guess, washing dishes was one of your chores as a kid."

"How'd you know?" he asked as she giggled helplessly.

"Cooking was my chore once I was old enough to handle it. But unlike you, that only made me love it."

"That's because it's possible to lend a little imagination to cooking, and it's a lot more gratifying. There's only so many ways to wash a dish. It's not much fun."

"It can be." She shrugged, biting back a smile.

"How?"

She splashed him with sudsy water. "That's how!"

"No fair!" He reached into the sink and splashed her, then blew a mountain of suds toward her face.

Laughing uncontrollably, she tried to duck out of the way, but the wet floor had ideas of its own. She slipped, arms pinwheeling as she lost control of her body.

"Careful!" Brax was still laughing when he caught her before she hit the floor. "See? That's what you get for trying to be cute."

She looked up into his shining eyes, breathless and giggling and having more fun than she'd had in a very long time. Something she saw there silenced her. She could hardly breathe.

He hooked a finger under her chin, tipping her head back. Her eyes drifted to his lips a heartbeat before those lips touched hers.

He was so different from Robert.

The fact that Robert came into her thoughts at all seemed like a sacrilege, but there was no helping the comparison at first. It came up on its own, without her consciously thinking about it.

Robert had been slick. Forcing his way into her mouth like he was staking a claim on her. Caring only about how it made him feel. Brax was in an entirely different league— no big surprise, since he was in a different league in every other way imaginable.

He took his time, moving his lips against hers in a firm but gentle way. Wanting, but not forcing. Coaxing her.

The hand under her chin cupped her cheek while the other pressed against the small of her back and pulled her closer. She reveled in it, since there was no way to be close enough to him. Her hands rested against his chest where his heart hammered away. Hers did too, slamming against her ribs, leaving her weak and fluttery.

It was the most thrilling sensation. The sort of first kiss a woman dreamed about after reading about it in books or seeing it in movies. The sort of kiss she'd never imagined anybody would give her.

When his arm tightened around her and the kiss deepened, her entire body came alive. Yes, this was what she wanted. This was right and perfect. The scent of his cologne, his warm breath on her face, the sense of safety in his strong arms.

It ended too soon.

She leaned in a little further, chasing after what he was taking away. Her heart ached almost as much as her unsatisfied body.

"I'm sorry," Brax murmured, stroking her cheek one more time before letting his hands fall to his sides.

"Is it me?" she whispered. Was she not what he wanted?

"Oh, no. No, that's not it at all." He crammed his fists into his pockets, shoulders raised near his ears. "Believe me. I want you, Tessa. Badly."

"You do?"

He managed a faint smile. "Too much, maybe. But it wouldn't be right this way. You're caught up in a situation beyond your control. Let's get that settled and clear your name, and then we can focus on...us. If that's what you want."

That was what she wanted—that and so much more.

Before she could say anything to embarrass herself, the sound of Walker's cries came from the monitor on the counter. It was almost a relief having an excuse to leave the kitchen and gather herself a little. She made a quick escape with her cheeks still flushed and her lips tingling from Brax's kiss.

Just when she thought there couldn't be more of a reason to clear her name.

Chapter Sixteen

Two days of looking into Tessa's story had left Brax more certain of one thing than he'd ever been: Robert needed a good throttling. He'd needed one for a long time.

"I knew he wasn't exactly a sweetheart," he murmured, passing files back and forth among his brothers. "But this takes being a rotten human being to a new level."

"He's playing in the pros," Luke grunted.

"He could manage an entire team." Chance blew out a low whistle at the report of the accident that had killed Tessa's parents. "Wild. No matter how many times I see something like this, it always shakes me up a little. One minute they were on their way to dinner. The next? It's over."

Brax only half heard his brother's musings. What concerned him was Tessa. How it must've felt to lose her parents so suddenly. How terrified she must've been. How alone.

One of those little reminders of life's unpredictability. "Never get too comfortable. You never know when it'll end."

"Wow." Weston rubbed his temples with a rueful grin. "We're a cheerful team today."

Brax sank into the chair behind his desk. "What I can't understand is why Robert would go to all the trouble of taking Walker away—setting Tessa up, concocting stories for CPS—if he was planning on leaving the kid with me. He stole his son. Not an easy thing to do, and punishable by law if it turns out the reports were faked. Up to two years in jail, a sizable fine. He took a real risk."

"He probably didn't count on getting himself in trouble." Luke shrugged. "Though knowing him, even as little as I do, I can't imagine why, considering he was always in trouble for something or other."

"Arrogant." Weston sighed. "That sort of person has to be arrogant. They have to believe they're untouchable. That they'll be able to get out of any situation—and, of course, that this close call will be the last close call. Their luck will turn around."

"A lot of good that's ever done him," Luke muttered, flipping through the falsified reports Robert had called in. "He'd gone into detail too, like it had taken real thought to put this plan together."

When Brax looked over the signature on the paperwork terminating Tessa's parental rights, that part made a lot more sense. "Look who it is. Robert's cousin Ray. He must've coached Robert on what to say, how to make an effective case."

"At least that works in Tessa's favor," Weston pointed out. "It'll take time, no doubt, but just the fact that the judge is Robert's cousin is a positive for us. No way should anyone remotely related to one of the parties be involved in a legal proceeding."

"I know that'll make her happy." She deserved a little happiness, a little hope, after everything Robert had put her through.

He looked around at his brothers. "So, the best we can come up with is Robert didn't figure on getting himself in trouble and having to leave town. I guess running with a baby would slow him down."

Luke nodded. "I guess we can assume it wasn't for Walker's sake that he ended up on your doorstep."

"Let's say that if Robert took his son's safety into consideration, I'd just about fall over in surprise." Brax smiled, but it was a grim smile. Bitter.

There were people out in the world just dying to have kids of their own, while others treated their children like possessions. Pawns to be used in a larger game.

Just as there were men like his biological father who refused to accept a son's existence and left him to suffer out of sheer selfishness.

"I can't believe Tessa kept all this to herself." Luke shook his head. "So much for one person to carry on their shoulders."

Brax nodded. "She's been through a lot. I wonder what those thugs must've thought when she didn't scare easily. And the way she slipped past them and out of Eagle Pass."

Even he could hear the pride in his voice. He *was* proud of her. She'd done well.

Once he was alone in his office, he opened his laptop and pulled up the list of dates Tessa had been terrorized. He'd asked her to compile the list in case there was a way of cross-referencing those dates with security footage in the areas in which she'd been accosted or attacked.

License plates, images of the men involved, anything—as long as he could get an idea of exactly who they were dealing with. It had been too dark to make out much about the two attackers who'd found Tessa in his car.

Brax wanted to see them. To know them before he taught them what happened to men who terrorized women.

He recognized one of the dates immediately. The night they'd gone to Nick's. Her account of the situation confirmed this. She'd been inside the office building with Walker when two men had tried to get inside.

He sat up straighter, eager now, digging into the network to find their security footage. There were cameras mounted at each corner of the building, along with one over the front door. Perfect.

"There you are," he muttered, staring at the men. One who glared in through the window, one who tried to force the door open.

The longer he studied them, going back and forth through the feed from all three cameras, the more certain he was that these were the men who'd attacked him behind the strip mall.

One of them had a pockmarked face—Tessa had mentioned him, had described what he'd done to her outside the mall before taking her purse. He was the one who'd tried to open the doors.

Brax was no expert in body language or reading facial expressions, but he knew pure frustration when he saw it. The sort of frustration that could turn into violence with little provocation.

Knowing she'd been inside the building and able to see the men who wanted to hurt her sent his blood pressure soaring. Oh, yeah, he was going to enjoy teaching them what happened to men who terrorized women.

He rolled back the footage in hopes of catching sight of the car the men had arrived in, but it was out of the camera's range.

He switched to another camera, this one mounted at the corner of the building, and rolled the footage back to before he'd arrived with Walker. Just in case the car had passed in the distance, in case they'd been watching even then.

It wasn't the two men he ended up catching sight of. It

was Tessa, emerging from the alley next to the office building. Where had she come from?

He switched feeds, watching her emerge from the alley from a different angle. But there was no footage of her entering the alley, like she would if she'd come up behind the building.

He moved to the camera at the other end of the alley, mounted at the rear of the building, and watched the time-stamp at the top of the screen. She hadn't entered the alley from back there.

So where had she come from?

A sick feeling bloomed in the pit of Brax's stomach. He rolled the footage back to the time they'd left the office together earlier that night.

There they were, talking. He'd asked if she could come in early, and she had accepted. Then he'd walked away, carrying Walker to the car. Tessa had watched for a moment or two before turning and heading for the alley. Only she'd never come out at the other end.

No wonder it had been so easy for her to get to the office in a hurry. And why she hadn't even let him finish asking her to move in before accepting. It wasn't just motherly love.

She'd been sleeping in the alley all along.

His fists tightened hard enough to make his joints ache. Robert had so much to pay for.

Brax was still furious enough when his phone rang that he practically barked into it on answering. "Yeah?"

"Brax. It's Janice Morgan."

He forced his anger away. "Hi. How's it going?"

"About as well as can be expected when dealing with the Riviera cartel." She sighed. Somehow, the DA sounded even more exhausted than she had the last time they'd spoken—considering that he'd noted her exhaustion then, too, that was saying something.

"What happened?"

"Our shopkeeper passed away last night."

He closed his eyes, stricken. "I'm sorry to hear that."

"So am I, considering that the poor guy was recovering well as of yesterday afternoon. I checked in with his doctors to see about his progress, and they were pleased with the way things were going. They told me he might be able to go home as early as tomorrow."

"You're kidding."

"It happens that way sometimes," she allowed. "But the doctors expressed surprise when I talked to them a few minutes ago."

"We know what we're talking about, then."

"I think we can safely say this has 'the cartel' written all over it."

He couldn't think of anything to say except to offer a single reassurance. "You can count on me. I don't plan on backing down from testifying."

"Thank you for that—but remember, be careful. Now's the time to grow an extra pair of eyes in the back of your head. With Prince out on bail until the trial, there's no telling what else he's put into motion."

He took this to heart and was still thinking about it hours later when he left for the night. A quick call home confirmed everything was okay there. Tessa and Walker were waiting.

They were quickly becoming the center of his world, if they hadn't already firmly planted themselves there. What a time to need eyes in the back of his head.

The ride home normally helped clear his mind. It wasn't a heavily traveled route—he liked it that way, liked not having to sit in traffic the way some commuters did.

The wash of high beams took him by surprise, almost blinding him when the light hit the rearview mirror. He threw an arm up, blinking hard to clear away the spots in his vision.

"What do you think you're doing?" he asked, tapping the horn. Some people...

His car jolted forward, pushed by the car behind him.

That was no accident.

He floored the gas, determined to outrun them. There was an on-ramp for the freeway about a mile ahead. He could lose the tail there.

The driver had other ideas, ramming him harder than before and almost driving Brax off the road. He corrected in time, swinging the wheel to the left, kicking up clouds of dust. In the end, though, it gave the car behind him just enough room to slide in alongside and force him into the ditch.

Brax's chest hit the wheel when the car pitched forward, and pain exploded in his shoulder when he hit the door. He pushed the pain aside and brought the car to a stop.

His heart hammered wildly. At least the adrenaline kept the pain at bay, but he knew that he'd be bruised come morning. If he made it to morning.

Looking around, he tried to spot the car that had caused this. There was light up on the road, telling him they'd come to a stop with the high beams still on. The best thing to do was stay in the car, doors locked. He was armed, but there was no way of telling how many people were up there.

Was this because of Robert? Or Prince Riviera?

He found out soon enough. A familiar figure reached the edge of the road, standing just where it dropped off into the ditch. The high beams created a sort of halo around him. But there was nothing holy about the head of the Riviera cartel.

Prince stared down at Brax's car. What was he waiting for? To see how badly Brax was hurt?

How had the cartel found him?

Rather than descending to the car or sending somebody down in his place, Prince called out from where he stood, "You have the choice not to testify."

With that, he walked away, and seconds later the sound of a car door closing came as a relief. The glow of the headlights faded to darkness, leaving Brax alone.

Chapter Seventeen

It was so quiet at night. Blessedly quiet. Better than an alley. Or the back seat of a car.

Tessa propped her head up on one bent arm, staring up at the ceiling. How much time had passed since she'd gone to bed? Hours, probably.

Hours of worrying. Wondering.

What was Brax hiding from her?

Something was going on. He had that tense, cagey energy about him, the way he'd acted while tracking that bail jumper. Like something was very wrong. Whatever it was, he wasn't sharing it with her.

And that left her feeling slightly insulted. Wasn't he the one who'd made her promise there would be no more secrets? Yet there he was a few days later acting secretive, putting up an invisible wall between them.

Why?

Naturally, her mind went first to the most likely answer: he blamed her for what had happened with Robert. Given time to think things over, he'd decided she was untrustworthy and too stupid or gullible to care about.

Why else would he have been so distracted when he'd gotten home from work last night? Distant. Like he was only half with her, half someplace else.

Weston had called to tell her Brax had had car trouble and would be late getting home. While she'd appreciated the call, why couldn't Brax call for himself? Was he that dismissive of her?

He'd acted like it after finally showing up. She might as well have not been there at all. So much for looking forward to him getting home.

Not that he'd been mean or rude. That might've been easier to deal with. She was used to rude men. Being ignored, especially by Brax, wasn't as easy to swallow.

He'd gone to bed not long after getting home. He hadn't eaten, but that didn't seem to matter half as much as getting away from her had. His movements had been stiff, like there was something physically wrong.

He hadn't told her what it was. He'd hardly said a word.

She'd hoped to ask him about it in the morning, but he'd been gone by the time she'd woken up. That was early even for him.

He'd worked late again, not getting home until nearly ten o'clock. So yeah, seemed like he was avoiding her. If he hadn't been so different before then—friendly, warm, curious about her and about how her day had gone—this sudden change wouldn't have come as such a shock.

It looked like the more time he had to think about what she'd told him, the more distant he'd become.

Even now, lying in a darkened bedroom, just the thought of Brax losing respect for her and thinking she couldn't be trusted was enough to make her chest ache. Tears stung behind her eyes. All they did was frustrate her.

Her stomach started growling. She hadn't eaten dinner. She'd waited for Brax until it was clear he wouldn't be home, and then decided to sleep instead. The stew was in the fridge now, though that wasn't exactly what she wanted to eat at this time of night.

Or the morning. She'd finally checked the time—usually, she avoided looking at the clock since it only made her more anxious while she was lying awake—and found she'd been staring at the ceiling for three hours. It was almost half past two.

The thought of Walker waking up before the sun wasn't pleasant, but now that her stomach was growling, she knew sleep wouldn't be coming. Only eating would settle her down. She tiptoed downstairs in the dark house toward the faint glow of the kitchen. She was careful to be quiet, not wanting to take a chance on waking up Walker or Brax.

She stopped short when she saw Brax in the kitchen, bent over in front of the fridge like he'd had the same idea about food. He hadn't eaten dinner either.

The impulse to run swept over her. Why did her mind go there right away? Why would she run from him? He was the last person she should want to avoid. Two days ago, she would've laughed at the idea. But that was before he'd started ignoring her.

He didn't know she was there. She could get away and sneak back upstairs and avoid any awkwardness. She would have if it hadn't been for something rooting her to the floor.

Him wearing low-slung sweatpants that looked like they were a moment away from sliding off his hips. No shirt. She could make out the lines of his slim waist, broad shoulders and muscular arms in the light from the refrigerator.

She could hardly breathe. Her mouth went dry. Good thing, since she might've started drooling otherwise.

He looked back at her over his shoulder. "Oh. Hi."

She struggled to respond. "Hi," she murmured.

Brax turned toward her and the sight of his left side made

her gasp. A mass of bruises covered his shoulder and arm, then bloomed again on his chest and ribs. There were lacerations along his biceps and elbow. It was ugly and had to be painful.

"What happened to you?" she whispered with her heart in her throat. Seeing him that way was enough to cause her actual pain. If she had only known…

He looked down at himself, wincing. "Yeah." He frowned, cleared his throat, looked anywhere but at her. "That car trouble I had two nights ago?"

"Yeah?"

"It was more like an accident."

"Brax!"

"I'm fine."

"Fine?" She gestured to him. "You don't look fine. No wonder you walked around like a reanimated corpse when you got home. How did it happen? What sort of accident?"

"It was nothing." He still wasn't looking at her. "One of those things. Dark, empty road. Driving too fast. I get a little cocky sometimes, I guess."

She studied him. Watched his subtle movements.

He was lying.

"There aren't many things I'm really good at," she admitted in a low voice. "But if there's anything I know, it's when somebody's lying. You'd think I would've been smarter about Robert because of that, but…" She shrugged, then pointed at him. "You're not telling the truth. Come on. You got away from those thugs who were following us without coming close to another car. You're an excellent driver."

He shrugged. "Things happen."

"You won't look at me. That's another way I can tell you're hiding something. No secrets. That was your rule. I can follow it. Can you?"

"You're tough." He sighed before finally looking her in the eye. "Okay. I wanted to keep you out of it, but I see that's a waste of time. I didn't run off the road. I was run off the road. By Prince Riviera."

Her heart sank like a stone. "Oh, no. Brax..."

"I'm okay. See?" He spread his arms—even now, in the back of her mind, she couldn't help but notice how very okay he looked.

Except for the hideous bruises that monster had given him.

"Why don't you sit down?" She reached out and took one of his hands. "Come on. I'll make you a sandwich. You need to eat, no matter how stressed you are."

"I'd argue, but I really am hungry. You should be asleep, though."

She giggled softly while pulling food from the fridge. "Why do you think I came down in the first place?"

He was quiet for a while as she put turkey and Swiss cheese together. "I'm sorry," he eventually mumbled as she put the finishing touches on the sandwich and cut it in half.

"For what?"

"For keeping you in the dark. I didn't know what to do or how to manage this, so I figured it was better to keep you out of it."

"I understand." Her relief was almost physical. Not relief at him being hurt, but at there being a reason he had avoided her. Especially since that reason was to protect her.

She started with her own sandwich, but a glance in his direction stopped her. "You okay?" she asked when he winced as he rubbed his neck.

"Stiff, you know? Nothing I can't manage."

"So stoic." She went to him. "Eat your sandwich. I'll rub your neck."

"As long as you can manage not to strangle me."

"Don't tempt me."

She was already massaging his neck before the realization that she was touching him registered on her awareness. It was innocent, of course, but still. He was shirtless and she was very close to him, and her heart didn't know what to do with that.

"This is a great sandwich," he grunted around a mouthful of food. "Just what I needed."

"I'm glad."

He looked up at her, touching one hand to hers. "I needed this too."

"I'm not very good at it."

"You're just fine." He pulled her around and into his lap before she could think to stop him.

Not that she would've wanted to stop him. Not for anything.

Even so, she had to know. "You told me a few nights ago you didn't want us to go anywhere until all these problems were worked out."

"I did say that." His arms locked around her, pulling her close to his bare chest.

She touched a gentle hand to his bruised shoulder. "This doesn't look like things are worked out."

"Sometimes I wish I'd keep my mouth shut," he grumbled.

There was no way to fight it. Not that she tried very hard or wanted to try.

Not when she was so close to him, and he was so warm and firm and strong.

His face filled her awareness an instant before his lips met hers and pulled her down, down into a sweet, soft kiss.

Maybe it was two days spent thinking he hated her that made it so sweet. So special.

Soreness didn't seem to slow him down. His arms tightened as the kiss deepened. She was careful not to hurt him but couldn't possibly resist the urge to touch him. To feel for herself his smooth skin, the muscles warm underneath.

She was hungry for more than a sandwich. The sort of hunger he stirred in her couldn't be satisfied by anything but him.

Her hunger deepened. The way he kissed her. The way he held her. The way his hand burned a trail down her back. Would she ever be able to get enough of him? Or would every touch and kiss leave her wanting more? The way they did now.

There was nothing in the world that could've stopped them.

Except for somebody who couldn't speak, but could certainly make his presence known.

Tessa giggled when Walker's cries came through the monitor. "He has a sixth sense, I swear."

Brax blew out a sigh, then laughed. "His timing is impeccable."

"He's probably hungry. It's almost three. I could heat up a bottle."

There wasn't much she felt less like doing than working her way off Brax's lap, but it had to be done. What was she going to do otherwise? Their first time couldn't be on the kitchen floor.

By the time she had water simmering on the stove and the bottle warming up in the pan, Brax brought Walker down to the kitchen.

She tried not to care that Brax now wore a T-shirt, but it wasn't easy.

"Hey, buddy. You hungry?" Tessa stroked Walker's smooth, soft cheek before kissing the top of his head.

"Yeah, he was telling me upstairs he had a craving for a turkey sandwich, but I reminded him about the whole teeth thing. They help when it comes to chewing." The way Brax smiled at the baby melted her heart.

The three of them jumped when one of the living room windows shattered.

Brax handed a screaming Walker to her and positioned himself between her and the living room. Tessa might've screamed a little, too, out of surprise, but it was all a blur.

She followed a step behind Brax as they moved toward the sound. Her heart raced, and her stomach churned as she clutched Walker to her chest, cupping his tiny head and tucking it under her chin.

His arm shot out, stopping her before they reached the living room.

The smell of gasoline and burning carpet filled her nose. A dancing, flickering light reflected off the walls.

Fire.

Chapter Eighteen

Fire was spreading in the living room, catching the throw rug, the curtains. Brax caught sight of a terrified Tessa holding a screaming Walker.

The smell of gasoline almost overwhelmed them. It must have been a Molotov cocktail that had smashed through the window. Common sense told him to get out of the house, but his gut told him somebody was outside. Waiting. Planning to do more harm than the fire.

Acting purely on instinct, he steered Tessa and the baby back into the kitchen. "Stay in here." He shoved them into the pantry. It was safer in there: no windows, no way for anybody to get to them from outside.

But also no way to escape if the fire raged out of control.

"The fire!" Tessa clung to Walker as he squalled.

"I'll handle it. Stay in here." He closed the door and ran into the living room. Grabbing a pillow off the couch, he flailed at the fire on the rug and the bits of curtain that had fallen to the floor.

The room was smoky, but the fire hadn't spread. Whoever had thrown the bottle hadn't tossed it hard enough for the glass to shatter when it hit the floor.

Lucky break. Literally.

Once he was sure the fire was out, he moved to his safe,

took out his gun and slid his back along the wall to a window. The soft light from the kitchen glowed behind him as he peered out into the moonless night.

"Where are you?" he muttered to himself. No one would go to the trouble of sending a message like this without sticking around to see if the message had been received.

Through one of the front windows, he caught the outline of a car sitting on the road leading away from the house. Far enough away that they'd be safe from the fire, but not so far that they couldn't pick him off if he'd bolted from his burning home.

Hugging the wall again, he made his way back to the kitchen for the one phone he knew he could always find: his landline. He punched the speed dial button for Chance.

"Can't talk long," he barked. "Somebody threw a Molotov cocktail through my living room window. It's not terrible, but I need you to call the fire department and the cops and get them out here. You guys too. I think whoever did this is hanging out waiting for me."

Chance let out a string of curses before asking, "What's your next move?"

"I have to get Tessa and Walker out of here." He coughed on thickening smoke. He must have missed a smoldering ember. "Make the call. I have to get out."

"Be careful."

Brax returned to the living room. The curtains had reignited and the wall behind them had started to blacken. He fought through the building fear and focused on the only thing—the only people—who mattered right now: Tessa and Walker.

Why was Walker so quiet? Had someone gotten to them?

Forgetting about the flames that threatened to burn his home to the ground, Brax raced to the kitchen and flung open the pantry door. Tessa, sitting cross-legged on the floor, fed Walker the bottle she'd been warming before the chaos had erupted. Even in the middle of a blazing hellscape, her first concern had been for her son.

And somebody wanted to hurt them. His rage alone could've set the house on fire all by itself.

"Come on. We have to get out of here," he whispered through clenched teeth, careful not to scare the baby again.

"What are we going to do?" Tessa's eyes widened with terror.

That was a good question. "We'll go out the back. There's someone waiting in a car in the front."

He reached down to help her up and hurried toward the kitchen door. Before rushing outside, he paused to check the backyard. It was clear. So far. "Keep him as quiet as you can and follow me. Don't say a word."

Even though everything looked quiet behind the house, he constantly scanned the area and listened hard, but he didn't pick up the slightest hint of an intruder. Riviera's men were either lazy or stupid.

No surprise. Not that Brax was in any position to complain.

He took Tessa's arm and led her away from the house as he continued to survey the grounds. Every crunch, every footstep rang out like a gong.

Somebody would be sent to cover the back when nobody had come running out of the front—Brax was sure of it, so he wasn't surprised when he heard a heavy tread coming their way from the side of the house. Brax pushed Tessa toward the trees. "Go!" he whispered. She darted off.

He turned and crouched behind a massive smoker that had provided the food for so many raucous gatherings, praying that Walker didn't choose this moment to become raucous himself.

Nobody was going to hurt his family.

He waited, hardly daring to breathe, gun at the ready. A tall, heavyset man rounded the corner with a cigarette hanging out of his mouth like he was taking a walk in the park. A Sunday stroll.

Brax used this to his advantage, waiting for the man to pass him before hitting him across the back of the head with the butt of his gun. The man crumpled at Brax's feet.

There was no one with him. No one following close behind. Everybody was out front waiting in that car.

For a split second, Brax was torn. Part of him wanted to make this goon—and all of the goons waiting in the car—pay for threatening his family, but the bigger part urged him to run for the trees so he could be with Tessa and the baby. They were too vulnerable out there, even while hiding.

The goons or Tessa and Walker?

Tessa and Walker of course. "Tessa?" he whispered once he was close enough to risk speaking.

"Over here." He could just make out the sound of her voice. "He's sleeping."

Tessa crouched between a pair of thick tree trunks, so hidden in the deep shadows he almost tripped over her before realizing she was there.

He squatted next to her and wrapped his arms around them both. "You okay?"

"Fine." The trembling he felt under his hands told a different story. She was still terrified.

Smoke billowed from the house now, drifting out through the broken window. Another window shattered as the flames grew. He hated thinking of what was happening to his home, but what truly mattered was with him in his arms.

They were his, both of them, and he would die if it meant keeping them safe.

He stiffened at the sight of the unconscious man stirring, working his way to his knees. "Shh," he hissed into Tessa's ear. A glance at Walker showed he was fast asleep now that he'd eaten.

A second man came around from the other side of the house. "Hey, what are you doing?" His voice carried toward them as he helped his buddy up.

"...hit me...don't know where he went..." The guy sounded confused, dazed. He was lucky. Brax would've liked to have done a lot worse to him—to both of those thugs.

"It's okay," he whispered to Tessa, his arms tightening around her and the baby. "We're safe. They can't hurt us."

She nodded then buried her face into his neck. It was better that way. For her to hide her eyes and pretend none of this was happening. Otherwise, the baby might sense her agitation, and there was no telling how long their safety would last once he started screaming.

Sirens wailing in the distance calmed most of Brax's anxiety. Beyond the house, he could make out the faint glow of the red lights on top of the fire trucks. The men froze for a second before taking off. It was the first smart thing they'd done all night.

When they were out of sight, Brax breathed a little easier, but there was no way he was going to lead Tessa and Walker out into the open before he knew with absolute certainty that they were safe. Which meant waiting and watching and listening.

It wasn't until Weston and Luke appeared that he stood, helping Tessa to her feet. "We're here!" he called out to them.

Seeing his brothers chased away the last of his apprehension. It also brought the grim realization that he could have lost Tessa and Walker. Now that he could think straight, now that their safety was assured, he could afford to think about what might have happened.

What if they'd all been upstairs asleep when the Molotov cocktail had come through the window? What if Tessa had been in the kitchen alone with Walker, fixing his bottle? Would she have panicked and run out the front door?

So many what-ifs bombarded him, it was a relief to be distracted by the pair of officers looking for answers.

He told them everything he could. He described both men he'd seen behind the house and what little he had been able to make out of the car that had been parked on the dirt road.

"What reason would anyone have to attack you and your family, Mr. Patterson?" one officer asked.

His family. That was what they were. He didn't bother correcting the officer who'd asked.

"I'm scheduled to be the prime witness against Prince Riviera and his cartel," he explained. "District Attorney Morgan will tell you all about it if you give her a call. Riviera and his men ran me off the road two nights ago." He pulled up his shirt to show them his chest.

"Why didn't you alert us to that before now? This could've been prevented," the second officer said.

Weston spoke before Brax could, and that was for the best. "We've worked most of the past thirty-six hours straight trying to figure out how to protect my brother without making the situation worse for him or the people close to him."

When he looked at Tessa and Walker, the officer softened. But not by much. "All the more reason to bring us in on this."

"The shopkeeper who was set to testify went to you—" Brax cut himself off when Weston shot him a look.

No. He wasn't helping things by mouthing off.

Though he believed he had a strong point.

"We'll pick up Riviera now that we have a statement based on the encounter you had with him," the second officer stated. "We can offer protection."

"I've already arranged for a safe house," Weston assured them. "That's the first step. You take care of Riviera and his men. We'll take care of our own."

Chance wrapped Tessa and Walker with a blanket he'd brought from his car.

Luke looked grim when he approached Brax. "It could've been much worse."

"I know."

"It's going to take some work to restore the living room. You did well putting out what you could before getting out."

"I couldn't let the place burn down with Tessa and Walker in it." Just the thought made Brax's stomach twist.

Luke clapped a hand over Brax's uninjured shoulder. "I know what you're going through, brother. I know how it is to feel like there's somebody whose safety is more important than your own. Not that it helps you any, but… I understand."

It didn't help. Not in any concrete way. But it did ease Brax's mind a little. He wasn't completely out of his head for wanting to kill everybody involved in what had happened tonight. Not for his own sake. Not even for the sake of his home, which he'd always been proud of and thought of as a sanctuary.

But for them. For Tessa and Walker.

First and foremost, he had to get them to safety. Then he'd make it his mission in life to make sure something like this never happened again.

Chapter Nineteen

A police radio squawked. Tessa jumped at the sound. Her heart lodged in her throat. Her arms shook so hard she was afraid she might drop the baby.

She would break into a million pieces soon. All it would take would be one more thing. One more menacing face in the dark. One more emergency. One more panicked run at nighttime. It would destroy her.

Then there were the questions. The what-ifs. When she wasn't jumping at the slightest sound, she asked herself what could have happened.

If they hadn't been downstairs when the bomb had come through the window. If it had shattered on impact with the floor. If they'd gone out the wrong door and one of those men had cut them off. If Walker had cried out while they were hiding in the trees.

If, if, if. An endless string of them, stretching into infinity.

She'd lose her mind if this didn't stop. There was another what-if. What if this never stopped and she ended up losing what was left of her sanity?

No.

Some people had the luxury of falling apart when life threw them curveballs. Some people didn't have a baby depending on them.

She nuzzled Walker's head, tucking it protectively under her chin, and marveled at his ability to sleep through so many things. A blessing, considering he'd fallen asleep while they'd been hiding. "Thank you, sweetheart," she whispered before kissing him.

Who had tried to kill them? Robert's enemies or Brax's? More than likely something so vicious would have come from the cartel, but there was no way to tell.

Did it matter? If they'd died, would it have mattered who had killed them? The result would've been the same.

A slight touch on her shoulder made her jump again.

"Sorry." Brax held up his hands, coming around in front of her. "I didn't mean to scare you."

A stunned little laugh bubbled up from her chest. "You're the least of my worries."

"Understood." His brows drew together. "Come on. Weston's going to get you two to a safe house. You'll be fine there."

Fine. As if anything could be fine. She almost laughed again, but the little bit of self-possession she still had told her it wouldn't be a good idea.

He walked her to Weston's car and opened the passenger side door for her to sit inside while Luke set up the car seat in the back. When Brax reached for Walker, she only held on tighter.

Brax's face fell, which was what got through to her. Knowing her reaction had hurt him. He had never done anything to hurt her or the baby. He didn't deserve this.

She extended her arms and held Walker out to him. Brax took the baby and fastened him into his car seat. He would be safe. Her son would be safe. Even if she still felt like she was going to fall apart.

The impulse to scurry over the center console, get behind the wheel, and tear off into the night with her son was so strong she almost couldn't resist it.

All that mattered was keeping him safe. She had to keep him safe. His life meant more than hers—after all, what had she ever done that was worth anything?

Giving birth to Walker had been the only worthwhile thing she'd ever done. He was her one good thing. And she'd come so close to losing him. Again.

She studied Brax's face as he looked down at her from outside the car. He had that look in his eyes. That sad, fallen sort of look like when she'd held Walker away from him. Brax hated this as much as she did. Maybe more, since he felt responsible. Nobody had to tell her that. She just knew.

He crouched beside the vehicle. "It's going to be okay, I swear. Once we get you and Walker to the safe house, there won't be anything to worry about."

His hand covered hers. "You're not in this alone. I'm going to keep you both safe. I swear on my life, Tessa. Nothing matters more to me than you and Walker. You're my priority, and I intend to make your safety my life's mission. Do you understand?"

The conviction in his words shook her to her core. The strength in his voice. His confidence. A man with a mission was a powerful thing.

And he had the power to make her believe him.

She turned her hand upside down so they were palm-to-palm and laced her fingers with his. "Yes. I do."

"Good." He cupped her cheek with his free hand and sealed his promise with a kiss that soothed her aching heart.

"Let's roll." Weston slid behind the wheel. "Meet you there."

Brax gave his brother a nod, stood and looked at her one

more time before closing the door. He lifted his hand in a wave before backing away.

"Don't worry. We'll split up on the way, just in case anybody's watching—which they aren't, but we can't be too careful." Weston stole a glance her way and cleared his throat. "Why don't you get some rest while we drive?"

"Where are we going? I mean, exactly where. Don't take it personally, I'm curious."

"I don't blame you. You have the right to be curious about where we're placing you for the time being. It's an apartment on the north side of San Antonio."

"Okay."

He eyed her. "Seriously. You look like you're ready to fall over."

"I didn't get any sleep tonight, even before this whole nightmare started."

"Then by all means." He gave her knee a gentle pat. "Rest while you can. Something tells me that come morning, your little guy isn't going to care very much what went on tonight."

He made a good point. Walker couldn't exactly tell time. She'd close her eyes for just a minute…

"Tessa? We're here."

Her eyes snapped open. Not a second had passed.

Or hadn't it? Because they were in a parking garage now. "Wow. I dropped right off."

"You needed it. Come on. Brax texted a few minutes ago. He's already inside." Weston helped with the car seat, and Tessa was all too happy to follow him into the apartment building.

"It's not the biggest or fanciest," Weston offered as he unlocked the door. Like he was apologizing in advance.

If she hadn't been half-dead from exhaustion, she

might've told him this apartment was at least three times the size of the one she'd left in Eagle Pass. Furnished better too.

Brax was waiting, just like his brother had promised. He pulled her in for a hug. "You'll be safe here. I promise."

"I'm going to head out." Weston placed the car seat on the coffee table. "You have everything under control?"

"Sure." Brax shook his hand.

"Thank you," Tessa whispered. Weston touched two fingers to his temple in a quick salute before leaving them alone.

She turned to Brax with a heavy sigh. "Alone at last."

He offered a brief smile. "I hate to say it, but I'm going to have to leave you too."

"Really? Already?" Except a look over his shoulder told her it was close to dawn. It had been a long night.

"I'll be back soon. I promise."

She should let him go. She knew she should.

That didn't make it any easier to release the hold she had on his shirt.

"Tessa." He touched her hair, her face. "Nobody knows about this place except for people I trust—which pretty much means my brothers and that's it. You'll have to stay inside. No going out. But otherwise, you'll be safe here."

"I don't care that I can't leave. I'm worried about you."

His smile was more genuine now, and for a second he was his usual, charming self. "I'm the least of your worries, trust me. It's the bad guys you should be worried about."

"Unlikely." No amount of humor could ease the cold fist gripping her heart. "Please be careful."

"I will." He kissed her forehead and held her tight for a moment before letting her go. "I'm going to figure out how to keep us safe long-term. In the meantime, I'll send somebody with supplies for you and Walker. There's a burner phone on the nightstand in the bedroom that I'll call to contact you. All you have to do is sleep now. Okay?"

"Okay." She tried to be as brave as she could so he wouldn't have one more thing to worry about.

After all, she'd given him enough to worry about already.

IT WAS PAST noon when she woke up.

Her first thought, as always, was of Walker. He was next to her on the big bed, surrounded by pillows just in case he decided today was the day he'd start rolling all over the place.

"Hey, little man." She relaxed when she found him cooing to himself, playing with his feet. "I used to be that flexible once."

At least he was feeling good. No memory of last night's trauma.

That made one of them.

There was a message from Brax on the burner phone. Supplies on their way. Trusted sources.

Whatever that meant. She knew she could trust him—and anybody he trusted.

There was time to change Walker and take care of her own needs before a knock sounded at the front door. Tessa tiptoed to the door with her heart in her throat and peered out through the peephole.

It was Maci, from the office, along with a woman who looked vaguely familiar. They were loaded down with bags and boxes. She hurried to open the door so they could put everything down.

"Hi," Maci whispered as she hurried through to the kitchen. "Whew! That was my arm-day workout right there."

"You don't have to whisper. He's awake." Tessa went to the bedroom and brought Walker back.

"There he is! My best buddy!" Maci held out her arms, which didn't seem to be all that sore from carrying the packages after all.

Meanwhile, the other woman—small, blonde, with a face Tessa recognized from somewhere—held out a hand. "Hi. I'm Luke's fiancée, Claire Wallace."

Right. Tessa might've been half out of her mind with grief and pain after Robert had stolen Walker, but she remembered seeing Claire on the news around that time. There were stories about her supposedly killing somebody she'd worked with and then killing a cop, but she'd been cleared of all charges.

And had managed to simultaneously bring down one of the most crooked businessmen in Texas. Now Tessa understood how the woman had not only survived but had come out the other side smiling. She shook Claire's hand gladly.

"I've never seen Brax like this," Maci admitted as Claire and Tessa put the groceries and supplies away.

"Same here. I mean, I haven't known him for too long, but he's on a whole other level right now." Claire winced when she met Tessa's gaze. "Not to make you feel bad or anything. It isn't your fault."

"No, but he's definitely determined to get you out of this okay," Maci continued. "You have nothing to worry about. Believe me. Those boys do not give up."

Claire set aside the packs of diapers and wipes, then went back to stocking the pantry. "I'm surprised, honestly. Brax is usually the laid-back one, isn't he? I mean, I've always seen him that way. Charming and smiling. He could convince anybody of just about anything."

"True. Luke's usually the cranky one—with everybody but you, anyway," Maci teased with a wink at Claire. "Weston's Mr. Serious. And Chance…" She blew out a long sigh, rolling her eyes.

"You two don't get along well, do you?" Tessa asked, remembering them bickering during her time at the office.

"We get along fine. When I don't want to kill him."

Claire giggled. "Oh, please. You two have it bad for each other. You just don't want to admit it."

"'Oh, please' yourself!" Maci turned her attention to Walker, clearly eager to change the topic. Not fast enough, though, her flushed cheeks betraying her words.

Tessa exchanged a look with Claire. "I don't know," she said. "Sometimes it's those denied attractions that are the most explosive."

Claire's eyebrows moved up and down. "Remind me not to be around when a spark ignites the fuse."

"Okay, enough." Maci's face glowed redder as she turned back to them. "Believe me, I'm not the sort of woman a guy like Chance would ever look at twice. Men prefer women like you two, or didn't you know that?"

Tessa assumed Maci was referring to her figure, which could be described as plus-size. "You have curves I would kill for. Chance would be blind not to notice you."

"Anyway." Maci's voice was a little louder than it needed to be, which Tessa took as a signal that this part of the conversation was over. "Brax has taken your safety to heart. Big time."

Tessa looked at Walker, who clearly loved the attention of three women at once. The thought of him being a ladies man like his father crossed her mind, and she hated it. "Brax is concerned about his nephew. It's only right."

Claire frowned. "You're kidding. You think that's all he's worried about?"

"Seriously. I've seen the way he looks when he talks about you. He's just as concerned about you as he is about Walker—but in a different way." Maci shrugged. "It's the truth."

Suddenly, Tessa's knees felt weak. Could it be true? She collapsed into a seat at the kitchen table.

She wanted to believe them, to think that Brax cared about her. A few kisses were one thing. But deep, serious emotion? That was something else.

"I doubt Brax could ever trust me again after the way I lied," she confessed.

"Listen." Claire sat across from her, and she wasn't kidding anymore. "If there's one thing the Pattersons understand, it's survival. I mean, anybody would lie in your situation—so there's that right there. You had to be with Walker, but you didn't know what Robert had told Brax and whether Brax believed him."

Maci handed Walker to Claire, who looked like she was just about dying to hold him. "Those men respect people who do whatever it takes to survive. They're survivors. So are you. I know Brax respects you."

"Agreed." Claire beamed at the baby while bouncing him in her arms.

Were they right? She hoped so, since one thing was clearer every single day, and it scared her a little.

She was falling in love with Brax Patterson.

Chapter Twenty

If Brax had his choice of anybody in the world to work alongside, he would've chosen his brothers every time.

Things usually got intense when the stakes were high, but it had never been like this. For one thing, he was normally the one breaking the tension. Trying to pick up everybody's spirits, keeping the group from splintering due to emotions running high and hot.

Now? It was his brothers' turns to calm him.

"When I think of what could've happened…" He ran his hands through his hair before resting them on top of his head, almost like he was holding it in place. That was how it felt. Like his head might fall off because of everything going on inside.

"Here's an idea—stop thinking about it." Chance didn't bother softening this with a smile.

"He's right. You're driving yourself crazy." Luke patted Brax's shoulder on his way to the break room for fresh coffee.

Easy for them to say. Like he could let go of everything he'd seen and felt last night. There wasn't much in the world powerful enough to scare him. Last night qualified.

"But what if I'd been working late? What if it had been just Tessa and the baby at home? What if I hadn't been there?" He looked around the conference room, where they were working together to put a plan in place.

Weston blew out a long sigh. "It could've been much worse."

"What if we hadn't been awake at the time?" he continued, remembering the kisses in the kitchen, how sweet it had been to have Tessa in his arms. Close to him.

How right it had felt, bringing Walker downstairs for his feeding. How…satisfying. Like having a little family of his own. It had all fallen to pieces so fast. But like Weston had pointed out, it could've been so much worse.

Chance had his whiteboard out and the thing looked like some abstract masterpiece. Multicolored words and phrases scrawled everywhere. It was like he was planning an invasion.

Alibi. Witnesses. Testimony.

Brax's insides twisted at the sight of the word *alibi*. It referred to the iron-clad alibi Prince Riviera had presented to the cops during questioning. For both events. There'd been a dozen people hanging out together at that time of the morning. A dozen people willing and eager to offer proof of their late-night partying. How convenient.

And even if Prince had been partying like he'd said, it didn't matter. He didn't have to be physically present at the scene for his thugs to do the dirty work for him—if anything, it was more likely that he would send them on ahead to keep his hands clean.

Like a man in his position ever had clean hands. He was the weakest, most cowardly one of them all.

Weston noticed Brax staring at the whiteboard. "You know, not a single cop in San Antonio believes a word that comes out of Riviera's mouth. Or his so-called associates."

Brax shook his head. "It doesn't do anybody on their

hit list much good to know the police don't believe the bad guys. Not when there isn't enough evidence to tie said bad guys to anything. Doesn't make them any safer."

"Agreed. But law enforcement are on your side."

"I hope they still are when I need them again." Though if he had it his way, he wouldn't need them. Brax would take care of Prince Riviera on his own. With his bare hands if necessary.

Brax gladly accepted the fresh coffee Luke brought back for him. "Why is it that when we need to be our sharpest, it's usually when we're lacking sleep? Is it just me or is that the way it goes?"

Luke gave a one-shouldered shrug. "I know what you mean. You saw how I was when Claire was in the thick of it."

"As long as I make it through the next five days and get the pleasure of testifying against Riviera, at least one of my problems will be solved."

Luke didn't share Brax's hopeful grin. In fact, he looked downright pained when he sat. He frowned at Brax. "I know this isn't what you want to hear, but do you think it's a good idea to look at the trial as the end of the road?"

"What do you mean?"

"I mean Riviera isn't the sort of guy who lets bygones be bygones. Let's say he goes to prison thanks to your testimony. You think he'll let it all go because he's behind bars? If anything, he'll be more determined than ever to get back at you."

The coffee went sour in Brax's mouth. Not that it had been all that great in the first place.

"Why didn't I think of that?" He looked around at his brothers as if any of them could give him an answer. "What's wrong with me?"

"There's nothing wrong with you. You're stretched thin, is all." Luke offered a slow nod. "I know what you're feeling. You can only think as far ahead as the solution for the most pressing problem you're facing at this moment."

"Think too far into the future and you're liable to think yourself into inertia—or madness," Weston added with a grim expression.

Unable to sit still, Brax jumped to his feet and paced the length of the room. "If I'm not safe after my testimony, that means Tessa and Walker won't be safe either. Not if they're anywhere near me."

It tore him up inside just thinking about them being in greater danger. Especially when he realized he was the reason for that danger. There was one thing he'd learned in the past twelve hours or so: Tessa and Walker were his world, and he couldn't live without them.

"I think it's time we get the police department on this for real."

Brax turned toward Weston at his suggestion. "Meaning what?"

"Meaning we have them watch you. And Riviera. We'll know every move he makes, and we'll have eyes on you at all times to make sure you're okay. I think that's our best bet at the moment."

"You're probably right about that," Brax agreed. "I know I'd feel better if we had eyes on him and his associates." He rolled his eyes at that. *Associates.* Like the cartel was some sort of legitimate business.

"That doesn't change what might happen after you testify," Luke pointed out. "We need to think long-term."

"All right. Let's think long-term." Chance, always the strategist. He would be the one to jump on the idea of putting a plan together. "We can keep you hidden for a few years, if that's what it comes to. We have the resources. You could virtually vanish."

"Riviera's got connections, but there's no way he'd have enough to look for you all over the country," Luke mused. "It would be like looking for a needle in a haystack. He'd have to give up after a while, especially if the cartel implodes without him."

"Which is exactly what the DA is hoping will happen," Brax agreed. "His resources will only take him so far once he's inside, and the jackals will eat each other in his absence."

"But—"

They went silent. Weston drew a deep breath before continuing. "You'd have to go it alone. By yourself."

The implication hung heavy over their heads. No Tessa. No Walker.

On the one hand, he knew that was for the best. Riviera's thugs could still find him.

On the other hand, there was no other hand. He loathed the idea of being away from Tessa and Walker. What was the use of finding what he never knew he'd been waiting for if he ended up losing it so quickly?

"I don't know. This is a lot to process at once." He kept pacing like it would do any good, like it would help him make sense of the thoughts crashing into each other in his mind.

Saying goodbye to them or sticking around and exposing them to greater danger. They might not be so lucky next time, and he knew it.

He looked around the conference room. This was his business. These were his brothers. He was proud of what they'd built, just like they were. He didn't want to give up the results of their hard work. He couldn't abandon his brothers either. They were a team.

Not to mention the thought of losing Tessa and Walker completely gutted him.

"It's funny." He spoke more to himself than to any of them, looking at his feet as he walked the room. "For a minute there, I almost tricked myself into believing I had a normal life. Like this little game of house I've been playing with Tessa wasn't a game. It was comfortable. I felt normal."

"You are normal."

He chuckled at Weston without looking at him and replied, "Come on. You know what I mean."

"This won't be forever. You can have your normal life back once this blows over."

"I don't want to wait for it to blow over. I don't want to have to hide."

Luke snorted. Brax's head snapped around. "Is that funny?"

"Whoa, whoa." Luke held up his hands. "Don't shoot. I was reading a text from Claire. She's checking in from the apartment."

Brax scrubbed his hands over his face. "Sorry. I didn't—"

"It's okay."

He jerked his chin toward the phone. "What'd she say? How are things?"

"She says all is well over there. She and Maci dropped off the supplies."

"Great." That was one load off his mind, anyway. Maybe he'd overdone it with the list he'd given the women before sending them out, but Tessa and Walker's comfort meant too much for him to care.

"Claire likes her." Luke grinned. "And she thinks Walker's so cute she might want to reconsider her whole no-kids stance."

That got a laugh out of Brax. "She should've met him a few weeks back when all he could do was scream. Man, was it only a few weeks ago? It feels like a lifetime."

"A lot can happen in a month." Luke spread his arms. "Again, I know all about it."

A buzzing sound cut through the air, surprising them all. The front door normally wouldn't have been locked, but this wasn't a typical workday, and their office manager wasn't at the front desk to greet visitors. It had made sense to keep things locked up.

For that and for other reasons. Which was why they'd given Maci a little paid time off. If Riviera decided to pay a visit to the office...

Chance headed out there. "I'll see who it is."

"We don't get a lot of walk-ins, do we?" Luke asked, sitting up straighter than before, like he didn't trust the situation.

"Could be a delivery. Maci would have a better idea than we would of whether something was on its way." Weston started out like he wanted to back Chance up, but Chance's voice floated their way from the front door.

"Brax? Could you come out here?"

Brax looked at the others before going out to see what Chance wanted. He didn't sound panicked or even anxious. If anything, his voice had sounded...flat.

It took all of three seconds for Brax to understand why. The sight of somebody very familiar told him everything he needed to know.

"Hey, bro." Robert offered one of his typical greasy smiles. "Long time, no see."

Chapter Twenty-One

Brax rocked back on his heels. Not much in life had the power to render him speechless, but the sight of his lying, stealing, cheating, runaway half brother standing in front of him with the nerve to smile and act like nothing was wrong came pretty close.

Close enough to leave Brax at a loss for words.

Fortunately for him, he wasn't alone. "What do you think you're doing, showing up here like you didn't turn Brax's entire world upside down?" Chance demanded.

"Not just his world either," Luke muttered, dangerous and low, his hands curling into fists.

That made two of them—no, four of them, because a look around the entry area told Brax that all of his brothers wanted to take a swing at Robert.

Robert, meanwhile, glanced around and sighed. "Can we talk privately?" he asked Brax, ignoring the others.

Brax's blood only simmered harder than before. "If you have anything to say to me, you can say it in front of them."

Robert smirked. "Yeah, but you know how certain people are. Hot-blooded. Not able to listen to sense."

Weston's short, nearly silent hiss spoke volumes at Robert's racist comment. Brax lunged forward, taking Robert by his shirt collar and dragging him to the conference room.

"You're lucky I need information from you, or else I'd let the three of them pull you apart while I watched and laughed."

"What's that supposed to mean?"

The fact that he could feign ignorance after his racist comment ratcheted Brax's fury to another level. He threw Robert into a chair and slammed the door behind them, knowing his brothers would be able to watch and listen to everything through the surveillance equipment installed in there. They'd probably be observing from Weston's office.

"So," he grunted while turning to face Robert. "What'd you come back for? You here to saddle me with more kids?"

The remark had its intended effect. Robert winced. "Hi to you too." He adjusted his clothes like Brax might've somehow hurt them.

Everything Robert did made Brax more inclined to kill him. His attitude, his racism, then preening like he was the injured party. Of all the nerve.

"People like you are good at playing the victim, aren't you?" Brax asked, forgetting everything else for the moment in favor of trying to understand his brother just a little.

"What do you mean?"

"If you can jump in and pretend to be hurt first, you're deflecting from the problem at hand. It's how you go through your life, isn't it? Always trying to stay a step ahead, trying to distract people long enough so that they won't have the opportunity to kill you for the harm you've caused."

Something flickered in Robert's eyes. Something like understanding. Maybe even fear.

It cleared quickly. "I don't know what you're talking about."

"Of course, you don't." Brax pulled out a chair. "You have a lot of explaining to do."

The trick to this little interrogation would be avoiding the topic of Tessa. He couldn't let Robert know she was back in Walker's life or that he'd even met her. Tessa was supposed to be dead, according to the little story Robert had told, and if Brax had any hope of prying the truth from somebody so disassociated from truth, it would mean stepping carefully.

A shame, since it would've been gratifying to see him sweat over the legal ramifications of falsified documents.

But no, what mattered more was Tessa. If Robert contacted CPS and they took Walker away from her again, it would break her. Brax had no doubt.

He glanced up at one of the discreet cameras mounted in the corner of the room. They'd be watching.

It was Robert who spoke first. "I want Walker back."

Brax whirled on him. This was the last thing he'd expected. An explanation, maybe. A sob story, likely. But this?

"What are you talking about? You had the paperwork drawn up and everything. Is this some kind of a game to you?"

"Things have changed." How the man could sit there, unblinking, and deliver such a load of…

Brax shook his head. "That doesn't matter. You don't drag the law into something and then up and change your mind. What gives?"

Robert didn't respond.

Brax took a chair, straddled it, facing his brother. "I mean it. Fess up. What's this really about?"

"I told you. Things have changed." Only now he was shifting slightly in his chair. Uncomfortable.

Brax decided to press harder on that uncomfortable spot. "You just decided you want your son back? After awarding me guardianship? It doesn't seem like the sort of decision a person randomly changes their mind about."

"It wasn't random."

"So why, then? Why is he suddenly convenient to your life?"

Robert rolled his eyes with a heavy, put-on sigh. "I miss the little guy. He's my son. Isn't it right that I miss him? I mean, you're the moral authority. You tell me."

Brax snorted. "Moral authority? Fine. I'll give you moral authority—you can't pass your kid off like an inconvenient house plant whenever you feel like it, then decide you made a mistake and want him back. I know he's just a baby, but it's not good for him to lose his routine like that. You've already done it once. Now, he's in a routine with a nanny he likes." That was as much as he could admit about Tessa.

"You just said it yourself. He's a baby." Robert drew this out like he was talking to one just then. "It doesn't matter yet. He won't remember any of this."

"Because you're an expert in child development now?"

"Are you?"

"You might be surprised what I've had to learn on the fly," Brax murmured, holding Robert's gaze. "When a few days turned into this many weeks."

"Okay, okay, I admit I lost my head a little." Robert sat back, hands in the air. "It happens to everybody. I couldn't see myself making it work. I figured I was no good for the kid and you would be a better parent. I mean, look at you. All settled into your fancy office and your bros out there."

"Watch it," Brax warned, always aware of those cameras.

"But I changed my mind," Robert continued. So intense, like he believed himself.

Not that it mattered.

"You can't change your mind. What about this isn't getting through to you? What happens if you decide to change your mind again? That's not how this works."

"Where is he?" Robert's eyes narrowed. "I went to the house but it was empty. It looked like there was a fire there."

Brax's jaw tightened. What would've happened if there hadn't been a fire and Tessa had been at the house with Walker when Robert had showed up? The thought made him sick.

"He's somewhere else, with the nanny. They're doing fine. The fire was just an accident, but it didn't spread beyond the living room."

"That's good to hear. I hate to think of my son being in danger."

"Accidents happen," Brax muttered, teeth clenched at the nerve of the man in front of him. "He's perfectly safe and happy right now."

"Where's he staying?"

"Why does it matter when I have legal guardianship and you don't? You handed him over to me, and I take that seriously. When you decide to float in and out of his life, I have to question why."

Robert laughed. "I'd think you would be happy to be free of him. No more daddy duty. You should be thanking me!"

Brax held onto the arms of the chair to keep from throwing a punch. "I'm pretty happy with the way things turned out, actually. Sorry if you thought I'd throw the kid at you and run in the other direction, but that's not how this is going down."

Robert swallowed, eyes darting back and forth over Brax's face like he was trying to sense whether this was a game or not.

It was like magic. Robert deflated bit by bit. The shoulders slumped. His mouth tugged downward at the corners into something like a sad clown's grimace. He slouched in the chair.

"I need him back."

They were getting closer to the truth, finally. "Why? Why now? What changed?"

"There's people after me. Bad people."

What a big surprise. Brax glanced at one of the cameras, knowing what his brothers would be thinking then. It took long enough for him to admit what they'd known for days, ever since Tessa had revealed all.

"That's all the more reason to leave Walker with me, isn't it? To protect him from the people after you?"

"It's not like that."

"Are you kidding? How else could it possibly be? You're in danger. Why would you want to bring your son back into it?"

Robert shook his head, looking at the floor. "It's complicated."

"When is it not?" Brax leveled his gaze, staring straight at Robert. "Who are these people?"

He drew a deep breath and let it out slowly before answering. "The Solomon family."

Brax rocked back for the second time that day. He hadn't expected this. "The family that owns casinos all over the country? That Solomon family?"

"Yes."

"They're insanely wealthy."

"I know."

"And you got on their bad side? I mean, I can see rubbing elbows with them, but you'd have to be a real idiot—"

"Okay, okay. I don't need the insults."

Brax gritted his teeth. It was one thing to be a professional gambler, but to get on a casino owner's hit list? It took a special kind of stupid to cross a family with that kind of power and influence.

"Do you owe them money?" It was the easiest guess.

Robert nodded. "Yeah. That was the money I was trying to scratch together when I left Walker with you."

"Right."

Still, Robert stared at the floor, fingers picking at the armrests. There was more to the story. "What else? This isn't all about money. Don't bother lying and wasting my time."

A heavy sigh. "I was sort of involved with a member of the family."

For the sake of everything. "Okay."

"Gabrielle Solomon. She was visiting the Eagle Pass casino. I don't know if you've ever seen her, but she's hot. And smart. Into the business side of things, not just spending the family money. I couldn't keep my eyes off her."

Or his hands, Brax would've bet.

"The first time I talked to her, she told me she loves kids. Babies, you know. I told her I had a kid. She lit up."

A sick certainty started unfurling in Brax's gut, but he needed to hear it from Robert. He wouldn't let him off the hook.

Robert lifted a shoulder. "So I played up the single-dad thing. She fell in love with Walker, and it brought us closer."

Which was why he'd stolen Walker away from Tessa. So he could seduce some wealthy woman, who might've been smart, but wasn't smart enough to see through him.

If there had ever been a time Brax wanted to kill Robert, this was it. All the agony he'd put Tessa through, and all so he could rope a woman.

"I screwed things up," Robert admitted, rubbing his temples. "I was so stupid. I cheated on her."

"On Gabrielle Solomon?"

"Just the one time. A couple nights before I went to you. She threw a fit, told me she's not the sort of woman guys cheat on and get away with it. Threw me out. She told her brother Victor, and he decided all the money I owed them was due immediately."

"Do I even want to know how much?"

Robert cringed. "Fifty thousand."

Brax closed his eyes for a moment as this washed over him.

"I've been running from them ever since. I don't know what I'm going to do." Robert shrugged before bending forward, resting his elbows on his knees and his face in his hands.

Brax thought it over for a little while before pointing out, "They're not going to kill you, if that's what you're worried about. That's not how they'll get their money back. If I were you, I'd go back and take my beating, then work out a plan."

When Robert flinched, Brax added, "I know it's easier said than done, but they won't let this go. Would you rather live on the run for the rest of your life?"

"Well…"

"Don't tell me there's more to this."

"One of the guys on their security team…hates me. It's personal."

"What does that mean?"

"I said some things back in the day, he took it the wrong way. Overly sensitive," he scoffed.

Brax rolled his eyes. "What's his name?"

"Jakob Hawkins. He wants to kill me."

"Robert."

He looked up, his face hard. "He does. When he finds me, he's going to kill me. He's made that clear to everybody he knows."

"And you thought what? Get Walker back and make up with Gabrielle? Or use him as a human shield, hoping this

Jakob would change his mind when he saw the baby? That was your big plan? What if this Jakob found you and killed you anyway? What would happen to your son?"

Robert had no answer for that, which hardly came as a surprise. Brax knew he hadn't thought about his son, not really. Walker's future meant nothing when compared to Robert getting himself out of the latest crisis.

No way would Brax let that happen. Robert wasn't about to get his hands on Walker, not ever again. Even if he hadn't known about the history with CPS and Tessa, this situation on its surface was more than enough for Brax to keep Walker as far from his father as possible.

Still, the longer the Solomon family was after Robert, the longer they'd be after Tessa. He couldn't let that continue. Especially since they'd asked her where Walker was when they'd threatened her in the mall parking lot.

Did they want to use Walker as a pawn to get to Robert?

Brax wouldn't let that happen either.

"Well, I don't have the money, if you were wondering." Brax stood. "But I think there might be something I could do for you."

Robert's eyes lit up. "What's that?"

"Give me forty-eight hours. I was lying about the nanny having Walker right now. My parents do, and they're out of town. It'll take time to get him."

"Your parents?" Robert scoffed. "Great. I hope they don't take him out anywhere, or people might wonder."

Brax's patience snapped. "What's that supposed to mean?"

"Hey, hey!" Robert held up his hands in mock self-defense. "I'm not the one saying it. I just bet other people are, is all. Like why are they out with a little white kid? You need to get a sense of humor."

He grinned on his way out of the conference room. "See you in forty-eight hours, bro."

It took every scrap of self-control not to break Robert's head open. He waited until he heard the front door open and close before leaving the room.

Weston's office door opened at the same time, and his brothers filed out. They didn't say a word about Robert's comments, though the set of their jaws made words unnecessary.

Chance cleared his throat. "Weston found information on this Jakob Hawkins." He nodded toward the laptop Weston had brought with him.

One look at the photo on the screen was enough. "That's the guy. I recognize the pockmarked skin."

"Now we probably have a good idea why he hates Robert so much," Luke muttered. Everything about him screamed tension, from his voice to his folded arms.

"Yeah, imagine the sort of so-called jokes Robert made at his expense." Brax's lip curled in disgust. "You have no idea how much of me wants to let him get what's coming to him, but as long as he's on the run and they're not finding him—"

"It affects Tessa," Weston confirmed.

Brax sank into a chair and blew out a long breath while looking at the ceiling. There were bits and pieces of a plan moving around in his head, but it was still shadowy. Sketchy. He didn't have much time to solidify things.

"Do you think the Solomon family itself want Robert dead?" Chance posed. "Is this coming from them, or is it strictly because Hawkins hates Robert and wants an excuse?"

"The Solomons are rich," Brax mused. "But not stupid. And they're powerful, but they're not a crime family per se.

I don't know whether murder is in their bag of tricks, but wouldn't we know if it was? Word spreads."

"Odds are they don't care one way or another about Robert," Chance decided. "The money is a drop in the bucket. A lot to us, but nothing to them. They probably wouldn't blink an eye if he ended up dead. Especially after he cheated on Gabrielle."

"An honor thing," Weston muttered. "But if they'd put their money behind finding Robert, he'd be dead by now. No question. This sounds like Hawkins and a buddy of his working on their own."

"Not to rain on anybody's parade, but you have bigger problems than this Hawkins guy being after Robert." Chance offered a shrug when Brax looked his way. "Prince Riviera?"

"Of course, but this Hawkins might be a threat to Tessa, and I can't let him hurt her. I can deal with the cartel after I know she's in the clear. Besides, there's still the idea of me having to go away. I don't want to, but if things come down to that, I'll need to know Tessa and Walker are free of Robert forever. I couldn't stand it otherwise."

He stood, slid his hands into his pockets, and looked at his brothers. "I have a plan."

He turned to Weston. "I think you were right about involving the police in this. Can you call some of your old colleagues with the San Antonio PD?"

Chapter Twenty-Two

Tessa jumped like a skittish rabbit when the key turned in the lock on the front door.

Brax had texted to let her know he was leaving for the apartment, with two of his brothers following him. Then he'd texted to tell her he was in the garage and on his way up.

Even with his thoughtful warnings, she couldn't breathe until he opened the door and poked his head into the living room.

Then, it was like her feet had a mind of their own. She closed the distance between them before she knew what was happening.

She stopped short before she could do anything stupid. What if he didn't want her to jump all over him like an overexcited puppy the minute he walked through the door?

The flash of his smile told her otherwise. He pulled her into a hug, wrapping her up tight. He filled her world. Pressed against him, she could forget about everything for a little while.

"Hi," he murmured against the top of her head before planting a kiss there. "How's it going?"

"Would it be too unforgivably corny if I said it's going better now that you're here?"

Laughter rumbled in his chest up against her ear. "Corny, but not unforgivably."

"Good." She snuggled closer, breathing in his scent, drinking in his warmth. "How are you?"

"Not the worst I've ever been. Not anymore." He pulled back enough to look down at her. How would he feel about staring at each other this way for the rest of their lives?

If being held in his arms was balm for her wounded soul, his kiss was nothing short of heaven. His arms tightened. A groan from the back of his throat awakened something deep in her core. This was all she needed—this and her son.

The three of them. What if this could be their life?

Not this, exactly. The thought of it pulled her back to reality. They were standing in a safe house because she was hiding from all sorts of bad guys. No, she didn't want this exact situation to be her life.

She smiled when the kiss was over, standing on tiptoe to brush her nose against his. "Did you eat?"

"Not yet. I'll dig up something."

"You'll do no such thing. Let me. You look so tired." He followed her toward the kitchen, stopping to check the bedroom where Walker slept before joining her.

"How was your day? I see you're good and stocked up now."

"It was sweet of Maci and Claire to go out and shop. And sweet of you to make them a list."

"It's the least I could do."

Tessa didn't exactly agree. She was in this apartment thanks to him. She had her son thanks to him.

"Claire and Maci are great. It's been a long time since I chatted with the girls. They made me feel like we were old friends." She couldn't suppress a grin.

"I knew you would get along." He smiled, too, but she'd

been right. He did look tired. The overhead light made the circles under his eyes more prominent.

She stopped making his sandwich to touch his scruffy cheek. "You really do need some rest. I'm starting to become a little worried about you."

"This is nothing. You've never seen me exhausted. I'm only slightly tired right now."

"I know you think you're helping your cause, but you aren't."

"I'm the last thing you need to worry about. I've been handling myself for a long time."

"I need you to know I'm here for you." He smiled in an indulgent, "aren't you cute" sort of way. "Seriously," she insisted. "So far, you've been super involved in my problems. I want you to know I'm here for you. This goes both ways. It can't be all me, me, me."

"I don't see you that way. I never would."

"Well, thank you, but you get what I mean." She turned to him, plate in hand, and it was plain he leaned against the wall to prop himself up. "Come on. Let's sit in the living room where you can be more comfortable."

He joined her on the couch, kicking off his shoes with a sigh before taking the huge sandwich she'd fixed. "My favorite." He grinned, taking in the sight of the turkey, Swiss cheese, coleslaw and Russian dressing on rye.

"Maci told me it's what you always order when she goes for sandwiches. She figured she'd buy the ingredients in case you had a hankering."

"She's a godsend." He closed his eyes after taking a bite and groaned. "Oh, yeah."

"That good, huh?"

"Sometimes a simple thing like this really hits the spot."

He looked genuinely happy while devouring the sandwich in far fewer bites than Tessa could have managed.

She sat facing him, legs crossed in front of her. "So now that you've gorged, can you tell me what's going on? Share a little something with me? I know bad guys are after you, but I'll go nuts without updates on anything new."

"I appreciate you caring." He leaned over, leaving the plate and napkin on the coffee table, then sank back against the cushions with a sigh. "I don't want to burden you."

"It's not a burden."

He shot her a knowing look, stopping just short of rolling his eyes.

"Even if it is a burden, that's fine. I have pretty strong shoulders." She wiggled them around, hoping to get a smile from him.

And she did, though it was brief.

"I know you're a strong person." His hand found hers. "But you've already handled so much."

"I can handle more. Please. Let me in. Tell me what's happening."

He let out a long breath, puffing out his cheeks. "Okay. It's not going to be easy."

She braced herself.

His hand tightened. "Robert's back in town. He came to the office today. He wants Walker back."

Her head snapped back. Her body went into panic mode: heart racing, blood roaring in her ears, her stomach in knots, muscles twitching. She had to move. She had to leave before Robert found her.

Before he took Walker away from her again.

"Hey, hey." Brax moved closer until she was practically in his lap. "It's going to be okay. Just because he's back doesn't mean he'll get Walker. That's not going to happen."

"I…" She looked away from him because his face was so earnest, and she liked looking at it so much, but she was going to have to leave. How could she leave him?

"I know what you're thinking right now." With his free hand, he cupped the back of her head and drew her close, touching his forehead to hers. "I get it. I do. Just breathe. No way in hell am I or my brothers—my real brothers—going to let that happen. You can trust me on that, okay? We will never let him take Walker away."

She breathed the way he'd asked her to, and after a few minutes, was calm enough to ask, "How? He has documents on his side. Even if they're fake, it'll take time to prove they are, and in the meantime, he could take the baby and go anywhere. What if he runs and is never found?"

"I'm telling you. We're not going to let that happen. He won't so much as put his hands on Walker."

"No offense, but how can you be so certain?"

"I have a plan."

Hope stirred in her still-racing heart.

He continued, "We'll get it on record that Robert went through illegal channels to take the baby from you. That he falsified information. Once that's done, you'll get full custody back. The Patterson brothers are going to make sure of it."

It was so easy to believe him because she wanted to believe. She wanted what he said to be true with every ounce of her being.

That didn't mean she missed his choice of words.

"The Patterson brothers will make sure of it?" She pulled back just enough to look him in the eye, searching for answers.

"Right."

"Not you, personally?" She narrowed her eyes at him.

"I'm not saying you have to do it all yourself. But you've always made it sound like you were the one fighting for me and Walker. Why shift it to your brothers now? What am I missing?"

The way his brows drew together spoke volumes. So she was right. Brax Patterson wasn't exactly an open book, but she'd learned enough about him to know how he operated.

He took the situation with her and Walker seriously. Personally. He might rely on his brothers for help, but he would never straight up outsource.

"Things are getting more dangerous with Riviera and the cartel. You of all people know that." He stroked her hair, looking deep into her eyes. "I might have to go off the grid for a while because of it. I won't do it until you're completely in the clear. I swear it."

Her chest ached. Her throat went tight.

He was leaving her.

Maybe he had never been with her in the first place.

Sure, those few kisses had been mind-blowing, but that was all they had. No promises.

She sat up straighter, patting the hand on the back of her head. He let it fall away. "So you're going away to keep yourself safe. That's smart. It's what I would want you to do. Those guys—"

"Tessa—"

"—Those guys won't stop until they shut you up. I mean, it won't be easy on you."

"Would you listen to me?"

She tried to turn away, to reposition herself on the couch so he couldn't see the emotion she fought against. The disappointment crushing her insides.

He wasn't having it. "Listen, please." Taking her by the shoulders, he turned her to him. "Do you think I'm trying to run away from you? Nothing could be further from the truth. Don't you know by now how much I want to be part of your life? Not just Walker's life, but yours. I want us to be together. But not if it means putting you in jeopardy. You are my number one concern right now. Do you believe me?"

There was no other way to answer. "Yes."

"Good."

"So what's your plan?"

He shot her a rueful smile. "Funny you should ask, since it involves you. Don't worry," he was quick to add at her sharp intake of breath. "It's nothing huge. You don't have to show your face, and you don't have to even speak to Robert. For the record, he has no idea you're even in town, and we're going to keep it that way."

"Okay." But her voice sounded shaky even to her.

"I'm going to need you to call that guy. The one who tracked you down. We have his name now, thanks to Robert, and his contact information. Don't bother asking."

Her mouth snapped shut, because she'd been about to ask how they managed it. The Pattersons had their ways.

"You'll call him and tell him you know where Robert is. That's all you have to do. My brothers and I and the police will handle the rest. If all goes as planned—and there's no reason it shouldn't—both Robert and this Jakob Hawkins who's been terrorizing you will be arrested. And you'll be free."

"Free." The word fell from her lips like a prayer. It felt foreign, like a language she hadn't learned yet.

"That's what I want for you." He kissed her forehead, her cheeks. "I want you to be free and to feel safe. You deserve nothing less than the whole world. I might not be able to give you the whole world, but I can give you this."

And she would accept it gladly, though she wanted more. She wanted the man whose arms she was now in. The man who would put his plans to keep himself safe from the cartel on hold to ensure she was taken care of first.

He was her miracle. Everything she could ever want.

She kissed him, melting into his arms. She kissed him over and over. Every time their mouths met, she only wanted more. Like a thirst that got worse the more she drank.

She'd never have enough.

He held back a little, eventually pulling his head away and taking her by the shoulders, holding her in place. "You don't have to do this. You don't owe me anything."

She ran her hands over his arms, his shoulders. "I know that."

"It's just that I don't want you to feel like you don't have a choice."

Her hands moved to his face, one on either side. She stroked his scruffy cheeks with her thumbs and wondered what she'd ever done to deserve a man like him in her life. Before meeting Brax, she'd had no idea men like him existed.

There was so much concern in his eyes. It was almost enough to break her heart, the way he cared about her.

"I know I have a choice," she whispered, and she meant it with all her heart. "And I choose you."

A soft smile touched the corners of his mouth before he pulled her in, and this time there was no hesitation as his mouth crushed against hers and his arms held her tight against his unyielding chest.

His heart pounded there—she felt it when her hand slid over his chest, then up under his shirt as she worked it over his head.

Her heart pounded too. But for once, it wasn't fear. Fear was the last thing on her mind as Brax lowered her to the couch and stretched out on top of her, wiping away all thoughts of anything but him. And her. Together.

Chapter Twenty-Three

Time had never moved so slowly. Brax was certain of it.

"One hour." As if Chance needed to announce it. Like Brax hadn't looked at the time every few minutes since they'd arrived at the office.

"And Robert knows where you're supposed to be meeting him?" Tessa asked, standing at Brax's side. They had been joined at the hip the past two days.

Not that he would've complained for anything, since it had been the happiest two days he'd ever spent. There hadn't been anything in the world but her and Walker.

Mostly her. They hadn't been able to keep their hands off each other since that first night together, which had resulted in two days of jumping in and out of bed.

And the couch. And once on the kitchen counter, but that had been completely spontaneous.

Now, she was more precious to him than ever. He would've done anything for this woman who'd become his world. The fact that this would involve putting his useless half brother behind bars was gravy at that point.

He clasped her hand, squeezing once to reassure her. "He does. He said he's familiar with the area. An old warehouse just outside of town."

"Why would he be familiar with that?"

"Who knows?" Chance shrugged. "There could've been any number of illegal activities going on out there. Gambling, drugs, you name it. Robert isn't exactly discriminating when it comes to how he gets his fix."

"What bothered me was how glad he sounded when I told him where to meet," Brax admitted. "Once he knew it would be an empty place, he seemed relieved."

"What could that mean?" Tessa looked around the room.

Chance pursed his lips, his brow furrowing. "He's suspicious, maybe? Then again, somebody who's left nothing but havoc in his wake for so long is bound to be suspicious by nature."

"Don't worry. I'll do whatever it takes to calm him and get him talking." He squeezed Tessa's hand again, and the smile she offered went a long way toward easing his concerns for her.

She was handling this like a champ. He should've known she would. The pride he felt when he looked at her knew no bounds.

"You ready to make the call?" Chance asked.

She responded with a firm nod, her jaw tight. "Absolutely."

Her hand didn't so much as tremble as she punched in Jakob's number. The phone's speaker was turned on so they could all hear what he had to say and could coach Tessa through any sudden changes in the script.

Brax caught her eye as the phone rang. *You can do this*, he mouthed, giving her a thumbs up. She stood a little straighter, nodding once.

"Yeah?" The voice rang out in the conference room.

Tessa lifted her chin. "Jakob Hawkins?"

"Yeah, this is him. Don't tell me. Tessa?"

"You know my voice?" Her lips pursed.

"I do. Although I never thought you would be the one reaching out to me. What's this about?"

Her tongue darted out over her lips. "I know where Robert is, and I figured I should pass the information on to you."

Right, right, stick to the script. Brax nodded, hoping to encourage her.

"Oh, really?"

"Yes, really. I told you before that I didn't know, and that was the truth. But he's in town again, and I know where he's going to be exactly one hour from now. I thought you'd want to know."

"I got to admit, you've piqued my interest."

"Not so fast. I want a little something for my trouble. You've put me through the wringer, and I deserve at least a little something."

"What did you have in mind?"

Brax prayed this would work.

"A thousand dollars," Tessa announced, closing her eyes briefly when she said it. Brax had settled on this amount, thinking it was enough to make her sound serious but not so much that Hawkins would balk at the number.

"Sounds good to me. As long as I can get my hands on that loser." He paused. "Where's he going to be?"

"There's a warehouse outside of town. He's meeting somebody there." She rattled off the directions as Brax had written them down.

"So he'll be in the middle of nowhere is what you're telling me."

"I'm only telling you what I know."

"Who's he meeting?"

Tessa glanced at Brax. "Like I said, that's all I know. That he'll be there in an hour."

"You expect me to walk into a situation without knowing who I'm going to find there? No way, baby. I'm going to need a little more than that."

Brax shook his head, making sure Tessa saw him when he did it. No way was he going to let this scum set the terms.

"Like what?" she asked. Brax shook his head harder, waving his hands back and forth in a "no way" motion.

"Like you meeting me there."

Chance held Brax's arm, signaling him to stay quiet. It was easy for him, wasn't it? If Luke had been there, he might get it, but he and Claire were at the safe house with Walker.

To his horror, Tessa asked, "And what would happen once you see Robert there, just like I promised?"

"You'd be free to go. I don't need anything from you but a little bit of insurance. I'm not walking into some empty warehouse without knowing I'm covered."

Brax vibrated with rage. Was he supposed to stand back and let this happen? How could he live with himself if Tessa got hurt? Or worse. Why would she want to breathe the same air as this scum?

"Okay," she agreed, and Brax gritted his teeth against the torrent that threatened to pour out. Every filthy word he'd ever learned wanted to make itself heard, plus a few that might not have existed.

"Meet you there," Hawkins promised before ending the call.

Brax managed to wait until a series of beeps signaled the line had gone dead before exploding. "Why would you do that? Why would you agree to anything he asked?"

Her eyes went wide, her mouth falling open in surprise. "Because he wouldn't have gone if I wasn't going to be there. Weren't you listening?"

"You never let the target dictate the terms, Tessa. I don't want you going anywhere near him."

"Do you think I want to be near him? This isn't something I'm looking forward to, you know."

"Okay, you two." Chance tried to get in between them, but all Tessa did was sidestep so she could continue glaring at Brax like he was the bad guy.

"I'll do anything to keep Walker safe. Got it?" she asked, hands on her hips. "Don't ask me not to do whatever it takes. If showing my face is going to get Hawkins to relax and believe Robert's there and he isn't in any danger, that's fine by me."

"It's a solid plan," Chance reminded him. "Weston's already out there with Rick and his guys. We've wired the entire warehouse, and you'll be wearing a wire and recording every word Robert says. The cops will pick up Robert and Hawkins a couple miles from the warehouse. And I'll be outside watching Tessa. Once Hawkins leaves with Robert, I'll follow and keep Hawkins from killing him before they reach the police."

Brax nodded. "Right, right. I know that. But there was a plan in place for this call, wasn't there? And here we are, going completely off-script. I don't want Tessa there."

"You might want to try not talking about me as if I am not here," Tessa suggested, raising an eyebrow.

He scrubbed his hands over his head, at a loss. "You know it's not like that. I'm not trying to talk around you or like you don't matter. If you didn't matter, I wouldn't be so against you getting yourself wrapped up in this."

"Newsflash—" she went to him, looping her arms around his waist "—I'm wrapped up in it. I'll show my face, Hawkins will trust Robert is inside, and that'll be it."

"Come on. We'd better get moving." Chance motioned for them to follow him outside.

Brax knew there was nothing more he could do. No time.

The plan was already in motion. He had to be there before Robert showed up.

They walked outside together, hand in hand. "Listen to me, please," he urged on the way to the car. "You can't get too close to Hawkins. Play your part, show your face, then get out of there. Okay?"

"Okay."

"You promise?" He turned to her, taking her precious face into his hands. She would never understand how important she was. How her well-being meant more to him than his own. Why, if it seemed like he came down too hard on her, it was done out of love.

"I promise." She covered his hands with hers, smiling. "Hey. After all I've been through to be with my baby, to be with him without looking over my shoulder, do you honestly think I'd risk getting killed? Risk leaving him alone? No way. I promise you I will play it safe."

He kissed her once, firmly, before letting her go. There would be time for everything else later. He could show her and tell her everything she meant to him. How his life had meaning now thanks to her and Walker. How he'd waited so long without knowing he was waiting, because he could never have imagined somebody like her existed.

Somebody so perfect for him. So perfect in general.

As long as she stuck to her word and Hawkins didn't decide to do something crazy, he'd have the opportunity to tell her everything he held in his heart.

Chapter Twenty-Four

"Weston. Come in." Brax adjusted the earpiece, setting it deep inside his ear.

"I hear you, brother. Loud and clear. ETA?"

Brax checked the GPS on the console. "Five minutes."

"Great. We're ready and waiting out here. You know what you're doing once he shows?"

"I've been through it a hundred times in my head, beginning to end. Believe me."

"Remind me anyway."

Brax rolled his eyes. Weston, ever the cop. "I have to get Robert to confess to what he did. Trust me. I know. I have my wire, and there's recording equipment all over the warehouse. Chance will watch the exterior. Tessa will meet Hawkins outside the warehouse so he knows—"

"Tessa?"

Right. He didn't know. "Believe me. I don't want her involved. Hawkins insisted she show her face so he'd know she wasn't lying."

"Wonderful. I should have guessed he wouldn't let it go that easily."

"I have to get as much information from Hawkins as possible. He has to admit he's been tracking Robert because he intends to kill him. I'm telling you, I'm on it."

"All right. Just checking. We have everything covered on our end, as well. You focus on your part, and we'll take care of the rest."

Sure. It would be easy.

Brax didn't believe it for a second. Nothing about this went easy. Ever.

Then again, maybe this meant they were due a little good luck. It would certainly be welcome.

He reached the warehouse a minute earlier than the GPS had predicted. He'd beaten everybody else, which was a good thing. The car seat was in the back, and he made a big deal of unloading it and carrying it into the warehouse.

He even talked to the doll and bundle of blankets inside, just in case Robert was watching from somewhere nearby. Not that he'd give Robert credit for thinking that far ahead, but anomalies happened, and now would be the worst time to get caught in a lie.

He had barely stepped foot inside when Chance's voice rang out in his ear. "He's coming. Just about to reach the warehouse."

Brax took one deep breath after another, forcing himself to relax. Telling himself he was there to give the baby to Robert—the way he was supposed to be. That he cared about his half brother and only wanted what was best for him.

A sick joke, but one he had to at least pretend to believe if he had any hope of coming off believable.

"We're a go," Weston announced. "You've got this, Brax."

"Yeah, and now I just have to figure out what to do with it." The fact that he could make a joke had to be a good sign. He hoped.

Robert stepped through the open door, his head sweeping from side to side. "I had half an idea you brought me here to set me up," he giggled like a little girl once he found they were alone.

"This is too serious for anything like that."

Robert shrugged. "So? Hand him over."

Brax took a step back. "Not until you tell me how things turned out this way. You're still my brother. I can't let you walk out of my life again without knowing how you got into this situation. And what you plan on doing after this."

"Why does it matter all of a sudden?"

"Call me sentimental. Now more than ever, since I happen to have formed an attachment to your son. I want to know what his father's planning on doing after he leaves this warehouse."

That greasy smile. "I'm gonna stay alive, bro. You know me. Always one step ahead of the bad guys."

Brax withheld comment. He had to keep things moving in the right direction, ideally before Hawkins showed up. "You said Walker's mother is dead? Is that true? Be honest with me now, please. This might be the last time we see each other for all I know. I think after you dropped your kid on my doorstep and disappeared, you owe me that much."

Robert's eye roll was visible from the open door and the dim light filtering through the few filthy windows lining the walls. "What do you want me to say? She was a loser. She didn't know how to handle herself, much less our kid."

Brax stopped short of snarling, but just barely. "It doesn't say much about you that you were hooking up with a loser who couldn't handle herself."

"She was cute. What can I say? Anyway, she was no good, so I got custody."

"You must've had proof of her being no good. Judges don't up and grant custody to a professional gambler—no offense—over a baby's mother."

"Like her being a waitress at a casino was any better?" Robert scoffed. "Please. It took no time. My cousin, you remember. He's a judge."

He was making it so easy, it was hard not to laugh. "Oh, so it was like that? You got him to fix things for you?"

"Listen, Brax. Don't get up on your moral high horse now. I did what I needed to do."

"What does that mean? Did you steal this baby from his mother? Does she even know what's going on with you and the Solomon family?"

"No, why would she? For all I know she's in a hole somewhere. What does it matter? The important thing is I got Walker and that's that."

"Even though you had to lie to do it?"

"What do you want me to say? Yeah. I did what had to be done. I had my cousin fix things. He told me what to tell CPS, what they would listen to, and I told them. Bing, bang, boom, I got full custody of my son."

"You lied to Child Protective Services?" Always good to have clear confirmation.

"Yes, okay? I told them she was an addict and fixed it so CPS would show up while she was high on something. She didn't even know I had a buddy inject her as she was leaving work that night. I called CPS and had them go to her place, and they saw with their own eyes what a waste she was. It was easy after that."

He had just signed his own arrest warrant. Brax took pains to calm himself. "And the judge who helped you get away with it is the same cousin who accepted my forged signature on those guardianship documents?"

Robert sighed. "Why do you have to make it sound the way you do? 'Forged.' I mean, come on."

"I never signed those guardianship documents, yet he

approved and signed them. He granted me guardianship sight unseen."

"He knew you're my half brother."

"It doesn't matter. I never met him, yet he was on board with doctoring those papers."

"This is a waste of my time. I should've known it wouldn't be enough for you to hand the kid over and be done with it. You had to let me know what a scumbag you think I am and how much you hate me."

"I don't hate you," Brax insisted. "I feel sorry for you, if anything."

"Spare me your pity." Robert strode over to him, hands out. "I need the kid. I have places to be."

"Brax?" Chance murmured in his ear. "Tessa and Hawkins are on their way in."

Perfect timing.

Brax handed the car seat to Robert, watching with pleasure as his expression changed from snide arrogance to confusion. "What is this?" He peeled back the blankets, revealing the doll in Walker's place. "What do you think you're doing?"

"I'm protecting people who aren't scum," Brax fired back.

A moment later, Hawkins walked in with Tessa behind him. Robert's mouth fell open. He dropped the seat, the sound echoing in the empty space.

He turned to Brax, snarling. "What have you done?"

Meanwhile, Hawkins let out a satisfied breath. "You were as good as your word." He turned to Tessa with a grin. "Thank you. And sorry for all the trouble I put you through. You can go." He handed her a fat envelope.

Tessa withdrew a wad of cash from the envelope, counted it and exchanged a look with Brax before glaring at Robert. She didn't say a word, only stood there with her arms wrapped around herself, hate burning in her eyes.

Brax let out a relieved breath when she backed out of the warehouse. A moment later, Chance reported, "She's safe. She's cleared the building and gone to her car."

Robert turned on Brax, sweating like he'd just run a marathon. "Why would you do this to your own brother?" he snarled.

"You stole your son from his mother and used him as a pawn," Brax snarled back. He didn't have to pretend anymore. "You did everything you could to destroy her. How am I supposed to have sympathy for you? You deserve everything you're going to get."

"I agree." Hawkins advanced, but Brax held up a hand to stop him. This wasn't over yet.

"You can't get the money he owes the Solomon family if you kill him," Brax reminded him.

Hawkins shrugged, then took Robert by his shirt collar and drove a fist into his face once, twice. Robert dropped to the floor.

Hawkins turned to Brax. "If you wanted your brother alive, you shouldn't have brought him to me. You probably know better than most how much he deserves to die—hell, what you just said now about his kid is reason enough. I've got my own personal issues with Robert."

He kicked Robert in the ribs to punctuate his statement. "Don't I?" he shouted, the sudden change making Brax jump. "I warned you I'd kill you if you didn't quit saying the things you were saying. Making a fool out of me. Then you made a fool of the family. Of Gabrielle. That was all the reason I needed to go after you. They know I'm gonna kill you, Robert, and guess what? They don't care as long as they never have to set eyes on you again."

A chill ran through Brax.

Weston broke in. "That's all the police need. We'll pick them up once they're out of there. Chance will follow them."

"On my way out to meet them on the main road," Chance confirmed.

"Then get him out of my sight." Brax turned to Hawkins. He needed to keep the man from killing Robert right now. "Just do me a favor? Call it what I'm owed for giving you what you want."

"What is it?"

"Get him far from here before you do what you plan to do. He's still close enough to San Antonio that there could be blowback on me just because we're related. I'm trying to run a business, you know?"

It was a risk, but Hawkins appeared to appreciate this. "Fair enough. I'll get him far enough from here that the blowback won't fall on you. Seems he made your life difficult enough already."

"Don't get me started." Brax removed his earpiece when neither of the other men were looking and glanced down at the empty car seat.

Was this all that was left of his life? An empty car seat? The memory of what had brought him indescribable happiness and contentment? Even if it was, Tessa and Walker would be together and safe. The way it was meant to be. He could take that with him wherever he went.

His family would be safe. Brax might be alone, but they would be safe.

"Who are you?"

His head snapped up at Hawkins's question.

And everything turned upside down.

"Wow," Prince Riviera chuckled as he dragged a gagged Tessa into the warehouse with a pistol to her head. "I thought you were supposed to be a good guy, Patterson. But you just sold your brother out even though you know he's gonna end up dead."

Chapter Twenty-Five

Tessa had no idea what had happened.

One minute she was hurrying to her car, glad everything had gone okay and Hawkins had let her go so easily. Imagining being reunited with her son, living with him. No fear. Nobody to keep them apart anymore. She could be his mother openly.

Then, while she'd been waiting in the car for Brax or one of the others to come for her like they'd promised, the door had opened. She'd screamed as Prince Riviera had reached in and pulled her out by her hair.

Not that she'd ever had the displeasure of meeting him before then—she'd recognized Riviera from the news. Tall, thin, with a mouth that was curled up in a permanent sneer. Like he knew something the rest of the world didn't.

She would've screamed again to signal Brax, but Prince had a gun, which was the only thing that could have silenced her. He'd pressed it to her temple with a laugh, and one glimpse of his dark, empty eyes had chilled her to the bone.

"I don't know what the hell's going on here," he'd whispered, holding her close, "but you and I are going inside to have a little talk with Patterson."

He'd then shoved her back into the car, sitting her sideways so her feet were on the ground, his gun still at her head while the friend he'd brought with him went over to the warehouse to listen in. He'd come back, reporting what had gone down.

Prince had laughed softly, shaking his head. "Maybe we were coming at this Brax the wrong way. I didn't think he had it in him to do something like that."

Then, holding her arm in a painful grip that had hurt as much as the patch of scalp he'd pulled her hair from, he had dragged her to the warehouse. "Come on," he'd snorted. "Let's go in and have a talk with your boyfriend."

Just when she'd convinced herself a future with Brax was possible, probable—maybe even certain— the gun at her head had turned her insides to water.

All she could do as Prince had pulled her into the warehouse was thank the heavens that Walker wasn't there. That he was safe.

She couldn't say the same for herself.

It was Brax's worst nightmare come true.

Not because he'd had any fear for himself. It didn't matter what happened to him, not now. But Tessa…he couldn't live if anything happened to her. And right then, with her mouth gagged and a gun to her head? A gun held by none other than Prince Riviera?

A beyond-worst nightmare come true.

"What's this all about?" Hawkins demanded. "What do you think you're doing?"

"Shut up," Riviera spat. "I'm talking to my friend over here, Mr. Patterson. He's a tough man to get a hold of, you know? I've been looking for him ever since my friends paid him a visit a few days ago."

"Yeah, thanks for that." Brax's gaze moved to Tessa, whose eyes were wide enough to bulge. "Did you hurt her?"

"Nothing she won't recover from given enough time," Riviera sneered. "Don't worry about it. You wouldn't want to waste your final moments worrying, would you?"

"Just…just lower the gun, okay? You want to talk? You want to work something out?" Brax took one tentative step toward them. Then another. "Fine. We can talk this out. But I can't concentrate if she has a gun shoved in her face. That's just how it is."

"Like I care what you want or don't want." Riviera's laughter was cold, empty, just like his eyes and his smile. He reminded Brax of a shark.

A shark that smelled blood. He could probably sense Brax's barely concealed panic.

Except a shark didn't toy with its prey. It didn't take any pleasure from watching people squirm.

"Lower the gun, and we can work this out. She hasn't done anything. She's no threat to you." Another tentative step. Another.

Riviera pulled Tessa closer to him. Bile rose in Brax's throat at the thought of that monster touching her. Hurting her. There was pain in her eyes, no doubt from the way Riviera's fingers dug into her arm.

"Okay. Fine. Talk to me." He lowered the gun, letting his arm hang at his side. "What do you have to say?"

"I'll back out of testifying," Brax offered. "No worries. You can have your little cartel to yourself and continue doing whatever it is you do without having to concern yourself with me."

Riviera looked him up and down. "Really? Just like that? This was all I had to do, huh?" He laughed softly, looking at Tessa. "Your boyfriend isn't so hard to get along with as long as a guy knows where his soft spots are. And he's obviously got a huge soft spot for you, cutie."

Brax bit his tongue.

If only he could hear Weston or Chance in his ear, but he'd already taken the earpiece out. Putting it back in now would give away the entire plan. Hawkins and Robert were behind him, both of them silent. Probably frozen in shock.

"Would it make you feel better if I told you I want money to keep quiet?" Brax asked with a shrug. Anything to stall. The best he could hope for right now was for one of his brothers to hear what was happening and call in backup.

But what if they weren't listening anymore? What if they were waiting for Hawkins, unaware of what was going on here?

Riviera smirked. "Now you're speaking my language, Brax. Money. That's what lies at the heart of everything, doesn't it? My man outside overheard you talking about money in here. Your, uh, what is it? Brother? Your brother can't give the people he owes what he owes them if he's dead."

"That's right," Brax said, thankful that for once Robert knew enough to keep his mouth shut.

"That's an astute observation on your part. That's the kind of thinking an intelligent man does. You can't get your money from someone if he's dead."

Riviera looked at Tessa, a nasty smile tugging at the corner of his mouth. "Then again, why would a smart man bother giving somebody money when he could just kill him and get it over with?"

Brax's insides went cold when Riviera raised the gun again and pointed it at Tessa. "But I'll take care of you first, cutie, since I've learned an important lesson. Never leave a witness alive."

There was no time to think about it, no time to try to get Riviera to listen to reason. There was no reasoning with a monster—something without feelings, without morals—anyway. He was going to kill Tessa. This was not a man who made idle threats. He wouldn't think twice about killing an innocent woman in cold blood.

There was no backup and nobody to help him. He'd be taking a bullet.

But if there was one thing Brax knew with complete certainty, it was that life without Tessa wasn't worth living. He had no desire to even try it. Even the idea of going off the grid and being without her was unthinkable. He doubted now, in this moment of clarity, that he would ever have managed it.

Which was why he threw himself at Prince Riviera, gun and all. If he got shot, he got shot.

As long as *she* didn't.

A shot rang out. Brax hit the floor with Riviera under him, bouncing the crime boss's head off the concrete, knocking him unconscious.

He waited for the pain from the bullet to set in, but there was no pain. Why wasn't there pain? There'd been a shot. Everything had happened too fast.

He looked up at Tessa, who was still standing. No blood. Just a lot of fear.

"Brax! Report!" Weston's frantic voice coming from outside.

"All clear!" he managed. He stumbled to his feet and rushed to Tessa.

She fell against him as he worked the gag from her mouth. He took her face into his hands and looked her over. "Are you okay?"

"I'm okay. I'm okay." But she jumped when Weston rushed into the warehouse with his gun drawn.

"He had a friend with him," Weston reported. "He had a

bead on you from outside the building. I took care of him."
Seconds later, red and blue flashing lights flooded through the windows and the open door.

So that was where the shot had come from. It had been his brother saving his life.

Brax could only wrap his arms around Tessa, wanting to pull her inside of him and keep her there forever.

"You're safe now," he whispered into her ear as she trembled. "You're safe. It's all okay."

"You could've gotten yourself killed!" She glared up at him. "Don't you know that? What would've happened if you had ended up dead?"

"I didn't care about staying alive as long as you had a chance to get away."

Her eyes welled up with fresh tears. "Don't say that. Don't say you were willing to die for me."

"What if it's the truth?" He tucked her hair behind her ear, letting his fingers linger against her smooth jaw, her throat, her cheek. "I knew when you were standing there with that gun to your head that I wasn't interested in living if it meant being without you. Because I love you."

"Yeah?" In spite of the tears now pouring down her cheeks, she smiled.

"Oh, yeah," he whispered. "I love you, Tessa Mahoney. And I would face a hundred armed gunmen for your sake. You and Walker are my entire world. You're all I want. All I'll ever need."

He caught her lips in the sweetest, most tender kiss. As precious as she'd been to him before then, having almost lost her only made every moment she was in his arms more meaningful.

"I love you so much," she beamed before falling against him, her wet cheek on his chest. He held her, stroking her hair, watching as Robert, Hawkins and Prince Riviera were led away in zip ties.

"You managed to get Riviera's confession too." Weston grinned, striding over to them. "Talking all about how he planned to kill a witness. You don't need to testify now, brother. I'd call that a solid day's work."

Brax could only laugh. "Yeah. A solid day's work."

Chapter Twenty-Six

"Let me help you with that." Tessa handed Walker off to Brax before hurrying to help Sheila with the food she was taking from the oven.

"You've gone to so much trouble." Claire marveled, looking over the spread Brax's mother had prepared.

"It's no trouble, fixing my boys' favorite dishes." Sheila beamed as she looked over the full kitchen. "Having everybody here at once is more than enough reason to celebrate. But today is important. Worthy of a feast."

Tessa grinned over at Brax, who lifted Walker's hand in a wave.

"That's right, pal," he murmured. "You and Mama are going to be together for always now."

"It only took four weeks." Clinton shook his head as he entered the room. "Let it never be said the wheels of justice turn quickly."

"We know all about that," Sheila reminded him. "Not so much the justice bit, but waiting for red tape to be cleared. We went through it four times, remember?"

Clinton slid an arm around his wife and kissed the top of her head.

Brax marveled, and not for the first time, at how lucky he'd been. He had a couple of parents who'd always been an example of a loving partnership. One based on mutual respect, friendship, and affection.

Claire paused in the middle of putting together a fruit salad. "How does it feel now that the judge has restored your parental rights?"

"Like I've been given the whole world." Tessa glowed. She might as well have floated above the floor she was so overjoyed.

Brax knew how she felt. He'd felt that way once he was certain that she was safe, that there was nothing and no one who could hurt her anymore.

Knowing she had full custody again brought him deep satisfaction too. This was how it should be.

"Game's on," Luke announced before rummaging through the fridge for a drink.

"That's all you have to say when we're in here toiling away for you?" Claire clicked her tongue and shook her head.

"Hey, I never claimed to be great in the kitchen. My announcement of the game being on was my contribution. That and, well, eating." He leaned in and kissed Claire's cheek. She only laughed and shook her head again.

"Here, you can contribute this way." Brax handed Walker over to his brother and did what he could not to laugh at the look of panic on Luke's face.

He wasn't successful. "I didn't hand you a bomb," he snickered. "Take it easy."

"I have to say—" Sheila dropped a broad wink in Claire's direction "—you look good holding a baby, son."

Tessa met Brax's gaze, and they both grinned. It was almost too obvious the way Sheila hinted heavily at Claire and Luke giving her grandkids.

Luke's face went red. "Good thing there's a baby around to hold." Though he wasn't fooling anybody. The way he looked at Walker, who waved his fists and babbled happily, told the real story.

Chance and Weston set the table as per their mom's orders. Clinton pulled one casserole dish after another out of the oven while Sheila fretted over whether they had enough wine. Tessa put the finishing touches on a pan of macaroni and cheese, sprinkling buttered breadcrumbs on top. Claire and Luke fussed over Walker.

Brax had never felt happier and more at peace in his life.

Which was why what he planned to do that special day was the easiest move he'd ever considered. There wasn't a scrap of doubt in his mind.

Tessa was his home. She was just as much his family as the rest of the people around them.

The tricky part was how to do it.

After serving themselves from the array of dishes and platters on the counter, they gathered around the table.

"It's all delicious." Tessa marveled. "I love to cook, but I don't think I've ever cooked this much food at once. How do you manage?"

"It's practice." Sheila shrugged. "I had to feed four growing boys at once, not to mention a husband with a healthy appetite."

"If you didn't cook so well, I wouldn't want seconds all the time," Clinton pointed out.

"Seconds? Try thirds, Clinton Patterson."

"Whatever magic you work, I would love to learn some of your recipes. Like this mac and cheese." Tessa let out a soft groan as she took a bite.

"I guess if you're going to spend time with my Brax,

you'd better learn how to cook my recipes." Sheila gave Brax a very knowing, very motherly look.

He made a mental note to ask just how she managed to read their minds the way she did. There was no keeping secrets from the woman.

Tessa fed Walker mashed bananas, which was a fairly new development and needed her complete attention or else everything in a three-foot radius would end up covered in Walker's snack.

It was now or never, he realized. This was the moment. With his family together, laughing, happy. With Tessa secure, knowing no one could take her son away. With everyone who had tried to hurt the ones he loved behind bars, Brax's life had never been more perfect.

Which was why he slid the box from his pocket while Tessa's back was turned. He opened it then placed it on the table where she couldn't help but see it when she turned away from Walker.

Claire clamped a hand over her mouth.

Sheila held her hands up, signaling for silence. She didn't need to, since everyone went quiet once they realized what was going on.

Finally, Tessa noticed. "Is everything okay?" she asked in a panicked tone.

Then she saw the box and the ring inside.

"Oh, my goodness." She looked at Brax. "What is this?"

"What do you think it is?" he asked, more nervous than he'd ever been in his entire life. Why was he shaking?

"Brax…oh, my goodness." She crossed her hands over her chest as tears started to flow.

"You know by now that I love you," he murmured, "and that you and Walker are my world. I want us to be a real family. I want you to be my wife. I want Walker to be my son. You'd make me the happiest man who ever drew breath if you would agree to marry me."

"Agree?" She burst out laughing. "Like there was any doubt?"

"That's a yes?" he asked, still tentative.

"Of course, it is!" She nearly knocked him off his chair when she threw her arms around his neck and squeezed until he could hardly breathe.

But that was just fine. He could take it.

"Oh, it's about time!" Sheila crowed, laughing and crying and clapping.

"About time?" Chance laughed. "It hasn't been all that long that they've been together."

"Sweetheart, if there's one thing I've learned, it's this—when you know, you know. And I knew the minute that woman stepped foot in this house that she was right for my Brax."

"See?" Brax whispered in Tessa's ear. "Mom knew. I guess that means we're both on the right track. She's never wrong."

Tessa loosened her grip on him enough to pull back with an ear-to-ear smile. "Then I guess she has more to teach me than recipes."

"Nah. You're pretty perfect just the way you are." He pulled the ring from the box and slid it over her finger. Everyone in the room broke out in cheers and applause.

Even Walker raised his tiny fists and shouted.

Brax and Tessa leaned against each other and laughed. "He approves," Tessa noted. "We're definitely on the right track."

* * * * *

COMING SOON!

We really hope you enjoyed reading this book. If you're looking for more romance be sure to head to the shops when new books are available on

Thursday 1ˢᵗ April

To see which titles are coming soon, please visit

millsandboon.co.uk/nextmonth

MILLS & BOON

LET'S TALK

Romance

For exclusive extracts, competitions
and special offers, find us online:

f facebook.com/millsandboon

𝕏 @MillsandBoon

◎ @MillsandBoonUK

♪ @MillsandBoonUK

Get in touch on 01413 063 232